LUCY GORDON

DAPHNE CLAIR

JOANNA NEIL

&MILLS
BOON

First published in Great Britain 2013
by Mills & Boon, an imprint of Harlequin (UK) Limited,
Eton House, 18-24 Paradise Road, Richmond, Surrey TW9 1SR

SWEPT AWAY! © by Harlequin Enterprises II B.V./S.à.r.l 2013

Accidentally Expecting!, *Salzano's Captive Bride* and *Hawaiian Sunset, Dream Proposal* were published in Great Britain by Harlequin (UK) Limited.

Accidentally Expecting! © Lucy Gordon 2009
Salzano's Captive Bride © Daphne Clair de Jong 2009
Hawaiian Sunset, Dream Proposal © Joanna Neil 2010

ISBN: 978 0 263 90449 9
ebook ISBN: 978 1 472 00815 2

05-0113

Printed and bound in Spain
by Blackprint CPI, Barcelona

ACCIDENTALLY
EXPECTING!

BY
LUCY GORDON

Lucy Gordon cut her writing teeth on magazine journalism, interviewing many of the world's most interesting men, including Warren Beatty, Charlton Heston and Sir Roger Moore. She also camped out with lions in Africa and had many other unusual experiences which have often provided the background for her books. Several years ago, while staying Venice, she met a Venetian who proposed in two days. They have been married ever since. Naturally this has affected her writing, where romantic Italian men tend to feature strongly.

Two of her books have won the Romance Writers of America RITA® award.

CHAPTER ONE

HORNS blared, lights flashed in the darkness and Ferne ground her hands together as the cab battled its way through the slow-moving Milan traffic.

'Oh no! I'm going to miss the train. *Please!*'

The driver called back over his shoulder, 'I'm doing my best, *signorina*, but the traffic here is like nowhere else in the world.' He said it with pride.

'I know it's not your fault,' she cried. 'But I've got a ticket on the night train to Naples. It leaves in a quarter of an hour.'

The driver chuckled. 'Leave it to me. Twenty years I am driving in Milan, and my passengers do not miss their trains.'

The next ten minutes were breathless but triumphant, and at last the ornate façade of Milan Central Station came into view. As Ferne leapt out and paid the driver, a porter appeared.

'Train to Naples,' she gasped.

'This way, *signorina*.'

They made it to the platform looking so frantic that heads were turned. But suddenly Ferne stumbled and went sprawling right in the path of the porter, who sprawled in turn.

She wanted to yell aloud at being thwarted at the last moment, but miraculously hands came out of nowhere, seized her, thrust her on board, the bags following after her. A door slammed.

'*Stai bene?*' came a man's voice.

'I'm sorry, I don't speak Italian,' she said breathlessly, clutching him as he helped her to her feet.

'I asked if you are all right,' he said in English.

'Yes, but—oh heavens, we're moving. I should have given that poor man something.'

'Leave it to me.'

There was a narrow opening at the top of the window and the man slid his arm through, his hand full of notes which the porter seized gratefully. Her rescuer waved and turned back to face her in the corridor of the train that was already gathering speed.

Now Ferne had a moment to look at him, and realised that she was suffering delusions. He was so handsome that it was impossible. In his thirties, he stood, tall and impressive, with wide shoulders and hair of a raven-black colour that only Italians seemed to achieve. His eyes were deep blue, gleaming with life, and his whole appearance was something no man could be permitted outside the pages of a novel.

To cap it all, he'd come galloping to her rescue like the hero of a melodrama, which was simply too much. But, what the heck? She was on holiday.

He returned her gaze, briefly but appreciatively, taking in her slender figure and dark-red hair. Without conceit, but also without false modesty, she knew she was attractive; the expression in his eyes was one she'd often seen before, although it was a while since she'd responded to it.

'I'll refund you that tip, of course,' she said.

A woman had appeared behind them in the corridor. She was in her sixties, white-haired, slender and elegant.

'Are you hurt, my dear?' she asked. 'That was a nasty fall you had.'

'No, I'm fine, just a bit shaken.'

'Dante, bring her to our compartment.'

'OK, Aunt Hope. You take her, I'll bring the bags.'

The woman took Ferne gently by the arm and led her along the corridor to a compartment where a man, also in his sixties, was standing in the doorway watching their approach. He stood back to let them in and ushered Ferne to a seat.

'From the way you speak, I think you are English,' the woman said with a charming smile.

'Yes, my name is Ferne Edmunds.'

'I too am English. At least, I was long ago. Now I am Signora Hope Rinucci. This is my husband, Toni—and this young man is our nephew, Dante Rinucci.'

Dante was just entering with the bags, which he shoved under the seats, and then he sat down, rubbing his upper arm.

'Are you hurt?' Hope asked anxiously.

He grimaced. 'Pushing my arm through that narrow space has probably left me with bruises for life.' Then a grin broke over his face. 'It's all right, I'm only joking. Stop fussing. It's our friend here who needs care. Those platforms are hard.'

'That's true,' Ferne said ruefully, rubbing her knees through her trousers.

'Would you like me to take a look?' he asked hopefully, reaching out a hand.

'No, she would not,' Hope said, determinedly forestalling him. 'Behave yourself. In fact, why don't you go to the restaurant-car and order something for this young lady?' She added sternly, 'Both of you.'

Like obedient little boys, both men rose and departed without a word. Hope chuckled.

'Now, *signorina*—it is *signorina*?'

'Signorina Edmunds. But, please, call me Ferne. After what your family has done for me, let's not be formal.'

'Good. In that case—'

There was a knock on the door and a steward looked in.

'Oh yes, you want to make up the berths,' Hope said. 'Let's join the men.'

As they went along the corridor, Hope asked, 'Where is your sleeping berth?'

'I don't have one,' Ferne admitted. 'I booked at the last minute and everything was taken.'

By now they had reached the dining-car, where Toni and Dante had taken a table. Dante stood up and graciously showed her to the seat beside him.

'Here's the ticket inspector,' Hope said. 'Let's get the formalities out of the way before we eat. They may be able to find you a berth.'

But from that moment things went horribly wrong. As the others showed their paperwork, Ferne scrabbled hopelessly in her bag, finally facing the terrible truth.

'It's gone,' she whispered. 'Everything. My money, the tickets—they must have fallen out when I fell on the platform.'

Another search produced no result. Disaster!

'My passport's gone too!' she gasped. 'I've got to go back.'

But the train was now travelling at full speed.

'It doesn't stop until Naples,' Hope explained.

'They'll stop to throw me off when they find out I've no ticket and no money,' Ferne said frantically.

Hope's voice was soothing. 'Let's see what we can do about that.'

Toni began to speak to the inspector in Italian. After a while he produced his credit card.

'They're issuing you another ticket,' Hope explained.

'Oh, that's so kind of you. I'll pay you back, I promise.'

'Let's not worry about that now. First we have to find you a berth.'

'That's easy,' Dante said. 'My sleeping-car is a double, and I'm only using one berth, so—'

'So Toni can come in with you and Ferne can come in with me,' Hope said, beaming. 'What a splendid idea!'

'Actually, Aunt, I was thinking—'

'I know what you were thinking and you should be ashamed.'

'Yes, Aunt, anything you say, Aunt.'

But he winked at Ferne, and she couldn't help being charmed. The mere idea of this handsome, confident man doing what he was told was so idiotic, and his air of meekness so clearly an act, that she had to smile and join in the joke.

The inspector exchanged some more words with Toni before nodding and hurrying away.

'He's going to call the station now and tell them to look out for your things,' Toni explained to Ferne. 'Luckily you discovered the loss quickly, so they may pick them up before anyone else finds them. But, just in case, you must cancel your credit cards.'

'How can I do that from here?' Ferne asked, baffled.

'The British consulate will help you,' Dante declared, taking out his own mobile phone.

In a few moments he had obtained the emergency number of the Milan consulate, dialled it and handed the phone to Ferne.

The young man on duty was efficient. Quickly he looked up the numbers of the credit-card companies, assigned her a reference number and bid her goodnight. Calls to the finance companies achieved the cancellation of her cards and the promise of new ones. This was as much as she could hope for for now.

'I don't know what I'd have done without you,' she told her new friends fervently. 'When I think what could have happened to me.'

'Don't think about it,' Hope advised. 'All will be well. Ah, here is the waiter with a snack. Hmm, cakes and wine are all very well, but I should like a large pot of tea.'

'*English* tea.' Toni gave instructions to the waiter, who nodded solemnly, evidently familiar with this peculiarity among his customers.

The tea was excellent, so were the cakes, which the others piled onto her plate.

'When did you last eat?' Hope asked.

'Properly? Oh—some time. I left on the spur of the moment, caught the train from London to Paris, then Paris to Milan. I don't like flying, and I wanted to be free to stop and explore whenever I wanted. I had a few days in Milan, shopping and seeing the sights. I meant to stay there overnight and go on tomorrow, but I suddenly changed my mind, packed up and ran.'

'That's the way to live!' Dante exclaimed. 'Here today, gone tomorrow; let life bring what it will.' He took Ferne's hand and spoke with theatrical fervour. '*Signorina*, you are a woman after my own heart. More than a woman—a goddess with a unique understanding of life. I salute you—why are you laughing?'

'I'm sorry,' Ferne choked. 'I can't listen to that guff with a straight face.'

'Guff? *Guff?* Is this a new English word?'

'No,' Hope informed him, amused. 'It's an old English word and it means that you need a better scriptwriter.'

'But only for me,' Ferne chuckled. 'I expect it works wonderfully on the others.'

Dante's face was the picture of outrage.

'The others? Don't you realise that you are the only one who has inspired me to lay my heart at her feet? The only— Oh, all right; I usually get a better reception than this.'

His collapse into realism made them all laugh.

'It's nice to meet a lady with such an adventurous approach to life,' he added. 'But I expect it's only while you're on holiday. You'll go back to England, your sedate nine-to-five life, and your sedate nine-to-five fiancé.'

'If I had a fiancé, what would I be doing here alone?' she demanded.

This made him pause, but only for a moment.

'He betrayed you,' he said dramatically. 'You are teaching him a lesson. When you return, he will be jealous, especially when he sees the compromising pictures of us together.'

'Oh, will he indeed? And where will these pictures come from?'

'It can be arranged. I know some good photographers.'

'I'll bet you don't know anyone better than me,' she riposted.

'You're a photographer?' Hope asked. 'A journalist?'

'No, I do theatrical work.' Some inexplicable instinct made her say to Dante, 'And he wasn't sedate. Anything but.'

He didn't reply in words, but his expression was wry and curious. So was the way he nodded.

'Let the poor girl eat in peace,' Hope admonished him.

She watched Ferne like a mother hen, finally declaring that it was time for bed. The four of them made their way back along the corridor and said goodnight. Ferne and Hope went into one sleeping car, Toni and Dante went on to the next.

As Ferne hung up the trousers she'd been wearing, a few coins fell out onto the floor.

'I'd forgotten I had some money in my pocket,' she said, holding them out.

'Three euros,' Hope observed. 'You wouldn't have got far with that.'

They sat down on the bed, contentedly sipping the tea they had brought with them.

'You said you were English,' Ferne recalled. 'And yet you speak as though you've been here for some time.'

'Over thirty years,' Hope told her.

'Do you have any children?'

'Six. All sons.'

She said it with an air of exasperated irony that made Ferne smile and say, 'Do you ever wish you had daughters?'

Hope chuckled. 'When you have six sons, you have no time to think of anything else. Besides, I have six daughters-in-law and seven grandchildren.

'When our last son married, a few months ago, Toni and I decided to go on our travels. Recently we've been in Milan to see some of his relatives. Toni was very close to his other brother, Taddeo, until he died a few years ago. Dante is Taddeo's elder son, and he's coming back to Naples with us for a visit. He's a bit of a madman, as you'll discover while you're staying with us.'

'I can't impose on you any further.'

'My dear, you have no money or passport. If you don't stay with us, just what are you going to do?'

'It just seems dreadful for you to be burdened with me.'

'But I shall love having you. We can talk about England. I love Italy, but I miss my own country, and you can tell me how things are there now.'

'Ah, that's different, if there's something I can do for you.'

'I look forward to you staying with us a long time. Now, I must get some sleep.'

She got into the lower bunk. Ferne climbed to the top one, and in a few minutes there was peace and darkness.

Ferne lay listening to the hum of the train speed through the night, trying to get her bearings. It seemed such a short time since she'd made the impulsive decision to leave England. Now she was here, destitute, reliant on strangers.

While she was pondering the strange path her life had taken recently, the rhythm of the train overtook her and she fell asleep.

She awoke to find herself desperately thirsty, and remembered that the snack bar was open all night. Quietly she climbed down and groped around in the darkness for her robe.

The three euros she'd found would just be enough for a drink. Holding her breath and trying not to waken Hope, she crept out into the corridor and made her way to the dining-car.

She was in luck. The snack bar was still open, although the tables were deserted and the attendant was nodding off.

'I'll have a bottle of mineral water, please,' she said thankfully. 'Oh dear, four euros. Do you have a small one?'

'I'm afraid the last small bottle has gone,' the attendant said apologetically.

'Oh *no*!' It came out as a cry of frustration.

'Can I help?' asked a voice behind her.

She turned and saw Dante.

'I'm on the cadge for money,' she groaned. '*Again*! I'm desperate for something to drink.'

'Then let me buy you some champagne.'

'No, thank you, just some mineral water.'

'Champagne is better,' he said in the persuasive voice of a man about to embark on a flirtation.

'No, water is better when you're thirsty,' she said firmly.

'Then I can't persuade you?'

'No,' she said, getting cross. 'You can't persuade me.

What you can do is step out of my way so that I can leave. Goodnight.'

'I apologise,' he said at once. 'Don't be angry with me, I'm just fooling.' To the bartender he added, 'Serve the lady whatever she wants, and I'll have a whisky.'

He slipped an arm about her, touching her lightly but firmly enough to prevent her escape, and guided her to a seat by the window. The barman approached and she seized the bottle of water, threw back her head and drank deeply.

'That's better,' she said at last, gasping slightly. 'I should be the one apologising. I'm in a rotten temper, but I shouldn't take it out on you.'

'You don't like being dependent on people?' he guessed.

'Begging,' she said in disgust.

'Not begging,' he corrected her gently. 'Letting your friends help you.'

'I'll pay every penny back,' she vowed.

'Hush! Now you're getting boring.'

Fearing that he might be right, she swigged some more water. It felt good. .

'You seem to be having a very disorganised holiday,' he observed. 'Have you been planning it for long?'

'I didn't plan it at all, just hurled a few things into a bag and flounced off.'

'That sounds promising. You said you're a photographer…' He waited hopefully.

'I specialise in the theatre, and film stills. *He's* an actor, starring in a West End play. Or, at least, he *was* in a West End play until—'

'You can't stop there!' he protested. 'Just when it's getting interesting.'

'I was taking the pics. We had a thing going—and, well, I

didn't expect eternal fidelity—but I did expect his full attention while we were together.'

'A reasonable desire,' her companion said solemnly.

'So I thought, but an actress in the play started flashing her eyes at him. I think she saw him chiefly as a career step-up— Oh, I don't know, though. To be fair, he's very handsome.'

'Well known?' Dante asked.

'Sandor Jayley.'

Dante's eyes widened.

'I saw one of his films on television the other day,' he said. 'He's supposed to be headed for even greater things.' He assumed a declamatory voice. 'The man whose embrace all women dream of—whose merest look—'

'Oh, shut up!' she said through laughter. 'I can't keep a straight face at that twaddle, which used to really annoy him.'

'He took it seriously?'

'Yes. Mind you, he has plenty going for him.'

'Looks, allure…?'

'Dazzling smile, more charm than was good for him—or for me. Just the usual stuff. Nothing, really.'

'Yes, it doesn't amount to much,' he agreed. 'You have to wonder why people make such a fuss about it.'

They nodded in solemn accord.

He yawned suddenly, turning so that he was half-sideways and could raise one foot onto the seat beside him; he rested an arm on it and leaned his head back. Ferne studied him a moment, noticing the relaxed grace of his tall, lean body. His shirt was open at the throat, enough to reveal part of his smooth chest; his black hair was slightly on the long side.

She had to admit that he had 'the usual stuff', with plenty to spare. His face was not only handsome but intriguing, with well-defined, angular features, dark, wicked eyes and a look of fierce, humorous intelligence.

Quirky, she thought, considering him with a professional gaze. Always about to do or say something unexpected. That was what she'd try to bring out if she were taking his photograph.

Suddenly he looked at her, and the gleaming look was intense.

'So, tell me about it,' he said.

'Where do I start?' She sighed. 'The beginning, when I was starry-eyed and stupid, or later, when he was shocked by my "unprincipled vulgarity"?'

Dante was immediately alert.

'Unprincipled and vulgar, hmm? That sounds interesting. Don't stop.'

'I met Tommy when I was hired to take the photographs for the play—'

'Tommy?'

'Sandor. His real name is Tommy Wiggs.'

'I can see why he changed it. But I want to know how you were unprincipled and vulgar.'

'You'll have to wait for that bit.'

'Spoilsport!'

'Where was I? Ah, yes, taking pictures for the play. Thinking back, I guess he set out to make me fall for him because he reckoned it would give an extra something to the photographs. So he took me to dinner and dazzled me.'

'And you were taken in by actorly charm?' Dante asked, frowning a little, as though he found it hard to believe.

'No, he was cleverer than that. He made a great play of switching off the actor and just being *himself*, as he put it, saying he wanted to use his real name because Sandor was for the masses. The man inside was *Tommy*.' Seeing his face, she said, 'Yes, it makes me feel a bit queasy too, but that night it was charming.

'The thing is, Tommy was made to be a film actor, not a stage actor. He's more impressive in close-up, and the closer you get the better he seems.'

'And he made sure you got very close?'

'Not that night,' she murmured, 'but eventually.'

She fell silent, remembering moments that had been sweet at the time but in retrospect felt ridiculous. How easily she'd fallen, and how glad she was to be out of it now. Yet there had been other times that she still remembered with pleasure, however mistakenly.

Dante watched her face, reading it without difficulty, and his eyes darkened. He raised a hand to summon the attendant, and when Ferne looked up she found Dante filling a glass of champagne for her.

'I felt you needed it after all,' he said.

'Yes,' she murmured. 'Maybe I do.'

'So what was the film actor doing in a play?' Dante asked.

'He felt that people didn't take him seriously.'

'Heaven help us! One of them. They make a career out of being eye candy but it's not enough. They want to be *respected*.'

'You've got him to a T,' Ferne chuckled. 'Are you sure you don't know him?'

'No, but I've met plenty like him. Some of the houses I sell belong to that kind of person—"full of themselves", I believe is the English expression.'

'That's it. Someone persuaded him that if he did a bit of Shakespeare everyone would be impressed, so he agreed to star in *Antony and Cleopatra*.'

'Playing Antony, the great lover?'

'Yes. But I think part of the attraction was the fact that Antony was an ancient Roman, so he had to wear little, short tunics that showed off his bare legs. He's got very good legs.

He even made the costume department take the tunics up a couple of inches to show off his thighs.'

Dante choked with laughter.

'It was very much an edited version of the play because he couldn't remember all the long speeches,' Ferne recalled. 'Mind you, he made them shorten Cleopatra's speeches even more.'

'In case she took too much of the spotlight?' Dante hazarded a guess.

'Right. He wasn't going to have that. Not that it really mattered, because everyone was looking at his thighs.'

'I don't think you're exactly heartbroken,' Dante commanded, watching her intently.

'Certainly not,' she said quickly. 'It was ridiculous, really. Just showbusiness. Or life.'

'How do you mean?'

'It's all a performance of one kind or another. We each live by pretending something's true when we really know it isn't, or not true when we know it is.'

A strange look came into his eyes, as though her words carried a particular resonance. He seemed about to say something, but then backed off. She had the impression that a corner of the curtain to his mind had been raised, then dropped hastily.

So there was more to him than the charming clown, she thought. He presented that aspect to the world, but behind it was another man who hid himself away and kept everyone else out. Intrigued, she wondered how easy it would be to reach behind his defences.

The next moment he gave her the answer.

Seeing her watching him, he closed his eyes, shutting her out completely.

CHAPTER TWO

SUDDENLY he opened his eyes again, revealing that the tension had gone. The dark moment might never have been. His next words were spoken lightly.

'You're getting very philosophical.'

'Sorry,' she said.

'Were you talking about yourself when you said we each live by refusing to admit the truth?'

'Well, I suppose I really knew that another woman had her eye on him, and I ought to have realised that he'd give in to flattery, no matter what he'd said to me hours before. But it was still a bit of a shock when I went to meet him at the theatre after the performance and found them together.'

'What were they doing—or needn't I ask?'

'You needn't ask. They were right there on the stage, stretched out on Cleopatra's tomb, totally oblivious to anyone and anything. She was saying, "Oh, you really are Antony—a great hero!"'

'And I suppose they were—' Dante paused delicately '—in a state of undress?'

'Well, he still had his little tunic on. Mind you, that was almost the same thing.'

'So what did you do?' he asked, fascinated. 'You didn't creep away in tears. Not you. You went and thumped him.'

'Neither.' She paused for dramatic effect. 'I hardly dare tell you what I did.'

'Have we got to the bit where you're unprincipled and vulgar?' he asked hopefully.

'We have.'

'Don't keep me in suspense. Tell me.'

'Well, I take my camera everywhere…'

Dante's crack of laughter seemed to hit the ceiling and echo around the carriage, waking the barman from his doze.

'You *didn't*?'

'I did. They were wonderful pictures. I took as many as I could from as many different angles as possible.'

'And he didn't see you?'

'He had his back to me,' Ferne explained. 'Facing downwards.'

'Oh yes, naturally. But what about her?'

'She was facing up and she saw me, of course. She loved it. Then I stormed off in a temper, went straight to the offices of a newspaper that specialised in that sort of thing and sold the lot.'

Awed, he stared at her. 'Just like that?'

'Just like that.'

His respect grew in leaps and bounds; a woman who reacted to her lover's betrayal not with tears and reproaches but with well-aimed revenge was a woman after his own heart.

What couldn't she do if she set her mind to it?

Would any man of sense want to get on her wrong side?

But her right side—that was a different matter!

'What happened?' he demanded, still fascinated.

'There were ructions, but not for long. The seats had been selling reasonably well, but after that it was standing-room only. *She* gave an interview about how irresistible he was, and he got offered a big, new film-part. So then he walked out on the show, which annoyed Josh, the director, until the understudy took over and got rave reviews. He was Josh's boyfriend, so everyone was happy.'

'Everyone except you. What did you get out of it?'

'The paper paid me a fortune. By that time I'd calmed down a bit and was wondering if I'd gone too far, but then the cheque arrived, and, well…'

'You've got to be realistic,' he suggested.

'Exactly. Mick—that's my agent—said some people wait a lifetime for a stroke of luck like mine. I've always wanted to see Italy, so I planned this trip. I had to wait a couple of months because suddenly I was much in demand. I'm not sure why.'

'Word had spread about your unusual skills,' he mused.

'Yes, that must be it. Anyway, I made a gap in my schedule, because I was determined to come here, chucked everything into a suitcase, jumped on the next train to Paris and from there I got the train to Milan.

'I spent a few days looking over the town, then suddenly decided to take off for Naples. It was late in the evening by then and a sensible person would have waited until morning. So I didn't.'

Dante nodded in sympathy. 'The joy of doing things on the spur of the moment! There's nothing like it.'

'I've always been an organised person, perhaps too organised. It felt wonderful to go a bit mad.' She gave a brief, self-mocking laugh. 'But I'm not very good at it, and I really messed up, didn't I?'

'Never mind. With practice, you'll improve.'

'Oh no! That was my one fling.'

'Nonsense, you're only a beginner. Let me introduce you to the joys of living as though every moment was your last.'

'Is that how you live?'

He didn't reply at first. He'd begun to lean forward across the table, looking directly into her face. Now he threw himself back again.

'Yes, it's how I live,' he said. 'It gives a spice and flavour to life that comes in no other way.'

She felt a momentary disturbance. It was inexplicable, except that there had been something in his voice that didn't fit their light-hearted conversation. Only a moment ago he'd shut her out, and something told her he might just do so again. They had drifted close to dangerous territory, which seemed to happen surprisingly easily with this man.

Again, she wondered just what lay in that forbidden place. Trying to coax him into revelation, she mused, 'Never to know what will happen next—I suppose I'm living proof that that can make life interesting. When I woke up this morning, I never pictured this.'

His smile was back. The moment had passed.

'How could you have imagined that you'd meet one of this country's heroes?' he demanded irrepressibly. 'A man so great that his head is on the coins.'

Enjoying her bemused look, he produced a two-euro coin. The head, with its sharply defined nose, did indeed bear a faint resemblance to him.

'Of course!' she said. 'Dante Alighieri, your famous poet. Is that how you got your name?'

'Yes. My mother hoped that naming me after a great man might make me a great man too.'

'We all have our disappointments to bear,' Ferne said solemnly.

His eyes gleamed appreciation at her dig.

'Do you know much about Dante?' he asked.

'Not really. He lived in the late-thirteenth to early-fourteenth century, and he wrote a masterpiece called *The Divine Comedy*, describing a journey through hell, purgatory and paradise.'

'You've read it? I'm impressed.'

'Only in an English translation, and I had to struggle to reach the end.' She chuckled. 'Hell and purgatory were so much more interesting than paradise.'

He nodded. 'Yes, I always thought paradise sounded insufferable. All that virtue.' He shuddered, then brightened. 'Luckily, it's the last place I'm likely to end up. Have some more champagne.'

'Just a little.'

A train thundered past them, going in the opposite direction. Watching the lights flicker on him as it went, Ferne thought that it wasn't hard to picture him as a master of the dark arts; he was engaging and more than a little risky, because he masked his true self with charm.

She'd guessed he was in his early thirties, but in this light she changed the estimate to late thirties. There was experience in his face, both good and bad.

'What are you thinking?' he asked.

'I was wondering what part of the other world you might have come from.'

'No doubt about it, the seventh terrace of purgatory,' he said, one eyebrow cocked to see if she understood.

She did. The seventh terrace was reserved for those who had over-indulged in the more pleasurable sins.

'That's just what I thought,' she murmured. 'But I didn't want to suggest it in case you were offended.'

His wry smile informed her that this was the last accusation that would ever offend him.

For a few minutes they sipped champagne in silence. Then he remarked, 'You'll be staying with us, of course?'

'As Hope says, I don't have any choice, for a few days at least.'

'Longer, much longer,' he said at once. 'Italian bureaucracy takes its time, but we'll try to make your stay a pleasant one.'

His meaning was unmistakeable. *Well, why not?* she thought. She was in the mood for a flirtation with a man who would take it as lightly as herself. He was attractive, interesting and they both knew the score.

'I'll look forward to it,' she said. 'Actually, Hope wants me to talk to her about England, and it's the least I can do for her.'

'Yes, she must feel a bit submerged by Italians,' Dante said. 'Mind you, she's always been one of us, and the whole family loves her. My parents died when I was fifteen, and she's been like a second mother to me ever since.'

'Do you live here?'

'No, I'm based in Milan, but I came south with them because I think there are business opportunities in the Naples area. So after looking around I might decide to stay.'

'What do you do?'

'I deal in property, specialising in unusual places, old houses that are difficult to sell.'

He yawned and they sat together in companionable silence. She felt drained and contented at the same time, separated from the whole universe on this train, thundering through the night.

Looking up, she saw that he was staring out into the darkness. She could see his reflection faintly in the window. His eyes were open and held a faraway expression, as though he could see something in the gloom that was hidden from her and which filled him with a melancholy intensity.

He looked back at her and smiled, rising reluctantly to his feet and holding out his hand. 'Let's go.'

At the door to her carriage, he paused and said gently, 'Don't worry about anything. I promise you, it's all going to work out. Goodnight.'

Ferne slipped into the carriage, moving quietly so as not to waken Hope, who was asleep. In a moment she'd skimmed up the ladder and settled down in bed, staring into the night, wondering about the man she'd just left. He was likeable in a mad sort of way, and she didn't mind spending some time in his company, as long as it was strictly casual.

But she didn't brood. The rocking of the train was hypnotic, and she was soon asleep.

Next morning there was just time for a quick snack before they arrived. Hope looked eagerly out of the window, wondering which of her sons would meet them.

'Justin's in England and Luke's in Rome,' she said. 'Carlo's in Sicily and won't be back for a couple of days. It'll be one of the other three.'

In the end three sons were waiting at the station, waving and cheering as the train pulled in. They embraced their parents exuberantly, clapped Dante on the shoulder and eyed Ferne with interest.

'These are Francesco, Ruggiero and Primo,' Toni explained. 'Don't try to sort them out just now. We'll do the introductions later.'

'Ferne has had a misfortune and will be staying with us until it's sorted out,' Hope said. 'Now, I'm longing to get home.'

There were two cars. Hope, Toni and Ferne rode in the first, driven by Francesco, while the other two brothers took Dante and the luggage in the second.

All the way home Hope looked eagerly out of the window,

until at last she seized Ferne's arm and said, 'Look. That's the Villa Rinucci.'

Ferne followed her gaze up to the top of a hill, on which was perched a large villa facing out over Naples and the sea. She was entranced by the place; it was bathed in golden sun, and looked as though it contained both beauty and safety.

As they grew nearer she saw that the house was larger than she'd realised at first. Trees surrounded it, but the villa was on slightly higher ground, so that it seemed to be growing out of the trees. A plump woman, followed by two buxom young girls, came out to watch the cars arriving, all waving eagerly.

'That's Elena, my housekeeper,' Hope told Ferne. 'The two girls are her nieces who are working here for a couple of weeks, because there will be so many of us—and plenty of children, I'm glad to say. I called Elena while we were still on the train, to tell her you were coming and would need a room.'

The next moment they stopped, the door was pulled open and Ferne was being shown up the steps onto the wide terrace that surrounded the house, and then inside.

'Why don't you go up to your room at once?' Hope asked. 'Come down when you're ready and meet these villains I call my sons.'

'These villains' were smiling with pleasure at seeing their parents again and Ferne slipped away, understanding that they would want to be free of her for a while.

Her room was luxurious, with its own bathroom and a wide, comfortable-looking bed. Going to the window, she found she was at the front of the house, with a stunning view over the Bay of Naples. It was at its best just now, the water glittering in the morning sun, stretching away to the horizon, seeming to offer an infinity of pleasure and unknown delight.

Quickly she showered and changed into a dress of pale

blue, cut on simple lines but fashionable. At least she would be able to hold her head up in elegant Italy.

She heard laughter from below, and looked out of the window to where the Rinucci family were seated around a rustic wooden table under the trees, talking and laughing in a gentle manner that made a sudden warmth come over her heart.

Her own family life had been happy but sparse. She was an only child, born to parents who were themselves only-children. One set of grandparents had died early, the other had emigrated to Australia.

Now her father was dead and her mother had gone to live with her own parents in Australia. Ferne could have gone too, but had chosen to stay in London to pursue a promising career. So there was only herself to blame that she was lonely, that there had been nobody to lend a sympathetic ear when the crash had come with Sandor Jayley.

There had been friends, of course, nights out with the girls that she'd genuinely enjoyed. But they were career women like herself, less inclined to sympathise than congratulate her on the coup she'd pulled off. She'd always returned to an empty flat, the silence and the memories.

But something told her that the Villa Rinucci was never truly empty, and she was assailed by delight as she gazed down at the little gathering.

Hope looked up and waved, signalling for her to join them, and Ferne hurried eagerly down the stairs and out onto the terrace. As she approached the table the young men stood up with an old-fashioned courtesy that she found charming, and Dante stepped forward to take her hand and lead her forward. Hope rose and kissed her.

'This is the lady who joined us on the train and who will be staying with us for a while,' she said.

She began to introduce the young men—first Primo, stepson from her first marriage, then Ruggiero, one of her sons by Toni. Both men were tall and dark. Primo's face was slightly heavier, while Ruggiero's features had a mobility that reminded her slightly of his cousin, Dante.

Francesco had a brooding quality, as though his mind carried some burden. Like the other two, he greeted her warmly, but then said, 'I'd better go now, Mamma. I want to get home before Celia.'

'Doesn't she ever get suspicious about how often that happens?' Hope asked.

'Always, and she tells me to stop, but—' He gave a resigned shrug. 'I do it anyway.' To Ferne he added, 'My wife is blind, and she gets very cross if she thinks I'm fussing over her, but I can't help it.'

'Go on home,' Hope told him. 'Just be sure you're at the party tomorrow.'

He embraced her fondly and departed. Almost at once another car appeared and disgorged two young women. One was dark, and so gracefully beautiful that even her pregnancy-bump couldn't detract from her elegance. The other was fair, pretty in a way that was sensible rather than exotic, and was accompanied by an eager toddler.

'This is my wife, Olympia,' Primo said, drawing the pregnant woman forward to meet Ferne.

'And this is my wife, Polly,' Ruggiero said, indicating the fair young woman.

At this distance she could see that Polly too was pregnant, possibly about five months. Her husband's attitude to her seemed protective, and again Ferne was pervaded by the feeling of contentment that she'd had earlier. Just being here, among people so happy to be together, was enough to create it.

It was soon time for lunch. Hope led the way indoors to inspect the meal Elena was preparing, taste things and give her opinion. In this she was joined not only by her daughters-in-law but her sons, who savoured the dishes and offered advice freely—sometimes too freely, as their mother informed them.

'So it's true what they say about Italian men,' Ferne observed, amused.

'What do they say about us?' Dante murmured in her ear. 'I'm longing to know.'

'Why, that you're all fantastic cooks, of course. What did you think I meant?'

He gave a disillusioned sigh. 'Nothing, nothing. Yes, we're all interested in cooking. Not like Englishmen, who eat sausage and mash on every occasion.' Suddenly he looked closely at her face. 'What is it?' he asked. 'Why are you looking troubled?'

'I just suddenly thought—perhaps I should telephone the consulate. They might have some news by now.'

'This afternoon I'll drive you into Naples and we'll visit the consulate here. They can get onto the Milan consulate. Now, let's forget boring reality and concentrate on the important things—enjoying ourselves.'

'Yes, let's,' she said happily.

Dante was as good as his word, borrowing Toni's car after lunch and driving her down the hill through the streets of the old town until they reached their destination near the coast.

There the news was bleak. Neither her passport nor her credit cards had been recovered.

'Considering how quickly they were reported, it looks as though someone made off with them,' Dante observed. 'But hopefully they won't be any use to them.'

'We can arrange a temporary passport,' the young woman

at the desk said. 'But it will take a few days. There's a kiosk over there for the photograph.'

'No need, I'll take it,' Dante said. Eyeing Ferne's bag, he added, 'If you'll lend me your camera.'

She handed it to him. 'What made you so sure I had it?'

'You told me you always had it. And the woman who was smart enough to record her lover's infidelity wouldn't miss a trick like this.'

She showed him how to work it, and they spent a few minutes out in the sun while she turned this way and that at his command.

'Pull your blouse down this side,' he said. 'You've got pretty shoulders; let's see them. Good. Now, shake your head so that your hair fluffs up.'

'This is no good for passport pictures,' she objected.

He grinned. 'Who said anything about passport pictures? Maybe I have a wicked purpose of my own.'

Back inside, they switched the camera to 'view' and showed the results to the woman at the desk, who regarded them with saintly patience.

'None of these are suitable. I think you should use the kiosk,' she suggested.

'We could have done that to start with,' Ferne pointed out.

'But then my wicked purpose wouldn't have been fulfilled,' Dante said unanswerably. 'Come on; go into that kiosk and take some shots that make you look dreary and virtuous.'

'Are you suggesting that I'm *not* dreary and virtuous?'

'Which part of that question do you want me to answer?'

'Let's just get on with it,' she said hastily.

When the formalities were complete, Dante took her to a café by the beach and they relaxed over coffee.

'If you think the villa's a madhouse now,' he said, 'wait until tomorrow when the rest of the family get here.'

'There's quite a lot of them, isn't there? Six, I think Hope said.'

'That's right, although they don't all live around here. Luke and Minnie will be coming from Rome. Justin and Evie from England, with Mark, Justin's son, and their baby twins.'

A terrible thought struck Ferne. 'Where will they be staying?'

'At the villa, of course.'

'And you're there too, so whose room have I been given? Someone will end up sleeping on the sofa because of me, and I can't have that. I've got to go.'

'And stay where—in a hotel? With no money or paperwork?'

'Well, if you could lend me some money I'll pay it back…'

Dante shook his head firmly. 'Sorry, no. To tell the hotel that you're a trustworthy person, when actually I don't know if you are, would be most improper. And we must always behave with propriety, mustn't we?'

Despite her agitation, she couldn't help laughing.

'You,' she said in a slow, deliberate voice, 'wouldn't recognise *propriety* if it came up and whacked you on the nose— which I am strongly tempted to do right now.'

'Curses!' he said theatrically. 'She's seen through me. All right, I'll admit my true motive. I plan to keep you here, a prisoner, subject to my will. Cash would help you to escape, which doesn't suit my evil purpose.'

'I wonder if I can guess your evil purpose,' she said dryly.

'Well, I'm not exactly subtle, am I? But do I need to be? You're in my power.'

'In your dreams!' she chuckled.

'In those too,' he said with a yearning look.

'No, I didn't mean— Oh, you know what I meant.'

'Well, a man can dream, can't he?' he asked, eyeing her significantly.

'He can dream all he likes, as long as he doesn't confuse dreams with reality,' she said, also significantly. 'And you didn't answer my question. Whose room have I been given?'

He didn't reply, but his mouth twisted.

'Oh no, please, don't tell me…?'

'If you feel that way, we could always share it,' he suggested.

'Will you just stop, please?'

'All right, all right, don't eat me. You can't blame a man for trying.'

'I can. I do.'

'You wouldn't if you could sit where I'm sitting, looking at you.'

She gave up. How could you talk sense to a man who had that wicked glint in his eyes?

But it could be fun finding out.

CHAPTER THREE

'IF YOU'RE going to reject me, I'll just have to console myself with those pictures of you that I took,' Dante remarked.

'I deleted them,' she said at once.

'Like hell you did! If you didn't delete the evidence of your lover misbehaving, you aren't going to wipe out the pics of you looking like every man's dream of sexy.'

'Will you stop talking to me like that?'

'Why should I?'

What could she say? *Because it gives me a fizz of excitement that I'm not ready for yet.*

He was a clever man, she reckoned; he made it clear beyond doubt that he was sexually attracted to her, yet with such a light touch that she could relax in his company, free from pressure. She didn't doubt that he would jump into her bed in an instant, if she gave him the barest hint. But without that hint he would sit here talking nonsense, biding his time.

She wondered how many other women had been beguiled into his arms, and what had happened to them when it was over. She suspected that Dante would always be the one to say goodbye, treating love easily, never lingering too long. But there was more to him than that; instinct, too deep to be analysed, told her so.

His tone changed, becoming what he would have called 'prosaic'.

'While I think of it—' he reached into his wallet and handed her a wad of notes '—you can't walk around without any money.'

'But you just said you wouldn't—'

'We're back in the real world. You must have something. Here.'

Staggered, she looked at the amount. 'So much? No, Dante, please—I can't take this.' Accepting some of the notes, she tried to thrust the rest back at him.

'You don't know what you may need,' he said firmly, pushing her hand away. 'But what you will definitely need is your independence, and with that you'll have it. Put it away safely.' He sounded like a school master.

'But what about keeping me in your power?' she asked, tucking it into her bag. 'Making me independent isn't going to help your evil purpose.'

'True,' he mused. 'On the other hand, nothing gained by force is really satisfying. It's better when she knocks on his door and says she can't live any longer without his wild embraces. Much more fun.'

'And do you think I'm going to do that?'

He seemed to consider this. 'No, I think you'll go to the stake before you yield an inch. But, as I said before, a man can dream.'

They regarded each other in perfect, humorous understanding.

Afterwards they drove back to the villa slowly, where supper was just being prepared.

'Some people only turn up just before a meal,' Francesco jeered, giving Dante a friendly thump on the shoulder.

He'd gone home and returned with his wife, Celia, whom he now drew forward.

Ferne would hardly have guessed that Celia was blind. She was bright and vivacious with a way of turning her head, clearly aware of what was happening around her. They fell easily into conversation, sitting on the terrace and chatting about their work. Celia's career was making the world accessible to the blind.

'I'm working on a scheme to make theatres more friendly,' she said. 'It involves an ear-piece with a description of the action. Francesco and I were in London a couple of months ago, going to lots of shows so that I could get some ideas, and we went to a performance where everyone was going crazy over the star, Sandor Jayley. They said he looked incredibly sexy in a little Roman tunic.

'But Francesco wouldn't tell me that, and I had to find out afterwards when apparently there were some deliciously scandalous pictures of Sandor in the papers. Why, what's the matter?'

Dante had drawn a sharp breath. The sight of his appalled face made Ferne burst out laughing.

'Have I said something wrong?' Celia begged.

'No, not at all,' Ferne choked. 'It's just that…'

Briefly she told the story and Celia covered her mouth in horror.

'Oh no! What have I done? I never meant— Please, please—'

'It's all right,' Ferne hurried to say. 'I saw the funny side of it ages ago. Oh heavens!' She went off into gales of laughter again, then calmed down and tried to reassure Celia that she wasn't in a state of collapse. It took a while, but at last she managed it.

When she looked up Dante was observing her with a strange smile and a look in his eyes that might have been admiration.

From inside the house they heard Hope's voice.

'Ferne, dear, are you there? I need your help.'

'I'll be back in a minute,' Ferne said, hurrying away.

Celia listened as Ferne's footsteps faded, then turned to Dante.

'She's gorgeous,' she said. 'You're a lucky man.'

'What makes you think she's mine?'

'Francesco says you can't take your eyes off her.'

'And with reason. She's worth looking at.'

'I think her face is gentle and kind, like her voice, when she went to so much trouble to reassure me. She sounds lovely.'

'She is lovely,' Dante murmured.

'Is she really all right about that man—the one they call "sexy legs"?'

'Would you mind not saying that?' Dante said in a strained voice.

'You've really got it bad, haven't you?'

'I decline to answer,' he said after a moment. 'Shall we go in to supper?'

That evening was one of the most pleasant Ferne had ever spent. As the sun faded, lights came on in the garden and at last everyone drifted away from the table to drink their wine under the trees.

'I think your family has found the secret of happy marriage,' Ferne murmured. 'They all look like courting couples—even Hope and Toni, after all these years.'

Dante nodded. 'Hope says that's all down to Toni, the sweetest-natured man in the world. He's always been very kind to me. I'm glad he has happiness now, even if it's in the sunset rather than the sunrise.'

'I wonder if that could be better.'

'I doubt it. Who can ever tell what their own sunset is going to be?'

'Perhaps wondering about it is one of the pleasures of life?' she suggested.

He gave a little shrug. 'Perhaps. Let's go where we can watch the Naples sunset.'

Totally content, she let him lead her to a place where they could stand beneath the trees and watch the miracle that was happening over the bay. For a dazzling moment the light was deep red, seeming to set the sea on fire, and they watched it in awed silence.

'No matter how often I see that,' he murmured, 'it never fails. As long as there's so much glory in the world…' He fell silent.

'Have you spent much time here?' Ferne asked.

'Since my parents died I've kind of moved around the family, living with aunts, uncles, grandparents. This was where I came in the summer, and I loved it. It felt more *home* than anywhere else.'

'But it sounds sad to be moving around the family, not really having a settled base.'

'I like having a big family. There's nothing to compare with the feeling that you have the whole tribe behind you.'

'Isn't there one member of the tribe you need more than the others?'

'Hope and Toni have been like second parents. Apart from them, no. Like you, I'm an only child, but I thrive on having plenty of cousins.'

At last everyone drifted back to the house. There were children to be put to bed, and Hope wanted an early night. Ferne was glad of the chance to go to her room to be alone and think about everything that had happened to her.

To think about Dante Rinucci.

He was attractive, amusing, sexy and clearly in the mood for a diversion. Since she felt the same, there was really no problem, except for the little voice in her head that kept saying, *Beware*!

But beware what? she asked herself.

There's something about him that doesn't add up.

Nonsense. I'm just being fanciful.

She put on a night-gown, took out her laptop and connected it to her digital camera. In a moment she was looking at the pictures Dante had taken of her, trying to recognise herself.

Who was this woman with the come-hither look, giving the man that teasing smile because she was basking in his attention? It was an illusion. Dante had summoned that look from her in the joking spirit that seemed natural to him, and somehow he'd persuaded her to glance sideways, smiling, to intrigue him as he intrigued her. This man was a natural showman with the gift of luring everyone else into the show. There was no more to it than that, and she mustn't forget.

There was a knock on the door and Dante's voice called, 'It's me.'

She drew a slow breath of dismay. She'd half-expected him to appear at her door, but not so soon. Where was the skilled, sensitive man with the light touch that she'd pictured? Was he going to be vulgarly obvious after all? Her disappointment was severe.

As she was preparing the words of rejection, he knocked again. 'Can I come in?'

'Yes,' she said hastily, reaching for her robe and whisking it on as his head appeared cautiously around the door.

'Ah, you've got the pictures on-screen,' he said. 'I was hoping to see them. Am I any good as a photographer?'

'Er, yes, some of the pictures are very nice,' she said, trying to marshal her thoughts.

He was still fully dressed and didn't seem to notice that she was attired for the night. He studied the computer screen eagerly.

'Nice,' he said. 'You photograph well, and the light was good just then.'

He ran through to the end of the pictures, then back, then forward again, until he found one that seemed to please him especially. She had just shaken her hair so that it fell in soft curls about her face, framing her laughter.

'I'd like to have a copy of that one,' he said. 'You look just great.'

Here it was: the first move. *Be careful.*

But it was hard to be careful when she was suddenly conscious of her nakedness beneath the flimsy night-gown. Her whole body seemed alive to him and oblivious to her efforts at control.

'I'm afraid that may take a while,' she said. 'I don't have a printer with me.'

'No problem. Here's my email address. Send it to me as a file attachment and I'll take care of the printing. Now, I should get to bed if I were you. You've had a long day, and tomorrow is going to be even busier.'

He turned in the open door.

'Sleep well. Sorry I disturbed you. Goodnight.'

The door closed behind him.

Just down the corridor, the sound of that door closing was heard by two who lay contentedly in each other's arms.

'Leaving so soon?' Toni observed. 'Dante's losing his touch. Usually he can have any woman he wants—for a little while.'

'I know,' Hope sighed. 'As soon as it looks like getting serious, he vanishes. But how can we blame him? Think what it must be like for him, living with the knowledge that— Oh, it's terrible! Of course he can't be like other people.'

'He won't let anyone mention the subject,' Toni said sombrely. 'If you try, he becomes cold and angry. He wants to pretend that nothing is wrong, but if you catch him off-guard it's there in his eyes, the knowledge and the fear.'

'Should we tell Ferne?' Hope said. 'Just in case?'

'Warn her, you mean? Not now. Perhaps later. Dante would be furious to know that his secret was out.'

'Won't it have to come out in the end?'

'I don't know,' Toni said sadly. 'Perhaps it will never be spoken of at all—until it's too late.'

Dawn was the best part of the day, when the bright, clear air gave the view across the bay to Vesuvius a new vividness. How peaceful the volcano looked now it was sleeping, and how hard won that peace must be. The previous night had taught Ferne that.

She'd thought herself so well prepared, so ready to fend off any advance from Dante. But when he'd bid her a gentle-manly goodnight she'd been ill prepared for any of the reactions that had coursed through her.

Starting with disbelief, they had exploded through to outrage, deprivation and finally insult. At the mere prospect of making love with him, her body had flowered. And he hadn't been interested. It was sheer bad manners.

She could cheerfully have hurled something at the door he'd closed behind him. It had taken the rest of the night to calm the volcano inside her, and now the sight of the real one in the distance didn't improve her temper.

Had he suspected her moment of weakness? The thought made her go hot and cold.

She felt an urgent need to get away from where he might be. He'd come out last night to watch the sunset. Suppose he came out again at dawn?

Turning to hurry inside, she saw him standing behind her. How long had he been there?

'Good morning,' she said hurriedly, trying to get past him.

But he detained her with a light hand on her arm. 'Stay.'

'You're very free with your commands,' she said tersely.

'Have I offended you?'

'Of course not. But I expect you want to be alone.'

'Not alone from you.'

He turned her so that she faced the sea and then he stood behind her, his arms crossed over her breast, holding her gently against him. Mysteriously his touch seemed to soothe her annoyance, and Ferne put up her hands, not to push him away but to hold his forearms.

'So near and yet so far,' he murmured.

'How far is Vesuvius really?'

'Only about six miles in earthly distance, but it comes from another universe. Once, years ago, I heard it rumble, and it was like magic. I'm always hoping for another one.'

'No luck?'

'Not yet. It keeps you waiting.'

'Maybe it can't decide what it wants.'

'Or maybe it knows what it wants and can't decide what to do about it,' he mused. 'Even when you want something badly, the way isn't always clear.'

Now she had her answer about the night before. He didn't want to keep his distance from her, but for some reason seemed to feel that he should. So the next step was up to her. Nothing else mattered now; she was content.

They returned to find the villa already awakening. Everyone was agog at the arrival of the two remaining sons, Justin from England, Luke from Rome. As many of the family as possible were going to the airport to meet Justin, his wife and children. Dante and Ferne remained at the villa to greet Luke.

In the early afternoon Primo and Olympia arrived, soon followed by another car, out of which stepped a powerful-looking man and a petite, fair-haired young woman.

'Luke and Minnie,' Dante said.

It was clear from the interested looks Ferne was getting that her story had spread throughout the family. When Minnie came downstairs from settling into her room, she comman-deered Ferne's company, demanding to be told everything. But before there was time to say much there was a shout and everyone hurried outside to welcome the party from England.

Justin, Hope's eldest son, was an austere-looking man who at first seemed out of place in this convivial gathering, but Ferne noticed that his eyes followed his mother with a pos-sessive look that contrasted curiously with his bearing. He had the same look for his wife, Evie, a brisk young woman with an air of friendly efficiency.

They were accompanied by Mark, Justin's son by his first marriage. He was twenty, handsome, with dark wavy hair and brilliant eyes that made both the young maids give him yearning looks.

'He's just discovering his powers as a ladykiller,' Justin said with a groan, yet also a touch of fatherly pride. 'It makes him very difficult to live with.'

'Don't be hard on him,' Evie protested. 'It's not his fault he's good-looking. He's just finished his first love affair with a girl who teaches ballroom dancing. He started learning as a way of getting close to her, and now he's really good.'

The young man's presence changed the atmosphere,

making it livelier. Later, when the meal was over, Toni rummaged through some old tapes, made in the days before rock 'n' roll, and played them on an ancient tape recorder.

'Go on,' he told Mark. 'Let's see how good you are.'

Without hesitating, Mark extended a hand to Ferne, whom he'd been admiring across the table all through supper.

'Dance with me?'

Pleased, she accepted. She was a good dancer, and Mark was an expert. Soon they were spinning around in perfect time.

'Let's go really fast,' he said suddenly, swinging her around and around.

Gasping, she just managed to keep up. When they finished there was applause from the others, who had retired to sit down and watch them with admiration.

'What is that dance?' Dante asked, coming forward hastily. 'Could you teach it to me?'

'It's basically the quick-step,' Mark told him. 'You do it like this.'

Someone switched the music on again, and there were more cheers and applause as Mark gave a dazzling demonstration, with Ferne as his partner. Then Dante took possession of her and proceeded to show how well he'd learned.

Ferne had to admit that he was a natural, mastering the fastest steps with ease, and taking her flying across the floor as if they had been doing this all their lives.

With this partner the most intricate steps became easy to her, and her feet flashed in and out, sometimes between his own feet, so that she felt they must surely trip each other, yet never did. She had the glorious sensation that no mistake was possible while Dante held her. He was a powerful man, but that power lay not in muscles and brawn but in quicksilver.

That was how he lived his life, she was sure. If trouble

loomed, he would dance around it, or over it, or past it, then vanish into the shadows, leaving everyone wondering if he'd ever really been there. It made him both enchanting and dangerous.

At last Toni changed the tape, and they slowed into a waltz.

'I'm impressed,' she gasped. 'Have you really never done the quick-step before?'

'No, but I love dancing; the faster, the better.'

'Waltzing's too dull for you, huh?'

'Much. Who needs it? You have to hold her close.'

'As you're doing with me?'

'Naturally. And you have to pay her compliments, like she's the loveliest woman in the room.'

'But you're not doing that!' she protested indignantly.

'Why should I bore you with what you've heard a hundred times before? Besides,' he added more slowly, 'you know exactly what you look like.'

He was right. She'd taken time over her appearance, and was pleased with the result. The honey-red of her hair was perfectly set off by the floaty chiffon dress with its mixture of autumnal colours. It was knee-length, revealing that her legs were long and elegant, her ankles perfect, and she had a natural balance for the high-heeled sandals that many women couldn't have risked wearing.

In the arms of this tall man, those heels were an advantage, helping her match his height and see his face more closely.

'Maybe I know and maybe I don't,' she teased. 'That's for me to say.'

'So you want me to tell you that you're a dream of beauty, a goddess of the night?'

'Oh, shut up!' she chuckled.

'I'm just trying to do the proper thing here.'

'And you're always so proper, aren't you?'

'Well, somebody did once say that I wouldn't recognise propriety if it came up and whacked me. I can't recall her name just now.'

'Ah! One of those instantly forgettable females. She was probably just trying to provoke you to get your attention.'

He gave a self-mocking smile. 'I wish I could believe she wanted my attention.'

'Or she might be playing cat-and-mouse with you.'

'I'd like to believe that too. You don't know what fun cat-and-mouse can be.'

'You think I don't?' she asked, eyebrows arched sardonically.

'No, forget I said that. Of course you do.' He added hopefully, 'You could probably teach me a thing or two.'

'No, I don't think I could teach you anything about playing games.'

'The game of love has many different aspects,' he suggested.

'But we're not talking about love,' she whispered. 'This is a different game altogether.'

It was a game that made her pulses race and her whole body sing from the close contact with his. Reason argued that her physical excitement was due to the movement of the dance, but reason fell silent before the pleasure of his clasp about her waist and the awareness of his mouth near hers.

'What do you call the game?' he whispered.

'I'm sure we each have our own name for it.'

'Tell me yours.'

She glanced up, murmuring, 'I'll tell you mine if you'll tell me yours.'

'I asked first.'

This time she didn't reply, but her look was full of mischief.

'You're going to tease me, aren't you?' he said. 'You're a wicked woman.'

'I know. I work at it.'

'No need. I reckon a certain kind of wickedness comes naturally to you.'

'True. It's one of the great pleasures of life.' Exhilarated, she provoked him further. 'Almost as much fun as cat-and-mouse.'

A gleam of appreciation came into his eyes. 'Cat-and-mouse; I wish I knew which one I was.'

'I'll leave you to work that one out.'

He gave a shout of laughter that made everyone stare at them, and began whirling her fast again until they spun out onto the terrace, where she broke from him and darted away, running down the steps and under the trees. She was high on excitement, and the sound of him pursuing her was a delight. She ran faster, challenging him to follow her, and he accepted the challenge.

'Woman, are you crazy?' he demanded, winding his arms around her waist in a grip of velvet and steel. 'Just how much do you think a man can take?'

She responded not with words but with laughter, that rang up to the moon until he silenced her mouth with his own. Somehow the laughter continued, because it was there in the kiss, passing from her to him and back again. It was there too in the skilful movements of his hands that knew how to coax without demanding, persuade without insisting.

He had the gift which so many men lacked, of kissing gently. Her return kiss was joyful, curious, teasing just a little.

'I'm not crazy,' she whispered. 'And perhaps a man should exercise a little self-control.'

'Not while you're making it hard for him,' he growled, moving down her neck.

She was unable to say more, because his lips had found the spot where she was most sensitive. Shivers went through her, defying her efforts to control them as his mouth caressed the hollow at the base of her throat, touching it softly again and again while she clung to him and her head whirled.

He was wicked. Even with all her nerves shouting warnings, he could still make her want him. Her hands had a will of their own. They clasped his head, drawing him closer against her so that his lips continued their skilled work. She should push him away, but, just another minute…

She felt the ground beneath her. She didn't know when he'd drawn her down, but suddenly she was lying in his arms, and he was looking at her with an expression on his face that she couldn't see through the darkness.

That was so like him, she thought feverishly—always keeping one part of himself a secret. And right now she wanted to know his secrets, wanted to know everything about him, to feel his hands on her body, all over, wanted everything there was to want.

His fingers were at the neck of her dress, trying to draw it lower. When it would go no further, he drew the shoulder down and laid his lips against it. Now she could feel his hair brushing her face and she ran her hand deliciously through it, sighing with satisfaction.

But then she heard something that froze her blood: laughter, soft and merry, coming from a little distance away. The family was appearing in the garden, getting nearer.

CHAPTER FOUR

'DANTE,' she hissed. '*Dante*! Get up.'

Frantically she pushed at him and he drew back, frowning.

'They're coming,' she said. 'They mustn't find us like this.'

Muttering a curse, he wrenched himself away and got to his feet, drawing her up with him. He would have run, but Mark's voice came through the trees.

'Ferne, Dante, are you there?'

'I'm going to murder that boy,' Dante muttered. 'He's doing this on purpose.'

'Don't be paranoid.'

'I'm not paranoid,' Dante said in a soft, enraged voice. 'He fancies you.'

Despite her jangling nerves, she nearly laughed.

'Nonsense. His heart's given to his dancing-girl friend.'

'He's twenty,' Dante snapped. 'He forgot her the minute he left England.'

'You don't know that.'

'Of course I know. I've been twenty.'

'So *that's* what young men of twenty do. And thirty. And thirty-five.'

Dante flung her the look of a man driven to madness.

Now the others were calling them. There was no choice but to walk back into the light, looking as cheerful and natural as possible. Ferne had a worrying feeling that her voice was shaking and she was sure that her smile looked unnatural.

But, more than that, she was shaking inside. She felt like someone who'd found herself unexpectedly on the edge of a cliff, and had backed off without knowing how she'd got there.

The family settled down for final drinks under the stars. Mark tried to get close to Ferne but was deterred by a scowl from Dante. If Ferne's nerves hadn't been jangling, she might have felt flattered and amused.

Hope ordered a pot of tea and Ferne drank it thankfully, feeling the warm liquid soothe her. Hope was looking at her kindly, and her eyebrows raised in surprise when Ferne took four sugar-lumps instead of her usual one. She needed them.

'I'm feeling a little tired,' she said as soon as she decently could. 'You won't mind if I go to bed?'

'I'm tired too, after the flight,' Evie said, and the party began to break up.

Ferne escaped upstairs, unable to meet Dante's eyes. Once in her room, she plunged into an icy-cold shower. That would soon put her right.

It did, to the extent that it cooled down her flesh, but her mind remained as disturbed as before. She was accustomed to thinking of herself as calm and collected. Even in the throes of passion for Sandor she'd felt in command—something which their grande finale had surely proved.

But Dante had upset that unruffled composure, making her wonder if it was really such a virtue. Had she perhaps become a trifle smug? If so, he was rescuing her from that danger, surprising her again and again.

He insisted on haunting her mind, despite her stern orders

for him to depart. But that was Dante: awkward. When she stepped out of the shower and caught a glimpse of herself in the mirror, he seemed to be there, eyeing her nakedness longingly, making her regret that she hadn't allowed him to see her, because he would have liked her so much.

She pulled on her nightdress and in her mind's eye his face fell.

'Get out!' she told him. 'Go away and leave me alone.'

He obeyed, but not without a final glance over his shoulder. There was a soft knock at her door.

'Who is it?'

'It's me,' said Dante.

She nearly said, 'Are you back already?' but stopped herself in time.

'What do you want?'

'Can I come in? There's something I need to talk about.'

She stood back to let him in, first making sure that her robe was securely fastened. Even so, she felt as though her garments were transparent.

He was still in shirt and trousers, but now the shirt had been torn open at the throat, showing several inches of his chest. It was an attractive chest, she had to admit that, but now she was trying to be cautious. In his arms tonight she'd almost lost her head. There had been a moment in the grass when she would have done anything he wanted, because he could make her want it too.

She was sure he knew it. This was one clever, manipulative man, and she must never let herself forget that.

'What did you want to talk about?' she asked demurely.

'Us,' he said at once. 'And what you're doing to me. I don't think I can stand it much longer.'

Now she was glad she'd taken the cold shower, for her body

had regained its equilibrium and her mind was able to view him rationally.

'If you can't stand being with me, it was hardly wise of you to come here,' she pointed out.

'I didn't say that,' he replied, imitating her tone of reasoned argument. 'It's the "so near and yet so far" aspect that's shredding my nerves. It should be one or the other, and I thought we might discuss it sensibly and come to a rational decision.'

The bland innocence of his face might have fooled anyone less alive to his tricks than Ferne. But by now she was back in command.

'I quite agree,' she said seriously. 'One or the other. And, since I'll be gone fairly soon, I think it we should opt for the second choice.'

'Pardon?'

'It would be wise for you to leave my room.'

He nodded. 'It would be wise, wouldn't it? If I were a wise man I'd flee and never look back. But I was never wise.'

'Then this would be a good time to start.'

He slid an arm around her waist.

'I know I shouldn't have come,' he murmured. 'But I had to. You were so wonderful tonight. I watched you and knew I had to dance with you—and then I danced with you and knew I had to hold you in my arms and kiss you and love you…'

He drew her close as he spoke in a grip that was gentle and implacable together.

'That's going a little too far, surely?' she asked lightly.

'But I want to go too far with you. How could I want anything else when you're so beautiful and you fire me up? I want to go too far and then further—'

'Hush,' she said suddenly. 'I thought I heard a noise in the corridor. Could anyone have seen you?'

'Not a soul. Don't worry, I'll be as quiet as a mouse.'

'You, a mouse?' she jeered softly. 'Who do you think you're fooling? Dante, I like you a lot, I really do, but I am not some daft little bimbo to be overcome by your charm. Don't forget, I've been seduced by an expert.'

'Are you suggesting I'm not an expert?' he asked in outrage.

'Well, you're not doing brilliantly right now.'

He gave a sigh and a rueful look, much like a schoolboy caught playing truant. She almost capitulated there and then, but thankfully managed to hold firm.

'It was worth a try, wasn't it?' she teased.

'I don't know what you mean.'

'Like hell you don't! You came in here saying to yourself, "Go on, give it a whirl. She might say yes, she might say no, she might slap my face. Let's find out".'

His sheepish expression confirmed her suspicions.

'Well, I found out, didn't I?' he said. 'But at least I didn't get my face slapped.'

'That's the next stage. Now, depart while we're still friends.'

'Friends? Is that really all you—?'

'*Go!*'

He went. Hastily.

As an attractive woman working in the entertainment business, Ferne had had a fair amount of experience in saying no to over-enthusiastic gentlemen, and she'd discovered that you could tell a lot about a man by how he behaved at the next meeting, assuming there was one. Some behaved well, some badly, some pretended that nothing had happened.

Dante, of course, had to be original, hopping behind her from tree to tree as she walked through the garden, darting out of sight when she turned until she cried, exasperated, 'Come out, you idiot.'

'If you're calling me an idiot, does that mean I'm forgiven?' he asked, presenting himself hopefully before her.

'I guess it does.'

From behind him came a shout. 'Dante, are you coming?'

'On my way,' he yelled back. 'I'm going into town with Carlo and Ruggiero, but I couldn't go until I knew I was back in favour.'

'I didn't say you were back in favour,' she told him sternly. 'I said you were forgiven—just.'

'Yes, of course, there's a difference. I'll work on it when I get back. Bye.'

He kissed her cheek and fled, leaving her laughing and wondering what she had to do to get the last word.

But then, she reflected, did she really want the last word? It had a melancholy sound.

She spent an enjoyable day with Hope and the other women, talking about England and fussing over the children. Dante's behaviour to her that evening was restrained and impeccable. He seemed completely oblivious to her as a woman, which was how she preferred it, she tried to tell herself.

Ferne had said she was never without her camera, and it was true, so when she came across Toni playing with Ruggiero's baby son she hurried into action and produced some swift, spontaneous shots that had everyone exclaiming with delight.

'I've been thinking what I can do to thank you for your kindness,' Ferne said to Hope. 'And now I know. I'm going to take pictures, dozens of them—everybody alone, in couples, with their children, without their children. Then I want you all to gather in the garden so that I can take a big one.'

'And I'll always have a memento,' Hope cried, overjoyed. 'Oh, yes please.'

Ferne started at once, going around the house, working on her idea until everyone had a solo shot, down to the tiniest child.

To these she added pictures taken secretly, when people had been unaware of being photographed and were therefore more natural. The final result was a triumphant collection that made Hope weep with joy, and give a special dinner in Ferne's honour.

'That was a very kind thing you did,' Dante said as they sipped wine together. 'Hope's family is everything to her.'

His praise made her slightly embarrassed.

'I did it for myself, really. Taking pictures is a kind of compulsion, and when I can't do it I get restless.'

'Why do you put yourself down? Who are you hiding from?'

'Since when were you an expert in psychoanalysis?' she asked, amused. 'I'm not hiding.'

'Some people would say you were hiding behind the camera, getting everyone else into focus but staying safely concealed. I'm just playing with ideas. If you want some good pictures, let me take you into town and show you old Naples, where the historic buildings still exist. You'll find all the pictures you want.'

She agreed eagerly and they went the next day, driving down into the *centro storico*, as historic Naples was called. As he'd guessed, she was enthusiastic and began clicking, enchanted by the narrow, winding streets with washing strung from side to side, and the stalls selling fish and fruit.

At last they collapsed into chairs at a roadside café, and revived themselves on cake and coffee.

'I'm so glad you thought of this,' she sighed blissfully. 'It's been wonderful. This place is almost too picturesque to be true.'

Dante nodded. 'Naples has its modern districts, places full of soulless, efficient buildings. But it also has these corners where people can still be human instead of cogs in a wheel. People here don't just know each other, they're neighbours, practically family. A lot of them *are* family. You tend to get whole apartment-blocks populated by relatives. Let's have some—'

He stopped as a wild scream came from somewhere nearby. Suddenly there was chaos. People were running down the little streets, waving their arms and indicating something behind them.

'Incendio!' they screamed. *'Incendio!'*

'There's a fire somewhere,' Dante said.

Following the pointing hands, they began to run until they came to a five-storey building on one side of a narrow alley, where the ground was entirely made of steps. Smoke was billowing from the windows and people were streaming out, shouting to each other.

'They've called the fire brigade,' Dante said, picking up a few words. 'But these lanes are too narrow for the machines. The nearest they'll get is that corner, then they'll have to carry the ladders into this street and set them on the ground. Let's hope their ladders are long enough. Luckily, everyone seems to be escaping the buildings fast.'

Behind them a woman was screaming, 'Piero, Marco, Ginetta, Enrico—*mio dio!*'

From the bags cast aside on the pavement, it seemed that she had been shopping when the news had reached her and had run back to her children. Now they were hurling themselves into her arms and she was sending up frantic prayers of relief.

'Salvo,' she wept. Safe. *'Oh, dio! Salvo. Ma no! Dove Nico?'*

Nico? People began to look around. Nico? Where was Nico?

One of the boys said something and recoiled as his mother slapped his cheek.

'What is it?' Ferne asked, horrified.

'Nico was coming down with them, but they lost sight of him,' Dante explained. 'She's blaming them for going on without him.'

'Nico!' the woman screamed, gazing up at the building. *'Nico!'*

Suddenly there was a mighty rumble followed by a crash from inside the building, and smoke billowed out of the windows.

'The inside has collapsed,' Dante said grimly. 'Let's hope Nico got out.'

But the next moment there was a shout of horror. Everyone looked up to see a little boy standing on a rickety wrought-iron balcony at the top, looking down.

'Nico!' his mother screamed again. 'Come down.'

She was too hysterical to realise that this was impossible, but everyone else understood, and groans went up at what seemed inevitable.

People were running to fetch ladders which they leaned up against the wall, but the boy was five storeys up and nothing reached him. Another ominous rumble from within the building warned how close danger was.

'Move that ladder!' Dante yelled. 'Push it over here.'

'But it's not long enough,' someone protested.

'Don't argue,' he roared. 'Just do as I say.'

Impatiently he yanked the ladder from their hands and set it up against the wall.

'Hold it,' he snapped.

Recognising the voice of authority, they scurried to obey. This was a new Dante, one Ferne had never seen before, a man of grim determination; his eyes were hard, his attitude set, brooking no argument, and woe betide anyone who got in his way.

She ventured to say, 'But what will you do when the ladder runs out?'

For a moment he looked at her as though he'd never seen her before.

Then recognition kicked in, and he said curtly, 'I'll climb.'

He turned away without waiting for her reply and the next moment was climbing the ladder swiftly, two rungs at a time, until he reached the base of the third balcony. Seizing the wrought iron, he managed to haul himself to the upper rim while the crowd below gasped. Ferne gazed in awe, thinking how strong his arms must be to manage that.

Having mounted the balcony, he climbed up onto the rail and leapt upwards. It was only a small distance, but it was enough to take him to the base of the next balcony where he did the same thing, managing to climb up there too.

One more to go. Thank goodness, Ferne thought, that he was so tall and so long in the leg. A shorter man could never have managed those leaps.

Now he was there, soothing the child. But how was he going to descend with him? Those watching below saw Dante take a hard, considering look down, then nod as though the decision was made. He turned and knelt down so that the child could climb onto his back; his arms wound tightly about Dante's neck. The next moment he'd swung over the balcony, going down the iron railings inch by inch until he reached the bottom and hung there.

Everyone below held their breath, wondering what he could possibly do now. He soon showed them, swinging back and forth until he could risk releasing the rail, and taking a flying leap onto the balcony below. It seemed an impossible trick, yet he managed it, throwing himself forward at the last minute so that he landed on his knees, and that the child on his back was safe and unhurt.

Nearly done. One more leap before they reached the safety of the ladder. Could he make it, or would they both plunge to earth? Down below hands were raised up as if everyone feared the worst and would try to catch them.

Dante didn't hesitate, swinging over the balcony, working his way down the railings, then taking the leap. A roar broke from the crowd as he landed safely.

A man had climbed the ladder and now reached out to take Nico, helping him down to safety while Dante remained on the balcony, breathing hard. Cheers and applause broke out as the child reached the ground, but nobody could relax until his rescuer was also safe. At last Dante reached for the ladder and climbed down to a deafening roar.

Ferne felt the tears pouring down her cheeks. She couldn't have said why she was weeping, whether it was fear for Dante or pride in him, but she was filled with feelings that threatened to explode.

He gave her a brief smile and went to the mother, who was in transports of delight, uttering passionate thanks that seemed to embarrass him. She was clinging to the child, who seemed dazed and unresponsive, but who suddenly seemed to awaken and look around him, searching for something. When he didn't find it, he began to scream.

'Pini?' he cried. 'Pini! He'll die—*he'll die!*'

'Is that another child?' Ferne asked. 'Does he mean someone's still in there?'

'No, Pini is his puppy,' said his mother. 'He must be out here somewhere.'

'No, *no*!' Nico sobbed. 'He's still in there. He'll die.'

His mother tried desperately to soothe him.

'*Caro*, it can't be helped. Nobody can risk their life for a dog.'

Nico began to scream. 'Pini! Pini, Pini…!'

'He's probably dead already,' somebody said. 'He must have been overcome by the smoke—he won't have suffered.'

'No, *there*!' came a shout from the crowd.

Everyone looked up, gasping at the sight of the little dog appearing at the window. He was barking and looking around him in fear and bewilderment. Screams rose from the crowd as his inevitable fate approached, and Nico began to struggle, trying to escape.

'Pini, Pini—I'm coming!'

'No!' cried his mother, clutching him tightly.

'Stay there,' Dante said sharply. 'Just don't move.'

The next moment he was running headlong back to the building.

There were more screams from the crowd as they realised what he meant to do.

'He's crazy—does he want to be killed? Does he know what he's doing? Stop him!'

But Ferne had seen the reckless determination in his eyes and knew that nothing could have stopped him. Terrified, she watched as he reached the house and began climbing up the ladder through the smoke that now seemed to surround everything. Every time he vanished, she was convinced she wouldn't see him again, but somehow he always managed to reappear, higher and higher, closer to the place where the dog was looking down, yelping with terror.

By now two fire-engines had arrived, but had to stop at the end of the narrow street. Seeing what was happening, the firemen came running along the street with a detachable ladder and sent it shooting up towards Dante. Mercifully it was longer than the first one, but when they shouted at him to climb onto it he merely glanced down at them, shook his head and turned back, heading up again.

He'd reached the last balcony, but now his luck ran out. As soon as he seized it, the wrought iron pulled away from the crumbling brickwork so that one end came completely free, swinging down violently. Screams came from the crowd as Dante hung from the iron, seemingly with no way to save himself. The firemen were working the ladder, trying to get it closer to him.

Ferne watched, her heart in her mouth, unable to endure looking, yet equally unable to turn away. It was surely impossible that he could come through this alive?

Then he kicked against the wall hard enough to swing out and up. From somewhere he found the strength to reach higher, and begin to climb up the swinging balcony. He did it again and again, inching closer to the window where the dog was shivering.

Cheers rose as he finally made it, but as he reached for the dog the animal vanished into the building. Dante hauled himself in, also vanishing, and everyone below held their breath. The next moment there came a crash from inside. Smoke billowed from the window, and an appalled hush fell over the onlookers. He was dead. He must be.

Ferne buried her face in her hands, praying frantically. He couldn't die. He mustn't.

Then a shout of triumph went up. *'There he is!'*

Dante had reappeared at another window, further down, with the dog in his arms. Now he was closer to the ladder with the fireman at the top. A little more manoeuvring, and it was near enough for him to reach down and hand the animal to the fireman, who began to back down the rungs, leaving the top of the ladder free for Dante to follow.

It was nearly over. He reached the ladder, climbed onto it and started the descent. In another moment, he would be safe.

But then something seemed to halt him. He froze and stayed there, clinging on, leaning against the metal, his eyes closed, his head hanging down.

'Oh heavens, he's passed out!' Ferne whispered. 'It's the smoke.'

The fireman passed the dog to another man further down, then climbed back up to Dante, positioning himself ready to catch him if he fell, reaching up to touch him.

To everyone's relief Dante seemed to come out of his trance and look around him. At last he managed to move and complete the journey down.

As he reached the ground, the cheers broke out again. He shook his head as though to clear it and, seeming to return to reality, took the dog from the fireman and carried it to the child, who screamed in ecstasy.

If the crowd had cheered him before, they now went completely mad. A man who risked himself for a child was a hero; a man who took the same risks for a dog was a wonderful madman.

Yes, a madman, Ferne thought, trying to still her thumping heart. A glorious madman, but still a man who didn't live on the same planet as everyone else.

He seemed strangely unwilling to enjoy the praise he'd won. They tried to hoist him shoulder-high, but now all he wanted was to escape.

'Let's go,' he said, grasping her hand.

CHAPTER FIVE

THEY ran from the crowd, dodging the outstretched hands, darting through street after street until they were lost and their pursuers were far behind.

'Where are we?' she asked.

'Who cares? Anywhere.'

'And where's the car?'

'Anywhere. What does it matter?'

'Will you talk sense?' she laughed. She was on a high of relief.

'No. Why talk sense? When was it ever sensible to be sensible?'

'Never for you; I can see that,' she said tenderly. 'Come on, let's get you somewhere safe.'

'Wherever you say. Lead on.'

She suddenly felt protective. Taking his hand as she might have taken the hand of a child, she led him until they found a small café with a table on the pavement where they could let the sun drench them.

'I need this,' he said, 'after all that smoke. I also need a drink, but I suppose I'd better not have one since I have to drive home—when we find the car.' He began to laugh. 'Where are we going to find it? Where do we start?'

'I think I remember the street. Don't worry about it now.'

When the waiter had taken their order, he leaned back, looking at her. There was exhilaration in his eyes.

'Dante, for pity's sake,' she said, taking hold of his hand again. 'Will you come down to earth?'

'I thought that was what I'd just done.'

'You know what I mean. You're up in the stratosphere some-where. Come back down to the same planet as the rest of us.'

'What for? I like it up here.' He turned his hand so that now he was holding her. 'Come up here with me. It's a great life. I've never had such fun.'

'Fun? You could have died!'

'Well, the strangest things can be fun if you look at them the right way.'

'You could have died,' she repeated slowly, as if to an idiot.

'But I didn't. I could have, but I didn't. Don't you under-stand? It's been a great day.'

'How can you *say* that?' she exploded. 'How can you sit there as if it was nothing? Of all the mad things to do! To save a child, yes, that's wonderful. But to take such a risk for a dog—what were you thinking of?'

'I'm a dog lover. And that little boy would have been broken-hearted if I'd left his dog to die.'

'And what about you? Don't you mind if you live or die?'

He shrugged. 'I don't worry about it. It'll happen when it happens.'

'It'll happen a lot sooner if you take crazy risks.'

'Maybe it will, maybe it won't. What's wrong with taking risks? Life's better that way. Think of it as doing the quick-step with fate as your partner. You go faster and faster, never knowing which of you is going to reach the edge first. Everything is possible; it's the only way to live.

And, if not, better to die like that than, well, some of the other ways.'

'You nearly came to grief,' she reminded him. 'When you were on top of the ladder you seemed to collapse. You just clung there and I thought you were going to fall. What happened?'

'Nothing. You imagined it.'

'But I didn't. You slumped against the ladder.'

'I don't remember. There was smoke everywhere and a lot of things passed me by. It doesn't matter now. Let's leave it.'

'I don't think we ought to leave it. You may have been affected in some way that isn't obvious yet. I want a doctor to have a look at you.'

'There's no need,' he said in a voice suddenly full of tension. 'It's over.'

'But you don't know that,' she pleaded. 'You passed out on the top of that ladder and—'

'How the hell do you know?'

The sudden cold fury in his voice was like a slap in the face, making her flinch back.

'You weren't up there; you don't know what happened,' he snapped. 'You saw me close my eyes against the smoke and give myself a moment's rest before climbing down the rest of the way. *And that's all!* Don't start dramatising.'

'I didn't mean— I'm just worried about you.'

'Do I look as if I need worrying about?' he asked in a voice that was now quiet and steely.

Ferne was struggling to come to terms with the terrible transformation in him, and she had to take a deep breath before she could reply bravely, 'Yes, actually, you do. Everyone needs worrying about. Why should you be any different? Something dreadful has happened to you. It might have made you ill and I simply want to find out. Why should that make you angry?'

'Why does any man get angry at being fussed over? Just leave it, please.'

His voice was still quiet, but now there was something in it that was almost a threat.

'But—'

'I said *leave it*.'

She didn't dare to say any more, and that word 'dare' told her what a dreadful thing had happened. The mere thought of being afraid of Dante was incredible, and yet she was. This was more than masculine irritation at being 'fussed over', it was bitter, terrifying rage.

But he was recovering himself. Before her eyes, the temper drained out of him.

'I'm sorry,' he said. 'I'm not quite myself. I'll be all right soon. Just promise me one thing—you won't say anything about this at home.'

'Not tell them about the fire? I think that story will get around somehow.'

'I don't mean that. I meant the other thing, that I had a bad moment on the ladder. Hope worries easily. Say nothing.'

When she hesitated he said, 'You *must* give me your word.'

'All right,' she said quickly. She had a fearful feeling that his rage was on the verge of rising again.

'You promise faithfully?'

'Yes, I promise.'

'Fine. Then everything's all right.'

Everything was far from all right, but she couldn't say so. She could never forget what she'd seen.

But now his mood was lightening, changing him back into the Dante she knew.

'Look on the bright side,' he said. 'Think what exciting pictures I must have given you.'

Pictures. Stunned, she realised that she'd never once thought of them.

She, to whom photography was such a part of her DNA that even her own lover's treachery had been recorded for posterity, had forgotten everything the moment Dante had started to climb.

'I didn't take any pictures,' she whispered.

'What do you mean?' he asked in mock outrage. 'You take pictures of everything. How come I'm not considered worth the trouble?'

'You know the answer perfectly well,' she snapped. 'I was too worried about you to think of photography.'

He shook his head. 'I don't know what the world is coming to,' he said sorrowfully. 'My great moment and you missed it. Shall I go back up and give you a second chance?'

'Don't bother,' she said crisply. 'The second take is never as effective as the first.'

They both knew what they were really talking about. The woman who let nothing get in the way of a good picture had missed this because she'd forgotten everything but his being in danger.

Now he would know, and how he would love that! But when she met his eyes she saw in them not triumph, but only bleak weariness, as though a light had gone out. He was struggling to present his normal, jokey self, but it was an effort.

'Come on,' he said tiredly. 'Let's go home.'

They found the car and drove back in silence. At the villa he immediately went for a shower. While he was away, Ferne outlined the events to the family but, remembering her promise, said nothing about what had happened at the end.

'Trust Dante to go back for the dog,' Hope said.

'He loved it,' Ferne said. 'It was as though risking his life gave him some sort of kick.'

'His father was the same,' Toni sighed. 'Always finding excuses to do crazy things.'

'Yes, but—' Hope began to speak, then stopped.

Puzzled, Ferne waited for her to continue. Then Hope met her husband's eyes and he gave an almost imperceptible shake of the head.

'If a man is like that, he's like that,' she finished lamely. 'I'll just go up and see if he's all right.'

She returned a moment later saying, 'I looked in. He's asleep. I expect he needs it.'

Then she deftly turned the conversation, leaving Ferne again with the impression that where Dante was concerned there were strange undercurrents.

Next morning he'd already left for town when she rose. She tried not to believe that he was avoiding her, but it was hard.

Her new credit cards arrived in the post, and news came from the consulate that her passport was ready. She drove down and collected it, then went to a café by the water and sat, considering.

Surely it was time to move on? Her flirtation with Dante had been pleasant but it would lead nowhere. Forgetting to take pictures was an ominous sign, because it had never happened before. But the mere thought of a serious affair with him was madness, if only because of his habit of withdrawing behind a mask.

On the surface he was a handsome clown who could tease his way into any woman's heart. But, when she'd given him her heart, what then? Would she be confronted by the other man who concealed himself inside, and whose qualities were beginning to seem ominous? Would he frighten her? Or would Dante keep her at bay, allowing her only to see what suited him? Either prospect was dismaying.

She thought of their first meeting on the train when they had sat together, thundering through the night, talking about the circles of heaven and hell. It had seemed a trivial conversation, but now she had the conviction that Dante was mysteriously acquainted with hell. Yesterday he had looked into its fiery depths not once but twice. Unafraid. Even willing.

Why? What did he know that was hidden from the rest of the world? What was his hell, and how did he confront it?

She was sunk so deep in her reverie that it took a while to realise that her mobile phone was shrieking.

'Ferne—at last!'

It was Mick Gregson, her agent, a cheerful, booming man.

'You've got to get back here,' Mick said. 'There's a great job coming up, big time, and I've put your name forward.'

He outlined the job which was, indeed, 'big time'. Following Sandor's example, a major Hollywood actor had just signed up for a West End play, seeking the prestige of live theatre. Next to him Sandor Jayley was peanuts.

'The management wants only the best for the pics, and when I mentioned you they were very interested.'

'I'm surprised anyone wants me after last time,' she observed wryly.

'I've heard that they value your "self-sacrificing honesty". Don't laugh; it's doing you a world of good. Seize this chance, sweetie. Gotta go.'

He hung up.

So there it was, she thought, staring at the silent phone: the decision was made for her. She would say farewell to Dante and return to England, glad to have escaped.

Escaped what?

She would have to learn to stop wondering about that.

The phone rang again. It was him.

'Where are you?' he asked in a voice that sounded agitated. When she told him, he said, 'Don't move. I'll be there in a few minutes.'

She was waiting for him, baffled, when he drew up at the kerb.

'Sorry to hassle you,' he said as she got in. 'But I need your help urgently. I've had a call from a man who owns a villa a few miles away and wants me to sell it. I'm going up there now, and I need a great photographer, so of course I thought of you.'

'I'm flattered, but my experience is showbiz, not real estate.'

'Selling a house can be a kind of showbiz, especially a house like this. In the nineteenth century, it was notorious. The owner had a wife and three mistresses and kept each one in a different wing. Then he was murdered.'

'Good for them.'

He laughed. 'It's odd how people always assume that it was the women.'

'If it wasn't, it should have been,' Ferne said without hesitation.

'It probably was. The police never found out. I want you to bring out the drama, while also making it look a comfortable place to live.'

After an hour they came to the villa, set on a hill with an extravagant outline, as though it had been built as part of a grand opera. Inside, the place was shabby with few modern comforts. The owner, a tubby, middle-aged man, followed her around, pointing out what he considered the attractions, but she soon left him behind and made her own way. The atmosphere was beginning to get to her.

It took three hours. On the way home, they stopped off for a meal and compared notes. Now Dante was a serious businessman. His notes were thorough, and he was going to do a first-class job with the house.

'My text, your pictures,' he said. 'We're a great team. Let's get back home and put it all on my website.'

'Fine, but then I've got something to tell—'

'Naturally, I'll pay you.'

'So I should hope.'

'Of course, I can't afford your usual fees. I expect you get top-dollar now for the *right* kind of picture.'

'I'll ignore that remark.'

'But you're the best at this kind of thing, and I could sell these houses much faster with your help.'

'I'm trying to tell you—'

'I'm going to leave soon, driving all over this area, drumming up business. Come with me. Together we'll knock 'em all dead.' When she hesitated, he took her hands in his. 'Say yes. It's time to have a little fun in your life.'

This was the Dante she'd first known, the chancer who faced life with a smile. The darkness of the recent past might never have been.

'I don't know,' she said slowly.

She was more tempted than she wanted to admit. Just a little longer in his company…

'Look, I know what you're thinking,' he said persuasively. 'But you're wrong. I've accepted your rejection.' His voice became melodramatic. 'Bitter and painful though it is.'

Her lips twitched. 'Oh, really?' she said cynically.

'Why don't you believe me?'

The mere idea of Dante meekly accepting rejection was absurd. It was a ploy, telling her that he was settling in for a long game, but if she admitted that she would be conceding a point in that very game. If there was one thing she knew she mustn't do, it was let him win too easily.

'Are you seriously asking me to believe that you'll act like a perfect gentleman at all times?'

'Ah, well, I might not have been planning to go quite that far,' he hedged cautiously. 'But nothing to offend you. Just friendly, I promise.'

'Hmm,' she observed.

'Hmm?' he echoed innocently.

'Hmm.'

In this mood, he was irresistible. On the other hand there was the promise of the biggest job of her life, maybe a trip to Hollywood eventually.

'I'll think about it,' she said.

'Don't take too long.'

They drove back to the villa and spent a contented hour at the computer, marrying his text and her pictures. The result was a triumph, with Ferne's flair for the dramatic balancing Dante's factual efficiency. He sent a copy to the owner, who promptly emailed back, expressing his delight.

At the end of the evening Ferne went out onto the terrace and stood looking up at the stars, wondering what she was going to do. It should have been an easy decision. How could any man compete with such a career opportunity?

She knew what would happen now. Dante would have seen her come out here, and he would follow her, trying to charm her into doing exactly what he wanted.

Just *friendly*, indeed! Who did he think he was kidding?

She could hear him coming now. Smiling, she turned.

But it was Hope and Toni.

'Dante has gone to bed,' Hope explained. 'He wouldn't admit it, but I think he has a headache.'

'Is something wrong?' Ferne asked. Something in the older woman's manner alerted her.

'He tells us that he wants you to travel and work with him,' Hope said.

'He has asked me, yes. But I'm not sure if I should agree. Perhaps it's time for me to be getting back to England.'

'Oh no, please stay in Italy for a while,' Hope said anxiously. 'Please go with him.'

Ferne's first thought was that Hope was matchmaking, but then she got a closer look at the other woman's expression and her amusement died. Hope's face was full of strange fear.

'What's the matter?' she asked. 'It's something serious, isn't it?'

Again that disconcerting silence; Hope glanced at her husband. This time he nodded and she began to speak.

'I'm going to confide in you,' she said, 'because we trust you, and we both think that you must learn the secret.'

'Secret?' Ferne echoed.

'It's a terrible one and it weighs on us. We try not to believe it, but the truth is—' She took a deep breath and spoke with difficulty. 'The truth is that Dante might be dying.'

'What?' Ferne whispered, aghast. 'Did you say—?'

'Dying. If that should happen, and we could have done something to prevent it and had not— But he will not have it spoken of, you see, and we don't know what to do.'

Ferne forcibly pulled herself together.

'I don't understand,' she said. 'He must know if he's ill or not.'

She could hear fearful echoes in her head. They were filled with warnings and told her that she was about to discover the dark secret that made Dante unlike other men.

'On his mother's side, he's a Linelli,' Hope explained. 'And that family has a hereditary problem. There can be a weak blood vessel in the brain that can suddenly start to bleed. Then the victim will collapse, perhaps go into a coma, perhaps die.'

'This has happened to several of them over the years,' Toni said. 'Some have died, but even the ones who survived have often been unlucky. His Uncle Leo suffered a major haemorrhage. His life was saved by surgery, but his brain was damaged. Now he's little more than a child, and to Dante he's an awful warning. He refuses even to consider that he might have inherited this illness and need treatment.'

'But has there ever been any sign?' Ferne asked. 'Or are you just afraid because it's hereditary? After all, not everyone in the family will have it.'

'True, but there was one frightening moment about two years ago. He had a headache so bad that he became confused and dizzy. This can mean a minor rupture of the blood vessel, and if that's ignored it can lead to a major one. But he insisted that he was perfectly recovered, and nothing else has happened since. That might mean nothing is wrong, or it might mean that he's been very, very lucky. He could go on being lucky for years, or…' Hope broke off with a sigh.

'But wouldn't it be better to find out?' Ferne asked.

'He doesn't want to know,' Toni said sombrely. 'He isn't afraid of death, but he is afraid of surgery, in case he ends up like Leo. His attitude is that, if death comes, it comes.'

'Doing the quick-step with fate,' Ferne murmured.

'What was that?'

'Something I've heard him say. I didn't understand it before. But I can't believe he'll go so far. Surely he'll be better having a diagnosis?'

'He's determined not to,' Hope said in despair. 'He doesn't want the family pressuring him to have surgery, even though it might not be so much of a risk. Surgical techniques have greatly improved since Leo's operation nearly thirty years ago, and Dante could easily come out of it well and whole, but he won't take the chance. He wants to get the best out of life while he can, and then, well…'

She gave a despairing sigh. Ferne was transfixed. This was worse than anything she'd feared.

'If only we knew for sure, but there's no way to be quite certain,' Hope resumed. 'Unless there's a definite symptom, like a dizzy spell. Have you ever seen him grow faint without warning?'

'Yes,' Ferne said, remembering with horror. 'He seemed to get dizzy when he was coming down the ladder when he saved the dog. But it seemed natural after what he'd been through—all that smoke.'

'It probably was natural,' Hope agreed. 'And his headache tonight is probably natural, just a delayed reaction to what he went through. But we always wonder. It's hard to say anything for fear of enraging him.'

'Yes, I've seen that,' Ferne murmured. 'I wanted him to see a doctor, and he was very angry. He made me promise not to say anything to the family, or I would have told you before. He got so furious that I had to give in. I could hardly believe that it was him.'

'He's going off alone,' Hope said. 'Please, Ferne, go with him.'

'But what could I do? I'm not a nurse.'

'No, but you'd be there, watching out for him. If anything worrying happens, you won't dismiss it as a stranger would. You can summon help, perhaps save his life. And you might even persuade him that he doesn't have to live this way.'

'He won't listen to me,' Ferne said. 'He'll probably suspect me from the start.'

'No, because he's invited you to go with him, so it will all seem natural to him. Please. I beg you.'

Ferne knew the decision had been made. This woman who had come to her rescue and asked so little in return was now imploring her.

'You don't need to beg me,' she said at last. 'Of course I'll do it. You must tell me all you can about this illness, so that I can be of most use.'

For answer, Hope flung her arms about Ferne's neck in a passion of thankfulness. Toni was more restrained, but he laid a powerful hand on Ferne's shoulder and squeezed tightly.

But Ferne was shaking, wondering what she'd let herself in for.

CHAPTER SIX

A SOUND from inside the house made them look up quickly, but it was only Primo, come to say goodnight before taking Olympia back to their apartment. Ferne took the chance to slip away among the trees. She needed to calm her thoughts and, more than that, calm her emotions.

For now there was a howling wilderness inside her, and she wanted to scream up to the heavens that it couldn't be true. It mustn't be true, for if it was true she couldn't bear it.

She'd wanted to know Dante's secret, and here it was. He was probably dying, and he knew it. At any moment of the day or night he could collapse without warning. That was the fact he lived with, refused to duck from, even laughed at. That was the quick-step he was dancing with fate.

Now she understood why he'd gone back into the burning house when anyone wiser would have stayed away. Inwardly he'd been yelling, 'Go on, then, do your worst!' to the gremlins who haunted him, trying to scare him, not succeeding.

If he'd died that day, he'd have called it a blessing compared with the fate he dreaded: permanent disability, being as dependent as a child, pity. To avoid that he would do anything, even walk into the fire.

This was why he chose light relationships. He couldn't allow himself to fall in love, nor would he risk a woman falling in love with him. He was at ease with her because she fended him off with laughter and seemed in no danger of serious feelings, which was just what he liked; it was safer for them both.

But he'd miscalculated, she thought in anguish. The news of his being in danger had brought a rush of emotion to her heart. Deny it though she might, the misery of knowing that he might be brutally snatched from her at any moment was tearing her apart.

She should fly this place now, run from him while she might still have even a little control over her feelings. Instead she had agreed to stay in his company, to watch over him, vulnerable to his charm which seemed even more potent now that she understood the tragedy that lay behind it.

She would probably fall in love with him despite her determination not to. And how would she bear what might happen next?

Flee! said the voice in her mind. *Forget what you've promised.*

'I can't,' she whispered, resting her head against a tree.

To go was to abandon him to whatever was waiting, leave him to face it alone. The fact that he'd chosen it that way would make it no less a betrayal.

'No,' she murmured. 'No, no, *no*!'

Suddenly she knew she couldn't keep her promise to Hope. She'd been mad to say yes, and there was still time to put it right. She would hurry back now…

'There you are,' came Dante's voice. 'Why are you hiding?'

She turned to see him walking towards her. He had the rumpled look of a man who'd recently been asleep.

'I came out for some air,' she said. 'It's lovely out here at night.'

'It is beautiful, isn't it?'

He didn't put his arms about her, but leaned against the tree, regarding her quizzically.

'Are you all right?'

'Yes, fine,' she said hastily. 'What about you? How's your head?'

'There's nothing wrong with my head. Why do you ask?'

'When you went to bed early, Hope thought—'

'Hope's a fusspot. My head is fine.'

Was his voice just a little bit too firm? She shouldn't have raised the subject. It was a careless mistake, and she must be more careful.

'You can't blame her for fussing,' she said lightly. 'You of all men, going to bed early! What kind of earthquake produced that?'

'I'm probably still suffering a touch of smoke inhalation. Even *I'm* not superman.'

'Now, there's an admission!' she said in as close to a teasing voice as she could manage.

She longed to take his face between her hands, kiss him tenderly and beg him to look after himself. But anything like that was forbidden. If she stayed she would have to guard every word, watch and protect him in secret, always deceive him. The sooner she was out of here, the better.

'Dante,' she said helplessly. 'There's something I must—'

'Oh yes, you were trying to tell me something this afternoon, weren't you? And I never gave you the chance. Too full of myself as always. Tell me now.'

It would have to be faced soon, but before she could speak blessed rescue came in the form of a commotion. Ruggiero's toddler son, Matti, came flying through the trees as fast as his short legs would carry him. From behind came Ruggiero's voice, calling to him to come back, which he ignored.

'I used to escape at bedtime just like that,' Dante said, grinning. 'Some rotten, spoilsport grown-up always grabbed me.'

He seized Matti and hoisted the toddler up in his arms, laughing into his face.

'Gotcha! No, don't kick me. I know how you feel, but it's bedtime.'

'It was bedtime hours ago,' Ruggiero said breathlessly, reaching them. 'Polly looked in on him and he made a run for it.'

'Parents can be a pain in the neck,' Dante confided to the tot. 'But sometimes you have to humour them.'

Reluctantly Matti nodded. Dante grinned and handed the child to his father.

'You really know how to talk to him,' Ruggiero said. Then, fearing to be thought sentimental, he added, 'I guess it's because you're just a great kid yourself, eh?'

'Could be,' Dante agreed.

Ferne, watching from the shadows, thought that there was more to it than a joke. Dante was part-child, part-clown, part-schemer, and part something else that she was just beginning to discover. Whatever it might turn out to be, he was a man who needed her protection. Somewhere in the last few moments the decision had been made.

'Now we're alone again,' he said, 'what were you going to say?'

Ferne took a deep breath and faced him with a smile.

'Just that I really enjoyed working with you. When do we leave?'

* * *

Be careful what you say in jest: it may return to haunt you.

That thought pursued Ferne over the next few days.

She'd teased Dante about being a perfect gentleman at all times, and he'd responded with an encouraging dismay. But as time passed she began to realise that he'd taken her seriously and was being, as he'd promised, 'just friendly'.

He bought a car, a solid, roomy vehicle designed for serious travel, and quite unlike the frivolous choice she might once have expected him to make. They headed south to Calabria, the rugged, mountainous territory at the toe of the Italian peninsular. One of Dante's techniques was to seek out places that had been on the market for a long time and offer his services.

'There are three villas there that my research tells me have been for sale too long,' he said. 'Let's try our luck.'

Their luck was in. The owners were getting desperate and were eager for Dante to add their properties to his books. They spent several days working up a sales pitch for each house, complete with glorious pictures. At the end of it, Ferne was exhausted.

'I seem to spend my life climbing stairs and walking mile-long corridors,' she complained. 'If I'd known it was going to be this tiring, I wouldn't have come.'

Dante himself didn't seem at all tired, and was clearly in such blazingly good health that she wondered if she was crazy to be watching out for him. He had a fund of funny stories which he directed at her over dinner, reducing her to tears of laughter, after which he would take her hand to lead her upstairs to their separate rooms, kiss her on the cheek and bid her goodnight.

No man could have behaved more perfectly. No man could have been more restrained and polite. No man could have been more infuriating.

For this she'd turned down the chance of a lifetime?

Mick Gregson hadn't been pleased.

'What were you thinking of?' he'd bawled down the phone. 'This man carries influence in film land. If he'd liked your work, you could have done anything you wanted.'

But I'm doing what I want, had been her silent thought.

'Ferne, I can't go on representing you if you're going to act like this.'

'That's your decision, Mick, and of course I respect it.'

They had parted bad friends.

Now she was on the road with a man who'd promised 'just friendly', and who seemed infuriatingly determined to keep his word.

There was no justice.

But one thing had changed—now she understood the true reason for Dante's restraint. He wouldn't make advances to her because his personal code of honour forbade him to ask for love when he might die without warning.

Here was the explanation for the way he slipped quickly in and out of relationships, never getting too close to any woman. It was his way of being considerate.

And he was right, she assured herself. If she wanted more from him, that was her problem.

'Where do we go next?' she asked as they turned north again, leaving Calabria behind.

'A place near Rome that I've promised to take a look at. There are some two-thousand-year-old ruins, plus a huge villa that the owner insists on calling a *palazzo*, that's "only" six centuries old. It may not be easy to shift.'

'If it's antique and historical, won't the atmosphere of romance help to sell it?'

'An atmosphere of romance is all very well in theory, but

people tend to want decent plumbing as well. I know the owner, Gino Tirelli, and he assures me that it's in a good state of repair—but he might, just possibly, be biased. Luckily I'm not due there until next week, so we can give ourselves a few days by the sea.'

'That sounds lovely. This heat is really getting to me.'

'Of course, we could always go sight-seeing in Rome. There are some really interesting historical buildings.'

'The sea, the sea,' she begged faintly.

He laughed. 'The sea it is, then. Let's go.'

A few hours' driving brought them to the Lido di Ostia, the beach resort about fifteen miles from Rome. It was a sunny place of level, pale-yellow sands that were adorned not only with umbrellas and loungers but the other trappings of civilization: wine bars and cafés.

Their hotel was close to the sea with a view over the ocean.

'They've got single and double rooms available,' Dante told her after a talk at the desk. 'A double room's cheaper.' In reply to her raised eyebrows, he said, 'How long can a man behave perfectly?'

'I think I can afford a single room.'

'You don't give an inch, do you?'

'You'd better believe it,' she said, laughing.

Not for the world would she have admitted her relief that his defences were finally crumbling.

The hotel had a shop that sold beach items. She lingered over a bikini that—for a bikini—was relatively modest, and a respectable one-piece. Dante eyed her hopefully as she hovered between them.

'Why don't you try it?' he suggested, indicating the one-piece.

She was slightly surprised that he urged her to try the

modest garment rather than the revealing one. Afterwards, she realised that she should have been more suspicious.

In the dressing-room she donned the costume, regarded herself in the mirror and sighed. It was elegant and showed off her figure, but didn't do her total justice. No one-piece could have done that. But, until she was sure how far along this road she was going to let Dante whirl her, she couldn't risk being a tease. That wouldn't be fair to him.

Nor was it fair on her, she realised, trying to calm the pleasure that fizzed through her as she thought of his eyes dwelling on her nearly naked body. It wasn't the only pleasure she was denying herself right now, and soon she must decide why.

She dressed again and went out, handing the costume to the assistant for wrapping. 'I'll take this.'

'I've already paid for it,' Dante said, whisking it out of her hand and putting it into a bag he was carrying. 'Now, let's be off.'

'I can't let you pay for my clothes,' she said as they crossed the road to the beach. 'It wouldn't be proper.'

'If we're going to have another discussion about propriety, I'd rather do it later over champagne.'

'Oh, all right.'

The sand was glorious, soft and welcoming. He hired a hut, two loungers and a huge umbrella, then handed her the bag with her purchase and stood back to let her enter the hut first.

When she opened the bag, she was reminded that this man was a talented schemer.

'They've given me the wrong costume,' she said, going outside again. 'Look.' She held up the bikini. 'But I don't see how it happened. I saw you put the other one into the bag.'

'I guess this one must have already been in there,' he said, eyes wide and innocent.

'But how…?' Light dawned and she stared at him indignantly. *'You didn't?'*

'If you've learned anything about me, you know that I did,' he said unanswerably. 'I bought the bikini while you were in the changing room.'

'But how dare you?'

'A case of necessity. You were going to buy that middle-aged thing that doesn't do you justice, so I paid for them both and slipped the bikini into the bag before you came out.'

'But what about the one I chose? Where is it?'

'No idea. It must have escaped.'

'You—you devious—'

'No such thing. Just a man who doesn't like wasting time. Now, are you going to get in there and change, or are you going to stand here all day talking about it?'

'I'm going to get in there and change,' she said promptly. And vanished.

It might not have been modern and liberated to let a man make her decisions, but that was a small sacrifice in return for the look in his eyes. He'd behaved disgracefully, of course, but all things considered she would forgive him.

The mirror in the hut promised everything to the beauty who gazed back, wearing just enough to be decent. Restrained as the bikini was, it didn't hide the way her tiny waist developed into curved hips, or the fact that her skin was perfect. Turning, she studied her rear view over her shoulder, noting that perhaps her behind was a fraction too generous.

Or, then again, perhaps not.

At last she was ready to make her grand entrance. Throwing open the door, she stepped out into the sunlight, only just resisting the temptation to say, 'Ta-Da!'

He was nowhere to be seen.

Oh, great!

'Ah, there you are,' he said, appearing with cans of liquid. 'I've been stocking up on something to drink. We can keep these in the hut until we're ready.'

'Do I look all right?' she asked edgily.

'Very nice,' he said in a courteous voice that made her want to thump him.

But his smile as he studied her told another story, so she forgave him.

While she waited for him to emerge, she let her eyes drift over the other men on the beach. Sandor had once told her that there were few men who appeared at an advantage in bathing trunks. He'd spoken with self-conscious grandeur, from the lofty heights of physical perfection.

But when Dante appeared she forgot everything else. He didn't show off; he didn't need to. His tall, lean figure was muscular without being obvious, and he seemed to have the tensile strength of whipcord.

Ferne's brief contacts with his body had hinted at power, not flaunted but always in reserve. Now she saw the reality and it pleased her, especially the long legs that moved with a masculine grace that hinted at his ability as a dancer.

For a moment she was back in his arms as they danced across the floor, feet between feet, spinning and twirling with never an inch out of place, because his control had been perfect. Watching him now, his body almost naked, she felt again the excitement of that night begin in the pit of her stomach and stream out to her fingertips.

'Shall we go in?' he asked, reaching out.

She took his hand and together they ran down the beach, splashing into the surf. She yelled aloud with ecstasy as the water laved her, and joined him in a race out to the horizon.

'Careful,' he said. 'Don't go too deep.'

But she was beyond caring. The feel of the water was so good that she wanted more and more.

'*Yee-haa!*' she cried up to the sky.

He laughed and plunged after her, keeping close, ready for the moment when she pulled up, treading water and puffing.

'All right now?' he called. 'Got it out of your system?'

'No way. Here goes!'

Kicking hard, she projected herself up as high as she could go, then dropped down deep into the water, down, down, until at last she kicked to start rising again.

But she was deeper than she'd guessed, and she didn't seem to be climbing fast enough. She became alarmed as her breath began to run out.

Suddenly there was an arm around her waist and she was being yanked up to the surface fast, until mercifully her head broke free and she could breathe again.

'All right, you're safe,' came Dante's voice. 'What were you thinking of, you crazy woman?'

'I don't know—I just wanted to— Oh, goodness!'

'Steady. Relax. I've got you.'

He trod water while keeping her well above the surface, holding her tight against him, his hands almost meeting about her waist.

'All right?' he said, looking up.

'Yes, I—I'm fine.'

It was hard to sound composed when the sensation of her bare skin against his was so disturbing. Her thighs were against his chest, his mouth was just below her breasts, and the waves were moving them about so that their contact constantly shifted; with every new touch the tremors went through her.

'I'm going to let you down,' he said. 'You can't touch the ground, but don't worry. Just hold onto me. Down—easy.'

She knew he meant only to be gentle and reassuring by lowering her slowly, but the feeling of her flesh gliding against his was just what she didn't need right now, she thought frantically. Control. *Control.*

'Ouch!' he said.

'What?'

'You're hurting me, digging your nails into my shoulders.'

'Sorry!' she said wildly. 'Sorry—sorry.'

'OK, I believe you. Let's get back to shore. Can you swim, or will you hold onto me?'

'I can manage fine,' she lied.

They made it back to the shore without incident, and she set her feet down on the sand with relief.

'All right?' Dante asked.

'Yes, thank you. You can let me go now.'

'I'll just support you until we reach the lounger. You had quite a shock.'

Her legs felt weak, but that was natural after her alarm. It surely couldn't have anything to do with her burning consciousness of his left hand about her waist while his right hand clasped hers?

What happened next was really annoying. By sheer ill-luck an unevenness in the sand made her stumble so that Dante had to tighten his grip to stop her falling.

'Let's do it the easy way,' he said, lifting her high into his arms and carrying her the rest of the distance.

This was even worse. Now she had no choice but to put her arms about his neck, which positioned her mouth close to his and her breasts against his chest, something a sensible woman would have avoided at all costs.

At last he eased her down onto the lounger and dropped on one knee beside her.

'You gave me a fright,' he said. 'Vanishing below the water for so long. I thought you'd gone for good.'

'Nonsense,' she said, trying to laugh it off. 'I'd have been bound to float up eventually.'

'Yes, but it might have been too late.'

'Then it's lucky for me that you were there. You do the "rescuing damsels in distress" thing really well.'

'It's my speciality,' he said lightly. 'And, just to show you how good at it I am, let me dry you off.'

He tossed the towel around her shoulders and began to dab.

'I can manage, thank you,' she said in a strained voice.

'All right. Do it properly, and I'll get you something to drink.'

He poured her some wine in a plastic container.

'Sorry it's a bit basic, but the wine is good,' he said.

She drank it thankfully, wishing he'd move away and not kneel there, so kind, so sweetly concerned, so nearly naked.

'Thanks,' she said. 'I feel better now. You don't need to hover over me.'

'Am I being too protective? I can't help it. I keep thinking what it would have been like without you, and I don't like that thought at all.'

'Really?' she asked quietly.

'Of course. How could I manage without your brilliant pictures?'

'My pictures?'

'You really enhance my work in a way that nobody else has managed to do. We make a great team, don't you think?'

'Fantastic,' she agreed dismally.

'So I'll just keep on watching out for you.'

Her head shot up. 'What—what did you say?'

'I said I'm watching out for you. You obviously need someone being protective. Hey, careful. You've spilled wine all down yourself.'

She seized the towel out of his hands and dabbed at her bare torso. Her head was in a whirl, and her senses were in an even worse whirl.

'Did you say you're keeping a protective eye on me?' she said.

'I think I need to, don't you? And it's what friends do, isn't it?'

'Oh yes, of course they do,' she babbled.

'It's time you had a rest.'

'Yes,' she said with relief. 'I think that's what I'll do.'

CHAPTER SEVEN

SHE was glad to escape by stretching out and closing her eyes. His words had unnerved her, reminding her that it was she who was supposed to be watching out for him.

She dozed for a while and awoke to find herself alone. Dante was further down the beach, kicking a rubber ball around with some boys. For a while she watched him through half-closed eyes, unwillingly admiring the lines of his body, the athletically graceful way he moved.

She was no green girl; Sandor hadn't been her first lover. At twenty-eight, she knew her own body well, knew how it could be most totally satisfied, knew exactly what it wanted.

But that could be a problem when it couldn't have what it wanted.

It would have been easier to observe Dante leaping about the beach if she didn't have to listen to the voice inside whispering how well he would move in bed, how subtle and knowing his caresses would be.

How fine would his tall body feel held close against her own long body? When she saw him give a mighty kick, she thought of his legs between hers. When he reached for the ball at an impossible angle, she could almost feel his hands against her skin, exploring her tentatively, waiting for her with endless patience, knowing exactly how to…

She sat up, trembling and annoyed with herself. What was the matter with her?

'Just friendly'. That was the matter.

When Dante returned, he found her fully dressed.

'I've had enough of this,' she said fretfully. 'I think I'll go into town.'

'Great idea,' he said. 'I'll show you the shops, then we'll go to dinner.'

She ground her nails into her palm. Why couldn't he at least show some ill temper, like any other man, thus giving her the chance to feel annoyed with him?

But the wretch wouldn't even oblige her in that.

Because he wasn't like any other man.

At least she'd made him put his clothes on.

They spent the rest of the day sedately, buying the odd garment, and also buying computer software. In one shop she discovered a superb programme that she hadn't expected to be available for another month, and snapped it up. Over dinner, she enthused about it to Dante, who listened with genuine interest. It was the high point of the day.

On reflection, she thought that said it all.

Afterwards he saw her to her door but made no attempt to come in.

'Goodnight,' he said. 'Sleep well.'

She went in, restraining herself with difficulty from slamming the door.

Furiously she thought of the signals he'd sent out that day, signals that had said clearly that he wanted her and was controlling it with difficulty. But the signals had changed. Now he might have been made of ice, and it was obvious why.

He was scheming. He wanted her to be the one to weaken. If either of them was overcome with desire, it must be her. In his dreams, she succumbed to uncontrollable lust, reaching out to entice him.

Hell would freeze over first!

Next day they promised themselves a lazy time in the sun.

'I could happily stay here for ever,' Dante said, stretching out luxuriously. 'Who cares about work?'

It was at that exact moment that a voice nearby called, '*Ciao*, Dante!'

He started up, looked around, then yelled, '*Gino!*'

Ferne saw a man in his fifties, dressed in shirt and shorts, advancing on them with a look of delight on his broad face.

'Is that…?'

'Gino Tirelli,' Dante said, jumping up.

When the two men had clapped each other on the shoulder, Dante introduced Ferne.

'Always I am pleased to meet English people,' Gino declared. 'At this very moment, my house is full of important English people.'

'So that's why you asked me to delay my arrival,' Dante said. 'Who've you got there? Members of the government?'

'A film company,' Gino said in an awed voice. 'They're making a film of *Antony and Cleopatra* and shooting some scenes in the ruins in my grounds. The director is staying with me, and of course the *big* star.'

'And who is the big star?' Ferne asked, suitably wide-eyed.

Before Gino could reply there was a squeal from behind them, and they all turned to see a young man of about thirty with curly, fair hair and a perfectly tanned body strolling along the beach in a careless way, suggesting that he was unaware of the sensation he created.

But he was fully aware of it, as Ferne knew. Sandor Jayley always knew exactly what effect he was creating.

'Oh no!' she breathed.

'What is it?' Dante asked her in a low voice. 'Good grief, it's—?'

'Tommy Wiggs.'

The young man came closer, pulling off a light shirt and tossing it to a companion, revealing a muscular body sculpted to perfection, now wearing only a minuscule pair of trunks. Regarding him grimly, Dante was forced to concede one thing: as Ferne had said, he did have magnificent thighs.

'I've got to get out of here before he sees me,' she muttered. 'That'll really put the cat among the pigeons.'

But it was too late. Sandor had seen his host and was starting up the beach towards him, doing a well-honed performance of *bonhomie*.

'Gino,' he called. Then, as he saw Ferne, his expression changed, became astonished, then delighted. 'Ferne! My darling girl!'

Arms open wide, he raced across the sand and, before she could get her thoughts together, she found herself enfolded in a passionate embrace.

It was an act, she thought, hearing the cheers around them. For some reason he'd calculated that this would be useful to him so he was taking what he wanted, selfishly indifferent to the effect it might have on her. For she was terrified in case she reacted in the old way, the way she now hated to remember.

Nothing happened. There was no pleasure, no excitement. Nothing. She wanted to shout to the heavens with joy at being free again!

'Tommy—'

'Sandor,' he muttered hastily. Then, aloud, 'Ferne, how wonderful to see you again!' He smiled down into her eyes, the picture of tender devotion. 'It's been too long,' he said. 'I've thought of you so often.'

'I've thought a few things about you too,' she informed him tartly. 'Now, will you let me go?'

'How can you ask me to do that when I've got you in my arms again? And I owe you so much.'

'Yes, those pictures didn't do you any harm, did they? Let me *go*!'

Reluctantly he did so, switching his attention to Gino.

'Gino, how do you come to know this wonderful lady?' he cried.

'I've only just met her,' Gino said. 'I didn't realise that you two were—are…'

'Let's say we're old friends,' Sandor said. '*Close* friends.'

Ferne became awkwardly aware of Dante standing there, arms folded, regarding them sardonically. After everything she'd told him about Sandor, what must he be thinking?

A little crowd was gathering around them as news went along the beach that the famous Sandor Jayley was among them. Young women sighed and regarded Ferne with envy.

'Sandor,' she said, backing away from him, 'Can I introduce you to my friend, Signor Dante Rinucci?'

'Why, sure.' Sandor extended his hand. 'Any friend of Ferne's is a friend of mine.'

Dante gave him an unreadable smile.

'Excellent,' he said. 'Then we're all friends together.'

'Let's all sit down.' Sandor seated himself on her lounger and drew her down beside him.

He was in full flood now, basking in the warm glow of what

he took to be admiration, oblivious to the fact that one of his audience was embarrassed and another actively hostile.

'Just think,' he sighed. 'If that house where we were going to shoot had come up to scratch, we'd never have moved to Gino's *palazzo* and we—' he gave Ferne a fond look '—would never have found each other again.'

'There were rats,' Gino confided. 'They had to find somewhere else fast, and someone remembered the Palazzo Tirelli.'

'Why don't you join us?' Sandor said suddenly. 'That's all right with you, isn't it, Gino?' Asking the owner's permission was clearly an afterthought.

Far from being offended, Gino nearly swooned with delight.

'And it will give Ferne and me the chance to rekindle our very happy acquaintance,' Sandor added.

'Sandor, I don't think—' Ferne protested quickly.

'But we have so much to talk about. You don't mind if I take Ferne away from you for a few days, do you?' he asked Dante.

'You mean Dante isn't invited too?' Ferne asked sharply. 'Then I'm not coming.'

'Oh, my dear, I'm sure your friend will understand.'

'*He* may, I won't,' Ferne said firmly. 'Dante and I are together.'

'So loyal,' Sandor cooed in a voice that made Ferne want to kick him in a painful place. 'Signor Rinucci, you're invited too, of course.'

'How kind!' Dante said in a voice that revealed nothing. 'I'll look forward to it.'

Ferne turned horrified eyes on him. 'Dante, you don't mean that?' she muttered.

'Of course I do. Getting really acquainted with the place may help me with the sale.'

'How? You've never needed it before.'

'Well, perhaps I have my own reasons this time,' he said, his eyes glinting.

Sandor didn't hear this exchange. Champagne had arrived and he turned to lift two glasses, one of which he handed to Ferne, saying, 'It's all settled, then. Here's to our reunion!'

A young girl detached herself from the swooning crowd on the beach and asked him for an autograph, handing him her lipstick so that he could write his name on her back. Beaming, he obliged, then gave Ferne a questioning look.

'No camera today? Not like you.'

'I left it in the hotel.'

'You? The lady who never moves without her camera? Well, well.'

His look was heavily significant, clearly meant to recall the last time she had turned her camera on him. She faced him back, her eyes full of anger.

Dante watched them and said nothing.

Having established the scene, Sandor didn't linger over the champagne. Indicating the crowd, he said modestly, 'You see how it is—wherever I go. I'll leave now, and see you at the villa this evening.'

He strode away, pursued by adoring fans, plus Gino.

'So that's him,' Dante said. 'He's exactly as you said, except worse.'

'I don't know what's going on here,' she said wildly. 'When we last met, he couldn't find words bad enough for me.'

'But that was three months ago, and he did pretty well out of it. He's a bigger star now than he was before, thanks to you. So clearly he wants to shower you with his favours. Tonight you'll be his honoured companion.'

'Are you trying to be funny?' she asked stormily. 'Do you think that's what I *want*?'

He gave a strange smile. 'Let's say I'm interested to find out. I didn't mean to offend you. Let's get going.'

It was late afternoon when they reached the Palazzo Tirelli, a magnificent edifice. Grander still were the ruins that lay nearby, dating back nearly two-thousand years. Ferne could just make out a film crew looking them over, making notes, rehearsing shots.

Gino came to meet them and show them over the place with its long, wide corridors and stone arches. In every room he was able to describe some notable historical episode, which sounded impressive until she saw Dante shaking his head.

Their rooms turned out to be on different corridors, the only ones left, according to Gino. His manner was awkward, and Ferne guessed he was acting on instruction.

At supper she was seated next to Sandor, with Dante on the opposite side of the table several feet down. There were about fifty people at the long table, most of them film crew and actors. Everyone was dressed up to the nines, making her glad she'd chosen the softly glamorous dress of honey-coloured satin that paid tribute to her curves, yet whose neckline was high enough to be tantalising.

'Beautiful,' Sandor murmured. 'But why aren't you wearing that gold necklace I gave you? It would go perfectly with that dress.'

'I'm afraid I'd forgotten it,' she said.

His self-assured smile made her want to thump him. She glanced down the table to see how Dante was taking it, but he wasn't looking at her.

He was having a good evening. Dinner jacket and bow-tie suited him, as the ladies nearby made clear. Ferne would have signalled her admiration if she'd been able to catch his eye, but he seemed happy with the full-bosomed creature who was laughing so uproariously at his jokes, that her attractions wobbled violently in a way that Ferne thought extremely inappropriate.

For a moment, she was nostalgic for Dante's jokes; sharing laughter with a man brought a special closeness. It was something she'd never known with Sandor, and it meant that she was always on Dante's wavelength, always inhabiting his world, even when they were bickering. In fact, the very bickering was a sign of that closeness, because they could always trust each other to understand.

As Dante had predicted, Sandor treated her as his honoured guest.

'I owe you so much, Ferne. If it hadn't been for what you did for me, I'd never have got the next step up.'

'That's not what you said at the time,' she observed wryly.

'I didn't appreciate your skill in turning a difficult situation into something that would benefit me.'

She stared at him, wondering how she'd ever taken this conceited booby seriously.

'Sandor, what are you after?' she demanded.

He regarded her soulfully. 'Destiny works in mysterious ways. We were fated to meet on that beach. Everyone was staggered by those pictures you took of me. Between us, we produced something of genius, and I think we could be geniuses again.'

She stared at him in outrage. 'You want me to…?'

'Take some more, as only you can. We'll go out to the ruins, and you tell me exactly how you want me to pose. I've been working out in the gym.'

'And I'm sure you're as fit and perfect as ever.'

'What did you think when you saw me today?' he asked eagerly.

It would have been impossible to tell him the truth, which was that he had seemed 'too much', because her ideal was now Dante's lithe frame.

To her relief, the maid appeared to change the plates for the next course. For the rest of the meal she concentrated on the elderly woman on her other side.

Afterwards the great doors were opened onto the garden, where coloured lights hung between the trees. People began to drift out to stroll beneath the moon. Sandor drew Ferne's arm through his.

The crowd congregated near the ruins, where blazing lights had been switched on, illuminating them up to the sky. The director, an amiable man called Rab Beswick, hailed Sandor.

'I like this place more every time I see it,' he said. 'Just think what we can make of these…' He indicated several walls, some of which stood at right angles to each other with connecting balconies.

'Just the right place to make a speech,' came a voice behind them.

It was Dante, appearing from nowhere.

'Antony was known for his ability to make the right speech at the right time,' he said. 'And his genius for picking the place that would be most effective.'

The director looked at him with awe.

'Hey, you're Italian,' he said, as though nothing could be stranger than finding an Italian in Italy. 'Are you an expert about this?'

'I've made a particular study of Marc Antony,' Dante said.

'Well, I'd be glad of anything you could tell me.'

'Let's not get carried away,' Sandor interrupted peevishly. 'This film isn't meant to be an historical treatise.'

'Certainly not,' Dante said suavely. 'Its selling point will be the personal charms of Signor Jayley.'

From somewhere there was a smothered choke. Sandor turned furious eyes in a vain attempt to detect who was making fun of him. Unable to locate a suspect, he turned back to Dante.

Which was what Dante had intended, Ferne thought. Whatever was he up to?

'Height is always effective,' Dante continued smoothly. 'If Antony was to make a great speech up there, silhouetted against the sky—'

'That's not in the script,' Sandor said at once.

'But it could be written in,' Dante pointed out. 'I'm not, of course, suggesting that you yourself should go up there. That would be far too dangerous, and naturally the film company won't want to risk their star. A double could be used for the long shot.'

Sandor relaxed.

'But it could look something like this…' Dante finished.

Before anyone realised what he was doing, he slipped out of sight, and a moment later reappeared on one of the balconies.

'You see?' he called down. 'What a shot this would make!'

'Great!' the director called up.

Ferne had to admit that Dante looked magnificent, standing high up, bathed in glittering spotlight. She only prayed that the balcony was strong enough to hold him and wouldn't start crumbling.

This time she really wished that she'd brought her camera, but one of the production staff had his and was snapping away madly. Sandor was livid, she was fascinated to notice.

'Come on down and we'll talk about it,' Rab called. 'Hey, be careful.' Dante was hopping down like a monkey, ending with a long leap to the floor, where he finished with a flourish.

'You're right, that's a great shot. You'll help us work on it, won't you?'

'Sure thing,' Dante said. 'I can show Mr Jayley how to—'

'It's getting late,' Sandor said hastily. 'We should be going inside.'

'Yes, let's go and look at the pictures,' Rab said eagerly. 'Come on, everyone.'

As the rest of them drifted away, Ferne murmured to Dante, 'What did you do that for?'

'You know exactly what I did it for,' he murmured back. 'I haven't enjoyed myself so much for ages. He's ready to kill me.'

His whole being was flooded with brilliance, as though he'd reached out, taken life by the hand and was loving every moment.

'Didn't anyone ever tell you not to repeat a trick?' she asked severely. 'Just because you climbed up into that building the other week, doesn't mean you have to keep doing it. You were just showing off.'

He grinned, and her heart turned over. 'You won't insult me by calling me a show-off. Too many have said it before you. As for repeating the trick? Sure, it was the memory of the fire that gave me the idea. It was actually a lot easier to get up there than it looks, but your lover wouldn't have tried it if you'd offered him an Oscar.'

'He is not my lover.'

'He wants to be.'

'Come on,' someone yelled from the retreating crowd. 'They're going to show the pictures.'

She would have argued further, but he slipped his arm about her, urging her forward irresistibly until they reached the villa, where someone had linked up the camera to a computer and had projected the pictures onto a screen.

There was Dante, high up, splendid, laughing down at

them. Whether his triumph lay in making the climb, or in making Sandor look absurd and diminished, only Ferne knew. One thing she was sure of—he'd done it in style.

She looked around for Sandor, wondering how he was taking this.

'He retired,' Gino explained. 'He's had a long day.'

Translation: he's sulking like a spoilt child, Ferne thought. Dante had hit the bull's eye.

Dante himself seemed oblivious to his success. He was deep in conversation with Rab, and by now Ferne was sufficiently in tune with his mind to recognise that this was another move in the game. He wouldn't say anything in front of an audience. But later…

'I've had a long day too,' she said. 'Goodnight.'

She slipped away and hurried up to her room. Sooner or later there was going to be a visitor, and she wanted to be ready.

First she needed a shower to wash the day off her. She turned it on as hard as she could and stood there, head back, arms wide, just letting it happen. It felt good.

She could have laughed aloud when she thought of how Dante had achieved his revenge—an Italian revenge—not violent, but skilled; a lithe, dancing movement, a quick thrust of the stiletto, unseen by anyone but his adversary, who had slunk away, humiliated.

Now she realised that she ought to have feared for Dante's safety when he'd been up high, but she hadn't, because she was under the spell he cast. And she was still under his spell, she thought happily.

She finished under the shower, pulled a robe around her and stepped out into the bedroom. But what she found there made her stop sharply.

'Sandor!'

He was leaning against the door, his arms folded, a look of happy expectation on his face. He'd removed his shirt so that his magnificent chest was presented for her approval in all its naked perfection, smooth, muscular, evenly tanned.

'What are you doing here?' She sighed.

'Oh, come on, sweetie. We both knew this was going to happen.'

'Tommy, I swear, if you try to touch me I'll thump you so hard you'll see stars.'

'You don't mean that.'

'Don't tell me what I mean. I'm warning you.'

He laughed and sauntered easily over to her, the king claiming his rights.

'I think I might just put that to the test— *Aargh*!'

He yelped as her hand struck his face.

'You bitch!' he wailed. 'I could get a swollen lip.'

She opened her mouth to reply, but before she could speak there was a knock on her door. She darted to open it and found Dante standing there. He was wearing dark-blue pyjamas, and his face had an innocent look that filled her with suspicion almost as great as her relief.

'I'm so sorry to trouble you,' he said, 'but there's no soap in my bathroom and I wondered if you'd mind— Oh dear, am I disturbing something?'

'Nothing at all,' Ferne said. 'Mr Jayley was just going.'

Dante regarded Sandor with apparent surprise, seeming not to have noticed him before, but Ferne wasn't fooled. He knew exactly what he was doing. In his own way, he was as much of an actor as Sandor, but a more subtle one.

'Good evening,' he said politely. 'Oh dear, you seem to have suffered an injury. You're going to have a nasty swollen lip.'

'Eh!' Sandor yelped. He tried to make for the bathroom,

but Dante was blocking his way so that he was forced to turn away and retreat from the room altogether, slamming the door behind him.

'That should keep him occupied,' Dante said with satisfaction.

CHAPTER EIGHT

'But how did you know? I didn't hit him that hard. He didn't have a swollen lip.'

'No, but he was afraid of it. I was just outside the door and I heard everything.'

'And was it coincidence that you were there?'

'Certainly not. I was lurking in the corridor. When I saw him go in, I listened. After all, you might have welcomed him.'

'And then you'd have just gone away, I suppose?' she said sardonically.

Slowly Dante shook his head, and there was something in his eyes she'd never seen before.

'No way. If you'd welcomed him, I'd have come in and thumped him myself a lot harder than you did. But there was no need. You dealt with him very efficiently—I'm glad to say,' he added softly.

'You didn't really think I wanted him, did you?'

He made a wry face. 'I hoped not, but I needed to know. When I saw how easily he entered, I did wonder.'

'I was in the bathroom, or he'd never have got in.'

'Are you really over him?'

'Of course I am. I just wish we'd never come here.'

'You were a big hit at dinner.'

'You weren't doing so badly yourself,' she flung at him.

'Just passing the time, keeping an eye on you, making sure you didn't misbehave. I had to know how you feel about him. It mattered.'

'And now you know.' She met his gaze, silently urging him on.

But the man who'd dismissed his enemy with a master stroke suddenly seemed to lose confidence.

'What happens now?' he said. 'It must be your decision. Do you want me to go?'

'I don't know what I want,' she said distractedly. It was almost true.

'Ferne.' His voice was quiet and suddenly serious. 'If you don't know, neither of us knows.'

'That's not fair.'

'Fair?' His voice was edgy. 'You stand there half-naked, doing heaven knows what to me, and *I'm* being unfair?'

The towel robe had opened just enough to show her breasts, firm and glowing with the need she could no longer hide. While she hesitated, he took the edges of the material and drew them apart, revealing the rest of her nakedness.

'*That* is being unfair,' he said in a shaking voice.

She couldn't move. Her whole being seemed to be concentrated on him, on his touch and the thought of where it would alight next. The feeling was so intense that it was as though he was already caressing her everywhere. It was almost a shock when he laid his fingers lightly at the base of her throat, leaving them there, seeming to wait for something.

She drew a long breath. None of Sandor's dramatic caresses had affected her one tenth as much as Dante's patience.

'Tell me,' he said softly.

'Tell you…?'

'Tell me what to do. Ferne, for pity's sake, if you want me to stop say so now, because I don't have that much control left.'

Her smile was deliberately provocative. 'Perhaps a man can have too much control. Maybe he even talks too mu—'

Her words were silenced by his mouth on hers. It was too late now, past the point of no return. Her own kiss was as fervent as his, speaking of desire held in too long, of frustration released in giddy, headlong joy.

While he kissed he was pulling at the robe until it fell to the floor and there was no barrier to his hands caressing her everywhere, setting off tremors that shocked her with their intensity. She managed to return the compliment, ripping away at his clothes until he was as naked as she.

Neither of them knew who made the first move to the bed. It didn't matter. They were running down the same road, seeking the same triumphant destination.

She had anticipated his skill, but her imagination had fallen far short of the reality. He made love as he did the quick-step, unfailingly knowing the right touch, the right movement, always in perfect understanding with his partner. Her body felt as though it had been made for this moment, this loving, this man, and only this man.

At the last moment he hesitated, looking down into her face as though seeking one final reassurance. By now her breathing was coming fast, and any delay was intolerable. She wanted him and she wanted him *now*.

'Dante,' she whispered urgently.

He gave a quick sigh of satisfaction, hearing something in her voice that he'd needed to know, and the next moment he was inside her, glorying in being part of her.

After he looked different. The teasing clown who enchanted her was also the lover who instinctively knew the secrets of her body and used them for his purpose in a way that was almost ruthless. He'd known what he wanted and been determined to have it, but what he'd wanted was her joyful satisfaction. Now he had it, which meant he knew his power over her, but she had no fears about that power. She trusted him too much for that.

She wondered if she looked different to him too. Then she caught the faint bewilderment in his eyes and knew that she did. That delighted her, and it was she who moved towards him for their second loving, caressing him in ways that had never occurred to her before, because he was like no other man. He laughed and settled himself against her, implicitly inviting her to do whatever she liked, an invitation she accepted with vigour.

Later, when they had recovered, he propped himself on his elbow, looking down at her lying beneath him with a mixture of triumph and delight.

'What took us so long?' he whispered.

How could she give him an honest answer when she was only just now facing the truth in her own heart?

It took time because I've been holding back, fearful of having too many feelings for you. I knew if I got too close I was in danger of loving you, and I don't want to. To love you is to risk heartbreak, and I don't have the courage. Even though—even though it may already be too late. Too late for me? Too late for you?

There was no way to say that.

She just opened her arms and drew him in so she could enfold him protectively until they fell asleep in the same moment.

* * *

As the first touch of dawn came into the room, Dante rose from the bed, careful not to waken her, and went to stand by the window. From here he could see the sun rising behind the ruins, casting its promise over the new day.

A new day. It was a feeling he'd thought he would never know. The circumstances of his life had bred in him a wary detachment, making it easier to stand back, observe himself wryly, often cynically, and sometimes with a melancholy that he fought with laughter.

But this morning the melancholy had lifted. Detachment was gone, leaving him at peace.

Peace: the very last quality he associated with Ferne. She teased him, haunted him, jeered and provoked him. Sometimes he wondered if she'd known how she tempted him, but then he would see the look in her eye—assessing, challenging, taking him to the next stage of the game they were playing.

The game was called 'who will blink first?' She'd played it with consummate skill, enticing him into indiscretions like buying her a bikini. That had shown his hand too obviously, and she'd played on it, luring him to the edge, closer to the moment when he'd had to abandon the control that ruled his life.

The luck of the devil had been on her side. Nobody could have predicted the arrival of Sandor and the fierce jealousy that had stormed through Dante. Seeing them together on the beach, Sandor's hands actually touching her body—the one he thought of as his own personal possession—he'd come close to committing murder.

She'd tried to refuse the invitation to stay here, but why? A demon had whispered in his ear that she was afraid to be in Sandor's company lest the old attraction overwhelm her. He'd insisted on accepting, driven by the need to see more of them together and know what he was up against.

It had been no satisfaction that so many lures had been cast out to him last night. There were at least three bedrooms at which he could have presented himself, sure of a welcome. Instead he'd haunted her door until inevitably Sandor had appeared, bare-chested, for seduction, and entered without knocking.

The moment when he'd heard her slap the man's face had felt like the beginning of his life.

It meant that in the game they were playing she'd won and he'd lost. Or possibly the other way around. Whatever! He couldn't have been happier.

He returned to the bed, sitting down carefully so as not to disturb her. He wanted to watch her like this, relaxed and content, breathing almost without making a sound. A wisp of hair had fallen over her face and he brushed it back softly. Somehow his hand stayed, stroking her face.

Her lips moved in a smile, telling him that she was awake. The smile turned into a chuckle and she opened her eyes to find him looking directly into them.

'Good morning,' he whispered, settling beside her and drawing her close.

No passion now, just her head on his shoulder in blissful content, body curled against body, and the sense of having come home to each other.

'Good morning,' she murmured.

'Is everything all right?'

'Mmm!' She hid her face against him.

'Me too,' he agreed. 'Very much all right.'

After a while she opened her eyes again to find him sunk in thought.

'What are we going to do now?' he wondered.

'Leave this place behind,' she said at once. 'Sandor will throw us out anyway.'

'A pity. Part of me wants to stay around for a while just to poke him in the eye. He had his turn making me jealous. Now it's my turn to pay him back.'

'Jealous? You?'

'Don't play the innocent. You knew exactly what you were doing to me. You loved seeing me on hot coals.'

'I'll admit it had its entertaining moments,' she mused. 'But that was because you were trying to play hard to get. Not always successfully, mind you, but you tried.'

'Of course,' he said, sounding shocked. 'Don't forget that I promised "just friendly", and a gentleman always keeps his word.'

'Gentleman? Huh!'

'Let's have that discussion later,' he said hastily. 'The point is, I couldn't break my word, so I had to get you to break it for me. You forced me into retreat, so I'm innocent.'

'Oh, *please*!' she jeered. 'The one thing I can't imagine is you being innocent. You are a scheming, manipulative, double-dealing, tricky— Oh, the hell with it! Who cares if you're a bad character? What are you *doing*?'

'What does it feel as if I'm doing? Hush now, while I prove what a bad character I am.'

Laughing, he proceeded to do exactly that with such vigour that she was left breathless.

'I suppose I ought to be grateful to Sandor,' Ferne said when they had recovered. 'He might be a clumsy oaf, but he did us a favour. Do you know, he actually wanted me to take some more pictures of him?'

'What, after you…?'

'Yes, apparently my photographs flattered him as nobody

else's did. Heavens, how did I ever fancy myself in love with that twerp?'

He suspected another reason why Sandor had tried to seduce Ferne. Such was the man's vanity that he wanted to believe that he could reclaim her whenever he liked. But about this Dante stayed tactfully silent.

'I suppose we should get up,' he said at last. 'It's a beautiful day.'

Gino was waiting for them downstairs, clearly on hot coals.

'Sandor had a restless night and he's gone for a walk in the grounds. He says he doesn't feel up to seeing anyone.'

'I wonder what could have brought that on?' Dante said sympathetically.

'Artistic sensibility,' Gino sighed.

'I understand,' Dante said solemnly. 'A true artist sometimes needs to be alone to commune with the universe. Did you speak?' This was to Ferne, who was displaying alarming symptoms of choking. She managed to shake her head and he continued. 'We'll leave at once. Give me a call when the filming has finished and I'll come back then.'

They didn't even stay for breakfast. Tossing their things into bags, they fled the Palazzo Tirelli like children making a dash for freedom.

As the car swung out of the gates Ferne caught a glimpse of a tragically noble figure standing on a hill, watching their departure with a look of passionate yearning. Not that she could see his expression at this distance, but she would have bet money on it.

'It's like your Shakespeare said,' Dante observed. 'Some men are born twerps, others achieve twerphood, and some have it thrust upon them. Well, something like that, anyway.'

'You've really got your knife in to Sandor, haven't you?' she chuckled.

Dante grinned. 'I did once. Not any more.'

Ferne leaned back in her seat, smiling. The jokey note of the conversation suited her exactly. This was a man to have fun with, nothing more. The gleam of danger was still far off on the horizon, but she knew it was there, throwing its harsh light over everything in anticipation. The only answer was to look away.

'Where are we going?' she asked after a while.

'Anywhere away from here.'

Safely out of Rome, he turned south and hugged the coast for about a hundred miles. There they found another beach, quiet, simple and delightfully unglamorous. The town was the same, a good place for strolling and buying toothpaste before retreating to their modest hotel and the room they shared.

'Thank goodness Sandor wasn't able to organise our accommodation this time,' Dante chuckled as they lay together in a cosy embrace late that night. 'It wasn't an accident that we were put miles apart.'

'Yes, I kind of worked that out. Low cunning.'

'Fatal mistake. I'm the master of low cunning. Someone should have warned him.'

'You're also an old-fashioned male chauvinist, now I come to think of it.'

'It took you long enough to find that out. When did you see the light?'

'You said that if I'd welcomed Sandor into my room you'd have come in and thumped him.'

'Good 'n' hard.'

'But who gave you the right to veto my lovers? What about my right to make my own choice?'

'My darling, you have an absolute right to choose any man you want.'

'Good.'

'As long as the one you choose is me.'

'And you think I'm going to put up with that nineteenth-century attitude?'

In the darkness she heard him give the rich chuckle of the triumphant male.

'Yes, because I'm not going to give you any option. Now, come here and let me make the matter plain to you.'

So she did. And he did. And after that they slept in perfect harmony.

Ferne had known from the first evening that there was more to Dante than met the eye. How many men discussed *The Divine Comedy* with a woman they'd known only a couple of hours, even if they were named after the poet?

Hope had mentioned that he had three academic degrees, and from odd remarks he dropped in their conversations she realised that this was no idle boast. His brain was agile and well-informed, and she could easily guess his horror at the thought of losing his high-powered skills.

Since she'd learned the truth about the threat to Dante's life, she'd come to see him as two men—one always standing behind the other, a permanent warning. When he was at his funniest, she was most conscious of the other man, silently threatening in the shadows, never allowing Dante to forget that he was there.

Sometimes it broke her heart that he must face his nemesis alone, and she longed to take him in her arms, not in the light-hearted passion that they usually shared, but with tender comfort. Then she remembered that he had chosen his isolation, however bitter it might be, and he wanted no comfort. Without her help, without anyone's help, he was complete and whole.

One evening he was unusually quiet, but he seemed absorbed in a book, so she'd put it down to that. Later that night she woke suddenly to find him sitting by the window, his head buried in his hands. He was completely still and silent, in such contrast to his normal liveliness that she knew a twinge of alarm.

Slipping out of bed, she went to kneel beside him.

'Is everything all right?'

'Yes, fine.' But he seemed to speak with an effort.

'You don't look well.'

'Just a bit of a headache.'

'Have you had it all evening? You haven't said much.'

'It'll go away. Just give it time.'

'Have you taken anything?'

'Yes.'

'And it doesn't work?'

'It will, in time.'

'Come back to bed. A sleep may do you good.'

'Later. Leave me now. I don't want to talk.'

'I'm only worried for you.'

'Will you drop the subject please?'

Dante's tone was light, but Ferne saw in his eyes something that reminded her of that other time. There was a steely anger, and a determination not to yield, no matter what the cost to himself or anyone else. Hastily she backed off, remembering Toni's words that to persist would be to endanger Dante, not help him.

She returned to bed, pulling the covers over her head so that she could huddle down and be alone with her thoughts.

She lay awake for a long time, telling herself that this must be just an ordinary headache, the kind everyone had.

It seemed that she was right, because the next day he was his normal self. Perhaps it was only her imagination that the 'other' Dante had been there, hostile, rejecting.

One evening they bumped into Mario, an old friend from Dante's college days. The two men plunged into academic conversation, occasionally remembering their manners, apologising and drawing her in. She laughed, not at all offended, fascinated by this new angle on Dante.

When he went to fetch more drinks, Mario said, 'We all thought he'd be head of the college by now.'

'Is he really that clever?' Ferne asked.

'He could think and write rings around anyone else. I know they offered him a professorship, but he wanted to go off travelling.'

Next day she claimed tiredness, urging Dante to spend some time with Mario. He said she was the nicest, most under-standing woman he'd ever known—which made her feel guilty, because she had an ulterior motive.

When she was safely alone she opened her laptop, accessed the Internet and looked up all she could find about his ailment. She had already done this once, on the day before they'd left Naples, but now she had a driving need to know far more.

A sudden bleeding into the space between the brain and an area of the lining that surrounds it; a weak blood vessel that suddenly ruptures.

Sometimes there are warning symptoms, such as headache, facial pain and double vision. This can happen minutes or weeks before the main rupture.

She read everything that she could find, forcing herself to understand every detail. The picture that kept returning to her mind was Dante going back into the burning building to rescue the dog, knowing that it might cost him his life.

When you lived with the possibility of death every moment, how much would you actually fear it? Welcome it?

There were three files that she needed to read again. Quickly she downloaded them, put them in a folder, titled it 'ZZZ', then shut everything down quickly. Finally she called Hope. Describing the headache, she said, 'I was worried at first, but he's been fine ever since, so maybe it was normal. He seems full of beans.'

'Thank you,' Hope said fervently. 'I can't tell you what it means to us to know you're with him.'

'I've got to go now. I can see him returning with his friend. I'll call again soon.'

Looking out of the window, she hailed the two men, who waved back and pointed up the street to a restaurant.

'Coming,' she called down.

It took a moment to slip the printed file into her drawer, then she was ready to leave.

The three of them spent a convivial evening, but at the end Mario seemed to forget Dante and become more interested in looking at Ferne's plunging neckline. After which, Dante said he needed an early night and swept her off to bed.

Mario departed next morning, but he left a legacy in Dante's mind. Stretched out on the beach, Ferne was startled to look up and find him doing a crossword puzzle in Latin.

'It's not difficult if you're Italian,' he demurred when she expressed her admiration. 'The two languages are so similar.'

'What's that?' she asked, pointing at a clue.

He translated for her and said, 'The answer is *quam celerrime*. It means "as quickly as possible".'

'*Quam celerrime*,' she mused. 'It has a nice, flowing sound, doesn't it? What a pity I was always useless at languages. What's the Italian version?'

'*Il più rapidamente possibile.*'

'No, I definitely prefer *quam celerrime*. Not that I could do anything with *celerrime* at the moment. I'm half-asleep.'

'Bad night?'

'No, it was a wonderful night, thank you. I just didn't get any sleep.'

He laughed, and she settled down. She was deep in happy slumber when the sound of her mobile phone reached her from a distance.

'Someone wants you,' Dante said, reaching into her bag for the phone. 'Here.'

It was a text:

Never thought you were the one to turn down the chance of a lifetime. The offer's still open and this time I want the right answer. Money, money, money. Mick.

'Who's Mick?' Dante asked, reading over her shoulder.

'Can't you tell?' Ferne asked sleepily. 'He's my sugar-daddy. He wants to cover me with diamonds and buy me an apartment in the West End, but I told him no. That stuff is old-fashioned.'

'Now I remember; he's your agent, isn't he? You mentioned him on the train the night we met.'

'Uh-huh!'

She was trying to sound half-asleep, but inside she was alert and wary. She didn't want Dante asking questions about why she'd refused a big job, in case he stumbled on the truth. Diverting him was going to be tricky.

'Why is he mad at you?' Dante asked. 'What have you turned down?'

She sighed as if it was too boring to be discussed.

'He wanted me to go back to London and do another theatre shoot with a big star who's condescending to do a live play. Sandor Jayley with knobs on. No way!'

'Who's the star?'

She told him. Dante stared.

'You rejected *him*? Just think what you might have—'

'He's bringing his fiancée with him,' she said, trying to sound petulant. 'No chance for me to be vulgar and unprincipled there.'

Dante grinned, slipping an arm around her.

'Can I flatter myself that you prefer to be vulgar and unprincipled with me?'

'I can't stop you flattering yourself,' she observed indifferently. 'Some men are so conceited.'

'Not me. I can't believe you'd choose me over the chance to make a lot of money.'

'You forget,' she said languidly. 'I already made my fortune with Sandor.' She drew a light finger down his bare chest. 'Now I'm in the mood to spend some of it on, er, the *pleasures of the moment*.' She uttered the last words in a seductive whisper.

'Oh, really?' he said, speaking with some difficulty, she was pleased to note.

'*La grande signorina* gives her orders?'

'Definitely. And she's very demanding.'

'So I'm here only for your pleasure?'

She surveyed him with wicked glee. 'Well, what else did you imagine you were here for? I expect my every whim to be obeyed.'

'I'm your willing slave.'

'And my first whim is to swim. Into the sea with us.'

'I was hoping for something better.'

'Hmm! Being my willing slave didn't last long, did it? Come on.'

She wriggled free of him and ran down the beach, hearing him just behind her. Once in the surf, he seized her and drew her further in, until the water was up to their chests; nobody else could have seen the way his hands were wandering.

'Just what do you think you're doing?' she challenged.

'Only my duty. I wouldn't want to disappoint you.'

'But you can't do *that* in public.'

'It's not in public, it's under water. Perfectly respectable.'

'There is nothing respectable about what you're doing,' she gasped.

After that she became incapable of speech and could only cling onto him, digging her nails into his shoulder in a way that left marks for days.

When they finally returned to their loungers, she asked him to fetch her a drink. While he was gone she texted Mick with shaking hands.

> Sorry, can't change my mind. Am out of action for a while.

She switched off the phone and hid it away safely, silently thanking a merciful providence for helping her get away with it this time.

Hopefully Mick wouldn't trouble her again, whatever he might guess.

Oh, to blazes with Mick and what he might think! To blazes with everything, except getting Dante back into her bed *quam celerrime*.

CHAPTER NINE

THE 'willing slave' fantasy kept them entertained for a while. Unlike many men, Dante was totally relaxed with it, his masculine confidence too powerful to be disturbed by such a joke.

They played it out in the bedroom, with her indicating her requirements and him following to the letter, both enjoying the challenge, laughing, not thinking any further. That was how they both preferred it.

One morning as they were preparing to go out the phone rang, and it was Gino.

'The film crew have left,' Dante informed Ferne when the call was over.

'Already?'

'There was some sort of a kerfuffle; Sandor threw a fit and everyone was out in an hour. Now we're needed to sell the place.' He looked at her, smiling. 'Ah, well, I guess it was too perfect to last for ever.'

'Nothing lasts for ever,' Ferne said lightly.

'That's what I say.' Then he sighed and added ruefully, 'But sometimes it would be nice if it did.'

They spent two days at the Palazzo Tirelli before heading

back to Naples, where they moved into a small apartment belonging to a friend of Dante who was currently away.

On the first night back they went to dinner at the Villa Rinucci. Hope broadcast the event to the family, inviting everyone to drop in. But for her the real point of the evening was to see with her own eyes that Dante was in good health, and even better spirits.

'He's told me all about it,' she said when she and Ferne had a moment alone in the kitchen. 'You actually slapped Sandor Jayley's face because you prefer Dante?'

'I'd have slapped his face anyway,' Ferne protested. 'It had nothing to do with Dante.'

'Oh, come! What about that big offer you turned down?'

'Well, I had to, after I made you a promise. Hope, Dante and I are ships that pass in the night, we both know that. We're having fun, but it can't last. He's not in love with me, and I'm not in love with him.'

Hope didn't reply in words, but her cynical gaze was answer enough. A moment later Toni called, and they both went out to where everyone was lounging in the garden as the evening wound down.

Ferne wished she could speak openly to Hope and tell her that love was impossible because she simply wouldn't allow it to happen.

She knew she had been lucky as few women were ever lucky. Dante was a gentle and considerate man. If she was tired, he would urge her to bed, kiss her gently and either hold her until she slept or creep away, leaving her in peace.

When they talked, he listened to her with every appearance of real interest. His own conversation was fascinating. Beneath the sometimes clownish exterior was a thoughtful, educated man who might well have been a professor in some serious subject.

In bed he was a skilled and tender lover, giving her a physical pleasure she had never dreamed possible, and treating her like a queen. On the surface no woman could have asked for more.

But in her heart she had the melancholy feeling that it was all a sham, an illusion, because he was hiding the most important part of himself from her. And while that was true it would protect her from falling deeply in love with him.

She reassured herself about that many times.

Their apartment was high up on the fifth floor of a block overlooking the Bay of Naples. From their bedroom window they could see the great volcano Vesuvius in the distance. Several times she woke to find him on the window seat, contentedly watching the full moon across the bay casting its glow on the volcano.

One night he stayed up late, leaving her to come to bed alone. She'd waited for him, then fallen into a half-sleep. Somewhere in that doze she'd thought she felt a gentle kiss on her cheek, but when she opened her eyes she was alone.

She'd slept again, and had finally woken to find him sitting by the window. This was different from last time, when he'd sat with his head in his hands, clearly in pain. Now he seemed content, gazing out, still in the same thoughtful mood as before. When he saw that she was awake, he didn't speak but held out an arm for her to come and join him.

'Do you remember when we looked at this before?' he murmured.

'Yes, and you told me you'd once heard it rumble and longed to hear it again,' she said. 'There's nowhere to get away from it, is there? Wherever you are in Naples, it's always there.'

'You think you're used to it,' he murmured. 'You know it in all its phases, but you can still be taken by surprise.'

She watched him, wondering what he would say next. He'd been in a strange mood for the last couple of days, with less to say than usual. He didn't seem sad or unwell, merely thoughtful. Occasionally she would look up to find him watching her with eyes that were almost puzzled, as though something had disconcerted him. If he caught her glance, he would smile and turn quickly away.

'What have you been taking for granted?' she asked him now.

'Everything, perhaps. You think you know how things are, but suddenly it's all different. You're not the same man you were—whoever that was.'

He gave a brief, nervous laugh, sounding mysteriously as though he had no self-confidence. 'I'm talking nonsense, aren't I?' he said.

'Mmm, but go on. It sounds good.'

'Yes, nonsense can sound very impressive. I learned that long ago. You can even impress yourself with it for a while. But—then the volcano rumbles and reminds you of things you've always known, and maybe wish you didn't.'

Ferne held her breath. Was Dante finally going to tell her the truth about himself, thus letting her come really close to him at last?

'Are you afraid of the volcano?' she whispered. 'I mean, the one inside?'

'Yes, although I wouldn't admit that to anyone but you. I've never even admitted it to myself before, but I feel I could tell you anything and it would be all right. I need never be afraid again.' He added wistfully, 'Could that ever really be true?'

'I suppose it would depend how much you wanted it to be true,' she ventured. 'If you trusted me…'

'I trust you as I've never trusted anyone in my life. If not you, then who?'

He took her hands in his, bending his head to kiss the palms.

'You have such tiny, delicate hands,' he whispered. 'Yet they're so strong, so welcoming. When they reach out, they seem to contain all the world.'

'I would give you the world if I could,' she said. It was a dangerous thing to say, but the words seemed to come out of their own accord. 'If it were mine to give.'

'Perhaps it is and you don't know it.' He stroked her face with tender fingers. 'Sometimes I think I know more about you than you know about yourself. I know how loving and honest you are, how brave, how open-hearted.'

'It's an illusion,' she said. 'That's a fantasy figure you've created.'

'Why do you say that?'

'Because nobody could be the way you see me.'

'Why? Because I think you're perfect?'

'That proves it's an illusion.'

'No, it proves I'm a man of insight and good sense. Now, don't argue with me. If I say you're perfect, you're perfect— and I do say it. I know you could never perform a deceitful or underhand action.'

His words, spoken so warmly and with such emotion, gave her a bad moment. The knowledge of her deception, however well-meaning, seemed to hang over them, poisoning the moment.

'Dante—'

His finger lightly touched her mouth. 'Don't spoil it.'

Don't spoil it. The words were like a bitter reproach.

But it wasn't her fault, she thought wildly. She was protecting him, but that innocent desire had led her up this path, fraught with danger.

'Let me say what I want to before I lose my nerve,' he murmured.

'I can't see you ever losing your nerve.'

'That's an act. Inside I'm a coward. If you only knew how much of a coward, you'd run away. And that's what you ought to do.'

'Isn't that for me to decide?'

'How can you, when you don't know the worst of me?'

'Then tell me the worst. I'm braced for anything.'

'You make a joke of it, but there are things…'

'Yes?' she said eagerly.

'Ferne…' She felt a tremor go through him. 'Have I imagined what's been happening to us?'

Now her heart was beating so hard that she couldn't speak, only shake her head.

'I know I said "just friendly",' he whispered. 'But I say a lot of things that are nonsense. I guess you know that by now. When we talk—and I've never talked to anyone the way I talk to you—I always feel that you understand everything I'm not saying. With you, I don't have to worry. I can be at peace.'

He made a wry face, aimed at himself. 'I never thought the day would come when I saw peace as a virtue. I was always one for racketing around. Yes, you knew that, didn't you?' His soft laughter joined hers. 'I don't suppose there's much about me you haven't worked out: clown, idiot, self-deceiver, overgrown schoolboy.'

'I could add a few others,' she teased.

'I'll bet you could.'

'Then how can you say I don't know the worst of you?

I probably think you're worse than you are. Why don't you put me right?'

'Tell you what a hero I am? What a strong, solid, upright character who never cut corners or skirted around the truth in his life?'

'No, I don't think I could quite believe that.' She was teasing him along the road, inviting him into the place where he would feel safe enough to tell her everything. When there was total honesty between them, the way would be clear for whatever lay in the future.

She wanted there to be a future. She could admit that now. She'd hidden her feelings, even from herself, behind a barrier of caution and sensible reasoning. But now Dante himself was demolishing that barrier. If she was only a little patient, there would be happiness soon.

'It you presented yourself as a stuffed dummy full of virtue I think I'd just laugh,' she admitted. 'And then I'd send you on your way, because I'd have no use for you.'

'For the stuffed-dummy part or the virtue?' he asked lightly.

'Guess.'

He smiled, but then his smile faded as emotion swept him.

'Oh, Ferne, don't change,' he said desperately. 'Promise me you'll never change, and then maybe I can dig deep in myself and find a little courage. Only it's going to take more than just a little. It's going to take a lot to show you myself as I really am, stupid and pig-headed, blind to what matters.'

'Stop,' she said, putting her fingers lightly over his mouth. 'Don't run yourself down.'

He didn't argue, just took hold of her fingers and moved his lips against them. His eyes were almost desperate. She stroked his face, willing him to take the last step that would join their hearts in the closeness that only honesty could bring.

'Dante,' she whispered. 'Please—please.'

Suddenly he gripped her tightly, drawing her to him and burying his face against her.

'Help me,' he said huskily. *'Help me.'*

She held him eagerly, flooded with emotion that made it impossible to speak. His carefully constructed armour was cracking, revealing the vulnerability he'd striven so hard to hide, and she wanted only to enfold him, to offer him the help he'd finally sought. Now the moment had come, she was almost dizzy with joy and gratitude.

'What's this?' he said, touching her face. 'You're crying.'

'No, I'm not, not really. I'm just—'

'Don't cry.' He was lightly brushing her tears away. 'I didn't mean to upset you.'

'I'm not upset.'

He took her face between his hands, looking down at her tenderly before dropping his mouth to hers. She kissed him back eagerly, trying to tell him silently that she was his in any way he wanted. If only they could take the next step.

'I'm so lucky to have you,' he said. 'If only…'

'If only…?' she echoed wistfully.

'If only I were worth it. There's so much I want to say to you, but not just now. My head's in a muddle—as usual,' he finished, turning it into a joke.

But she wouldn't let him get away with that.

'I don't think this is your usual muddle,' she persisted.

'No, I'm getting worse. Be a little patient with me.'

'All right,' she said, trying not to sound sad.

'Let's go to bed,' he said. 'We've got a long drive tomorrow.'

She was stunned, hardly able to believe that the emotion of a moment ago had vanished to nothing. They had come so close, and to see the prize snatched away at the last minute was hard. But she let him lead her unprotesting to bed. One incautious word from her, and the chance could be lost for ever.

He pulled the clothes up over her and got in beside her, holding her briefly before kissing her goodnight. Then he turned over and went to sleep.

She lay staring into the darkness, trying to come to terms with what had happened. It was disappointing to sense his withdrawal, yet she felt she understood. He'd meant to tell her—she was convinced—but he'd backed off, perhaps appalled by so nearly abandoning the caution of a lifetime.

Now she must be patient and it would surely happen, for there had been something in his manner that had never been there before, a new trust and tenderness. His eyes had shone with a different light, and somewhere Ferne had sensed a door opening.

How long had she loved him—right from the start? The signs had been there when he'd gone into the burning building and she, who'd coolly photographed Sandor's betrayal, had forgotten everything but Dante's danger.

She'd deceived herself, believing she was only doing this for Hope, when the truth was she yearned to be with Dante. How could she ever have imagined that it was possible to be with this man night and day and not love him?

The sadness had been to love him and hide from him, as he was hiding from her. But now that would soon be over, and she was feeling happy again as she fell asleep.

Next day they drove miles to a villa that was going to take all their joint skills to sell. But the challenge was exhilarating, and they returned home in a triumphant mood. On the drive back, Dante was in high spirits.

'We'll stop for a meal,' he said. 'But only a quick one. Let's not be late home.'

He said nothing about the day before, but there was something in the happy atmosphere that told her everything was different. He'd come to the edge of saying the words that would bind them closer, that it was almost as though they had already been said. Looking up, she saw him watching her with a contented smile that told her she was right.

When they reached home there was work to do, and they both settled down at computers.

'It's coming on really well,' he said, looking over her shoulder. 'How did I ever sell houses without you?'

'You don't have to butter me up,' she said sleepily. 'You're stuck with me, whether you want me or not.'

'That's what I like to hear. Why don't you go to bed?'

'I think I will.' She shut down her computer.

'Leave it,' Dante said. 'I'll put it away with mine.'

She kissed him and drifted away, yawning.

He watched her go, wondering if she would think it strange that tonight he didn't come to bed with her. In fact he was hatching a plan—reprehensible, no doubt, but he didn't think she'd mind too much when she found out.

She had never done as she'd promised and emailed him the pictures he had taken of her. Now he proposed to conduct a raid and claim them. Waiting until he could see that she'd turned the bedroom light off, he switched her computer back on.

He located the folder without difficulty, and within moments was looking at the pictures he'd taken. He'd thought he knew them, but now they struck him with new force. So much had happened since then. He hadn't meant to grow so close to her, but it had happened despite his resolutions. Perhaps it was fate. He, a man who believed in fate, had to believe in this possibility.

Now he couldn't understand why he hadn't seen her clearly

before. Entranced by her loveliness, he'd overlooked the strength and honesty in her face. It was this, as much as her passionate body, that had broken down his defences, so that only a day ago he'd been on the verge of telling her things he'd never told another living soul, things he'd sworn never to tell anyone in his life—however long or short that life might be.

He'd come to the very edge, then backed off. But not very far. The thought was still there in his mind that if he plucked up courage he could tell her everything, beg her to risk the future with him. If not her, then nobody, for there was nobody else in the world that he trusted as much.

She was smiling at him from the screen, her eyes wide and clear, offering hope where there had been none before, a future where there had been only blankness.

Quickly he connected the laptop to his portable printer and printed out a copy of the picture.

That was enough for now. Tomorrow he would confess what he'd done and they would laugh together, revelling in their private world where nobody else was allowed, and where they kept each other safe.

He was about to log off when he noticed the file called 'ZZZ'.

Through her light sleep Ferne was vaguely aware of the sound of the printer coming from the next room, then a long silence, until she heard the printer again. When it ended there was another silence that dragged on and on. Without knowing why, she was suddenly filled with fear.

Moving slowly, she left the bed at the same moment that Dante entered the room. Strangely, he too was moving slowly, as though struggling to recover from some terrible blow. He switched on the light, and she saw he was holding some papers, which he tossed onto the bed. She drew a sharp breath as she recognised some of the files about his condition that she'd stored on her computer.

At the sight of Dante's face filled with cold rage, her heart nearly failed her. It was the face of a stranger.

'I printed them off your computer,' he said. 'What are they?'

'Just—something I've been reading.'

'Just something you *happened* to be reading?' His voice was calm but as cold as ice. 'I don't think so. There are at least a dozen downloads in that folder. You've been searching the Internet for anything you could find on this one subject, and you didn't just chance on it by accident, did you?' When she hesitated, he added, 'Don't lie to me, Ferne.'

If only he would return to being the Dante she knew, and not this frightening stranger. She tried to find some warmth in his eyes, but there was only a cavern of emptiness that filled her with dread.

'I won't lie to you, Dante. I knew you had a problem.'

'Who told you? Hope, I suppose?'

'Yes, she was worried about you. You had that funny turn on the ladder the day of the fire, and then a bad headache.'

'And you both put two and two together and came up with five. I was sick with smoke that day, but you had to make a big thing of it.'

'All right, you think we were fussing about nothing, but people who care about you *do* fuss. That's how you know they care. You told me once that Hope has been the nearest thing to a mother that you've known since your own mother died. Well, mothers fuss. They may have to hide it, but it's what happens.'

'So, she told you—when? How long ago?'

'I—'

'How long ago?' he repeated relentlessly. 'Before we came away together?'

'Yes.'

'You've known all this time?' he said softly. 'There was I, like a fool, thinking I could guard my privacy, never dreaming you were spying on me.'

'I wasn't spying.'

'*This* is spying.' His voice was like the crack of a whip, making her flinch back.

'Is it wrong to care for you, to want to see you safe?'

'My safety is my own affair.'

'Not always,' she said, beginning to get angry. 'What you do affects other people. You can't spend your life cut off from everyone.' She drew a sharp breath. 'But that's what you've tried to do, isn't it?'

'That's my business.' His face was deadly pale, not white but grey. 'Is that why you came with me? As a kind of guardian, watching over me like a nurse with a child—or worse?'

'I never thought of you like that.'

'I think you did—someone so stupid that he has to be kept in the dark while he's *investigated* behind his back.'

'What did you expect me to do when you kept the truth from me?' she cried.

'*You've* been hiding secrets from *me*,' he shouted.

'I had to, but I didn't want to. I always hoped that you'd come to trust me.'

'But that's the irony; that's the ugly joke. I *did* trust you. I've never felt so close to anyone.'

'Then you were fooling yourself,' she said hotly. 'How could we be close when you were concealing something so important? That's not real closeness. That's just a pretence of it on your terms.'

'Exactly: "how could we be close when you were conceal-ing something so important?" That says it all, doesn't it?

When I think of you watching me, judging me, adjusting your actions to keep me fooled…'

He drew a sharp breath, and she saw sudden, bitter understanding overtake him. 'That's the real reason you refused to take that job, isn't it? And there was I thinking that maybe you wanted to be with me as much as I— Well, it just shows you how a man can delude himself if he's stupid enough. I must remember to pay you back the money you sacrificed for me.'

'Don't you dare say that!' she cried. 'Don't you *dare* offer me money.'

'Do you feel insulted? Well, now you know how I feel.' His voice rose on a note of anguished bitterness. 'But can you also understand that at this moment *I can't bear the sight of you*?'

CHAPTER TEN

As if to prove it, he turned away and began to pace the room, talking without looking at her.

'What a laugh I must have given you!'

'You don't really think that?' she said. 'You can't. I have never laughed at you.'

'Pitied, then. That's worse. Can't you understand?'

Wearily, she understood only too well. Dante was staggering under the weight of humiliation as he realised how close he'd come to opening his heart to her. For years he'd held off, never risking deep emotion and trust, until he'd met her. Now he felt betrayed.

She'd known that he guarded his privacy, but it was worse than that. He shut himself away from the world's eyes in a little cave where he dwelt alone, and even she wasn't allowed to venture. She thought of his loneliness in that bare cave, and shivered.

'I've always wanted to talk to you about it,' she said. 'I hated deceiving you. But I'd have hated it more if you'd died, and you might die if you don't have it properly checked.'

'What is there to check? I know the chances.'

'I wonder if you know as much as you think you do!' she

said in a temper. 'You're a conceited man, Dante, proud, arrogant and stubborn, in a really stupid way. You think you know it all, but medical science moves on. If you'd let the doctors help you, something could be done. You could be fit and strong for years ahead.'

'You don't know what you're talking about,' he said harshly. 'Don't tell me what happens with this, because I know more about it than you ever will. I've watched what it's done to my family, the lives it's ruined; not just the people who suffer from it, but those who have to watch them die. Or, worse, when they don't die, swallowing up the lives of the people who have to care for them. Do you think I want that? Anything is better. Even dying.'

'Do you think your death would be better for me?' she whispered.

'It could be, if it set you free, if I'd made the mistake of tying you to me so that you longed for my death as much as I did.' A withered look came into his face. 'Except that I wouldn't long for it, because I wouldn't understand what was happening to me, wouldn't know. Everyone else would know, but I'd know nothing. I'd just carry on, thinking I was a normal man. *And I would rather be dead.*'

Then he stared at her in silence, as though his own words had shocked him as much as they had her. When the silence became unbearable, Ferne said bitterly, 'What about what I want? Doesn't that count?'

'How can you judge when you don't know the reality?'

'I know what my reality would be like if you died. I know it because I love you.'

He stared at her with eyes full of shock, but she searched them in vain for any sign of pleasure or welcome. This man was dead to love.

'I didn't mean to, but it happened. Did you ever think of what you were doing to me?' she pleaded.

'You weren't supposed to fall in love,' he grated. 'No complications. We were going to keep it light.'

'And you think love is like that? You think it's so easy to say "don't" and for nothing to happen? It might be easy for you. You arrange things the way you want them, you tell yourself that you'll get just so close to me and no further, and that's how things work out, because you have no real heart. But I have a heart, and I can't control it like you can.

'Yes, I love you. Dante, do you understand that? I *love* you. I am deeply, totally in love with you. I didn't want that to happen. I told myself the same silly fantasies that you did—how it could be controlled if I was sensible. And it crept up on me when I wasn't looking, and, when I did look, it was too late.

'Now I want all the things I swore I'd never let myself want: to live with you and make love with you, marry you and bear your children. I want to crack jokes with you, and hold you when you're sleeping at night.

'You never thought of that, did you? And you don't think it matters. I wish I was as heartless as you.'

'I'm not—'

'Shut up and listen. I've listened to you, now it's my turn. I wish I didn't love you, because I'm beginning to think you don't deserve to be loved, but I can't help it. So there it is. What do I do now with this love that neither of us wants?'

'Kill it,' he snapped.

'Tell me how.'

His face changed, became older, wearier, as though he had suddenly confronted a brick wall.

'There is a way,' he murmured. 'And perhaps it's the best way, if it will convince you as nothing else could.'

'Dante, what are you talking about?'

'I'm going to kill your love.'

'Even you can't do that,' she said, trying to ignore the fear that was growing inside her.

'Don't be so sure. When I'm finished, you'll recoil from me in horror and run from me as far and fast as you can. I promise you that will happen, because I'm going to make sure it does. When you look back on this time, you'll wish we'd never met, and you'll hate me. But one day you'll thank me.'

The brutal words seemed to hang in the air between them. Ferne stared at him hopelessly, vainly looking for some softening in his face.

He checked his watch. 'We have time to catch a flight if we hurry.'

'Where are we going?'

'Milan.' He gave a frightening smile. 'I'm going to show you the future.'

'I don't understand. What is there in Milan?'

'My Uncle Leo. Have they told you about him?'

'Toni said he was a permanent invalid.'

'*Invalid* doesn't begin to describe it. They say that in his youth he was a fine man, a banker with a brain like a steel trap that could solve any problem. Women basked in his attention. Now he's a man with the mind of a child.'

'I'll take your word for it. I don't need to see him.'

'I say that you do, and you're going to.'

'Dante, please listen—'

'No, the time for that is passed. Now *you* listen. You wanted me to show you how to kill your love, and that's what I'm going to do.'

She tried to twist away but his hands were hard on her shoulders.

'We're going,' he said.

'You can't make me.'

'Do you really think I can't?' he asked softly.

Who was this man who stared at her with cold eyes and delivered his orders in a brutal *staccato* that brooked no argument? Why did he have Dante's face when he wasn't Dante, could never be him?

Or was he the *real* Dante who had lived inside this man all the time?

'Go and pack your things,' he said in a voice of iron.

She did so, moving like an automaton. When she came out with her bag, he was waiting.

'The taxi will be here in a minute,' he said.

Neither spoke on the way to the airport; there was nothing to say. Ferne had the feeling of coming to a huge bridge stretching so far into the distance that she couldn't see the other side. It led to an unknown place that she feared to visit, but to turn back now was impossible.

Worst of all was the sensation of travelling there alone, for there was no comfort to be found in the steely man beside her.

Then she caught a glimpse of his blank face, and remembered that he was the one in need of comfort. But he would accept none, especially from her.

On the flight to Milan, she ventured to say, 'What kind of place is he in?'

'A care home. It's clean, comfortable, kind. They look after him well. Sometimes his family visit him, but they lose heart after a while, because he doesn't know them.'

He added wryly, 'One strange thing that you may find useful, he still speaks excellent English. With all the damage that was done to the rest of his brain, that part has remained untouched. The doctors can't say why.'

At the airport he hailed a taxi to take them to the home, where a nurse greeted them with a smile.

'I've told him you called to say you were coming. He was so pleased.'

That sounded cheerful, Ferne thought. Perhaps Uncle Leo was better than Dante imagined.

She followed them through the pleasant building until they came to a bedroom at the back where the sun shone through large windows. A man was there, kneeling on the floor, solemnly decorating a Christmas tree. He looked up and smiled at the sight of them.

He was in his late sixties, plump and grey-haired, with twinkling eyes and an air of friendly glee.

'Hello, Leo,' said the nurse. 'Look who I've brought to see you.'

'I promised to come,' Dante said to him in English. 'And I brought a friend to see you.'

The old man smiled politely.

'How kind of you to visit me,' he said, also in English. 'But I can't talk for long. My nephew is coming, and I must get this finished.' He indicated the tree, immediately returning to work on it.

'It's his latest obsession,' the nurse said. 'He decorates it, takes it all down then starts again. Leo, it's all right, you can leave it for the moment.'

'No, no, I must finish it before Dante gets here,' Leo said urgently. 'I promised him.'

'I'm here, Uncle,' Dante said, going to him. 'There's no need to finish the tree. It's fine as it is.'

'Oh, but I must. Dante will be so disappointed otherwise. Do you know Dante, by any chance?'

Ferne held her breath, but Dante was unfazed. It seemed that he was used to this.

'Yes, I've met him,' he said. 'He's told me all about you.'

'But why doesn't he come?' Leo was almost in tears. 'He keeps saying he will, but he never does, and I so long to see him.'

'Leo, look at me.' Dante's voice was very gentle. 'Don't you know me?'

'No.' Wide-eyed, Leo stared at him. 'Should I?'

'I've often visited you before. I hoped you'd remember me.'

Leo's gaze became intense. 'No,' he said desperately. 'I've never seen you before. I don't know you—I don't, I don't!'

'It's all right, it doesn't matter.'

'Who are you?' Leo wailed. 'I don't know you. You're trying to confuse me. Go away! I want Dante. Where's Dante? He promised!'

Before their horrified eyes, he burst into violent tears, burying his face in his hands and wailing. Dante tried to take the old man in his arms but was violently pushed away. Raising his voice to a scream, Leo barged his way out of the room, racing across the lawn towards the trees.

The nurse made to follow him, but Dante waved her back. 'Leave this to me.'

He hurried out after Leo, catching up with him as they reached the trees.

'Oh dear,' Ferne sighed.

'Yes, it's very sad,' the nurse said. 'He's a sweet old man, but he gets fixated on things, like that tree, and things just go round and round in his head.'

'Is it normal for him not to recognise his family?'

'We don't see much of them here. Dante comes more often than anyone else. He's so gentle and kind to Leo. I shouldn't tell you this, but he pays the lion's share of the expenses here, plus any special treats for the old man; he gets nothing back for it.'

'And Leo has been like this for how long?'

'Thirty years. It makes you wonder how life looks from inside his head.'

'Yes,' Ferne said sadly. 'It does.'

'I suppose he doesn't really know, and that makes it bearable for him, poor thing. But then Dante visits him, and it brings him no pleasure because he never recognises him.'

Heavy-hearted, Ferne wandered out into the gardens, heading for the trees where she'd seen them go. She could understand the way Dante flinched from being reduced to this, being pitied by everyone. If only there was some way to convince him that her love was different. Inside her heart, hope was dying.

She heard them before she saw them. From somewhere beyond the trees came the sound of weeping. Following it, she came across the two men sitting on a fallen log. Dante had his arms around his uncle, who was sobbing against his shoulder.

He looked up as she approached. He said nothing, but his eyes met hers in a silent message: *now you understand. Be warned, and escape quickly*.

'Stop crying,' he said gently. 'I want you to meet a friend of mine. You can't cry when a lady is here—she'll think you don't like her.'

The gentle rallying in his voice had its effect. Leo blew his nose and tried to brighten up.

'*Buon giorno, signorina.*'

'No, no, my friend is English,' Dante said. 'We must speak English to her. She doesn't understand foreign languages as we do.' He emphasised 'we' very slightly, clearly trying to create a sense of closeness that would comfort Leo. 'Her name is Ferne Edmunds.'

Leo pulled himself together. 'Good evening, Miss Edmunds.'

'Please, call me Ferne,' she said. 'I'm so glad to meet you.' Floundering for something to say, she looked around at the trees. 'This is a lovely place.'

'Yes, I've always liked it. Of course,' Leo added earnestly, 'it's a lot of work to keep it in good condition. But it's been in my family for such a long time, I feel I must—I must—' He broke off, looking around in bewilderment.

'Don't worry about it,' Dante said, taking his hand and speaking quietly. 'It's all being taken care of.'

'I so much wanted everything to be right when he came,' Leo said sadly. 'But he isn't coming, is he?'

'Leo, it's me,' Dante said urgently. 'Look at me. Don't you recognise me?'

For a long moment Leo gazed into Dante's face, his expression a mixture of eagerness and sadness. Ferne found herself holding her breath for both of them.

'Do I know you?' Leo asked sadly after a while. 'Sometimes I think—but he never comes to see me. I wish he would. He said once that he was the only person who really understood me, and he'd always be my best friend. But he doesn't visit me, and I'm so sad.'

'But I do visit you,' Dante said. 'Don't you remember me?'

'Oh no,' Leo sighed. 'I've never seen you before. Do you know Dante?'

At first she thought Dante wouldn't answer. His head was bowed as though some terrible struggle was taking place within him, consuming all his strength. At last he managed to say, 'Yes, I know him.'

'Please, please ask him to come to see me. I miss him so much.'

Dante's face was full of tragedy, and Ferne's heart ached

for him. He'd been right; the reality was more terrible than anything she could have imagined.

'Let's go back inside,' he said, helping Leo to his feet.

In silence they made their way back across the lawn. Leo had recovered his spirits, as if the last few minutes had never been, and was chatting happily about the grand estate he believed was his.

The nurse came out onto the step, smiling kindly at Leo, welcoming him inside.

'We've got your favourite cakes,' she said.

'Oh, thank you. I've been trying to explain to my friend here about Dante. Look, let me show you his picture.'

From a chest of drawers behind the bed Leo took a photo album and opened it at a page containing one picture. It was Dante, taken recently. He was sitting with Leo, both of them smiling and seeming content with each other. Leo looked at it with pride.

'That was taken— Well, you can see that he's nothing like...' He looked at Dante sorrowfully.

Ferne felt her throat constrict and knew that in another moment she would be weeping. The picture was clearly Dante, and the fact that Leo didn't recognise him told a terrible story about his mental state.

'You see what a nice boy he is,' Leo said, running his fingers over the face on the page. 'He was always my favourite. Look.'

He began turning the pages, revealing earlier pictures. Ferne gasped as she saw Leo as a young man before his tragedy, sitting with a little boy on his knee. Even at this distance of years she could recognise Dante in the child. His face was the one she knew, bright and vivid with intelligence, gleaming with humour.

But the greatest tragedy of all was the fact that the man's face was exactly the same. Their features were different, but their expressions were identical. In his day, Leo had been the man Dante was now, dazzling, charmingly wicked, capable of anything.

And he had come to this.

Turning the pages, Leo revealed more pictures, including one of a beautiful young woman.

'That was my wife,' he said softly. 'She died.'

But Dante shook his head, mouthing, 'Left him.'

There was the child Dante again, with a man and a woman.

'My sister Anna,' Leo said proudly. 'And her husband, Taddeo Rinucci. They died in a car accident years ago.'

He switched back to the modern picture of Dante and showed it to the real man.

'You see? If you could remember what he looks like, and then—?' Tears began to roll down his face.

Ferne's heart broke for Dante, sitting there regarding this tragedy with calm eyes. When he spoke to Leo, it was with tender kindness, asking nothing, giving everything.

'I'll remember,' he said. 'Trust me for that. And I'll try to find some way of making things nicer for you. You know you can rely on me.'

'Oh yes,' Leo said brightly. 'You're always so good to me—who are you?'

'It doesn't matter,' Dante said with an effort. 'As long as we're friends, names don't matter.'

Leo beamed.

'Oh, thank you, thank you. I want—I want—'

Suddenly he was breathing wildly and shuddering. His arms began to flail, and it took all Dante's strength to hold him in his chair.

'You'd better go,' the nurse said tersely. 'We know what to do when he's like this.'

'I'll call later,' Dante said.

'By all means, but please go now.'

Reluctantly they did so.

'What happened to him?' Ferne asked as they left.

'He had an epileptic seizure,' Dante said bluntly. 'That's another thing that happens with his condition. He'll lose consciousness, and when he awakens he won't remember anything, even our visit. Once this happened and I insisted on staying, but my presence only distressed him. Possibly it's my fault he had the seizure, because seeing me agitated him.'

'That poor man,' she said fervently.

'Yes, he is. And, now you know, let's go to the airport. You've seen all you need to.'

She agreed without argument, sensing that Dante was at the end of his tether.

They spoke little on the short flight back to Naples. Ferne felt as though she never wanted to speak another word again. Her mind seemed to be filled with darkness, and she could see only more darkness ahead. Perhaps things would be better when they got home and could talk about it. She tried hard to believe that.

But, when they reached home, he stopped at the front door.

'I'm going for a walk,' he said. 'I'll be back later.'

She knew better than to suggest coming with him. He wanted to get away from her; that was the truth.

And perhaps, she thought as she opened the front door, she too needed to be away from him for a while. That was the point they had reached.

The apartment was frighteningly quiet. She'd been alone there before, but the silence hadn't had this menacing quality because Dante's laughing spirit had always seemed to be with her, even when he was away. But now the laughter was dead, perhaps for ever, replaced by the hostility of a man who felt he'd found betrayal where he'd thought to find only trust.

It had all happened so fast. Only hours ago, she'd been basking in the conviction of his unspoken love, certain that the trouble between them could be resolved and the way made clear. Then the heavens had fallen on her.

No, on them both. Even when Dante had been at his most cruel, she had recognised the pain and disillusion that drove him. Her heart cried that he should trust her, but life had taught him that the traps were always waiting at his feet, ready to be sprung when he least expected it.

In desperation she'd told him that she loved him, but now it hit her with the force of a sledgehammer that he hadn't said as much in return. He'd spoken only of killing her love, and had done his best to do it. With all her heart she longed to believe that he'd been forcing himself, denying his true feelings, but she was no longer sure what those feelings were. At times, she'd thought she detected real hatred in his eyes.

Perhaps that was the real Dante, a man whose need to keep the world at bay was greater than any love he could feel. Perhaps the cold hostility he'd turned on her was the strongest emotion he could truly feel.

She sat there in the darkness, shaking with misery and despair.

In the early hours she heard him arrive, moving quietly. When the door of the bedroom opened just a little, she said, 'I'm awake.'

'I'm sorry, did I wake you?' His voice was quiet.

'I can't sleep.'

He didn't come near the bed but went to stand by the window, looking out in the direction of Vesuvius, as they had once done together.

'That was what you meant, wasn't it?' she asked, coming

beside him. 'Never knowing when it was going to send out a warning.'

'Yes, that was what I meant.'

'And, now that it has, we're all supposed to make a run for it?'

'If you have any sense.'

'I never had any sense.'

'I know.' He gave a brief laugh. 'Nobody who knew us would imagine I was the one with common sense, would they?'

'Certainly not me,' she said, trying to recapture their old bantering way of talking.

'So I have to be wise for both of us. I should think what happened today would have opened your eyes. You saw what's probably waiting for me at the end of the road.'

'Not if you take medical help to avoid it,' she pressed.

'There is no avoiding it, or at least so little chance as not to justify the risk. To become like Leo is my nightmare. Maybe one day it'll happen, and if we were married what would you do? Would you have the sense to leave me then?'

Ferne stared at him, unable to believe that he'd really spoken such words.

'You'd want me to leave you—just abandon you?'

'I'd want you to get as far away from me as possible. I'd want you to go where you'd never have to see me, or even think about me, again.'

Shattered, Ferne stepped back and looked at him. Then a blind rage swept over her and she drew back her hand, ready to aim at his face, but at the last minute she dropped it and turned away, almost running in her fear of what she had been about to do.

He came after her, also furious, pulling her around to face him.

'If you want to hit me, do it,' he snapped.

'I ought to,' she breathed.

'Yes, you ought to. I've insulted you, haven't I? Fine, I'll insult you again. And again. Until you face reality.'

The rage in his voice frightened her. Part of her understood that his cruelty was a deliberate attempt to drive her off her for own sake. Yet still it stunned her in its intensity, warning her of depths to him that she had never understood because he had never wanted her to understand.

'Reality means what you want it to mean,' she said. 'Maybe I see things differently.'

'Marriage? Children? Holding hands as we wander into the sunset? Only I wouldn't just be holding your hand, I'd be clinging to it for support.'

'And I'd be glad to give you that support, because I love you.'

'Don't love me,' he said savagely. 'I have no love to give back.'

'Is that really true?' she whispered.

The look he gave her was terrible, full of despair and suffering that she could do nothing to ease. That was when she faced the truth: if she had no power to ease his pain, then everything was dead between them.

'Try not to hate me,' he said wearily.

'I thought you wanted me to hate you as the quickest way of getting rid of me.'

'I thought so too, but I guess I can't manage it. Don't hate me more than you have to, and I'll try not to hate you.'

'Hate *me*?' she echoed. 'After everything we've— Could you hate me?'

He was silent for a long moment before whispering, 'Yes. If I must.'

He looked away again, out of the window, to where the dawn was breaking. The air was clear and fresh; the birds were beginning to sing. It was going to be a glorious day.

She came up close behind him, touching him gently and resting her cheek against his back. Her head was whirling with the words that she wanted to say, and yet no words would be enough.

She could feel him warm against her, as she'd known him so often before, and suddenly, irrationally, she was filled with hope. This was Dante, who loved her, no matter what he said. They would be together because it was fated. All she had to do was convince him of that.

'Darling,' she whispered.

His voice was hard, and he spoke without looking at her.

'There's a flight to England at eleven this morning. I've booked your seat.'

He came with her to the airport, helping her to check in and remaining with her as they waited for the first call. There was no more tenderness in his manner than there had been before. He was doing his polite duty.

She couldn't bear it. Whatever might happen, there was no way she could go one way and leave him to go another, at the mercy of any wind that blew.

'Dante, please.'

'Don't.'

'Tell me to stay,' she whispered. 'We'll make it work somehow.'

He shook his head, his eyes weary and defeated. 'It's not your fault. It's me. I can't change. I'll always be a nightmare for any woman to live with. You were right. I shouldn't have lived with you and not warned you. I made the terms but didn't tell you what they were. Doesn't that prove I'm a monster?'

'You're not a monster,' she said fervently. 'Just a man

trapped in a vicious web. But you don't have to live in it alone. Let me come inside, let me help you.'

His face was suddenly wild.

'And see you trapped too? No, get out while you can. I've done you so much damage, I won't do more. For pity's sake, for *my* sake, go!'

He almost ran from her then, hurrying into the crowd without looking back even once. She watched as the distance between them grew wider, until he vanished.

But only from her sight. In her mind and heart where he would always live, she could still see him, making his way back to the empty apartment and the empty life, where he would be alone for ever in the doubly bitter loneliness of those who had chosen their isolation.

CHAPTER ELEVEN

IT WAS late at night when Ferne reached her apartment, to find it gloomy and cold. Locking the door behind her, she stood in the silence, thinking of Dante far away, locked in a chill darkness that was more than physical.

She'd eaten nothing all day, and after turning on the heating she began to prepare a meal, but suddenly she stopped and simply went to bed. She had no energy to be sensible.

Where are you? she thought. *What are you doing? Are you lying alone, your thoughts reaching out to me, as mine to you? Or are you passing the time with some girl you picked up for the evening? No, it's too soon. You'll do that eventually, but not just yet.*

She slept for a little while, awoke, slept again. Sleeping or waking, there were only shadows in all directions. At last she was forced to admit that a new day had dawned, and slowly got out of bed.

Her first action was to call Hope. She'd managed to keep her up to date about the disaster, Dante's discovery of her files, their trip to Milan and her return to England, and Hope had asked for a call to say she'd arrived safely.

'I meant to call last night, but I got in so late,' she apologised.

'Never mind. How are you? You sound terrible.'

'I'll be fine when I've had a cup of tea,' she said, trying to sound relaxed.

'How are you really?' Hope persisted with motherly concern.

'I'll need a little time,' she admitted. 'How's Dante?'

'He'll need time too. Carlo and Ruggiero went round to see him last night. He wasn't at home, so they trawled the local bars until they found him sitting in a corner, drinking whisky. They took him home, put him to bed and stayed with him until morning. Carlo just called me to say he's awake, with an almighty hangover, but otherwise all right.'

They parted with mutual expressions of affection. A few minutes later the phone rang. It was Mike.

'I've been hearing rumours,' he said. 'They say you might be back in the land of the living.'

She almost laughed. 'That's one way of putting it. I'm back in England.'

'Great! I have work piling up for you.'

'I thought you dumped me.'

'I don't dump people with your earning potential. That job you turned down is still open. They tried someone else, didn't like the result and told me to get you at any price. It's fantastic money.'

The money was awesome. If the Sandor episode had propelled her into the big time, her refusal of an even better offer had given her rarity value.

'All right,' she interrupted Mike at last. 'Just tell me when and where, and I'll be there.'

Later that day she went to the theatre, where the major star and his equally famous fiancée were rehearsing. From the first moment everything went well. They liked her, she liked them. Their genuine love for each other made them, at least for the moment, really nice people. They praised her pictures and insisted that she must take some more at their wedding.

The tale of her meeting with Sandor in Italy had got out. She began to receive offers to 'tell all' to the press. She refused them, but Sandor had heard rumours and become nervous, having given a self-serving interview to a newspaper, illustrated with several of Ferne's notorious pictures. Her fame had increased. So had her price.

All around her, life was blossoming.

No, she thought, not life. Just her career. Life no longer existed.

She talked regularly with Hope and gained the impression that Dante's existence was much like her own, outwardly successful but inwardly bleak.

But there was no direct word from him until she'd been home for a month, and then she received a text:

Your success is in all the papers. I'm glad you didn't lose out. Dante.

She texted back:

I lost more than you'll ever know.

After that there was silence. Desperately she struggled to reconcile herself to the fact that she would never hear from him again, but then she received a letter.

I know how generous you are, and so I dare to hope that in time you will forgive me for the things I said and did. Yes, I love you; I know that I shall always love you. But for both our sakes I can never tell you again.

Night after night she wept with the letter pressed against her heart. At last she replied:

> You don't need to tell me again. It's enough that you said it once. Goodbye, my dearest.

He didn't reply. She had not expected him to.

Her sleep was haunted by wretched dreams. In one she found that time had passed and suddenly there he was, older but still Dante. She reached out eagerly to him but he only gazed at her without recognition. Someone took him by the arm to lead him away.

Then she knew that the worst had happened, and he'd become the brain-damaged man he'd always feared. She longed for him to look back at her just for a moment, but he never did. She'd been blotted from his mind as if she had never been.

She woke from that dream to find herself screaming.

Struggling up in bed, she sat fighting back her sobs until suddenly her whole body seemed to become one gigantic heave. She flung herself out of bed and just managed to dash to the bathroom in time.

When it was over, she sat shivering and considering the implications.

It could be just a tummy bug, she thought. *It doesn't mean I'm pregnant.*

But it did. And she knew it. A hurried visit to the chemist, and a test confirmed it.

The discovery that she was to have Dante's child came like a thunderclap. She'd thought herself modern, careful, sensible, but in the dizzying delight of loving him she'd forgotten everything else. In a moment her life had been turned upside down. Everything she'd considered settled was in chaos.

A child of Dante's, born from their love, but also born with chance of the hereditary illness that had distorted his life: a constant reminder of what she might have had and had lost.

The sensible answer was a termination, but she dismissed the thought at once. If she couldn't have Dante, she could still have a little part of him, and nothing on earth would persuade her to destroy that. Fiercely she laid her hands over her stomach, still perfectly flat.

'I won't let anyone or anything hurt you,' she vowed. 'No matter what the future holds, you're mine, and I'll keep you safe.'

Then she realised that she'd spoken the words aloud, and looked around the apartment, wondering who she'd really been addressing. One thing was for sure: Dante had a right to know, and then, perhaps…

'No, no!' she cried. 'No false hopes. No fantastic dreams. Just tell him and then—and then?'

Once her mind was made up, she acted quickly, calling Mike and clearing the decks at work. Then she got on a plane to Naples, and booked into a hotel. She told nobody that she was coming, not even Hope. This was between Dante and herself.

It was still light when she walked the short distance to the apartment block and stood looking up at his windows, trying to discern any sign of life. But it was too soon for lamps to be on.

She took the lift to the fifth floor and hesitated. It was unlike her to lack confidence, but this was so vital, and the next few minutes so important. She listened, but could hear nothing from inside. The silence seemed a bleak forecast of what was to come. Suddenly her courage drained away and she stepped back.

But her spirit rebelled at the thought of giving up without

trying, and she raised her hand to ring the bell. Then she dropped it again. What was the point? Dante himself had believed that you couldn't buck fate, and now she saw that he was right. Fate was against them. Defeated, she headed for the elevator.

'Don't go!'

The words were almost a scream. Turning, she saw Dante standing there in his doorway. His hair was dishevelled, his shirt torn open, his face was haggard and his eyes looked as though he hadn't slept for a month. But the only thing she noticed was that his arms were outstretched to her, and the next moment she was enfolded in them.

They held each other in silence, clasped tight, not kissing, but clinging to each other as if for refuge.

'I thought you were never going to knock,' he said frantically. 'I've been waiting for you.'

'You knew I was coming?'

'I saw you standing down there. I didn't believe it at first. I've seen you so often and you always vanished. Then I heard the lift coming up, and your footsteps—but you didn't ring the bell, and I was afraid it was just another hallucination. I've had so many; I couldn't bear another. So many times you've come to me and vanished before I could wake and keep you here.'

He drew her into the apartment, and enfolded her in his arms again.

'Thank God you're here,' he said, words that carried her to the heights.

But his next words dashed her down again.

'I've longed to see you just once more. We parted badly, and it was my fault. Now at least there can be peace between us.'

So in that he hadn't changed. He was no longer denying

his love, but in the long term he was still determined to keep apart from her.

She took a deep breath. Relief at finding him here had undermined her resolution, but now the moment had arrived.

'It isn't that simple,' she said, stepping back and regarding him with loving eyes. 'Something's happened. I came to tell you about it—but then I'll go away if you like, and you need never see me again.'

His mouth twisted. 'That doesn't work very well.'

'No, with me neither, but when you hear what I have to say you might be so angry that you want me to leave.'

'Nothing could make me angry with you.'

'You were once.'

'I stopped being angry a long time ago. Most of it was aimed at myself. I forced you into an impossible situation, I know that. I should have stayed clear of you from the start.'

'It's too late for that. The time we had together has left me with more than memories.' Seeing him frown, she said, 'I'm going to have a baby, Dante.'

Just for a moment she saw joy on his face, but it was gone in an instant, as though he'd quenched it forcibly.

'Are you sure?' he breathed.

'There's no doubt. I did a test, and then I came here to tell you, because you have the right to know. But that's it. I don't expect you to react in a conventional way because I know you can't.'

'Wait, wait!' he said fiercely. 'I need time to take this in. You can't just— A baby! Dear God!'

'I did dare to hope you'd be pleased,' she said sadly. 'But I suppose you can't be.'

'Pleased—at bringing another child into the world to spend a lifetime wondering what was happening inside him?

I thought we were safe, that you were taking care; hell, I don't know what I thought. But I always swore I'd never father a child.'

'Well, you've fathered one,' she said quietly. 'We have to go on from there. You can't turn the clock back.'

'There is one way.'

'No,' she said firmly. 'Don't even mention that. If you think for a moment that I could destroy your child, you don't begin to know me. I told you I love you, but I could easily hate you if you ask me to do that.'

But she couldn't stay angry as she looked at him, saddened by the confusion in his face. He'd always insisted on being in control, quick-stepping with fate to the edge, but now he'd reached an edge he'd never dreamed of and he was lost. The thought gave her an idea.

'Fate doesn't always do what we expect,' she said, slipping her arms about his neck. 'It's had this waiting for you quite a while, and it's probably been laughing up its sleeve, thinking it's found the way to defeat you. But we're not going to let it win.'

He rested his forehead against hers. 'Doesn't fate always win?' he whispered.

'That depends who you have fighting with you.' She stepped back, taking his hand and laying it over her stomach. 'You're not alone any more. There are two of us backing you up now.'

He stared. 'Two?'

'Two people fighting on your side.' She gave a faint smile at the stunned look on his face, and pointed to her stomach. 'There is actually someone in there, you know. A person. I don't know if it's a boy or a girl, but it's yours, and it's as ready to defend you as I am. When you get to know each other, you'll be the best of friends.'

He was very still, and she sensed him holding his breath

as he struggled to come to terms with ideas that had always been alien to him.

'It won't be easy,' she urged, speaking with gentle persistence. 'It may have your family's inherited illness, so we'll find out, and if the news is bad at least you'll be there to help. You can explain things that nobody else can. The two of you will probably form an exclusive society that shuts me out, but I won't mind, because you'll have each other, and that's all you'll really need.'

'No,' he said softly. 'Never shutting you out, because we can't manage without you. But, my love, you don't know what you're letting yourself in for.'

'Yes, I do: a life of worry, always wondering how long the happiness will last.'

'If you know that—'

'But the other choice is a life without you, and I choose you. I choose you for me and as a father for our child, because nobody else can be the father you can. Nobody else knows the secrets you do.'

He held her close, where she belonged, where she'd dreamed of being all the long, lonely weeks. They neither kissed nor caressed, but stood still and silent, rediscovering each other's warmth, coming home. At last he led her into the bedroom and drew her down onto the bed.

'Don't worry,' he said quickly. 'I won't try to make love to you.'

'Darling, it's all right,' she said shakily. 'I'm in the early stages. It's quite safe.'

'Safe,' he whispered. 'What does "safe" mean? You can never be sure, can you? And we won't take any risks.' He gave a sharp, self-critical laugh. 'Listen to me, talking about not taking risks. But I'm such a selfish beggar; I've never had to think about anyone else's health before. I guess I'll have to get working on that.'

She kissed him in a passion of tenderness.

'You're almost there now,' she murmured.

'Almost?'

'There's something I want you to do,' she said, speaking quietly, although her heart was beating hard. 'We're going to find out the truth about your condition. I can't live with the uncertainty.'

'And if the worst is true?' he asked slowly.

'Then we'll face it. Not just for our sake, but for our child's too. This is your baby, born into the same heritage, and I want to know what it may face. If I don't know the truth, I shall worry myself sick, and that isn't a good thing for the baby. Do this for me, my love.'

In the long silence she sensed his agony and enfolded him protectively, trying to speak of her love without words.

'Be a little patient,' he begged at last. 'Don't ask me just yet.'

She understood. She was asking him to overturn the rules on which his whole life had been lived, and it was hard. All his major decisions had been taken alone. Now she'd told him that he had two supporters, but he was still struggling to adjust to that idea, or even understand it.

'Take your time,' she whispered.

They slept without making love, and when she woke at first light it was no surprise to find him sitting by the window, as he had often done before. She went to join him, sitting quietly. He didn't turn his head, but his fingers entwined with hers.

'It's still waiting there,' he said, indicating the silent volcano. 'I guess it finally gave me the rumble I wasn't prepared for. And, as I always feared, I have no answer. Why don't you despise me, run a mile, kick me out of your life?'

'Because without you I'd get bored,' she said, with a note of their old teasing. 'And, when our child asks where Daddy is, what do I tell her?'

'Say you chucked him out with the rest of the rubbish. Or you might recycle me into a sensible man.'

'Then how would I know it was you?' she asked with a hint of a chuckle.

'And what's this *her* business? Since when did she become a girl?'

'I've decided it's going to be a girl. We're better at being practical.'

He cocked a humorous eyebrow. 'I need another woman nagging me?'

'That's definitely what you need. Hope and I aren't enough. It's a task for three.'

Then her smile faded as she saw something on a nearby table and reached out for it. 'That's one of the pictures you took of me when I first came here.'

'We went to the consulate to get you a new passport,' he recalled.

'But how do you come to have it? I never did remember to give them to you.'

'No, and I raided your computer for them. This was the best, so I printed it out to keep.' He stopped and watched her for a moment, remembering. 'I'd never loved you as much as I did then. That previous night, I came to the edge of telling you everything.

'I backed off at the last minute, but when I went through those pictures and saw how you looked at me I knew I had to tell you, because you were the only person I could ever trust with the truth. Suddenly it was all clear, and I knew I could tell you everything.'

'Oh no,' she whispered, dropping her head into her hands. 'And then you found that folder and realised I'd betrayed you. No wonder you were so terribly hurt.'

'You didn't betray me. I've known that for a long time, but I was in such a state of confusion that I couldn't wait to be rid of you. You made me think, and I didn't want to think. It was only after you'd gone that I realised what I'd done—chosen safety and predictability over life. I kept that picture with me to remind myself what I'd lost.'

'But why didn't you call me and ask me to come back?' she asked.

'Because I thought I had nothing to offer you, and you were better without me.'

'That will never be true. I want you with me all my life.'

'If only…' he said longingly.

'My love, I know what I'm asking of you is hard, but do it for me. Do it for *us*.'

Without speaking, he slipped to his knees and laid his face against her, his hand gently touching her stomach. Ferne caressed him, also in silence. Nothing more was needed. He had given his answer.

Hope was in ecstasies as they reached the villa that evening, greeting them both, but especially Ferne, with open arms.

'Welcome to the family,' she said. 'Oh yes, you're a Rinucci now. You're going to have a Rinucci baby, and that makes you one of us.'

Ferne couldn't help smiling at the way she'd been taken over. Then Hope went even further.

'I'm so looking forward to another grandchild,' she said blissfully.

'But Dante isn't actually your son, is he?' Ferne said, startled.

'Oh, son, nephew, what does it matter? He's a Rinucci, and now so are you.'

Next day, she took over the preparations for Dante's tests, telephoning a contact at the local hospital. He moved fast, and Dante was admitted that day for a lumbar puncture and a CT scan. From behind a window, Ferne watched as he prepared for the scan; he kept his eyes on them until the last minute, as he was swallowed up in the huge machine.

After that the minutes seemed to go at a crawl until they were given the results. During that endless time, Ferne realised that she had always known what the truth would be.

'The tests show that you've already had one mild rupture quite recently,' the doctor said. 'You were lucky. You came through it. You might even go on being lucky. Or you could have a major rupture in a few weeks and possibly die.'

Dante didn't reply, but sat in terrible stillness, as though already dead. After a lifetime of avoiding this moment, he was forced to confront it.

'But surgery can make it all right?' Ferne's voice was almost pleading.

'I wish I could say that it was as simple as that,' the doctor replied. 'The operation is very difficult, and there's a high death-rate. But if he goes into a coma first then the rate is even higher.' He addressed Dante directly. 'Your best chance is to have it now before things get worse.'

Dante had been sitting with head sunk in hands. Now he looked up.

'And if I live,' he said, 'can you guarantee that I'll still be mentally normal?' He choked into silence.

Gravely the doctor shook his head.

'There's always a chance of complications,' he said. 'I wish I could give you a guarantee, but I can't.'

He walked out, leaving them alone, holding each other in silence. After all the dancing with fate, all the arguments, there was only the bleak reality left. With the operation or without it, the possibility of death was high. And, with it, there was a real chance of something Dante considered far worse.

Why should he choose to walk into the unknown? Ferne knew that there was only their love to make the risk worthwhile, but was that enough? Now he was really dancing to the edge of the abyss, but not with fate, with herself, trusting her to stop him plunging over. But even she had no power to do that.

At that moment she would not have blamed him for walking away.

'What am I going to do?' he asked desperately. 'Once I would have said that dying didn't worry me, and it would have been true. But now there's you—and her.' He pointed downwards, and a wry smile twisted his mouth. 'Who'd have thought that having something to live for could be so scary?'

She waited for him to say more. The only words that mattered would come from him.

'I've used my illness as a way of avoiding responsibility,' he said after a while. 'I didn't see it like that at the time. I thought I was doing the sensible thing. Now it just looks like a form of cowardice. My whole life has been a sham because I couldn't face the reality.'

He looked at her in agony, whispering fiercely, 'Where do you get your courage? Can't you give some to me? Because I don't have any. Part of me still says just walk away and let it happen as it will.'

'No!' she said fiercely. 'I need you with me. You've got to take every chance of staying alive.'

'Even if it means becoming like Leo? That scares me more than dying.'

She drew back and looked into his face.

'Listen to me. You ask me to give you courage, but can't you understand that I need *you* to give *me* courage?'

'Me? A clown, a chancer?'

'Yes, a clown, because I need you and your silly jokes to shield me from the rest of the world. I need you to make fun of me and trip me up, and take me by surprise and get the world in proportion for me. You made me strong and whole, so that now I need to be able to reach out and hold your hand for *my* protection, not yours.'

He searched her face intently, trying to discern the answer to mysteries. At last he seemed to find what he needed, for he drew her close, resting his head on her shoulder.

'I'll do whatever you wish,' he said. 'Only promise to be there.'

CHAPTER TWELVE

THE doctor emphasised that there was no time to lose, and a date was set for the next day.

They spent that evening at the villa, where the family had gathered to wish Dante well. He had apparently recovered his spirits, even making a joke of his new deference to Ferne.

'I don't believe this is Dante,' she said. 'It's so unlike him to keep agreeing with me.'

'He's turning into a Rinucci husband,' Toni said. 'However strong we look to the rest of the world, at home we all obey orders.'

Nobody knew which of the wives murmured, 'So I should hope,' but the others all nodded agreement, and the husbands grinned.

'But he's not a husband,' Hope pointed out. 'Perhaps it's time that he was.'

'You'll have to ask Ferne,' Dante said at once. He smiled up at her with a hint of the old, wicked humour. 'I just do as I'm told.'

'Then you'll be a perfect Rinucci husband,' she said in a shaking voice.

'But when is the wedding?' Hope asked.

'As soon as I come out of hospital,' Dante said.

'No,' Hope said urgently. 'Don't wait so long. Do it now.'

Everyone knew what she meant. It might be now or never.

'Can it be arranged so quickly?' Ferne asked.

'Leave it with me,' Hope said.

She had contacts all over Naples, and it was no surprise when after a few phone calls she announced that an emergency service could be arranged for the next day. The wedding would be in the afternoon, and Dante would enter the hospital straight afterwards.

It was all achieved in double-quick time, and Ferne was left worried that Dante felt he was being hustled into marriage. Her fear increased when he was quiet on the way home.

'Dante?'

'Hush, don't speak until you've heard what I have to say. Wait here.'

He went into the bedroom and searched a drawer, returning a few moments later with two small boxes. Inside one, Ferne saw two wedding-rings, large and small. Inside the other was an engagement ring of diamonds and sapphires.

'They belonged to my parents,' he said, taking out the engagement ring. 'I never thought the day would come when I'd give this to any woman. But then, you're not any woman. You're the one I've been waiting for all this time.'

He slipped it onto her finger, dropped his head and kissed the spot. Ferne couldn't speak. She was weeping.

'And these,' he said, turning to the other box, 'are the rings they exchanged on their wedding day. They loved each other very much. He got up to mad tricks, and she tried to stick with him whenever she could. She was afraid that he'd vanish without her.

'I used to blame her for that. I felt resentful that she took risks without thinking of me, left behind. But I understand now. I've come to understand a lot of things that were hidden from me before.'

His voice shook so much that he could barely say the last words. He bent his head quickly, but not quickly enough to hide the fact that his cheeks were wet. Ferne held him tightly, fiercely glad that in her arms he felt free to weep, and that she too had come to understand many things.

That night they made love as if for the first time. He touched her gently, as though afraid to do her harm. She responded to him with passionate tenderness, and always the thought lay between them: perhaps never again; perhaps this was all there would be to last a lifetime. When their love-making was over, they held each other tenderly.

Next morning a lawyer called with papers for Dante to sign, and also some for Ferne.

'They're in Italian. I don't understand a word,' she said.

'Just sign them,' he told her. 'If I become unable to manage my own affairs, this will give you complete control.'

She was a little puzzled, since surely as his wife her control would be automatic? But perhaps Italian law was more complicated. She signed briefly, and returned to her preparations.

There was no lavish bridal-gown, just a silk, peach-coloured dress that she already knew he liked. In a dark, formal suit, he looked as handsome as she'd ever seen him. Standing side by side, looking in the mirror together, they made a handsome couple.

Both of them tried not to look at the suitcase he would take with him, which contained his things so that he could go on to the hospital when the wedding was over.

At last the lawyer departed and they were alone, waiting for the taxi.

'I think it's here,' she said, looking out of the window. 'Let's go.'

'Just a moment.' He detained her.

'What is it?'

'Just one more thing I have to know before we go ahead,' he said quietly. 'I want to marry you more than anything on earth, but I can't face the thought of being a burden in your life. Will you give me your word to put me in a home if I become like Uncle Leo?'

'How can I do that?' she asked, aghast. 'It would be a betrayal.'

'I can't marry you to become a burden on you. If you don't give me your word, the wedding's off.'

'Dante…'

'Understand me, I mean it. One way or another, I'll leave you free.'

'And your child?'

'We just signed papers that will give you complete control, whether we're married or not. So you'll have everything that's mine to support you and our child.'

'Did you think I was talking about money?' she asked with a touch of anger.

'No, I know you weren't, but you have to know that my arrangements will look after you both, even without a wedding.'

She sighed. Even now he was setting her at a little distance.

'Do I have your word,' he asked again, 'that if I become *incapable*…?' He shuddered.

'Hush,' she said, unable to endure any more.

'I don't want people to see me and pity me. I don't want my child to grow up regarding me with contempt. Do I have your word that if this goes wrong you'll put me away?' He took her hand in his. 'Swear it, or I can't marry you.'

'What?' She stared, appalled at this unsuspected ruthlessness.

'I'll call it off right now if you don't give me your word. I can't go through with it unless I'm sure. You've never really understood what that dread means to me, have you? And I've never been able to make you.'

'I know it means more to you than I do!' she said wildly.

This should have been their most perfect moment, when they could be happy in their love despite all the problems. But she was saddened at his intransigence.

Perhaps he saw this, because his voice became gentler.

'Nothing means more to me than you,' he said. 'But try to understand, my love; you've done so much for me. I beg you to do this one thing more, to give me peace.'

'All right,' she said sadly. 'I swear it.'

'Promise on everything you hold dear and sacred, on the life of our child, on whatever love you have for me— promise me.'

'I promise. If it comes to that—' she paused, and a tremor went through her '—I'll do as you wish.'

'Thank you.'

The wedding was in the hospital chapel. All the Rinuccis who lived in Naples were there. The women of the family lined up to be the bride's attendants. The men scrapped for the privilege of waiting on Dante.

Toni gave her away, escorting her down the aisle with pride. Dante watched her approach with a look that took her breath away, and that she knew she would remember all her life. As she reached him and laid her hand in his, the problems seemed to melt away. Even the promise he'd imposed on her could not spoil this moment. She was marrying the man she loved, and who loved her. There was nothing else in the world.

Holding Dante's hand in hers, she declared, 'I, Ferne, take

you, Dante, to be my husband. I promise to be true to you in good times and in bad, in sickness and in health. I will love you and honour you all the days of my life.'

She knew he wasn't quite ready to understand that. She could only pray for the miracle that would give her the chance to show him.

Then they exchanged rings, the ones that had belonged to his parents, who'd chosen never to be parted. One after the other they recited the ritual wedding-vows, but then the priest looked a silent question, asking if they wished to add anything of their own. Dante nodded, took her hand and spoke in a clear voice for everyone to hear.

'I give you my life for whatever it's worth—not much, perhaps, but there's no part of it that isn't yours. Do with it whatever you will.'

It took her a moment to fight back the tears, but then she said in a shaking voice, 'Everything I am belongs to you. Everything I will ever be belongs to you, now and always—whatever life may bring.'

She said the last words with special significance, hoping he would understand, and she felt him grow still for a moment, looking at her, questioning.

Then it was over. It was time to turn and make their way out of the little chapel, followed by the family.

Instead of a wedding feast they all accompanied Dante to his room, where a smiling nurse showed them in. There was a bottle of champagne to stress that this was a party, but before long the laughter and congratulations faded, as they all remembered why Dante was there.

One by one they bid him goodbye, all of them knowing that it might be final. Hope and Toni embraced him heartily, then left them alone.

'You must rest well,' the nurse told him. 'So go to bed now, and drink this.' She held up a glass. 'It will help you sleep.'

'I want to stay with him,' Ferne said.

'Of course.'

She helped him undress, and suddenly it was as though a giant machine had taken over. It had started, and nobody could say how it was going to end.

'I'm glad you stayed with me tonight,' he said. 'Because there's still something I need to say to you. I want to ask your forgiveness.'

'For what?'

'For my selfishness. I've had a good look at myself, and I don't like what I see. You were right when you said I shouldn't have let you get so close without telling you the truth.'

'We were supposed to keep it light,' she reminded him.

'But that wasn't under our control. You and I could never have met without loving each other. I loved you from the start, but I wouldn't admit it to myself. Instead I selfishly found excuses, pretending that it wasn't what it was, and I led you into danger.'

'Don't talk of it as danger,' she interrupted him. 'You've been the best experience of my life, and you always will be, whatever happens. Do you understand that? *Whatever happens*.'

'But say you forgive me,' he said. 'I need to hear you say it.' He was already growing sleepy.

'I'll forgive you if you want, but there is nothing to forgive. Please—please try to understand that.'

He smiled but didn't answer. A moment later, his eyes closed. Ferne laid her head down on the pillow beside him, watching him until her own eyes closed.

This was their wedding night.

* * *

In the morning the orderlies came to take him to the operating theatre.

'One moment,' Dante said frantically.

As she leaned over him, he touched her face.

'If this should be the last time…' he whispered.

It hit her like a blow. This might really be the last time she touched him, looked into his eyes.

'It isn't the last time,' she said. 'Whatever happens, we will always be together.'

Suddenly he reached out, as though trying to find something. 'What is it?'

'Your camera,' he said. 'The one you always keep with you.'

Now she understood. Pulling it out, she fixed it to take a picture after a few seconds' delay, and set it up a little distance away. Then she took him into her arms, looking into his face.

His own eyes on her were quiet with a peace she had never seen in them before.

'Yes,' he said. 'We'll always be together. I may not be there again, but my love will be, until the end of your life. Tell me that you know that.'

She couldn't speak, only nod.

Then it was time. The orderlies wheeled him away. Suddenly it was all over; she might never see him alive again.

'Suppose he dies?' she said to Hope, distraught. 'Dies in an operation that he only had because I made him? He might have lived for years without getting sick. If he dies, I'll have killed him.'

'And if it goes well, you will have saved his life and his sanity,' Hope said firmly.

How slowly the hours passed. Many times she took out the camera and studied the last picture she'd taken. It was tiny, but she could see Dante's face turned towards her with an expression of adoration that startled her. Had it been there before, and had she just never noticed? Would it be the last of him that she ever saw?

What had she done to him?

She seemed to see her life stretching before her, with an empty place where he should have been. There was her child, asking where her father was, and not understanding that her mother had sent him to his death.

The years would pass and their child would grow, become a success, married. But without a father to show his pride and love.

'I took it away from him,' she mourned.

'No,' Hope said. 'You have to understand that Dante was right about doing the quick-step with fate. He's giving himself the best chance, or rather, you've given it to him. You were fate's instrument. Now it's out of our hands.'

At last he was wheeled out of the operating theatre, his head swathed in bandages. He looked pale, ghostly, and completely unlike the Dante they knew. But he was alive.

'It went well,' the doctor told them. 'He's strong, and there were no complications, so we were able to support the wall of the weak artery with less difficulty than usual. It's too soon for certainty, but I expect him to live.'

'And—the other thing?' Ferne stammered.

'That we'll have to wait and see. It's a pity he delayed treatment for so long, but I'm hopeful.'

That qualification haunted her as she sat beside Dante's bed, waiting for him to awaken. She didn't know how long she was there. It was a long time since she'd slept, but however weary she was she knew she couldn't sleep now.

Hour after hour passed. He lay terrifyingly still, attached to so many machines that he almost disappeared under them.

Part of his face was invisible beneath the huge plug clamping his mouth and attaching him to the breathing machine.

She had seen him wicked, charming, cruel, but never until this moment had she seen him totally helpless.

Perhaps it was for ever. Perhaps she had condemned him to this, although he'd begged her not to. He'd asked her forgiveness, but now, in the long dark hours, she fervently asked for his.

'I may have taken everything away from you,' she whispered. 'You tried to warn me, but now, if your life is ruined, it's my fault. Forgive me. Forgive me.'

He lay motionless and silent. The only sound in the room was the machine helping him to breathe.

Dawn broke, and she realised that she'd been there all night. A doctor came to detach the breathing machine, saying, 'Let's see how well he manages without it.'

Ferne stood well back while the plug was removed from his mouth and the machine pulled away. There was a pause, while time seemed to stop, then Dante gave a small choke and drew in a long breath.

'Excellent,' the doctor declared. 'Breathing normal.'

'How long before he comes round?' Ferne asked.

'He needs a bit longer.'

He departed and she settled back beside the bed, taking Dante's hand in hers.

'You've made a great start,' she told him.

Could he hear her? she wondered. Hearing was supposed to outlast all the other senses. Perhaps if she could reach him now she could even help to keep his brain strong.

'It's going to be all right,' she said, leaning close. 'You're going to wake up and be just the same as I've always known you—scheming, manipulative, dodgy, a man to be avoided by a woman with any sense. But I've never had any sense where you were concerned. I should have given in the first day, shouldn't I? Except that I think I did, and much good it did me. Do you remember?'

He lay still, giving no sign of hearing.

She went on talking, not knowing what she said or how much time passed. The words didn't matter. Most of them were nonsense, the kind of nonsense they had always talked—but he must surely hear the underlying message, which was an impassioned plea to him to return to her.

'Don't leave me alone without you; come back to me.'

But he lay so still that he might already have gone into another world. At last, leaning down, she kissed him softly on the lips.

'I love you,' she whispered at last. 'That's all there is to say.'

Then she jerked back, startled. Had he moved?

She watched closely. It was true; he moved.

A sigh broke from him, and he murmured something.

'What did you say?' she asked. 'Speak to me.'

'Portia,' he whispered.

'What was that?'

After a moment, he repeated the word. 'Portia—I'm so glad you're here.'

She wanted to cry aloud in her despair. He didn't know her. His brain was failing, as he'd feared. Whoever Portia was, she was there inside with him.

Slowly he opened his eyes.

'Hello,' he murmured. 'Why are you crying?'

'I'm not—I was just happy to have you back.'

He gave a sleepy smile. 'You were calling me names—scheming, manipulative, dodgy. Never mind. My little friend will stand up for me.'

'Your little friend?' she asked, scarcely daring to breathe.

'Our daughter. I've been getting to know her. I want to call her Portia. She likes it. Darling Ferne, don't cry. Everything's going to be all right.'

It took time to believe that his recovery was complete, for the news seemed too good to be true. But with every hour that passed Dante showed that his faculties were as sharp as ever.

'We played fate at his own game,' he told her. 'And we won. Or, rather, you did. You were the player. Before you came, I never had the nerve to take that game on. Without you, I should never have had it.'

He touched her face.

'I see you there so clearly, and everything around you; all the world is clear. I hadn't dared to dream that this would happen.'

'It's what I always believed,' she said.

'I know, but I couldn't be sure. There was always the chance that you might have had to put me in an institution.'

Ferne hesitated. It would have been so easy to let this moment slip past and be forgotten, but something impelled her to total honesty, whatever the risk.

'Oh no,' she said. 'I would never have done that.'

He frowned. 'But you promised, don't you remember?'

'I know what I promised,' she said calmly. 'But nothing would have made me keep that promise. Even now I don't think you begin to understand how much I love you. Whatever happened, I would have kept you with me. If you were ill, that would have been more reason to love you, but you were in no state to understand it then. So I had to practise a little deception.'

He looked stunned, as though the full power of her declaration was only just dawning on him.

'But,' he whispered at last, 'you promised on everything you hold dear and sacred.'

'I lied,' she said calmly. 'You wanted to be kept out of sight, so that's what I would have done—but you would have been in our home, where the world couldn't see you, but I could see you every day. Whether you were yourself, or whether your mind had gone, you would have been my husband and I would have loved you until the last moment of my life.'

Suddenly, shockingly, she found her temper rising. Why should she have to explain all this to him?

'So now you know,' she said. 'I lied to you. I wanted to marry you so much, I'd have said and done anything. I made that promise without the most distant intention of keeping it, because I loved you with all of my heart and all of my *life*—but you just couldn't realise, could you?

'Can you see it now? Or are you just too proud and arrogant—and too *stupid*—to understand? You think love is a matter of making bargains, and you can't get it into your head that love has to be unconditional. If it isn't unconditional, it isn't love.'

She waited to see if he would say anything, but he seemed too stunned to speak. Was she being foolish? she wondered. Was she risking their marriage for the satisfaction of getting this off her chest?

But she had no choice. If they were to stand a chance, the air must be clear between them.

'So now you know the worst about me,' she said. 'I tricked you into marriage by deceit. I'm a shameless, dishonest woman who'll do anything to get her own way.'

When at last Dante spoke, he said only two words, and they were the last words Ferne expected to hear.

'Thank goodness!'

'What was that?'

'Thank goodness you're a liar, my darling! Thank goodness you had the courage to be shameless and deceitful. When I think of the disaster that could have befallen me if you'd been truthful, I tremble inside.'

'What—what are you talking about?' she said, half-laughing, half-afraid to believe her ears.

'I never felt I had the right to marry you, knowing what I might be leading you into. It was my way of setting you free. If you'd refused to promise, I'd have forced myself to refuse the marriage, although to be your husband was what I wanted with all my heart. In life, in death, or in that half-life I dreaded so much, I want you, and only you, to be there with me.

'But that felt like selfishness. I demanded that promise because I believed I had no right to trap you and blight your life.'

'But you could never blight my life,' she protested. 'You *are* my life. Haven't you understood that?'

'I guess I'm just starting to. It seemed too much to hope that you should love me as much as I love you. I still can't quite take it in, but I know this: my life belongs to you. Not only because we married, but because the life I have now is the life you gave me.

'Take it, and use it as you will. It was you who drove the clouds away, and you who brings the sunlight. And, as long as you are with me, that will always be true.'

Two weeks later Dante was discharged from hospital, and he and Ferne went to spend a few weeks at the Villa Rinucci. Even when they returned to their apartment they lived quietly, the only excitement being the delayed wedding-breakfast, celebrated when the whole Rinucci family was present.

After that everyone held their breath for the birth of the newest family member. Portia Rinucci was born the next spring, a combination of her mother's looks and her father's spirit. At her christening, it was observed by everyone that it was her father who held her possessively, his face blazing with love and pride, while her mother looked on with fond tolerance, perfectly happy with the unusual arrangement.

If sometimes Ferne's eyes darkened, it was only because she could never quite forget the cloud that had retreated but not completely vanished. As her daughter grew, it might yet darken their lives again—but she would face it, strengthened by a triumphant love and a happiness that few women knew.

* * * * *

SALZANO'S CAPTIVE BRIDE

BY
DAPHNE CLAIR

Many thanks to Damarys Guerrero, Bryan DeNosky
and Kathie DeNosky for their help with information
on Venezuelan Spanish and life in Venezuela.

CHAPTER ONE

AMBER Odell had just washed up after her solitary evening meal when the doorbell sounded a long, imperative ring.

She closed a cupboard door with a click of the old-fashioned catch, hastily hung the tea towel on its rail and hurried along the short hallway.

The rimu floorboards beneath the faded carpet runner creaked under her bare feet. The old building in a once-fashionable Auckland suburb had endured a chequered career from grand home to orphanage to boarding house until, towards the end of the twentieth century, some crude renovations had converted it into flats. Amber was lucky to have leased one on the ground floor at a reasonable price, in return for some badly needed redecorating.

She switched on the porch light and hesitated at the sight of a large, dark shape behind the blue-and-red stained glass panes on the top part of the door. After a second or two the shape moved and raised a hand to rap on the wooden panel between the panes.

Cautiously she opened the door, braced to slam it shut again.

The porch light shone down on glossy waves of night-black hair combed back from an arresting olive-toned face with high cheekbones and a commanding nose. The forbidding features and uncompromising, beard-shadowed jaw were at odds with a sensuous male mouth, even though at the moment it was stubbornly set and unsmiling.

Vaguely she was conscious of broad shoulders, a pristine white T-shirt moulded over a toned chest, and long powerful legs encased in olive-green trousers. Casual clothes that somehow managed to convey a sense of style and expense.

But most of her attention was riveted by a nearly coal-dark gaze, burning with what looked like anger.

Which didn't make sense. She'd never laid eyes on the man in her life.

Not that he wasn't worth laying eyes on. She was perturbed by a stirring of unbidden female response to the potent aura of masculinity that invisibly cloaked him.

Pushing back a strand of fine, fair hair that flowed over shoulders bared by her brief tube top, she opened her mouth to ask what he wanted.

Before she could say anything, a comprehensive, searing gaze traversed downward over the wide strip of ribbed cotton hugging her breasts, and lingered on the pale flesh between the top and her blue shorts before quickly taking in the length of her legs and then returning to her face.

Amber went hot all over with anger of her own—and shock at the way her pulse points had leapt to life under the bold inspection. Lifting her chin—as she needed to anyway to look the man in the eye—she was about to ask again what he wanted when he forestalled her with the abrupt query "Where is he?" issued in a low, grating voice.

She blinked, startled. "I think you've—" *Made a mistake,* she'd been going to say, but she was cut off.

"I said, *Where is he?*" the man rasped. "Where is my son?"

"Well, certainly not here!" Amber told him. Maybe he was looking for one of the other tenants. "You've got the wrong place. Sorry."

She began to close the door, but the man reached out and with apparent ease pushed it back again and stepped into the hallway.

Amber instinctively retreated, then realised that was the worst thing to do as the intimidating stranger kicked the door shut behind him, and when she turned to flee along the passageway—not that it would do her much good—a hard hand clamped about her arm and swung her to face him.

She opened her mouth to scream, hoping the two students next door or the journalist in the flat directly above hers would hear and investigate.

All she got out was a choked sound before the intruder put his other hand over her mouth and crowded her against the wall. She felt the warmth of his lean, hard body almost touching hers, and smelled a faint whiff of leather with a hint of newly cut grass. Aftershave? Although he looked as if he hadn't shaved for a couple of days.

He said, moderating his voice with its slight foreign accent in an apparent effort to reassure her, "Don't be foolish. You have no need to fear me."

Now he looked exasperated rather than angry. Amber contemplated kneeing him, weighing her chances of disabling him and escaping, but suddenly he let her go and said, "Now let us be sensible."

Yes, let's! Amber thought grimly. "The sensible thing is for you to leave before I call the police!"

A frown appeared between his dark brows, and a flash of temper lit his eyes again. He said flatly, "All I ask is to see my son. You have—"

"*I told you*—" Amber raised her voice "—your son is not here! I don't know why you should think—"

"I don't believe you."

"Look—" she edged towards the door and kept talking "—you've made a mistake. I can't help you, and I'm asking you to leave."

"Leave?" He seemed affronted. "After flying from Venezuela to New Zealand? I have not slept since—"

"That's not my problem," she informed him.

She reached out to open the door again but he put a hand on it, holding it shut and looking down at her through narrowed eyes. "If he is not here," he said quietly, as though struggling to control himself, "what have you done with him?"

A new expression had appeared in his eyes—surely not fear? Or at least genuine anxiety.

"*Nothing!*"

Again the black brows drew together. Lucifer must have had that same terrible, ferocious male beauty.

She shivered, and he said, the harsh note back in his voice, "What are you up to?" His eyes made another hostile survey of her. "If you ever had a child it certainly does not show."

Amber gaped. "I've never had a child!" She reminded herself that most mentally ill people weren't dangerous.

Then he grabbed her upper arms and she thought, *But a few are!* and forced herself not to kick and hit. That might trigger him into real violence. If she kept calm maybe she could talk him into leaving. He muttered something that sounded suspiciously like swearing in Spanish. White teeth showed as his lips curled back in a near-snarl. "What devil's game are you playing?" he demanded. "Why did you write to me?"

"*Write* to you?" Amber's voice rose in disbelief. "I don't even *know* you!"

His hands tightened until she winced, and he dropped them, his tawny skin darkening. "In a sense that is true," he said with an air of hauteur, his eyes almost hidden by lowered lids that had the longest, thickest lashes she'd ever seen on a man. "But for a short time we *knew* each other intimately. That you cannot deny."

About to do so in no uncertain terms, she hesitated as a fantastic suspicion slithered into her mind. *Venezuela.* South America.

No. She shook her head to dislodge the shameful notion. The guy was raving.

"Very well," he said, impatient again and misinterpreting her action. "It is a matter of semantics. It was not…an emotional intimacy. But whatever you call it, you have not forgotten. What did you expect when you wrote that letter? That I would send money and put it out of my mind?"

"Wh-which letter?" Was it possible…? *No!*

"Were there others?" he asked, the lift of those almost satanic brows expressing cynical doubt. "The one," he continued with exaggerated patience, "that asked for a *contribution* towards the welfare of the child you had borne, apparently to me."

For a moment Amber felt dizzy, sick, and her hand involuntarily flew to her mouth to stop an exclamation escaping. Her voice shaking, she said, "I never sent you any letter, I swear."

Maybe she'd got through to him at last. He appeared briefly disconcerted, then his expression hardened again. "You were desperate, it said. Was it simply an attempt at extortion and there truly is no child?"

She breathed in, thinking, and slowly said, "Would you believe me if I told you that you have the wrong woman?"

His brows shot up again and he laughed. Not pleasantly. "I know I had far more wine that night than was wise, but I was not so drunk that I don't remember the face of the woman I shared a bed with."

Feeling sicker still, her heart pounding erratically, Amber couldn't speak.

Not that she'd have had a chance. His lips curling in a sneer, he asked, "Do you make a habit of asking men to pay you off after…I believe you would call it a one-night stand."

"I don't do one-night stands," she flashed, "and neither—" caution intervened "—neither do I try to blackmail…anybody."

"I'm the only one so privileged?" he asked, the harsh, accusative tone turning dark and silken, which paradoxically made her feel even more threatened. "And if it was not a one-night stand I'm not sure what you think it was. You yourself have denied any real connection between us, and we have had no contact since—until you claimed to have borne me a son."

"I haven't claimed anything of the sort!" Amber snapped. And as he made a move towards her, fright and anger sharpened her voice. "Don't you dare come near me!"

He stopped dead, as if she'd shot him. "I will not hurt you," he said.

"Oh, really?" She hoped her derisive tone didn't set him off, but she couldn't help adding acidly, "I expect I'll have bruises on my arms tomorrow."

To her surprise, a look of chagrin crossed his face. Stiffly, his accent stronger, he said, "If that is so, I apologise. I was…not thinking."

Not hard to guess he wasn't accustomed to apologising.

The change in him was at least marginally reassuring. Encouraged, Amber tried again, even more forcefully. "You're not listening to me, are you? I don't *know*—"

"Why should I listen to lies?"

"I'm not lying. You've got it all wrong!"

The sound he made in his throat was akin to an animal growl, alarming her again. He reached out, and long fingers closed about her wrist. "Then show me he is not here."

She wanted to snap at him again, but perhaps it would be safer to humour the man, persuade him he'd made a mistake, and he might leave. Or to distract him so she'd have a shot at escaping. "All right," she said finally. It wouldn't take long—the flat had only three small rooms besides the kitchen and bathroom. "Feel free to look around."

His gaze suspicious, he tugged at her imprisoned wrist. "Show me."

She wasn't going to be given a chance to flee outside and call for help.

Amber shrugged, hiding the fact that her heart was thumping, and led him to the doorway of her cosy sitting room, reaching aside to switch on the light.

A soft, cushioned olive-green sofa faced the fireplace, in front of which she'd placed a Chinese jar filled with white plumes of native toe-toe.

Two armchairs with calico slip-covers hiding their shabby upholstery were set at right-angles to the sofa, a couple of bright-red wooden boxes serving as end tables. Her TV and sound system sat in the chimney corners, and on the mantel a row of books was held by the South Island jade bookends she'd inherited from her grandmother.

The man glanced over the room without entering, and Amber took him across the hallway to her bedroom.

The bed was covered in white *broderie-anglaise,* and thick sheepskin rugs lay on the varnished floor. This time the man walked into the room as she tugged her wrist from his grip and stepped to one side, leaning with folded arms against the curve of the second-hand Queen Anne style dressing table.

The man threw her a glance that gave a silent warning and strode to the mirror-doored wardrobe, briefly looked at the clothes hanging there and closed it again. When his gaze went to the dressing table drawers she looked back at him defiantly and said, "You are *not* going through my underwear drawers. Are you some kind of pervert?"

For an instant fury flared in his eyes, then she thought he almost laughed, and she could see he was weighing whether he should ignore her ban before he headed for the door. Amber breathed a little more easily.

"Sure you don't want to look under the bed?" she inquired as he snagged her wrist again.

He didn't respond to the sarcasm, merely striding down the hall to the door opening into the minuscule bathroom.

Obviously no one was lurking in the shower cubicle behind its clear plastic curtain printed with coloured fish, or hiding in the cupboard beneath the washbasin.

Next was her office-cum-spare room, hardly large enough for the single guest bed, her filing cabinet, a compact desk that held her laptop computer, and the crowded shelves of reference books along one wall.

That left the narrow kitchen with a small dining area at one end. The man opened the back door onto the little walled and paved patio, saw the potted plants and the wrought-iron table and chairs for two, and on closing the door allowed her to free herself of his grasp and retreat against the sink counter.

He turned to the bank of cupboards on the opposite wall, and the counter below that held her toaster and bread-bin. Amber noticed how the glossy black hair was allowed to flow past his nape and curl at the neckline of his T-shirt.

Wondering if she could make a dash along the passage-way to the front door, she saw his shoulders stiffen, his entire body go utterly still. Had he stopped breathing?

He reached for something, making a hissing sound between his teeth, and turned abruptly to face her. "If you have no child, what is this?"

Oh, Lord! she prayed, staring at the baby's pacifier in his broad palm. *How do I get out of this?* "My…my friend must have left it when she brought her baby to visit."

His hand closed over the small object, then he dropped it onto the counter and began opening cupboard doors, shifting jars and bottles and tins, cups and plates, until in a lower cupboard he found a basket filled with small stuffed toys, a board book, rattles, a toy xylophone and a jumble of plastic blocks.

"For visiting children," she said. "Some of my friends have babies or toddlers. You won't find anything else. I keep telling you, you've made a mistake!"

He whirled then, fixing her with a glittering, hostile stare. "My mistake was almost two years ago, when I was *estúpido* enough to let cheap wine and a pretty tourist send my good sense and *disciplina* to the winds."

Bristling at his dismissal of the "pretty tourist" as on a par with "cheap wine," Amber said, "Whatever your problem is—"

"It is *our* problem," he argued, "if what was in that letter is true. No matter how often you deny it, or how distasteful I find it."

Distasteful? If that was how he thought of his supposed offspring, what sort of a father would he be?

The thought validated her caution. "Look," she said, making her denial as authoritative as she could, "it wasn't me. And I don't feel well." Brushing another strand of hair from her cheek, she realised her hand was trembling. Her stomach was battling nausea and her knees felt watery.

His eyes searched her face with patent distrust. "You are pale," he allowed grudgingly. His mouth clamped for a moment before he said, "Tomorrow then. I will come back. And I warn you, if you are not here I will find you again."

"How *did* you…?" Curious as to how he'd landed on *her* doorstep, she paused to reword the question. "You can't have had *my* address." She'd been too confused and alarmed to think about that.

A hint of that menacing sneer again distorted the firm male mouth. "It was not difficult. The post office box given as the return address was in Auckland, New Zealand. And you are the only A. Odell in the telephone book."

"I don't have a box," she said. "And not everyone is in the phone book." Which was lucky for them. It kept scary foreign men from pushing uninvited into their homes and flinging wild accusations.

She put a hand on the counter behind her. Her legs were still unsteady, and her voice lacked any kind of confidence when she said, "Please would you leave now? I…really can't talk to you any more tonight."

He took a step towards her, the Lucifer frown reappearing. "Are you ill? Do you need help?" One hand moved as if to touch her, but she shrank from it.

"All I need is for you to go!" And now she sounded shrill, dammit.

To her infinite relief he nodded curtly, but said, "You will be here tomorrow." As if he could order it. "In the morning?"

He was trying to pin her down. "I have to work," she said. "Some people do, you know." While some could afford to fly across the world at the drop of a hat—or a letter. "Tomorrow evening," she suggested randomly. "Eight o'clock." It seemed the only way to get rid of him, and next time she'd make sure she wasn't alone.

Another nod, and he turned to leave. Amber heard his footsteps recede down the passageway, and the door closing. Slumping against the counter, she felt as if she'd been picked up by a hurricane and dropped back to earth.

She straightened and made herself a cup of hot, black coffee, added a generous spoonful of sugar and took it to her bedroom. Sitting on the bed, she downed several steadying sips, before picking up the phone and keying in a number.

The ringing went on for a long time, but she didn't hang up. When it finally stopped and a voice as familiar as her own answered, she said without preamble, "Azzie, what on *earth* have you done?"

CHAPTER TWO

MARCO Enrique Salvatore Costa Salzano wasn't accustomed to being brushed off by women, much less being evicted from their homes.

But neither was he in the habit of forcibly invading those homes.

He'd spent the day brooding over last night's debacle even while he made a time-killing exploration of Auckland city and its environs, ending with a stroll on the waterfront path that curved in and out along several bays overlooked by well-kept houses wherever steep cliffs didn't border the road.

He'd found an underwater aquarium that featured such sea creatures as huge stingrays and even medium-size sharks swimming freely behind glass above and around the visitors. A short trolley ride in a fake Antarctic section allowed them to come eye to eye with king penguins. The animals were in every way a world apart from those he was accustomed to and to which he devoted a large part of his time. Yet they were sufficiently fascinating that for a short while he'd almost forgotten the mission that had brought him to the South Pacific.

Now the sun was inching downward and the eye-watering

blue of the sky over the Waitemata Harbour had gradually softened to a paler shade while he paced the thick carpet of his hotel suite. The hands of his watch crawled towards seven-thirty so slowly that he wondered if the several thousand dollars he'd paid for its world-renowned brand reliability, expensive platinum casing and flawless design had been misspent. There was still more than half an hour to his appointment with the woman who last night had inexplicably denied knowing him.

When he'd finally arrived in New Zealand after a seemingly endless flight, perhaps he shouldn't have left the hotel as soon as he'd had a hurried shower and pulled clean clothes randomly from his bag. Jet-lagged though he was, he hadn't been able to tolerate another night of angry anticipation mingled with regret and self-castigation—and something he refused to name as confused hope.

After all that, and despite her having appealed for his help in a way that suggested she and *his son* were suffering imminent if not actual penury, the woman had tried to shut the door on him!

Unable to conceal his simmering rage, he knew he had made her nervous. Although she'd mounted a valiant effort to hide that, standing up to him and threatening to call the police.

He almost smiled, recalling the defiant flash of her eyes—he hadn't remembered she had such striking eyes, truly jade green ringed with amber—and her determined efforts to oust him from that matchbox of a home. She'd deliberately goaded him with sarcasm and insults despite her slight though very feminine build and the fact that the top of her head barely reached his chin.

When he'd silenced her attempt to scream, and blocked

her escape with his body, her hair had been soft and silky against his throat and smelled of apricots with a hint of fresh lemon.

That scent had unexpectedly aroused him, as had the tantalising way her breasts rose and fell with her frightened breathing, under the scanty piece of cloth that barely covered them. He'd quickly stepped back, not wanting to add fear of rape to her perplexing reactions. It was not in his nature to terrorise women.

Admittedly last night's confrontation had been no ordinary visit. Perhaps he could have been less impetuous, but that letter had been a bombshell, coming long after he had written off the *Carnaval* incident as a lapse in judgement that, fortunately, had had no serious consequences.

Why be afraid of a man she'd happily allowed to take her to an unknown destination in a foreign city to have sex when they'd only met a couple of hours before? And why deny she'd sent that letter? Any logical reason eluded him.

Unless the story had been a lie. His fists clenched and he stopped pacing to stare moodily at the harbour, now calming into a tranquil satin expanse at odds with his chaotic thoughts. If this whole thing was a fabrication, he'd wasted his time making a long, time-consuming journey at great inconvenience to himself, his business and his family.

And the woman he'd done it for deserved no respect and no consideration.

Her apartment was old and the rooms cramped, her furnishings simple, but he'd seen no sign of true poverty. He wondered if New Zealanders knew the meaning of the word.

No one was dressed in rags, and although occasional

buskers performed, and a few street sellers displayed cheap jewellery or carvings, no whining beggars or persistent thin-faced children had accosted him.

Again he consulted his watch, seemingly for the hundredth time in the last hour, then left his room and took the elevator to the main entrance, where the doorman hailed him a taxi.

A couple of minutes before eight Amber's doorbell rang in the same imperious way it had the previous night.

All day her nerves had been strung to screaming point.

She loved her job as a researcher for a film and TV production company and usually gave it her all, but today her mind had kept straying to an exotic-looking, disturbing and driven male who would be on her doorstep again that night. During a team meeting she'd realised she hadn't heard a word for the past five or ten minutes, and the end of her ballpoint pen showed teeth marks where she'd been absently chewing on it.

And Azzie had been totally immovable about joining her tonight, leaving Amber to deal with the formidable Venezuelan on her own.

At the sound of the doorbell, she finished tying the white-and-green wraparound skirt that she'd teamed with a sleeveless white lawn top fastened with tiny pearl buttons. She slipped her feet into wedge-heeled casual shoes that gave her a few extra inches, and hastily pinned her hair into a knot while walking to the door.

The man who stood there was as striking as she remembered, but now he wore dark trousers, a cream shirt open at the collar, and a light, flecked cream jacket. The barely contained fury of last night had abated. He looked rigidly contained and rather chilly when she stepped back and said, "Come in, *señor.*"

His black brows lifted a fraction as he stepped into the hallway. "So formal," he said, "after having my baby?"

Amber bit her lip. "We…we can't talk here." She gestured towards the living room and he nodded, then placed a hand lightly on her waist, guiding her into the room ahead of him. A startling quiver of sexual awareness made her move quickly away from him to one of the armchairs, but she remained standing. Trying to match his self-possession, she offered, "Can I get you a coffee or something?"

"I did not come here for coffee. Please sit down."

Not expressing her resentment at being told to sit down in her own living room, she perched on the edge of one of the armchairs and waited while he took the opposite one.

Figuring that getting in first was the best plan of attack, Amber broke into speech. "I'm sorry you came all this way for nothing, but that letter was a mistake. I—"

"So you admit writing it?"

"It should never have been sent," she said, choosing her words as if picking her way through a minefield. "I'm sorry if it misled you."

His lips tightened, and for a moment she thought she saw disappointment in his eyes. "Misled me?" he said, and now she could see nothing in the dark depths but condemnation.

Her fingers clasped tightly together against a childish urge to cross them behind her back, she said, "The letter didn't say the baby was yours. Did it?" she added, trying to sound authoritative.

"The implication—" he started to say before she hurried on.

"I'm sorry if it wasn't clear, but it was written in haste and…and a silly panic. You had said in Caracas—" she paused to ensure she was quoting exactly "—'If you have any problem, contact me.'" Despite herself she felt her cheeks growing hot. Would he recall exactly how he had couched the offer?

A flash of incredulity crossed his controlled features.

Amber ploughed ahead. "The letter was just a stupid impulse. It wasn't necessary for you to come all this way. That was quite—" disastrous "—unexpected. So you can go home and forget about it. I'm sorry," she repeated under his hostile stare.

He stood up so suddenly she jumped, and stiffened her spine to stop herself shrinking from him.

Even though he didn't come nearer, his stance and the renewed anger in his blazing eyes, the stern line of his mouth, made her heart do a somersault. "Go?" he said. "Just so?" He snapped his fingers and again Amber flinched.

"I know you've come a long way," she said placatingly, "and I'm really sor—"

"Do not tell me again that you are *sorry!*" he snarled. "You claimed to have given birth to a baby boy nine months after we…met in Caracas. What was I supposed to think? And what did *you* think? That I'm the kind of man who would pay off the mother of my child and then wash my hands of them both?"

Amber swallowed hard. "I don't know what kind of man you are," she admitted. "Except that you're…" wealthy, aristocratic, and apparently some kind of power in his own country. Besides having a temper.

"That I have money?" he finished for her scornfully. "And you thought you could milk me of some of that money without giving anything in return. Was that why this letter promised never to bother me again?"

"It wasn't like that!"

He surged forward, gripping the arms of her chair, and now she instinctively drew back. "If there ever was such a child," he said, not loudly but in an implacable voice that sent a shiver down her spine, "where is he?"

Unable to meet his accusing eyes, she stared down at her entwined hands. "As I said last night, I've never had a baby." Despite doing what she'd been convinced was the right thing, she had a ghastly sense of wrongness.

"You wrote that you had debts you were unable to pay, that you were on the point of losing your home. It seemed my son was being thrown onto the street."

"Um," she muttered. "It wasn't as bad as that, exactly. Things are improving now."

"How? You found some other poor fool to fall for your tricks?" He lifted one hand from the chair arm, only to grasp her chin and make her look up at him.

"No!" she said. "Nothing of the sort."

His eyes, filled with accusation, were inches away. "The problem with liars," he said, "is that one never knows when they are telling the truth."

She forced herself to look straight into those dark eyes. "I did not have your baby. And I'm not lying." *I'm not,* she assured herself. "You saw last night there's no baby here."

He scrutinised her for what seemed like minutes. Then abruptly he released her chin and straightened, stepping back but still watching her with patent mistrust. "Are you a gambler?" he asked.

"What?" She didn't understand the switch of subject.

"Was that why you needed money?"

She shook her head. "It isn't important now."

"You have put me to a great deal of trouble and some expense. I think I have a right to ask why."

"I'm sor—" He lifted a warning hand and she stopped the apology leaving her tongue. She said instead, "If you want your airfare reimbursed…" It seemed only fair to offer.

The twist of his lips was hardly a smile, although he seemed to derive some kind of sardonic amusement from her reply. He made a dismissive gesture. "That is not necessary, even if it is possible."

She had been rash to suggest it. He'd probably travelled first class, and after paying off the student loan that had got her through university with degrees in history and media studies, and finally being able to afford her own place instead of grungy shared digs, her savings were on the lean side of modest. As for Azzie—no use even thinking about it.

Growing bolder, she stood up, still finding him much too close. Her knees were watery. "Thank you. I think you'd better go now. There's nothing more I can tell you."

"You mean there is nothing more you wish to tell me."

Amber shrugged. What else could she say without arousing further suspicion? And she needed him to leave. Marco Salzano's presence was unnerving in more than one way. While his scorn and disbelief were intimidating, he was a powerfully attractive man, and her female hormones ran riot every time he came near. She was beginning to have a new understanding of what had taken place in Venezuela.

Marco turned and took a couple of steps away from her. She inwardly sighed in relief, but then he stopped and faced her again. His gaze sharpened and he tilted his head. "Why," he said slowly, "have I a…a sense that you are hiding something? Perhaps something I should know?"

Her mouth dried and she said in a near-whisper, "There is no reason to involve you in my troubles."

As if on impulse he plunged a hand into an inside pocket of his jacket, took out a leather wallet and pulled a bundle of notes from it.

They were New Zealand notes. Reddish, hundred-dollar ones. Amounting to more money than Amber had ever seen anyone handle so casually.

"Take it," he said, holding the cash out to her, his expression unreadable. "Let us say for remembrance of a pleasurable encounter."

Amber recoiled. "I can't take your money!"

A gleam of surprised speculation lit his eyes and she knew she'd made a mistake. "But that is exactly why I am here," he said softly, "is it not?"

"I told you, everything's all right now." She fervently hoped so. Her hands were clasped behind her back, her mouth set in stubborn refusal.

He studied her as if she were a puzzle he had trouble figuring out, even while he tucked the notes back into the wallet and returned it to his pocket. Unnerved by the scrutiny, Amber lifted a hand to brush back a wayward strand of hair that was tickling the corner of her mouth.

His eyes tracked the movement, and when she made to lower her hand he suddenly covered the space between them in a stride, catching her forearm near the elbow so that it remained raised while he inspected the inside of her upper arm. Following his gaze, she saw a thumb-shaped bruise marring the tender skin.

Her cheeks warmed and she tried to pull away, but he retained his firm though careful hold. She saw him take a breath, and his mouth compressed. She guessed he was keeping back some vivid language.

In a low voice she'd not heard from him before, he said, "Is that my mark?" He was still looking at the bruise, as if unwilling to meet her eyes. The moment lengthened unbearably. She could smell again that subtle leather-and-grass aroma, mingled with a combination of male skin scent and freshly laundered clothing.

"It doesn't matter," she said.

Totally unexpectedly the dark head bent and she felt his lips touch the blue mark.

She almost choked on an indrawn breath, biting her lip fiercely to stop an involuntary sound escaping from her throat, where her heart seemed to have lodged.

His hair swept against her skin, and the sensation was like a lightning bolt arrowing through her body.

What *was* that? Did Marco Salzano's surprisingly soft hair hold an electrical charge like the one that made her own hair crackle sometimes when she brushed it?

He lifted his head and the glitter in his eyes made her pulse roar into overdrive.

Slowly he lowered her arm, slipping his hand like a caress down to her wrist. "Such delicate skin," he murmured. "Forgive me."

Unable to speak for the rioting of her senses, Amber dazedly wondered how a mere fleeting touch could arouse such an extravagance of feeling. No one had the right to effortlessly exude that much sex appeal.

He seemed a tad bemused himself. His jaw went tight, and the taut skin over his cheekbones darkened further.

Gathering her wits from wherever they'd dispersed themselves, Amber pulled at her imprisoned wrist, and with apparent reluctance he released it, thrusting his hand into the pocket of his trousers.

"I did not remember what a desirable woman you are," he said. "It is not so surprising I lost my head that night, and stepped outside the bounds of my normal behaviour."

Had he? "You weren't the only one," she told him dryly. And then warned herself, *Shut up!*

He looked at her consideringly. "The woman I took to my bed in Caracas was no spotless virgin, I think."

Amber snapped, "That doesn't make her a slut!" Momentarily she closed her eyes. Had she blown it with that automatic defence?

Apparently unperturbed, he said, "I did not mean to imply such a thing. Merely that I assumed you were a woman of the world. Capable of protecting yourself from any…inconvenience. You yourself assured me of that afterwards, if you remember."

That jolted her. "I…don't remember," she claimed truthfully, hoping to close the subject. "Now would you—"

"Had you had so much to drink?" he queried, frowning again. "I don't knowingly take advantage of drunken women. You appeared well aware of what you were doing. And I believe from your reactions at the time that you very much enjoyed our…brief encounter. You remember *that?*" The gleam that had entered his eyes intensified, and his mouth curved a little at the corners.

Heat rose again to Amber's cheeks. Desperately she said, "No. Now—"

"No?" Faint annoyance showed for an instant, and she supposed she'd offended his machismo.

The way he let his gaze roam over her body didn't help her flush subside. "Perhaps," he said in a reflective tone like a tiger's purr, "I can refresh your memory."

The sound she made when he swiftly closed the space between them again was something between a gasp and a squeal, but before she could say anything coherent he had his arms around her and had pulled her close, her body arching against the solid masculine warmth of his. Even as she opened her mouth to protest he covered it with his own, tipping her head back, his breath mingling with hers.

His lips were gentle but questing, moving across her startled ones even after she raised her hands to push at him.

The tip of his tongue was tracing an erotic path along her upper lip, igniting a shocking flare of answering desire before she rallied enough to clench her hands into fists and shove them against his chest.

His hands fell, and Amber shakily stepped back.

A glittering gaze met hers, and she swallowed before saying in a voice unlike her own, "I want you out of here right *now*."

As if he hadn't heard, he said, "I also seem to have forgotten much." She didn't know whether to be pleased or alarmed that he looked nearly as stunned as she felt. "You taste of honey…and passion," he said. "Something else I failed to remember."

He probably remembered nothing but wine, but she didn't want to go into that. Nor did she want to fall under the spell he'd woven with that oh-so-sexy, devastating kiss. "I said I want you to go," she stated precisely. "Please."

His expression became baffled, but he gave a jerky little bow of his head and said, "If you truly wish it."

"*Yes*." Not trusting herself to say more, she marched

past him to the hallway and flung the front door open. "Our business is finished," she said as he passed her.

He turned then, a half-amused, half-rueful smile on his lips, his eyes making another leisurely, perhaps slightly perplexed examination of her entire body before he gave a brief shake of his head, then descended the shallow steps and strode away.

Tempted to yell a rude word or two after him, she resisted and instead closed the door with a snap and leaned back against it until her legs regained some strength.

Never in her life had she imagined being caught in a trap like this.

One day she'd stop feeling so damned guilty, because wasn't it all for the best?

Of course, she assured herself. For him as well as for…well, everyone.

She hadn't said anything that wasn't true.

A flimsy excuse. But she ought to be happy at emerging unscathed and just forget the whole thing ever happened.

Forget?

She lifted the back of her hand to scrub at her lips, which still tingled with the memory of Marco Salzano's kiss.

CHAPTER THREE

THE following day, instead of driving home after work, Amber took the route to her sister's home.

The seventies house that Azure and her husband, Rickie, were gradually restoring with Amber's occasional help was in an outer suburb where real estate was less horrendously expensive than in more fashionable areas.

Sitting at the scarred auction-bargain table in the big kitchen, Amber sipped at the cheap wine her sister had poured. Azure was on her second glass, and was now smiling at the plump, rosy-cheeked baby on her knee—a smile so special it caught at Amber's heart—but the baby, unimpressed, wrinkled his face up and whimpered crossly.

Azure handed him over to his aunt while she poured milk into a plastic sippy cup.

Amber bent to kiss the amazingly smooth, warm skin of the baby's temple and studied him while he looked at her interestedly with round eyes so dark she couldn't determine their colour, and he babbled in his own private language interspersed with the odd Mama and Dada and even Namba which Amber hoped was his effort at Auntie Amber.

Rickie's eyes were dark too, inherited from his Maori

grandfather along with the black curls that Benny's soft fuzz promised to duplicate.

In the baby's blob of a nose, chubby face and tiny pouting little mouth there was certainly no hint of the man who had filled Amber's flat with his utterly adult male presence and striking features.

Seeing his mother approach with the cup, the little boy wriggled to the floor with a demanding "Ma!"

"At the table," she said firmly, perching him again on her own knee as she sat down.

"Azure," Amber felt driven to say, "you're sure there's no chance he's Mr. Salzano's baby?"

She recognised with a sinking feeling a flicker of fear in her sister's guileless eyes, belying Azure's defiant, "I told you, he misunderstood my letter. I never said that!"

"But you did have sex with him." Unbelievable though it seemed, Azure had confessed to that when Amber pressed her about the mysterious Venezuelan.

"*Once*. Oh, don't remind me!" Azure wailed. Benny stopped drinking his milk and began to wail too.

She soothed him, and when he settled again she said, "I didn't stop taking the pill until after that night. Once Rickie and I had decided we'd get married when we came home it didn't seem important. And I've never slept with anyone but Rickie before or since. So it can't be—"

"You did use a condom that night?" Something she'd assumed when she'd cornered her sister the day previously.

Azure shrugged. "What does it matter?" she muttered, her eyes fixed on the baby.

Amber was horrified. "You took an awful risk with a stranger!"

"We weren't thinking. Too much wine, I guess. He was

mortified when he realised… It's okay, I had all kinds of tests when I found out I was pregnant. I don't want to talk about it any more, now Benny's safe. You didn't tell Marco about him, did you? You promised!"

Amber *had* promised in the end despite huge reluctance, faced with an hysterical but persuasive sister whose reasoning seemed fireproof, and who fervently swore there was no way her baby's father could be anyone other than the man who was now her husband. "No. But if there's any chance Benny's his—"

"Everyone says Benny looks like his dad. *You* did!"

Amber had, before a dark-haired, dark-eyed man appeared on her doorstep with a fantastic accusation that Azure had later convinced her wasn't possible.

Amber closed her eyes—a mistake. The shadowy figure lurking in the back of her mind became a full-blown living-colour picture of a tall, gorgeous man with a blaze of anger in his almost-black eyes and a mouth that, despite its seductive contours, expressed an unbending will when it wasn't twisted in contemptuous disbelief.

A mouth that could also be gentle, persuasive, despite his suspicion of her and his angry frustration—a mouth that had wrought some kind of erotic magic on her senses.

And though his eyes had blazed in fury, they had shown unwilling but genuine concern when he'd seen she felt ill.

Opening her own eyes, she demanded, "*Why* ask Marco Salzano for money, then?"

"Like I said before," Azure retorted, "money's nothing to people like him. His family made a fortune mining gold and diamonds way back—and later, oil."

"He told you that?" Boastful on top of everything.

"Sort of. He was so casual about it I knew he wasn't having me on. And I picked up some information later about the family. They're big landowners, well-known and still seriously rich. You should have seen the place he took me to." Awe momentarily lit Azure's eyes, then she blushed. "And that was just his city pad."

No sleazy by-the-hour hotel, then. Of course not, for a man with his innate male elegance and what her and Azure's grandmother would call breeding, undiminished by the rough beard shadow and his cavalier attitude towards Amber. He had, after all, mistaken her for her sister.

Despite the three years' difference in their ages, people often mistook one of the Odell girls for the other.

Azure said, "It was lucky you hadn't told him who you really were. I'm sorry you had to get involved. I know you hated the idea."

Maybe, Amber thought, she should have stood firm in her initial shocked refusal, but Azure's denials had been very convincing, and since childhood Amber had taken seriously her role of elder sister, warning her younger sibling to look both ways when crossing the road, defending her in schoolyard scraps, and forever getting her out of trouble. A hard-to-break habit.

Benny pushed away the sippy cup, tipping it over. Righting it, Azure continued, "I'm really, really grateful you made him go away, Ammie."

From what Amber had seen of the man, it would take a team of wild horses to *make* Marco Salzano do anything. Whereas she herself had allowed her sister's reasoning to override her aghast objections, her deeply held principles and her better judgement.

The baby, who had been playing with his mother's hair, turned to Amber with a heart-melting dimpled grin.

A clutch of fear for him gave her a taste of Azure's terror when she'd learned of Marco Salzano's visit. "You could get a DNA test," she suggested.

Azure flatly vetoed that. "Rickie and I have only just got back together again. I daren't rock the boat. He'd go ballistic if he knew Marco was *here*. I *can't* ask him to take a test now!"

Amber had to concede the potential complications were horrendous. Surely Benny's welfare was the most important thing. "You didn't miss any of your pills before…?"

Azure didn't answer, apparently absorbed in adoring her son, making kissing noises that he tried to copy.

Amber's voice sharpened. "Azzie?"

Azure looked up impatiently. "Not really. Only it's difficult to keep track when you're travelling, changing time zones and everything. Do leave it alone, Amber!"

Amber bit her tongue. Too late now to berate her sister. It would only end in tears. Refusing another glass of wine, she was about to leave when Azure's husband came in, his good-looking face lighting up as Benny broke into a delighted chuckle, wriggled down to the floor and took a couple of shaky steps, then held up his arms to be lifted, and planted a sloppy kiss on Rickie's cheek.

They *were* so alike, surely Azure's certainty was justified. And with any luck Marco Salzano was already on his way back to Venezuela.

In fact Marco was in the bar of his hotel, having a couple of measured drinks and tantalised by the memory of the previous night.

After leaving the cramped flat with its cheap but rather charming décor and its infuriatingly inconsistent occupant, he'd almost booked a flight home. Something held him back, a niggling doubt that he couldn't quite pin down.

He'd tried to dismiss the persistent image of wide, startled eyes closing as his mouth found sweet feminine lips, and the memory of how surprisingly soft they'd been beneath his—an image not conducive to clear thinking.

The woman had lied the first night and been evasive on the second. She was a good actress—her bewilderment and fear when he'd brushed aside her futile pretence of not knowing him had seemed almost convincing, now that he thought about it. At the time he'd been preoccupied with finding his son.

He was inclined to believe the baby was fictitious—ridiculous to feel a pang of grief. Unless she'd had it adopted. Or worse, ended the pregnancy before the child was even born. Her figure was perfect, the skin between the skimpy top and shorts taut and unmarred by stretch marks. Anger heated his blood, along with another emotion aroused by the memory of her body, half-naked as it was, briefly coming in contact with his.

Deliberately he quelled both reactions. Emotion interfered with logical thought.

Why, after that begging letter, had she refused his money with something like horror? Nothing added up. In his experience two and two always made four. If not, he wanted to know why, and invariably something in the equation was wrong—a mistake or a deliberate obfuscation.

He had told the desk clerk he was extending his stay—a decision readily accepted. Marco Salzano didn't flaunt his wealth but he had never been ungenerous with it.

After spending the morning making expensive telephone calls and checking his e-mail, he had studied the phone book in his room and later interviewed a private investigator.

Marco had given him as much information as would be needed to do a background check on Azure Odell, vaguely suggesting she was suspected of fraud.

"Can't do much today, but I'll get onto it tomorrow," the detective promised, "since you say it's urgent."

And since Marco had laid down a handsome initial fee. Now all he could do was wait.

Moodily he swilled the wine in his glass, ignoring the chatter in the crowded hotel bar and avoiding the eyes of two women perched on high stools that showed off their legs, who had been covertly inspecting him for some time.

For almost two years he'd put out of his mind the memory of that single night shared with a stranger, scarcely remembering the details. Yet now, after meeting her again, his body seemed to have a memory of its own—and an inconvenient desire to repeat the experience.

She was an attractive woman, even beautiful. But the women of his own country were renowned for their beauty. There was something else about her, some indefinable quality that eluded his mind yet appealed to his senses. Something he'd missed during that first casual encounter. Because now he couldn't seem to get her out of his mind, couldn't stop his body growing hot and restless.

He scowled at an open portfolio of papers lying on the table in front of him, a clear sign that he was working and didn't want company, but for fifteen minutes he'd stared at the printed sheets without comprehension. Idly scanning the room again, his gaze chanced upon the two women at the counter. Neither evoked a flicker of interest.

Next morning he breakfasted early before returning to his room. It was too soon to expect a call from the investigator, but that didn't stop him staring balefully at the light on the phone that refused to obligingly blink.

He killed time checking e-mail and researching the New Zealand beef industry on his computer, noting possible contacts if he should be here for a few more days. It was afternoon when the man contacted him. "The lessee of the address you gave me is an *Amber* Odell," he said. "Single, twenty-seven, works for a film and TV company in the city. She does apparently have a sister named Azure, but—"

"A sister?" Marco queried sharply.

"Yeah. She—the sister—doesn't live at that address."

"A twin?"

"Uh, don't think so. I could find out, get her address. It might take a bit longer if she's married and changed her name, but which woman are you interested in? Or is it both?"

"Yes—no." There was a faster way. "You have the address of this…Amber's…workplace?"

After putting down the phone Marco swore in his mother tongue, left his chair to pace the floor and swear some more, opened the bar fridge, then slammed it shut. This whole thing had started because for once he'd gone over his usual strict limit. He had to think. To control his first instinct, which was to find the woman, whatever her real name was, and wring her smooth, graceful, deceitful neck!

He wouldn't, of course, do that. But, he vowed, disciplining his hot, out-of-control rage to a contained, ruthless anger, he would see that she paid in full.

No one played Marco Salzano for a fool and got away with it. Not even a beautiful woman who set his blood on fire.

He consulted a map and found the street address the investigator had given him for the film studio. Marco's lip curled. Wasn't the film industry notorious for its casual attitude to sex? Like sister, like sister. *Amber* Odell had probably had dozens of lovers.

His gut tightened. Why should it matter how many men she had slept with? Especially if he wasn't, after all, one of them? The only reason for his driving need to see her was to find his son. Who surely did exist. Obviously the two sisters had cooked up that charade he'd been subjected to.

Leaving the Filmografia building in central Auckland, Amber stopped dead when Marco Salzano loomed in front of her, his face looking as if some sculptor had chiselled it out of unyielding rock. In his eyes was the banked fire of the anger he'd displayed at their first encounter.

"Hello, *Amber*," he said, with dark, steely mockery in his tone.

"What are you doing here?" she gasped, her heart contracting into a shrivelled ball. "How did you find me?" She looked about her, but most of her colleagues had either already left or were still working. Filming wasn't the kind of business where working hours were cast in stone.

His expression changed slightly, as if she'd just satisfied him in some way. "We must talk."

He took her arm but she shook off his hand. "I don't need to talk to you," she said, trying to sidestep him, but this time he caught her arm in an unshakeable grip, trying to walk her along with him.

"Come, we cannot discuss anything here."

"I'm not going anywhere with you. Let go of me or I'll scream. Someone will call the police and I'll tell them you're stalking me." She opened her mouth and he dropped his hand from her arm, looking grimly amused.

"And I will tell them you are attempting to deprive me of my legal rights by fraud and deception. I'm not stalking you. I merely wish to talk about your sister."

Her *sister?* Of course, he'd called her by her own name, which she'd automatically reacted to. Not Azure's. How much did he know? "How did you find out where I work?"

"I hired an investigator," he said calmly.

"You…?" For a second she was stunned as well as angry. The idea of a stranger prying into her life gave her the creeps. "How dare you!"

"How else could I discover the truth? You lied to me."

"I didn't," she protested unconvincingly, her conscience stabbing. "I told you over and over you had the wrong person."

"*Sí.* The first time I came to your apartment. But the next evening you did not deny you had slept with me, written to me."

"What would be the point?" she said, pushing away a wildly inappropriate mental picture of herself and Marco in the same bed. "You'd jumped to a conclusion, and trying to set you straight hadn't worked before. I figured nothing I said was going to convince you."

"You did not say, *My sister* slept with you in Caracas and had your baby."

"How do you know there's a baby?" Her stomach went hollow.

Marco said, "Why else would you have played out that absurd pretence?"

Oh, hell! "Azure's *married.*" Surely he could understand that no married woman wanted a previous lover turning up on her doorstep?

He said, "To the boyfriend who abandoned her in a foreign city full of men who had been drinking heavily?"

"It was a misunderstanding." She was tempted to remind him that by his own admission he'd been one of those men.

Carnaval in Caracas is just so wild! Azure had said. *People dancing on the streets wearing fantastic costumes, and drinking like there's no tomorrow. We were in an outdoor bar, and this skank in nothing but make-up and a few feathers dragged Rickie up to dance. He didn't even resist. And enjoyed it far too much. We had a fight and he went off in a huff, but I was sure he'd be back as soon as he calmed down. I was sitting there all alone with a bottle of wine, and a guy in a devil costume came on to me, wouldn't take no for an answer. I was getting scared when Marco came along and got rid of him. I knew Marco was someone important because the staff treated him like he was a lord or something. And we...started talking.*

And more. Amber shut that part off.

"Her fiancé walked off to calm himself down," she relayed to Marco, "but then he got lost in the crowd and couldn't find his way back." Or even remember the name of the bar, and had been both contrite and frantic when in the early hours he and Azure were finally reunited at their hotel. "They shared their cell phone, so he couldn't call her."

Two hours after Rickie went off, Azure had told her, *I was still waiting and I was so mad at him! Marco's a very sexy man. We'd polished off another couple of bottles of wine and, well, one thing led to another.*

"She made a mistake," Amber told him now.

"You too made a mistake," he accused her. "Don't imagine I will be so easily deceived again."

"Please—she's happy now and the baby's happy."

"I will be happy also, if she proves it is not mine."

"She said she's certain he isn't!"

"And you believe her?"

Amber hesitated for a fatal second and saw his eyes narrow, his jaw tighten. She said, "Surely she should know?"

Two young women came out of the building. "Hi, Amber," one said, and they paused, obviously angling for an introduction. "We're going to Cringles for a drink with the usual crowd. Want to come along and bring your friend?"

Amber was unwillingly fascinated by the way Marco Salzano's demeanour instantly changed. He gave the other women a dazzling smile and a slight inclination of his head. "You are kind, but please excuse us," he said. "Amber is about to join me for a drink and a private discussion."

They looked both smitten and disappointed, and one mouthed *Lucky you!* at Amber as they turned away.

Marco had taken her arm again and he said rapidly under his breath, "Your sister cannot avoid me forever. This time you will tell me the truth."

Amber stiffened but remained mute. He loosened his hold. "If you prefer we will talk in a public place. My hotel is within walking distance. There is a small bar there that I have noticed is not crowded at this time."

Amber allowed him to steer her to the street. Somehow she had to persuade him to leave Azure alone. Her brain was telling her this was Azure's problem. She should just say so and tell her sister to sort it out. But it wasn't only Azure who would pay for her brief folly. "All right," she said at last.

At the hotel Marco headed for a bar tucked discreetly into a corner on the ground floor. Only a few people were sitting in tub chairs at the round tables.

Amber asked for a glass of white wine and sipped it cautiously as Marco picked up his red. He'd also ordered a plate of taco chips with sour cream and sweet chilli sauce and gestured for her to help herself before he took one.

Amber's taste buds awoke at the sight of the platter, and as Marco washed his mouthful down with a sip of wine she thought how oddly intimate it was to share food with a man she couldn't help thinking of as the enemy.

He put down his glass and regarded her with his head tipped slightly back, his eyes hooded. She recalled the smile he'd directed at her friends, not at all the way he looked at her, glaring with anger and suspicion.

She said, "My sister didn't say her baby was yours." Surely Azure hadn't lied to her about that.

His lip curled. "If she did not intend me to think so, why did she suggest I would be willing to give her thousands of dollars for the sake of the child?"

Amber inwardly winced. Azure did tend to rush into things without thinking. Her family had hoped that marriage and motherhood might temper that trait. "Desperation," she suggested.

"So?" he said scornfully.

"She…she'd told her husband about what happened in Caracas, and he was upset…angry." Sometimes Amber thought Azure and her husband were too alike. It hadn't been the first time in their long relationship that they'd temporarily split after a quarrel. But she supposed no other had been caused by such a devastating revelation. Certainly none had lasted so long.

Marco frowned. "Is he violent?"

"Oh no! No. But he left her and she panicked."

He said Benny might be anybody's, Azure had sobbed, finally confessing to her sister why Rickie hadn't been around for a while. Previously she'd told her family he was working out of town. The big industrial electrical firm that had employed him covered a wide area, and it wasn't unusual for him to be away for a few days. *He said he wasn't coming back. His family say they don't know where he is. He even left his job.*

"Then her marriage is no more?" Marco asked sharply. "The child is without a father?"

"No. He missed her, and the baby. He loves them both so much. After almost two months he came back. Azure asked if he wanted a DNA test and he said no."

Thinking she saw a flicker of disbelief in Marco's expression, she said passionately, "He's the only father the baby's ever known, and they're good parents. It would be cruel to take Benny from them. Cruel to him. And it would break my sister's heart." She couldn't keep the tremor from her voice, her eyes from stinging.

Azure's greatest fear was not losing her husband again, although Amber knew she'd be devastated, but that Marco Salzano would want to take Benny from her. *People with that much money can do anything!* she'd cried. *Pay top lawyers. Even kidnap him! Kidnapping's a business in South America.*

It was true other children had been spirited off illegally to a different country, some never returned.

Amber too loved Benny, and the thought of him being snatched away made her own heart ache unbearably. How much worse would it be for her sister?

Marco said, "The boy is very young. I have a right—" apparently confirming her worst fear.

"He has rights too! Who knows how a tiny baby feels about being torn from its mother's arms, taken from everything he's used to—what long-term effects it has?"

"You are being melodramatic. I don't mean to—"

Amber ignored that. "You can't possibly feel the same way they do. You've never even seen him." Repeating all the arguments Azure had used to persuade her to go along with Marco's mistaken identification of her sister.

"That is why I'm here," he said. "To see him. And should he be mine—"

"He *isn't* yours! If Azure hadn't written that stupid letter you'd never have known he existed."

"If she didn't want me to know, why did she write it?"

Momentarily Amber closed her eyes. If only… But it was spilt milk now. "Her husband had gone, she thought forever, maybe to Australia or further, and he hadn't paid the mortgage installment due on their house. Every cent they had—" Amber knew that hadn't been much "—went into buying it. My parents helped, and they guaranteed the loan. If the bank foreclosed, they would have lost their home too."

His frown deepened. "It was foolish of them to do so."

Her voice sharpening at the criticism, she said, "Parents will do anything for their children. Or grandchildren. Even if they're not lucky enough to have a family fortune." Her father had retired and sold his country house and farm contracting business after a heart attack, moving into a small town house that ate up nearly all the proceeds. "You don't know what it's like not to have a lot of money. Or how it would feel to lose a child."

A spasm seemed to cross Marco's harsh features. He took a moment to compose himself, rearrange his face into a grim mask. "You are wrong," he said, his voice almost expressionless. "I have lost a child. My seven-year-old son died some years ago, along with his mother, my wife."

CHAPTER FOUR

AMBER'S breath stuck in her throat. She could feel her face going cold, then hot. Marco had been married? Had a child? Children, perhaps. "I'm so *sorry*," she said, stricken. "I had no idea."

He shrugged, apparently in total control of himself. "How should you? Your sister and I did not talk about such private things during our brief…liaison. But the day we met was the anniversary of their deaths." Only a slight thickening of his voice suggested emotion. "I had been persuaded by friends to join them for the festival. They meant well, but I was not in the mood, and when we became parted I had no desire to find them and continue celebrating. Instead I kept drinking on my own. A mistake. And continued to drink with your sister—more than I realised at the time. Another mistake."

"I'm sorry," Amber said again, "about your family. Do you—did you and your wife have other children?"

"No. She had a difficult pregnancy and the birth was also not easy. I was not willing to see her suffer like that again. But the boy…" His tone softened, and in his eyes Amber saw both pleasure and pain. "The boy was remarkably healthy, quick to learn, but also loving, affectionate, like his mother. And always laughing." He stopped, and his hand went to his heart for a moment before dropping to the table.

"No," he amended, shaking his head, "that is not true of any child. Sometimes he wept—even roared." Briefly amusement mingled with sorrow in the dark eyes. "He had a temper, like his father." The beautiful male mouth curved self-deprecatingly at the admission. "But that is how I remember him. Laughing."

Amber was unable to speak. This aspect of Marco Salzano she would never have expected. A loving, grieving father.

Marco picked up his glass and drained it, then turned to signal a waiter for more. "What about you?" he asked, nodding at her half-empty glass.

Amber shook her head, and took a couple of tacos to hide her reaction. They seemed to lodge in her throat so she drank some more wine. She didn't feel she could ask how Marco's son and his wife had died. An accident?

He had banished the sadness from his eyes. Now they were neutral, all emotion hidden. Obviously he wanted to dismiss the subject.

But didn't this change everything?

A man who had lost his only child and then thought he'd been presented with another wasn't simply selfish and possessive. His insistence on seeing the little boy was understandable.

Yet so was Azure's fear of losing her baby.

Amber's loyalty must be with her sister. Marco had uncovered their deception, but was he still hell-bent on seeing Benny? And if he did, would he even try to resist a natural urge to claim him and take him home?

The waiter brought more wine, but instead of drinking,

Marco turned it with his fingers on the stem of the glass, his eyes lowered so Amber couldn't guess at his thoughts.

Again Azure's voice echoed in her head, high with panic, while tears ran down her cheeks. *Over there men are in charge of everything—the family, business, politics... Their laws might even favour the father. Especially if he's as rich and respected as Marco Salzano.*

Amber's own foray onto the Internet to look up international law had turned up nothing reassuring. Even though Venezuela was signatory to an international convention on child custody, it appeared to have had little effect.

To Marco, Amber said, "Even if he *were* yours, think about the baby."

"I could give him everything a child needs."

"Everything?" She let her scepticism show. "He has a loving mother and father now. Two parents. What would you do—hire a nanny? And when she left, another one? Set up a pattern for the poor kid of being loved and left...or taken away?"

He picked up a taco, but instead of eating it began stabbing it into the sour cream until it disintegrated. Scowling, he wiped his fingers on a red paper napkin.

Only then he looked at her and said, "I would love him. And ensure he is well and happy. If necessary I may marry again, if I find someone suitable."

"To give him a mother? He already has one. Pity the poor woman you marry for expediency."

"She would be very well cared for, have everything she wants."

"Except your love."

"Love has many faces."

"If you want to show love for this...this *barely possible*

child of yours, the best thing to do is to go away and forget about him."

He searched her face. "You truly believe this?"

"His mother and father adore him. They are good people. Not rich, but he'll be well looked after."

"His 'father' left them apparently without a penny, about to be thrown out of their home. That is irresponsible."

"It was a mistake."

His mouth twisted again into a sneer. "Yet another mistake?"

"He'd changed his job, arranged for the mortgage money to be taken out of his wages when they were banked by his employer, but someone slipped up and the payment was delayed. He explained it all to Azure when he came home and told her he couldn't live without her…and their baby."

His eyes flashed at the last few words. "His mother is a liar and an extortionist, and she cheated on her husband. A court may not see them as fit parents for my child."

"You make her sound like a criminal! She's not. And she and Rickie weren't married when…when they were in Venezuela! And it was the only time she slept with anyone else."

"You cannot be sure of that."

"That's what she said, and I believe her. They've hardly been apart since they met in high school."

His expression showed scepticism again, cynicism. "They took a long time to marry."

"These days people are marrying later, sometimes after they've lived together for years. I don't know about your country, but it's common here." Her parents had opposed a teenage marriage, and later, Amber suspected, regretted it when the couple appeared to have shelved the idea in favour of travelling the world. "They were married seven months before the baby was born."

Marco was still twirling the glass, then he picked it up and drank, one gulp. "I insist on a DNA test," he said.

"No!" Azure clutched Benny to her breast as though Marco were there in person, about to snatch him away.

"Why not?" Again Amber was sitting in her sister's kitchen. She'd promised Marco that she would relay his demand in return for his assurance that he wouldn't approach Benny's mother. "If Rickie really is the biological father you have nothing to worry about."

"I can't." Azure's eyes were wide, afraid. "I won't."

"But you offered Rickie—"

"Dig it all up again? Risk our marriage a second time? Rickie was there when I had Benny, he was the first one to hold him, even before me. He's got up in the night to change him, feed him, walk him back to sleep when he's fussing. Benny adores him! It's Rickie's name on the birth certificate, and anyway, legally a woman's husband is the father of her baby. I checked."

"Really? Surely if another man can prove—"

"Prove *what?*" Azure cried. "That by some biological freak accident, a thousand-to-one chance, another man's sperm produced my child? Rickie's his *real* father."

Amber said, "Wouldn't it be better to know for sure?"

Vehemently Azure shook her head. "Rickie said Benny is his son and nothing can change that, and it's true. *It's true.*" Sobbing, she buried her lips in Benny's fragile neck, while tears dampened his tiny blue shirt. "This is all my fault and it isn't *fair* to make them suffer for it."

Amber rose from her chair and swiftly enclosed both

mother and baby in her arms. "Maybe the test could be done without Rickie knowing. If you're right, there's nothing to worry about, Marco will leave." Inside her something trembled. "You said it's a thousand-to-one chance."

"*No.* I won't do that behind Rickie's back. *I* would know. And if…if it did turn out wrongly…" Her anguished eyes teared up again. "I couldn't bear it! Please, Amber, make him go *away!*"

The final wail sounded exactly like six-year-old Azure begging her nine-year-old sister to chase away the monsters under the bed. Amber had invented an invincible magic spell to banish them and persuaded the smaller girl to see for herself that the monsters had disappeared.

She didn't think there was any magic that would force Marco Salzano to disappear.

"I will come now," Marco said when she phoned his hotel and asked to see him, hoping a face-to-face meeting would be more persuasive than a telephone conversation. "Unless you prefer to meet me here?"

"I'll meet you at the hotel," she said. Neutral ground. And last time they had talked there, they'd managed to come to some sort of agreement.

He met her in the lobby, which was milling with people. "We'll have to talk in my suite," he said. "There's some kind of convention going on."

People wearing name tags occupied every sofa and chair in sight, and both bars buzzed, standing room only.

"I'm sorry," Marco said. "I did not realise earlier. They must have been in meetings, but now…" As Amber hesitated he added, "You will be quite safe."

"I know," she said quickly. Although she'd never felt

really safe with Marco Salzano, she was certain he wouldn't normally offer deliberate violence to a woman. Still, something deep inside her whispered as they ascended in the lift to his floor that if he offered her another kiss like the one he'd pressed on her before…

The doors swept apart and she stepped out, burying the wayward thought. Tonight he hadn't touched her, except for a light hand at her waist as they crossed to the elevator—a natural courtesy, she supposed, for a man like him. Even that had sent tiny shivers of awareness along her spine. She wondered if all his compatriots shared that potent aura of rampant masculinity.

The suite was predictably luxurious, a king-size bed visible through an open door from the main room. On a polished desk a laptop computer had its screen open, printed papers beside it. A mobile phone seemed to be connected to the computer.

"You've been working?" Amber couldn't hide her surprise.

"The Internet is a wonderful invention." Marco motioned her to a chair before seating himself at the other side of a low round table that held two wine bottles and glasses, and a plate of savoury nibbles. "It is possible to conduct some of my business while I am away from home."

"I thought…" She stopped there.

"You thought?" he queried, lifting one of the bottles.

"That you'd no need to work," she said, a little embarrassed.

"You imagine, perhaps, that I spend my time playing polo and partying?"

"I hadn't really thought about it. I have no idea how you spend your time."

He held up the bottle. "You asked for white last time. I ordered a white and a red, both New Zealand wines that the hotel sommelier assures me are excellent. But if you prefer something else I can have room service bring it."

"I'm sure that will be fine." She nodded at the bottle.

He poured and sat back, picking up the conversation. "I run a large *hato* belonging to my family. We run a tourist business and raise beef for export. You would call it a ranch."

Amber shook her head. "That's North American. Here we'd probably call it a cattle station."

"Station? Ah." He smiled, nodded as though absorbing the information. "We have other business and community responsibilities also. Since my father died I have been in charge."

"We?"

"I have two sisters, one with children, and my mother. Also uncles and cousins who have a financial interest in the family holdings."

"It sounds like an empire."

He laughed, and it transformed his face, making him look younger, happy. Something tugged at her heart, and she remembered the grief she'd seen when he talked about his dead son. Was this how he had been before that tragedy?

He said, "I am no emperor. Merely a hardworking *llanero*. A cowboy," he translated, and then smiled as at a small joke. He certainly didn't look like any cowboy she'd ever imagined. "Also," he added, "of necessity, we have various irons in the fire. It is unwise in these times to put all your eggs in one basket."

"Your English is very good." He had even mastered the clichés.

"I spent some time in the United States as a teenager,

learning how they run their cattle industry and picking up a few other things."

He looked at her over his glass, the light falling through the big windows catching on the rich red of the wine, making golden shimmers. "Your sister—" he said "—has she agreed to have the baby tested?"

Amber tensed, looking down into her glass, then took a quick swallow for Dutch courage. "She…she said no."

Rushing on, she reiterated Azure's objections, making them as persuasive as she could. "Try to see it her way," she begged, seeing Marco's face set into austere lines. "A few hours with you compared with a lifetime—she hopes—with her husband. It's too late for you to claim the baby now, even if he does share your DNA. He belongs to Azzie."

Marco's expression didn't change, and she couldn't read what he was thinking. She went on, praying to get through to him. "Azure nurtured him in her own body for nine months, brought him into the world, and she'll do *anything* to keep him safe and happy. She was wrong to sleep with you, wrong not to be more careful. But she isn't the only one to blame, and removing him now from his parents, his home, his country, won't make it right."

Marco got up, taking his wine with him to stand at the window, looking out to where the lights of the city reflected into the dark harbour.

Amber realised her hands were clenched hard in her lap.

Marco made a small movement and she held her breath, but he didn't turn. "I believe I could get a court order," he said, still without looking at her, "to enforce a test."

So he'd been doing some research too. She got up and walked over to him. Only then did he swing round to face her. She said, "You loved your son who died, must have wanted what was best for him. But you can't replace a person with another one. I know you still grieve for your little boy. Can you inflict that grief on a mother—and a father—who feel the same about their…about this child?"

His mouth finally softened slightly from its fiercely held line. "You are a passionate advocate," he said. "Your sister is fortunate you are so eager to plead for her."

"You don't know how terrified she is," Amber said. "If you could see how much she loves Ben—"

He lifted his free hand and put his fingers over her mouth, silencing her. "Enough."

She didn't understand the way he was looking at her, even after he dropped his hand to his side. "Wha-what are you going to do?" she asked, dreading to hear the answer.

His voice sounded odd, very deep and a little blurred. He was staring at her face as though memorising it. "I cannot give you an answer now," he said. "It is not a matter to be decided on a whim."

Amber swallowed any protest she might have made. He was right; it was asking a lot of a man. Especially this man, who had suffered the loss of his family and then discovered he might have an unknown child. She nodded. "I understand."

"I doubt it." A dry note that had become familiar reappeared in his tone.

"I suppose that was a stupid thing to say." How could she possibly know, who had never had a child herself?

"I don't think you are stupid," Marco said. "Loyal, perhaps to the point of folly. Compassionate…loving. You and your sister are close? And also, you are beautiful."

Amber brushed off the last bit as Latin hyperbole. "Azure and I are very close. There's only the two of us."

"You are very alike."

She nodded. "But if you'd known my baby sister better, you wouldn't have mistaken me for her."

"Baby?" His brows rose.

In his eyes of course Azure was very much a woman. She'd even given birth, a rite of passage to womanhood that was more than Amber could claim.

Perhaps it was time to let her sister fight her own battles. But despite her initial reluctance she didn't regret taking part in this one. "I should go," she said. "You will think about…all this?"

"I have thought about little else since I arrived in this country."

"And please," she added, "don't do anything before telling me what you've decided?"

"In return for a promise from you," he said.

"Oh?" Cautiously she asked, "What?"

"Two promises. One, that you will not spirit the child away, nor help your sister do so. And two…have dinner with me one night. Tomorrow, perhaps?"

"I'm busy tomorrow night." She'd been invited to a hen party for an old school friend.

"When?" he asked, leaving it to her.

"Well, Monday night is free." Was this a date, or did he have some kind of negotiations in mind? He'd called her beautiful. Again that kiss came to the front of her consciousness, in all its mind-blowing delight. If he planned to follow up on it…

A stirring of anticipation made her step back. That wouldn't do! The sooner this disturbing, far-too-attractive man went back to Venezuela the better.

"Don't look so worried." He smiled, and she felt her

response like a ray of sunshine entering her body. She'd seen the effect of that smile on other women, but now he'd turned it on her she thought Azure would have had to be superhuman to resist it. "Finish your wine," he said, "before you leave me to my thoughts."

"I've had enough." She was relieved that her voice didn't sound breathless. "Thank you, it was very good."

He followed her to the door and leaned forward to open it for her, giving her a whiff of his subtle masculine scent. "I will phone," he promised, and brushed his lips across her cheek before stepping back.

A current of electricity of some kind seemed to shoot through her, not painful but wickedly pleasurable. She stood looking at him, her lips parted in astonishment.

A glow in his dark eyes held her for a moment.

"Good night," she said in a muffled voice.

As the elevator carried her to the ground floor she tried to analyse what had happened then. She'd never experienced anything like it before. Did the man carry some sort of secret high-tech gadget that he used to extraordinary effect on women? Highly unlikely.

A man like that, who emanated sex appeal from metres away without even looking at a woman, hardly needed any help, electronic or otherwise. But he threatened to ruin her sister's life. She'd be mad to let him into hers.

All weekend, with a mixture of dread and something like the feeling she'd had as a kid on Christmas Eve, Amber kept thinking of the coming Monday. On Sunday she visited Azure and watched Rickie playing with Benny. When Rickie picked him up and held him high the baby was totally unafraid, giggling back at his grinning father until Rickie hugged him close and planted a smacking kiss on his rounded cheek.

Amber's throat ached. Glancing at her sister, she saw the haunted look in Azure's eyes behind her smile.

When she got home the phone was ringing and she caught it in her bedroom before the answer machine kicked in.

"Are you all right?" a deep masculine voice asked when she'd breathlessly answered.

"Yes, I just got in." Her heart quickened its pace.

"Ah," Marco said. "I tried several times to reach you."

"You could have left a message on the answer machine."

"I didn't want to talk with a machine. I wished to hear your voice."

A strange sensation travelled from her throat to her diaphragm, and her hand tightened on the receiver.

"Are you there?" Marco demanded.

"Yes."

"Tomorrow night," he said. "I will come to fetch you—"

"No!" It was instinctive. Already her home was haunted by the memory of his forceful presence. Each time she entered her sitting room she recalled his formidable expression when he accused her of lying, the leaping flame in his eyes before he kissed her. And when she glanced at Azure and Benny's photograph on her dressing table she remembered shielding it with her body from Marco's probing gaze while she prayed he wouldn't see it.

When he spoke again his voice had regained the harsh, implacable note it had carried that night. "We had a bargain," he said. "An agreement."

"I meant, don't pick me up. I'll meet you."

In the pause that followed she somehow knew he was scowling. "Very well," he said at last, the clipped tone conveying his displeasure. "Does seven-thirty suit you? I will meet you in the lobby of my hotel and we will get a cab. I have been told of a very good restaurant in Parnell."

The restaurant was fabulous. Amber was glad she had dressed up a little, in a peacock-blue silk dress with a swathed bodice and wide, low neckline that showed off a paua-shell pendant, carved into one of the intricate spirals favoured by Maori artists. The swirling blues and greens of the polished shell perfectly complemented the dress.

They were led to a table across thick carpet that sank under her high heels. The waiter seated her in a velvet-up-holstered chair, presented a large leather-backed menu, shook out the intricate folds of the white napkin standing upright in front of her and laid it on her lap, then did the same for Marco.

Occasionally with friends she'd splurged for a special treat on something more expensive than pizza or cheap ethnic cafés. She had dated actors trying to impress her after snagging a highly paid advertisement or feature film role.

This was way out of her experience. She had heard of the restaurant and the eccentric genius of the chef who owned it. But she'd never entered its august portals within one of the refurbished heritage buildings that made Parnell a haunt of tourists and wealthy locals.

If Marco had hoped to impress her, she reluctantly conceded that he had. But this was probably everyday for him. She supposed he was used to expecting and getting the best and was prepared to pay for it.

She looked across the damask-covered table and asked, "Are you going to tell me what you've decided?"

"Later," he said. "Let us enjoy our meal first."

Amber wasn't sure she could enjoy anything with that vital decision still hanging fire, but he smiled at her and said, "Please relax, Amber. Worrying will spoil your appetite, and there is no need."

Did that mean he'd given up his quest? Strangely the idea brought with it a hollow feeling mingled with the leap of hope. Contradictory and confusing.

He was perusing the menu and she turned her attention to hers. Already she knew he wasn't to be cajoled into changing his mind. If he didn't want to talk now she would have to wait.

They had drinks while waiting for their order, and Marco kept the conversation light, asking questions about New Zealand life and people, querying her about her job. She told him anecdotes about her research work and the world of film and TV, and once or twice he laughed, giving her a frisson of half-guilty pleasure. It didn't seem right to be enjoying Marco Salzano's company.

The food when it came was perfectly presented, perfectly cooked, and the wines Marco chose in consultation with the wine waiter complemented each dish, also to perfection.

Amber didn't finish all her wines, served in huge glasses. She was wary of the effect alcohol might have on her. Marco ate and drank with relish and appreciation, obviously savouring the various tastes, but had only one glass of each wine.

Over a light dessert she asked him about Venezuela and watched a new expression come into his eyes as he described growing up on the vast grasslands of the Los Llanos district—riding horses and helping to muster cattle, and from the age of twelve helping conduct tours of his ancestral land. It was—without exaggeration, she gathered—the size of a small country. Pumas, jaguars, monkeys, ocelots and some animal called capybara still roamed its plains and jungles.

"Many of our wild animals are endangered species," he said. "Eco-tourism is big business for Venezuela. Our *hato* has been a wildlife reserve for the past thirty-four years, and we don't allow hunting."

"What about your cattle? How do they co-exist?"

"We lose a few to the big cats. But cattle make little impact on the land. In some places we have made canals to trap water for them, and the wild animals share in that."

After they'd finished eating he pushed away his plate, laid his forearms on the table and fixed his gaze on her. "I have, as you suggested, given this matter much thought. But—" he looked around at the other diners, mostly businessmen entertaining one another, or parties of the young and rich who were becoming rather raucous "—perhaps this is not the right place. We can have coffee at my hotel. And afterwards I will send you home."

She thought about it, then nodded. "All right."

The hotel was quieter now, and they sat in a dimly lit corner of the small bar, away from the few other patrons. Tense again, Amber picked up a white marshmallow from her cappuccino's saucer and let it melt in her mouth.

Marco seemed in no hurry, stirring sugar into his coffee. Then he put down the spoon and drummed long, lean fingers on the table for a couple of seconds before looking up. "You may be right," he said, "that the boy is best left with your sister and her husband."

Relief washed over her, and impulsively she stretched out her own hand and laid it on his. "Oh, thank you! It *is* the right thing, though I know it's hard for you."

Suddenly conscious of the warm, tensile strength of his hand, she made to withdraw hers, but with a lightning-fast movement he caught her fingers, almost crushing them before his hold eased a little.

"Wait," he said. "There are conditions."

Caution took the place of relief. "What conditions?"

For a moment he didn't speak. His thumb was, apparently absently, caressing her skin, which reacted to the slight roughness of his, giving off tiny, invisible sparks. He looked down and said, "I wish to make you a proposition." Then he raised his eyes to hers, darkly probing as if trying to enter her mind.

Amber stiffened. His English, although formal, was fluent—he must know the word had more than one meaning.

She tugged at her hand, and this time he released it. Her heart hammered unevenly. Emotions and thoughts tumbled over each other—anger, dread, a piercing and puzzling disappointment, hope that she was mistaken, and a shameful stirring of something too much like excitement.

His expression turned to amusement. "Not that," he said. "You think I would insult you so?"

Mortified, and annoyed that he could read her so easily, she said more sharply than she'd intended, "What, then?"

"Your sister's letter," he told her, "said nothing about a husband. I understood she was a single mother."

"At the time—"

"I know." He held up a hand, then went on. "I hoped that if she was not willing to give up her child I might persuade her to marry me and return with me to my home."

Amber's mouth opened and closed again.

He said, "It seemed the most practical solution. For the child's sake. Then you told me her husband had returned. And you begged me to leave them alone."

He paused again, and she said, "What do you want?" What conditions did he have in mind that would persuade him to do that? Foreboding filled her.

"I want *you*," he said with quiet implacability. As she recoiled, he captured her hand again, saying rapidly, "Not as my mistress, Amber. I want you to marry me. And give me a child."

CHAPTER FIVE

AMBER sat stunned. Marry Marco Salzano? After several seconds she managed to croak out, "You can't be serious!"

The room—the whole world—seemed to recede into some distant sphere, leaving them isolated in a dizzying vacuum. The only reality was herself and Marco, his eyes intense and without a hint of irony or teasing.

"I do not offer women marriage for a joke," he said. "I am very serious."

Shock beginning to recede, her brain returned to something resembling working order, and a creeping cold assailed her body.

Of course he hadn't fallen madly in love with her in the course of a week or so. He was suggesting a solution to an insoluble problem—a monstrous solution. With herself as some kind of female sacrifice. "That's…it's blackmail," she said.

He frowned. "It is negotiation. You are at liberty to refuse, but that is my offer."

From icy cold she'd gone to raging mad. "A convenient marriage and a substitute child?"

"You are angry." Stating the obvious. "Why?"

"Why?" Angry didn't begin to describe what she felt. "What did you expect? That I'd be flattered?"

His back straightened and his head lifted, his proud *hidalgo* ancestry coming to the fore. "It is not an insult to be asked to marry a Salzano."

"You didn't ask! You *demanded.* As the price of…of…"

"Of my giving up my son." He looked immovable. "I do not think it is too high a price."

"He's not your son!" She leaned forward to emphasise the words.

"I do not know that. However, if you accept my proposal I swear I will relinquish any claim to him except that of a fond uncle. Has he been baptised?"

"What?" The change of subject threw her.

"Does he have godparents? I would like to—"

"Yes!" she answered. "I'm one. And Rickie's brother."

"Then I will be an honorary godfather as your husband."

"You are *not* going to be my husband! You're out of your mind! Find yourself another brood mare."

She pushed back her chair, swept up her wallet and keys, and stalked towards the lobby, then outside where several taxis waited for custom. Sliding into one, she discovered that Marco had been right behind her and was in beside her before she'd even closed her door.

Instinctively she moved away from him, saying between her teeth, "Get out!" But her voice was drowned by his deep one giving the driver her address.

"He's not with me!" she told the driver.

The man turned. "Sir? If the lady—"

Marco said to him in a man-to-man, indulgent tone, "We had a quarrel, but she will get over it."

"Ma'am?" the driver queried. "That's your address?"

"Yes, but—"

"Give us a minute," Marco said. He turned to Amber. "I would prefer to continue our argument in private. When you calm down you will be able to see this more rationally. Is there not a saying, Never let the sun go down on anger?"

"The sun *is* down," she retorted. Childishly.

He gave a low laugh that inflamed her further. Wasn't that advice usually given to couples? *Married* couples.

His voice low, he said, "We agreed I would not contact your sister until I made a decision. I have decided. If you turn this down…" He shrugged.

Amber was silent. It seemed he really was serious.

The driver asked impatiently, "Are we moving or not? Do I turn on the meter?"

"All right," Amber said, defeated. "Yes."

She fastened her seat belt and tried to think rationally. Could she secretly take a sample of Benny's saliva, get it tested? Behind Azure's back and against her wishes?

What if he was Marco's child? All the reasons Azure gave for refusing the DNA test were valid, but if she were really certain he was Rickie's, surely she'd have agreed?

Stealing a peek at Marco's profile, she saw he looked grimly determined. This wasn't some spur-of-the-moment whim. He'd looked at the angles, weighed up the options and found a bargaining chip he could use, like the business-man he surely was. So much for hot-blooded Latin passion.

Suddenly she wanted to cry. For her nephew, her sister. Herself. Even for Marco. Her chest was tight, and something inside hurt in a way she could neither describe nor understand. She gazed blindly out of the window at the streetlights, the passing cars. She was still angry—furious.

And wouldn't admit even to herself that the anger was largely fuelled by that hidden, aching hurt.

When they arrived at her apartment, Amber didn't even try to stop him coming inside. She switched on the sitting room light, dropped her wallet on a red-box side table and faced him. She didn't sit down and didn't invite him to, either. This was no cosy conversation.

She said, "You can't really expect me to give up my home, my family, my job. Even my country!"

"You will not need a job. Your family may visit as much as they wish. I will pay their fares if necessary. You may go home at any time—after you have my child."

"And leave him—her, whatever—with you?" There was no way she'd ever be able to do that. She even missed Benny if she'd been away from him for more than a week or two.

Marco shrugged, but she saw his jaw clamp tightly for a second. "It will be your choice. In my faith, marriage is for life, but I will not coerce you to stay. Nor forbid you to see the child whenever you wish."

"Oh, that's generous!"

"Perhaps," he said softly, "more than you know."

"Supposing I can't have children?" she demanded.

His brows drew together. "Do you have reason to believe you cannot?"

"No," she admitted. "But it happens."

"Then we will see what can be done. I should warn you, if I find you are deliberately cheating me, I will not be held by promises."

Amber couldn't believe they were actually discussing this. Of course she couldn't do it. This dilemma wasn't even her problem.

Then she remembered Benny's bright little face beaming

at Azure and Rickie, thought of how her parents doted on their only grandchild, and felt a tug of pain at the idea of not having him in her own life. Her entire family would be devastated if Marco took him to South America. Rickie's, too; he had a large and loving whanau—his extended family.

"There must be another way," she muttered.

"You know the only way." As she stood there chewing on her lip, he crossed the carpet and said softly, "Don't torture your lovely mouth so."

She stopped the unconscious action.

His thumb soothed her stinging lip with a featherlike touch. He lifted her chin and equally gently kissed her mouth. It was so comforting, so tender that she didn't pull away instantly, liking it far too much before coming to her senses and stepping back, her whole body tingling.

"It will not be too difficult," he said, his voice a seduction in itself. "I promise I will be a considerate lover. My home is comfortable and well staffed, and my country has its own beauty. You will want for nothing."

The mention of a well-staffed home, so casually dropped, made her conscious of the enormous gap between their lifestyles. She wouldn't have any idea how to deal with servants. "I would never fit in," she blurted out.

"I assure you, my family will welcome my wife. My sisters have been urging me to marry again."

"Oh, stop!" she cried. Her hands going to her temples, she closed her eyes. Surely this was some idiotic dream. For one thing she was tempted to say yes, and in real life only insanity would have let her entertain for a millisecond the notion of marrying a stranger—a stranger who threatened her entire family.

But when she opened her eyes, Marco Salzano was still solidly real and present, reaching for her hands and pressing the right one to his chest so she could feel the beat of his heart, making her own increase its rhythm as he kissed her forehead, then quickly both cheeks.

"If you need time to consider," he said, his eyes like dark, liquid fire, mesmerising her, "I will wait." Then his mouth captured hers for a long moment, very lightly, as though he remembered her lower lip was still throbbing, and was being careful not to hurt her.

He stepped back and lifted her hands one by one, kissing each of them before releasing it. "But not too long," he said, before he turned and left her.

Standing like a living but scarcely breathing statue, Amber watched him go, heard the front door close behind him. Only then did she move, trying to shake off the alternately hot and then cold, shivery sensation that enveloped her.

"He's mad," she said aloud. And she'd be mad to even contemplate such a thing. Whatever they did in Venezuela, she reminded herself, heading for the bathroom as though walking underwater, a marriage of convenience—*his* convenience—was out of the question.

One of her friends had seriously considered marrying a gay friend so she could stay on in the United States after her visa ran out. Some people married for tax reasons.

That was different. She splashed her face several times with cold water, and was annoyed and dismayed at her reflection in the mirror. Her cheeks bore a faint flush, her lips were full and soft and red, and despite the harsh light the pupils of her eyes were huge.

She looked like a sleepwalker, but there was no doubt she was awake and aware.

She remained wakeful all night, alternately trying to find ways out of the impasse, and fantasising about being married to a man who with a mere look made her more conscious of her womanhood than she had ever been, and who could shatter her equilibrium with a brief touch of his lips on her cheek, her forehead, her hand, set her entire body on fire when he took her mouth under his with tenderness and consideration for a bruised lip.

Sex doesn't last, she told herself sternly, and for the nth time turned over in bed. Not at that level of intensity, anyway.

Then she remembered that his main interest in sex with her was to create a baby. A baby made to order.

She thumped a fist into her pillow, stared through the window at a sickle moon high in the sky. Marco found her sexually attractive, she knew. He had called her beautiful, and other things besides—loyal, compassionate and loving.

He too was surely capable of being all those things. He'd loved and grieved for his son and surely for his wife. Even after she died he'd apparently been in no hurry to remarry. He had shown concern when Amber felt sick that first night he'd come storming into her life like a dark avenging angel, and again tonight when he realised even before she did that in her agitation she was hurting herself.

Yet he was also capable of using her love for her family to force her into a loveless marriage. He was that ruthless in getting what he wanted.

But he'd promised to let her go once she had his baby.

Which left her without any romantic illusions. Once she'd fulfilled his need for an heir he wouldn't care if she left or stayed.

She closed her eyes, willing herself to sleep, but unable to banish from her mind Marco's intense, dark gaze, his gorgeous, sexy mouth and his deep, black-velvet voice with the hint of iron beneath its seductive cadence.

After work the next day she spent a couple of hours with colleagues in a nearby bar, celebrating the wrap of their current project. It didn't stop her thinking about Marco and his extraordinary offer, but it helped.

Having had a couple more glasses than usual she took a bus, which dropped her a block from her home. When she opened the door her phone was ringing.

"Amber!" Azure's voice was hushed. "Did you talk to him again? What did he say?"

The extra alcohol made Amber reckless, and less tolerant of the sister who had got her into this. She said, "Marco? He asked me to marry him."

"*What?*" Azure squealed. Then in a hurried whisper, "That isn't funny."

"I'm not joking." Echoing his words. "He wants me to have his baby."

The silence at the other end was rather gratifying, although Amber knew it was unkind to feel that way. In the background she could hear baby squeals and splashing, and Rickie's laughter. He must be bathing Benny. It sounded as though they were both enjoying it.

Finally Azure said, "He can't mean it."

"Why not?" Amber asked airily, oddly annoyed. "He thinks I'm beautiful." Recklessly she added, "And actually I rather fancy him."

Azure gasped. "You *can't*, Amber. I won't *let* you! Don't you realise the only reason he's asked is to stay close to Benny? What do you mean, he wants you to have his baby?"

For some reason hearing Azure say what Amber already

knew increased her irritation. She said, "He lives in Venezuela—that's hardly close. Do you want to change your mind about DNA testing?"

"What's that got to do with it? I told you, I'll never…" A pause, then, "Why are you asking?"

"Because he swears he'll never bother you and Benny if I give him a baby."

Azure was silent again for what seemed an age. Then she said, seemingly shaken, "You can't marry a man like that. This is all my fault. I'll do whatever you want."

She sounded so defeated Amber's annoyance died.

"I'll have to tell Rickie first," Azure said unsteadily. "I don't know if our marriage will survive, but keeping this mess secret isn't worth ruining your life too. Thanks all the same, Amber, for trying. You're the best sister anyone could have."

"Wait!" Amber felt wretched now. "Azzie, I love you and I love Benny. Marco's not all that bad. You didn't know, did you, that he had a son—and a wife? They died."

"That's…awful," Azure said. "But—"

"This isn't over yet," Amber urged. "I'll be in touch."

She had hardly replaced the receiver before the phone rang again. Marco said, "Are you all right? I have been trying to contact you all evening."

"I've been partying with friends." Not that he needed to know about her social life. Booze made her talkative. "Having a good time," she embellished, just so he wouldn't think she'd spent all day chewing her nails about him and his diabolical plan. Although she had.

Bueno, he said. "That's good."

"What do you want?" she asked.

"I have told you what I want, Amber." His voice descended to a deep purr, and she remembered that puma and jaguars prowled parts of his ranch—his *hato*. "I cannot stay away from home very much longer."

"I hope," she said, "you've realised how impossible—"

"Nothing is impossible," he contradicted her, "if one desires it enough."

And if one had unlimited money and power, she thought. "I talked to Azure," she reluctantly told him.

"Ah." A short pause. "What did she say?"

I'll do anything you want. You can't marry a man like him. But Amber remembered how her sister's voice had wavered, the dejection and defeat in her tone.

Amber took a breath. "No test."

For a moment the line was silent. She couldn't even hear him breathing. Then, "So. Do you have a passport?"

"Yes." She swallowed hard.

"I filled in an application today for a marriage licence, which I am assured will be available in three days, and I am arranging a visa for you to enter Venezuela, which should be ready within a few more days, after you sign some forms and provide a birth certificate. We can be married, say, a week from today."

Feeling as though she'd just entered an alternate universe, she stammered, "You…you don't waste any time."

"As I said, I cannot spare too much of it."

"I'm willing to go to Venezuela with you, but I thought we'd be married there, after…well, after I've met your family and…got to know you better."

For a few seconds he said nothing, and she hoped he was considering the option.

But when he spoke he said, "You can meet them—and get to know me—after we are married. It is simpler to have the legal part taken care of here, so that you enter my country as my wife. Do not be concerned that I will insist on my rights against your wishes. We do, however, have things to discuss. May I visit you now?"

"I'm surprised you're asking my permission," she said. He never had before, since he'd barged into her life, turned it upside down and put her emotions into a constant merry-go-round.

"You are still angry with me," he said. "If it is not inconvenient I will be there in fifteen minutes."

"How can I tell my parents I'm marrying a man I've only just met and flying off to the other side of the world?" Standing in front of the fireplace in her sitting room, Amber spread her hands. *"Next week?"*

Marco hadn't sat down, either. He regarded her from a couple of metres away, his dark gaze steady and implacable. "We fell madly in love at first sight," he suggested. "We cannot wait to be together, and I am anxious to introduce my new bride to my own family."

"No! I won't do that. Anyway they'd never believe it."

"Then don't tell them we are getting married. Say you are to visit my home and we will come to know each other, as you suggested. Later we will tell them all they need to know."

"You're asking me to lie to them?"

He raised an ironic brow and she said defensively, "I never actually lied to you!"

"What you tell your family is up to you." Apparently losing interest. "I will book a time with the registrar. Do you have a preference? Morning, afternoon? Not too late. I would like to fly out the same day."

"I don't care." Her face suddenly felt cold and pinched, and Marco frowned, taking her arm. "You should sit down."

Amber shook his hand away. "I don't need to sit down. I can't believe you mean to go through with this."

"I do not easily change my mind." His voice lowered to a seductive tone. "I hope you will not change yours." He raised a hand and the back of one finger traced the line of her jaw to her chin, barely touching her skin.

Then he tipped her face, still with one finger, and kissed her so gently she felt her insides helplessly melting, before he drew her closer into his arms and kissed her more deeply, thoroughly. He took his time until she could bear it no longer and kissed him back, their mouths melding in an intimate slow dance.

When he drew away at last his hand pressed her head to his shoulder, and he kissed the tip of her ear, then her hair. Unbelievably she felt safe, not wanting to move out of Marco's warm embrace. He murmured, "It is not my intention to make you unhappy, *querida*."

She knew what that word meant—*darling*. Her heart did something weird, as though a tiny stiletto had pierced it. How could he do this to her so easily?

With an effort she stepped back.

It wasn't fair. His appalling proposition suddenly seemed not only possible but almost thrilling. The only time she'd felt remotely like this was when she was standing on a high bridge over a narrow river, seconds from her first and only bungee-jump. The same mixture of adrenaline, anticipation and sheer terror.

Then the terror had been mitigated by the knowledge that her ankles were comfortably secured to a strong, safety-tested rope.

This was like jumping without one.

She should tell Azure she couldn't go through with this after all, accept her sister's valiant offer to agree to the test. Then it would be all over. *If* Benny's DNA didn't match Marco's.

Instead she said through dry lips, "All right. Whenever you like. Now please leave me alone."

CHAPTER SIX

"BUT, *Amber*..." Azure's voice on the phone line conveyed her dismay. "I told you I'd—"

"I haven't married him yet." Prevarication. "I'm going to Venezuela to get to know him and his family. It's an interesting country and Marco's ranch—I guess you know it's called a *hato* over there—sounds fascinating. They have fantastic birdlife—parrots, flamingos, hundreds of others. I've been looking on the Internet." There was a lot more information on the wildlife than the custody laws.

The Salzano *hato* was mentioned on several travel blogs, and one site had a potted history of the family. On another she learned that Marco was a board member of an organisation dedicated to helping the native population dispossessed in past centuries by the Spanish invaders. Opening a large tract of Salzano land to small-farmers, he'd housed their families and built and staffed a school and medical clinic. It had made him unpopular with some other big landowners and even, it was hinted, members of his own family.

Azure said uncertainly, "You can't seriously be thinking of marrying him!"

Amber hesitated. "For Benny's sake. Yes."

"He'd be part of our family!" Panic filled Azure's voice. "What if—"

"Do you have a better idea?" Amber's tone sharpened in exasperation. "I don't want Benny caught in a custody fight any more than you do."

Then, contrite, she said, "It's okay. *I'm* okay. I've never done a proper OE like you and Rickie." Heading from their two-and-a-bit islands at the bottom of the Pacific for their "Overseas Experience" was for young Kiwis a rite of passage. "This is my chance. It'll be an adventure."

She told her parents she had the chance of working on an eco-heritage site in Venezuela, had to leave the following week and didn't know how long she'd be away. They weren't unused to her taking off at short notice, though previously she'd gone no farther than Australia—just across the "ditch," so-called, although the Tasman Sea was actually two thousand kilometres of notoriously rough water.

Skirting the truth was becoming a way of life for her. A distinctly uncomfortable thought.

When she gave a similar story to her studio boss, he was surprised and not pleased, but an assistant was happy to take over her job. She wondered about subleasing her flat, and decided keeping one option open gave her some sense of security, although possibly a spurious one. She'd ask Azure to keep an eye on the place.

The flight to Venezuela was long and exhausting, despite the unaccustomed, for Amber, comfort of first-class travel.

Too churned up to make small talk, she reflected with something close to panic that she didn't know her companion well enough for anything more personal.

She opened a Spanish/English phrase book, and now

and then asked Marco to check her pronunciation. Sometimes she could see her effort amused him, but apart from crinkling about his eyes he kept a straight face. And occasionally he pointed out a difference between the standard Spanish in the book and Venezuelan variations.

When the cabin crew dimmed the lights she dozed while listening to a basic Spanish primer through an MP3 player, hoping the lessons would permeate her subconscious. But her mind kept going over the events of the past several days—lunch with her parents, dodging their questions with vague answers and keeping a smile on her face when she said goodbye. Then a farewell to her sister's family, evading Azure's efforts to get her alone and ignoring her worried eyes while chatting to Rickie and playing with the baby.

She gave Benny a last hug and he snuggled into her, stiffening her resolve. Then she hugged Azure again, whispering, "It's okay, Azzie. Everything's fine."

The wedding ceremony had been brief. It had rained and she'd been chilled in the pale-green dress and jacket that, after a great deal of mind-changing, she had hoped would be appropriate.

Marco had a carnation tucked into the buttonhole of his superbly well-fitted suit, and had handed her a small bouquet of sweet-scented freesias and cream rosebuds.

For some reason she choked up, wordlessly shaking her head as she took the flowers, then burying her face in them to hide her emotion. He'd taken her hand and kissed it, saying, "You are nervous, but it will soon be over."

Amber clamped her teeth then to stop a hysterical laugh.

Over? This was just the beginning.

* * *

After crossing the dateline and changing planes in Los Angeles and then Miami, by the time they landed at Simón Bolivar airport in Caracas Amber had no idea what the hour or even the day was back home.

Marco somehow had a car waiting for them with a driver who took them to a hotel in Caracas. She recalled that he had a place of his own in the city where he'd taken Azure. Perhaps he was being tactful. She looked longingly at the two beds in the room they were ushered into.

Marco said, "You need to rest properly before I introduce you to my family. Also, I have some business to conduct in the morning. I will make it as brief as possible, and I hope you will not mind being alone for a short while. Which bed would you like?"

So he didn't intend to share one, but right now she was too tired to feel anything. She dumped her shoulder bag on the closest one and said, "Do you want the bathroom?"

"We have two." Indicating the nearest of two doors.

Amber showered, and left the bathroom wearing a synthetic satin nightshirt. By the time Marco emerged from the other bathroom she was in bed and drifting into sleep.

She woke to full daylight and saw him standing before the window, dressed in a white shirt and casual sand-coloured trousers. When she sat up he must have heard the rustle of the sheets, and turned. "Good morning," he greeted her. "Do you feel better?"

"What time is it?" she asked. "What *day* is it?"

"Eleven o'clock," he answered. "And it is Wednesday."

Still? They'd left on Wednesday. Crossing the dateline had gained them an extra day.

She ran a hand over her sleep-tumbled hair. "You should have woken me."

"As I said, I had business in Caracas, and you looked much too...blissful to be woken. You sleep like an angel."

Disconcerted that he'd been studying her while she slept, Amber said, "You've been out already?"

"Yes. Now I am yours for the rest of the day."

Hers? She was very sure Marco Salzano was his own man and no-one else's. On the other hand, she was his—bought and paid for—until further notice.

She threw back the covers, not missing the interested study he made of her legs as she swung her feet to the floor and the nightshirt slid up. Quickly she stood, and after grabbing some undies and clothes from her suitcase made for the bathroom again.

When she came out Marco was lying on the other bed, his hands behind his head. He watched her replace her things in the suitcase and take out a brush and hair tie. She could see him in the mirror as she brushed out her hair into a ponytail and twisted the tie around to hold it. She'd put on fawn cotton trousers and a sleeveless shirt patterned with forget-me-nots. Air-conditioning cooled the room but she suspected that outside it would be hot.

Marco said, "If you wish we can stay here for another day or two. I will show you our capital city."

Amber put away the brush without facing him. "I thought you were in a hurry to get home."

"Yes," he conceded, getting off the bed, so that he was by her side when she turned from the suitcase. His hands went to her waist, lightly holding her, and quickening her blood. "But I'm aware that you find our...circumstances difficult. At the moment you look like a doe facing a hungry puma. A little time together before returning to Hato El Paraíso may help you to adjust."

Amber wasn't thrilled at the analogy comparing her to a helpless animal, and had no particular wish to explore the city where he'd met her sister. Thinking about that made her voice cold, her words sharp. "A tour of Caracas won't help me adjust to being coerced into marrying you."

For an instant his hands tightened on her waist. Then he dropped them, stepping back, and said equally coolly, "Very well. I have some phone calls to make. Then we will eat lunch and this afternoon we will be home."

Over lunch the mood was strained. Marco's phone calls had been made in Spanish, and he had not told her what they were about. She let him order for her from the extensive, confusing menu, and he chose *empanada de pollo,* a sort of deep-fried turnover stuffed with chicken, saying it was a local dish he thought she would enjoy. She found it was a treat after airline food.

"Are your family expecting us—me?" she asked him. "Have you told them? Who actually lives at your… hacienda?" She was growing increasingly nervous, wondering what on earth his relatives would think of him bringing an unknown woman from the other side of the world home as his wife.

"My mother, my younger sister Ana Maria, my cousin Elena who organises the tourist part of our business and helps with the visitors. Another cousin, Diego, acts as a guide also. He has a degree in zoology, very helpful when scientists and ecologists come to the *hato.*"

"Your father…?" Amber asked tentatively.

"My father died some years ago," Marco said. "I spoke to my mother this morning. She will have informed my other sister that I am bringing home my bride. Paloma is married and has two delightful daughters. It would not surprise me if Paloma brings them and her husband to Hato El Paraíso as soon as she hears the news. She lives in Barinhas, our closest city. They will all want to meet you." He paused. "You will, *por favor,* not complain about your new husband to them. They are not to blame for my actions."

"Do you think I'd want to tell anyone I was forced to marry you?"

He said quietly, "I used no force. The choice was yours."

"Some choice!" She flashed him a hostile glance. "Between the devil and the deep blue sea."

"And I am the devil?" He gave her a sardonic look.

Amber remembered thinking when he first stormed into her life that he looked like Lucifer, the beautiful, arrogant angel so filled with pride he had challenged God Himself.

She shook her head. "You're only a man," she reminded him, and he laughed.

"That is true," he said, giving her a lazy, amused once-over that held appreciation. "And you, *querida,* are a woman. My wife."

He sounded so self-satisfied she flared again. "I may be your wife—legally—but I'm not your darling! This whole thing is a farce."

A brief shadow seemed to cross his aristocratic features. "I understand your resentment—" he said.

"Then why are you—"

Marco overrode her. "—But you will please curb it in front of my family. Or anyone else." Despite the phrasing, it was undoubtedly an order. "To the rest of the world we are passionately in love."

"That's difficult to fake."

"You are good at pretence."

She flushed, and he placed a hand over hers on the table.

"I will make it as easy for you as I can," he said. "Let us take one day at a time, hmm?" He lifted her hand and kissed it, sending a reluctant shiver of warmth through her, and smiled a little crookedly before releasing her.

When Marco turned coaxing this way he was hard to resist. She wished her stupid heart would behave itself instead of going mushy, and reminded herself how ruthless he was at getting his way.

They took another flight to Barinhas, and after leaving the city she saw distant snow-capped mountains, some towns and tiny settlements. Thick vegetation covered the lower mountain slopes and smaller hillocks, and Amber was surprised to see palm trees waving their distinctive fronds above the other trees. Marco pointed out places of interest on the changing panorama far below.

After landing again they were driven to a remote corner of the airport, where a twin-engine plane waited outside a hangar.

She saw the logo of a leaping jaguar on the side, its lean, golden hide spotted with black rosettes, the muscular body at full stretch and sharp teeth painted brilliantly white. Beneath it were the words "Hato El Paraíso."

"You have your own plane?" she blurted out.

He said matter-of-factly, "It is useful for transporting our guests. And sometimes we need to get from place to place quickly, even on our own land. We also keep a helicopter."

Marco piloted the small plane himself, flying over a vast, flat plain of grassland changing from blue-green to straw-coloured, studded with occasional trees, and here and there browsed by huge, scattered herds of cattle whose pale hides merged into the grass. Muddy rivers snaked across the landscape through stands of junglelike trees and shrubs along their banks.

Eventually the aircraft glided in over what appeared to be a village dominated by a large, U-shaped, tile-roofed building, before landing on a concrete airstrip several hundred metres away.

As Marco helped Amber out into warm, dry air, a truck took off from one of the outbuildings near the hacienda and, leaving a cloud of dust behind it, sped across the ground to come to a halt only a few metres from them.

A brown-skinned man with a crinkled face under a battered cowboy-style hat jumped from the driver's seat, directing a burst of rapid Spanish at Marco, who introduced the man as José.

José gave Amber two jerky little bows, and began enthusiastically unloading the luggage—mostly Amber's—and stacking it on the truck.

Amber and Marco climbed into the cab beside him and within minutes they arrived at the big house. An impressive colonnaded portico shaded wide steps leading up to a tiled terrace and a heavy, carved, open door, brass-studded and set into a whitewashed wall.

Two women appeared, one middle-aged with greying dark hair pinned in an elegant chignon, expertly applied make-up accentuating deep-set brown eyes and a full mouth. The other was young and also beautifully made up, with long curls arranged to look casual, like the perfectly fitted jeans she wore with a scarlet knit top.

"Buenas tardes, Madre," Marco said to the older woman, his hand on Amber's waist guiding her forward.

She said carefully, *"Buenas tardes, Señora Salzano."*

His mother's smile seemed strained as she greeted Amber with a kiss on her cheek.

Introduced to Marco's younger sister, Amber didn't miss the rather concentrated stare Ana Maria had given her, but the girl smiled when Amber held out her hand in greeting.

"You speak Spanish?" Ana Maria asked in English.

"I'm afraid not much," Amber confessed. "But I've been practising the basics. I will have to learn more."

Marco said, "You can help her, Ana Maria, and perhaps improve your English at the same time."

They moved inside and Amber was struck by how cool and dark it was. As her eyes adjusted she saw a wide passageway, its high ceiling supported by dark beams. An antique hall table with sturdy carved legs held a telephone and a bulbous terracotta bowl of flowers.

José was already on his way upstairs with several bits of luggage after consulting Señora Salzano, and Marco, his laptop slung over his shoulder and hers in his hand, led Amber the same way, saying they would rejoin his mother and sister in a few minutes. The room he took her to was spacious and featured an enormous carved bedstead covered with an elaborately embroidered spread and heaped with satin pillows in shades of red and gold.

All the furniture looked old, though lovingly polished, and the floor was dressed with a large woven rug. Two long, screened windows let in light and air, a breeze stirring the heavy curtains at the sides.

As José put down the cases and bags and quickly left, Amber skirted the bed, trying not to look at it, and went to stand at a window overlooking a courtyard surrounded by potted flowering plants. Beyond that a blue-tiled swimming pool shimmered in the afternoon sun.

"Do you want the bathroom?" Marco asked, indicating a door she hadn't even noticed.

"Later," she said.

He nodded, took a shirt from one of two huge freestanding wardrobes and entered the bathroom. The walls must be a foot thick, she thought, noting the depth of the door and window recesses.

When Marco emerged she scooted by him with an armful of clean clothing, make-up and toiletries. There was nothing wrong with what she had on, but the fresh-from-the-beauty-parlour appearance of the two Venezuelan women had made her feel like a country mouse.

When she emerged more than a few minutes later Marco gave an approving look at her jade-green silk shirt and bronze-coloured skirt worn with high-heeled gold sandals, taking in her smoothly brushed hair and re-done make-up.

Downstairs they found his mother and sister in what appeared to be a family room. Another young woman, about Amber's own age, was introduced as Elena, a cousin.

Not a hair was out of place in her smoothly combed-back coiffure, intricately plaited and pinned at the back. Bright lipstick highlighted her pretty mouth and flawless skin. A white blouse and wine-coloured skirt showed off an hourglass figure, the slim waist emphasised by a broad tooled-leather belt with an ornate brass buckle.

She gave Amber a cool smile before turning to Marco and speaking to him in rapid Spanish.

He said, "We will speak English, Elena. Amber does not know Spanish."

Elena's finely shaped brows rose. "*¿Qué?* None at all?"

"A few words," Amber said. "But I hope to learn it."

"I speak French, English, German and some Japanese," Elena told her. "As well as Spanish, of course."

Amber wasn't going to try competing with such a list of talents. She said, "You must be a great asset. Marco told me you organise the tourist business here."

"I help where I can." Elena looked cautiously pleased. "Marco is doing a wonderful job of protecting all the family's assets, even creating new ones. Although some of the old uncles make it difficult."

"Oh?" Amber was interested.

"They are stuck in the past, not understanding we must move with the times or lose our heritage." Elena gave a small laugh. "But of course you know nothing of the economics and politics of our country."

How could she be so sure? However, Amber was conscious that her knowledge was limited and not firsthand.

Marco took her arm and guided her to a wide cowhide sofa where he sat beside her.

A young woman introduced as Filipa brought in coffee on a tray, then left the room, and Señora Salzano poured for them. She asked Amber a few stilted questions in English, mostly about her family, but was obviously relieved to lapse into Spanish when addressing her son.

The room was large but comfortably furnished with deep chairs, convenient side tables, and a state-of-the-art entertainment centre complete with an enormous TV screen.

"You like television?" Ana Maria asked her, seeing her looking at it. "I love to watch the *telenovela*."

"English," Marco chided his sister. And to Amber, "She means soap opera. She and her girlfriends are all hooked on those silly stories. They like to cry over them."

Ana Maria protested, "You are a man! You cannot understand the emotions of women."

Suspecting that was true, Amber said, "Actually I like stories that deal with relationships." With a woman-to-woman smile at Ana Maria, she added, "Men do seem uncomfortable with them."

Marco gave her a piercing look and she wondered if the remark came under the ban on showing her family the real nature of their marriage, but he told his sister, "Amber worked in television."

Ana Maria's eyes widened, and even though she seemed a little disappointed when Amber explained she wasn't an actress but a behind-the-scenes worker, she was happy to chat on about TV, fashion and American film stars.

Later the other sister arrived as predicted, with her husband and children. Paloma had the same faultless appearance as Señora Salzano and Ana Maria.

The girls, aged seven and five—delectably attired in matching frilled dresses, their hair tied with ribbons—ran to their uncle Marco, who effortlessly lifted each of them high in the air before giving them a kiss and hug, and made them giggle with jokes in Spanish.

Amber shouldn't have been surprised. His longing for a child was the reason Marco had brought her here because he'd lost his own son. He was capable of loving children. And obviously fond of his sister and mother.

One day he might even be fond of her.

CHAPTER SEVEN

AT EIGHT o'clock Filipa, the maid, reappeared, and the whole family repaired to another big room where they sat down at a large table.

The meal was light and leisurely, with conversation in both English and Spanish. Everyone used their hands to illustrate a point—even Marco—although she hadn't noticed him doing so before. She guessed that he tempered his mannerisms to the company he was in. Trying to copy the local etiquette, she kept her hands above the table and when she was finished left a little food on her plate and placed her knife and fork sideways with handles on the tabletop like everyone else.

"Have you had enough to eat?" Marco asked her softly.

She nodded. "It was delicious."

He apparently relayed that in Spanish to his mother, and the *señora* smiled and nodded at her. No one seemed in a hurry to move, and Amber tried to hide a yawn. Embarrassed, she murmured, "Excuse me. It's been a long journey."

Marco gave a quiet laugh and pushed back his chair, saying, "I will take you up to our room." He spoke to his mother, then he pulled out Amber's chair for her to a chorus of understanding *"Buenas noches."*

Marco laid a hand on her waist as they ascended the stairs, and she wondered if he looked on this as their wedding night—the night she'd anticipated with very mixed emotions, encompassing dread and rather mortifying expectation and a whole lot in between.

A sturdy, grey-haired woman wearing a black dress was coming down the stairs, and Marco stopped to kiss her cheek and introduce her to Amber. "Concepcion has cared for the whole family," he said, "since my sisters and I were children. We could not do without her." He said something in Spanish to her, perhaps a translation, and she laughed and lightly slapped his arm before turning a bright, beady stare filled with curiosity on Amber. After a moment she gave a small nod and burst into a torrent of Spanish.

"What did she say?" Amber asked as she and Marco continued on their way.

"Too much," he answered. A glance at his face showed her an unsmiling, rather forbidding expression. But his voice changed to a lighter note and he said, "She wishes us well, and that you will give me many healthy children."

He opened the door of the room and switched on a light. "I will leave you to get yourself to bed," he said. "In an hour or so I will be back."

Did he expect her to wait for him? So they could consummate their bizarre marriage?

She stood indecisively where she was, and he touched her cheek with an index finger. "You are still tired," he said. "I will not disturb your sleep. Do you need anything?"

She said no, and he withdrew, closing the door.

The bedclothes had been turned down, her gold satin pyjamas laid across the left side of the bed, and the magnificent cover neatly folded on the box at its foot. Her luggage had gone, and when she opened a wardrobe she found her skirts and trousers and dresses hanging there. Her hairbrush and make-up were arranged on the dressing table.

She found her toiletries in the bathroom, alongside unused soaps, bath oils and bottles of bubble bath she'd noticed earlier. A fresh fluffy towel had replaced the one she'd hung on the brass rail after her shower.

Ten minutes later she slid into the big bed between crisp linen sheets and switched off the bedside light. Another glowed at the far side of the bed, and she turned her back to it.

Images of the past couple of days drifted across her closed eyelids: the various planes with their droning engines; the changing views from her window seats, which Marco had insisted she take; the seemingly arbitrary way night changed to day and then night again; and above all Marco, the volatile, determined, sexy and scary stranger to whom she was, unbelievably, married.

She woke to the sound of birds screeching and twittering. A chink between drawn curtains at the window showed a glimmer of light, and she could faintly hear the shower running.

Quickly she looked at the other half of the bed and dimly saw the sheet flung back in a heap, the pillow dented. Marco had slept there and she'd never even known.

Curious about this place that was his home, she left the bed and parted the curtains further. Daylight was turning the sky grey, edged with pale, luminous pink, and a tiny bird hovered at the window, its wings an almost invisible whirr of movement. She'd never seen a hummingbird before, and watched with fascination until it flew off and disappeared into a nearby tree.

Other birds were distantly silhouetted against the sky, soaring alone or erupting in dense flocks, and a group of multi-coloured parrots streaked across her vision as the bathroom door opened. She turned and Marco emerged, a towel slung about his hips, his hair damp and uncombed. He looked perfectly at ease and very sexy. She couldn't help appreciating his strong, muscular body.

"Ah," he said. *"Buenos días."* His gaze took in the enveloping pyjamas, a hint of amusement in his eyes when they met hers again, and he came towards her.

Her body tensed and something fluttered in her throat.

Marco halted, his eyes narrowing. "Don't look at me so."

"I don't know what you mean."

"As if you expect me to leap on you like some wild beast."

He turned away to stride to a massive chest of drawers and after dropping the towel pulled on underpants that fitted taut over his lean flanks, then jeans and a white tee.

"I have work to do," he said tersely, picking up a comb without looking at her. Dragging it through his hair, he said, "I will ask Filipa to bring you breakfast. What time would you like it?"

"I'd rather have my breakfast when everyone else does."

"Later, then. Eight o'clock. I thought you would sleep longer. This morning I must join the *llaneros*. I will try to be here for lunch. Go back to bed."

"I'm awake now," she said. "I might go for a walk, explore a bit."

"Not alone." He put the comb down and faced her. "Ana Maria may take you out. Or I will myself, later. I regret I must leave you now, but some problems have arisen while I was away."

She breakfasted a couple of hours later with his mother, sister and cousin, the table offering pineapple slices, scrambled eggs with corn patties called *arepas,* and cheeses, rolls and jam with iced fruit juice and coffee.

Afterwards Ana Maria took her on a tour of the house, its airy rooms cooled by large ceiling fans, the tiled bathrooms modernised by up-to-date plumbing and fittings.

One wing was for visitors, the rooms furnished simply but with comfortable beds and adjoining bathrooms. "We get a lot of bird-watchers and naturalists," Ana Maria said. "And backpackers, from all over the world."

The kitchen area, presided over by a small woman with a big smile, was vast. A long, scrubbed wooden table stood at its centre, and a huge old wood stove vied with a gleaming stainless steel electric cooker and oven, a huge dishwasher and two large fridge/freezers.

In the living rooms the heavy, dark furniture wasn't crowded together, nor cluttered by too many ornaments, adding to the cool, spacious look of the rooms. Pictures and woven rugs decorated the white walls.

Marco's office was on the ground floor. When Ana Maria knocked and opened the door, Elena looked up from a computer set on one of two large desks, asking rather abruptly, "What do you want, Ana?"

Amber said hastily, "Let's not disturb Elena."

"What else would you like to see?" Ana Maria asked.

"Is it dangerous to take a walk on my own, if I don't go too far?" It shouldn't be difficult in the flat landscape to keep the hacienda in sight. Amber hadn't forgotten Marco's warning, but his assumption she would obey his injunction not to walk alone rankled a little.

Ana Maria shrugged. "The big cats don't come near inhabited areas, usually. But it is not very interesting. If you want to see animals and birds I will show you."

"I don't want to take you from your studies."

"*No problema.* I can study another time. You will need a wide hat," Ana Maria advised, "to protect your complexion. I will lend you one of mine."

In a well-used, four-wheel-drive vehicle, they drove along a dusty unsealed road leading away from the hacienda. Amber saw a large brown form ahead, like a big fat dog sitting on the road, but as they drew closer it more nearly resembled a giant guinea pig. "Is that a capybara?" she asked.

"You know of them?" Ana Maria seemed surprised.

"From the Internet. The largest rodent on earth?"

"*Sí.*" Ana Maria stopped so they could get out and, after allowing Amber to photograph it, nudged the apparently sleeping animal aside. It huffed grumpily off on its short legs and settled in the grass beside the road.

It wasn't the last they saw, nor the last that had to be moved, after they began crossing the grass on narrow roads built several feet higher than the surrounding land.

"To trap some of the water after the wet season," Ana Maria explained, "so it doesn't dry up completely."

"Do you help guide the tourists?" Amber asked her.

"Sometimes, when I'm home. I am studying social science at university," she said, "but now I am between semesters."

A little later she told Amber, "Marco has been terribly secretive about you. We didn't even know he had a sweetheart until he telephoned and said he was bringing home his bride! It is so romantic! Did he really go all the way to New Zealand to ask you to marry him?"

"Something like that." Amber tried to smile. "What *did* he tell you?" They had better synchronise their stories.

"Only that he had met a New Zealand woman some time ago and had not forgotten her. She—you wrote to him, and I guess he wrote back. Or e-mailed. Love letters?" Curiosity and mischief danced in Ana Maria's dark eyes. "From my brother?" As if she found it difficult to imagine.

"Not exactly," Amber murmured.

Fortunately Ana Maria didn't demand any elaboration. "And you too were unable to forget."

Amber supposed she should make some comment. "Marco's not easily forgotten."

"He said you were beautiful and clever."

Clever? That could be a double-edged word. As for beautiful, perhaps there was novelty value in being fair-skinned and fair-haired where most people were darker.

"And," Ana Maria continued, "he had to marry you quickly so he could bring you back with him in case you changed your mind. But you wouldn't have, would you? You are in love with my brother, *sí?*"

"Why else would I have married him?" Amber made her voice light, erasing all trace of irony.

"Of course our mother would like a proper church wedding. But Marco said wait until you have settled, got used to us all. *Mi Madre* tried to insist, but Marco...once he makes up his mind—" Ana Maria shrugged "—he is like a rock. You can push and push but get nowhere."

Tell me about it. Amber forced a smile.

Eventually they left the road to go cross-country, where

tracks in the tall grass showed other vehicles had taken the same route to a riverside where capybaras swam with frogs and turtles, and butterflies floated like confetti through the trees. But most ubiquitous of all were the birds—parrots of all colours, wading birds and swimming birds, geese bending the branches of trees, storks and wrens, vultures, birds Amber had never seen nor imagined. She had used up all the storage on her video and still cameras by the time Ana Maria said it was time to leave.

Lunch was served to the women at two o'clock in the dining room. Filipa brought cool fruit drinks and a beef and rice dish, followed by a fruit dessert. Marco arrived late, going upstairs to change before joining them.

Afterwards Señora Salzano went to her room to rest. Elena disappeared too and Ana Maria took what looked like a textbook to the back of the hacienda, where a wide shaded terrace bordering the courtyard held chairs and small tables, and a couple of loungers.

Alone with Amber, Marco asked, "Can you ride a horse?"

"For a while my sister and I belonged to a pony club."

"I will take you riding when it is cooler and more animals are likely to be about. Now you should rest."

"Is that what you do in the afternoon?"

"Often I do paperwork, although much of it is done on a computer, not paper. My study is cool. But if you wish we can have a siesta together." A gleam entered his eyes, and hers shied from it.

"I'm not used to the idea of a siesta," she said. "I'd rather swim, if that's all right. I'm sure you have a lot to attend to after being away."

"As you say. Elena has left me a pile of correspondence." He turned towards his study, and Amber went upstairs for her swimsuit and a towel.

The pool was enclosed by a high, white-painted wall with a wooden gate. At one end of the enclosure a tile-roofed, open structure sheltered a barbecue and several chairs and tables, and sun-loungers were placed on the wide surround.

The water looked invitingly cool and sparkling clean, and after the first shock on diving in and a few laps of Australian crawl, Amber turned on her back and floated.

A flock of multicoloured birds passed across her vision, and she watched them out of sight. The sound of the gate clicking drew her attention, and she flurried upright as Marco, wearing bottle-green swim shorts that revealed rather than concealed his masculinity, discarded the towel slung over his shoulder and took a long, shallow dive, coming up less than a metre from her.

Water streamed from his flattened hair, which he shoved back with his fingers as he stood waist deep. His teeth gleamed white in a smile, and she could see herself in miniature, reflected in his dark, glowing eyes.

"I thought you were working," she said.

"It was hard to concentrate." He didn't touch her but she felt his gaze like a lingering touch as it encompassed her, taking note of the low cut of her flower-patterned bathing suit, and the way it clung to her breasts, waist and hips and was cut high at the thigh. "I thought of my new bride alone in the pool. It did not seem right."

She had thought the suit rather modest, falling for its splashy hibiscus flowers in hot-pink, orange and yellow against a blue background, and had chosen it instead of a bikini last summer. Yet she had never felt as naked as she did now, with Marco's eyes lit by the unmistakable flame of desire, and his much more nearly nude, magnificent body within touching distance.

He looked as though he'd like to devour her. Momentarily she recalled the white-painted teeth of the jaguar on the side of his plane, and a small shiver passed over her.

"You are cold?" he said.

"No." The water felt quite warm now. But her voice sounded thin, wary.

His smile vanished. "I will not rape you, Amber."

He'd seen her flash of alarm and correctly interpreted it. Chagrined that she'd shown panic, she said, "You have no need to, do you? You know you've got me over a barrel."

Marco cocked his head. "A barrel? The picture is—" He raised a dark eyebrow and broke off, shaking his head. "I don't know the expression."

"It means, I will have to sleep with you because you won't let me go until I have your baby."

His mouth compressed and she saw his jaw go tight. "It is what you agreed to," he acknowledged. "Are you contemplating breaking our bargain?"

"No. Unless you've thought better of it."

"That is not an option," he warned harshly. "We will not speak of it again." He turned and began swimming with long, somehow angry strokes to the deep end of the pool.

Amber lifted her feet and swam to the other end. She reached the short ladder and was climbing out when a hand closed around her ankle.

Marco said, "Come, it is too soon to leave. You have hardly begun to cool off."

"I'm cool enough."

He released her ankle, but before she could move he had his hands at her waist, hauling her back into the water.

Consumed by the anger that had been simmering below the surface since he'd first suggested she marry him, Amber tried to kick backwards, but the water made it a feeble effort and she heard Marco's low laughter, his breath at her ear. His arms went about her waist and her fury increased. She squirmed, turning to beat at him with her fists, thudding against his chest, his face, anywhere she could reach, until he drew in a hissing breath and she knew with a mixture of triumph and horror that she'd succeeded in hurting him.

He dragged her wrists down with implacable hands and clipped them behind her, pulling her against him. She could tell he was aroused, but his eyes glittered with temper that made her heart jump in fright.

CHAPTER EIGHT

"You will not strike me," Marco said, his voice deep and quiet but laced with steely purpose, "ever again. I will not allow it. You understand?"

Amber stared into his eyes, determined not to drop her gaze and let him win, think he'd cowed her.

"I'm not a servant!" she said. "Or a child. You can't—" *give me orders.* But he didn't allow her to finish.

"Then do not act like a child," he said.

He had a point—she'd never hit anyone since she was ten and Azure only seven and a quarrel had turned physical. Both of them ended up crying—not so much because the marks of Azure's teeth were clearly visible on Amber's arm, and Amber had a handful of Azure's hair, but because they'd upset themselves by hurting each other. Now she felt a similar mixture of rage and misery. But she said, "Then don't you act like a Neanderthal! Is that how Venezuelan men treat their women?"

"I did not harm you," he argued. "Another man might have hit you back. I will never strike a woman."

"You *grabbed* me to force me to do what you wanted." She glared defiance, and perhaps it was surprise at her standing up to him that momentarily flickered in his eyes.

"I merely wished to suggest you stay a little longer. On my way here I passed Ana Maria and she knew you were already swimming. It would have looked odd if you left immediately after I joined you. I 'grabbed' you in play. At first I thought you too were playing." The grimness in his expression was replaced by a rueful curve of his mouth. "I was not aware I had married a little hellcat."

"I'm not!" Amber protested. "It's years since I lost my temper like that." She shifted but he still held her. "I suppose," she admitted, "I overreacted. Sorry I hurt you."

"*De nada.* It was nothing." He paused, then said rather stiffly, "I also am sorry if I upset you."

Amber gave a jerky nod of acknowledgement. He'd apologised, and she didn't carry grudges.

"I think," Marco said thoughtfully, "that I may have a bruise…right here." Touching the skin just below his lower lip, he added lightly, "You could perhaps kiss it better, hmm?"

Amber went very still. There were a bare couple of centimetres between them, and she felt the heat of his body despite the cool water lapping about them.

"Is that not what you do after a quarrel?" he asked, scarcely above a whisper. "Kiss and make up?"

Somehow his words, and his almost nude body, so tantalisingly close to hers with its flimsy, wet Lycra covering, created a potent, sensual aura that she couldn't—didn't want to—resist.

This man was her husband, unlikely though that had seemed only days ago. She had promised to give him her body, make love with him—or at least have sex.

"Well?" he queried softly, and she realised he was waiting for her to make the first move, trying to demonstrate to her that he wouldn't coerce it.

Sometime she had to accept that this was why she was here, that he had a right to ask her to fulfil her part of the devil's deal they'd made. She should be grateful for his patience.

She tilted her head up, tiptoed and put her lips to the place he'd indicated, for the whole of one second. She smelled the scent of his skin, felt the slight roughness where he'd shaved. Her upper lip touched his lower one.

Amber hesitated, and then he shifted fractionally so that her mouth met his. Her breasts brushed against his chest, immediately reacting, and she knew he must feel it.

Marco's arms brought her closer again, his mouth taking over her tentative kiss, parting her lips to a passionate but controlled exploration, teasing and tantalising, inviting and demanding, gentle and yet passionate.

His hands roved over her back, bared by the bathing suit, and slid to her behind, then cupped her and lifted her to him, and her heart rate accelerated into a fast drumbeat. Her body was suffused by fire. She had her arms about his neck, and his hands went to her thighs, lifting her even further so that she instinctively wrapped her legs about him and felt the hardness of him at the apex where the myriad, unimaginable sensations that thrilled through her being had their centre.

But suddenly Marco was pushing her away, pulling her arms down, and her legs slid from him, her feet finding the bottom of the pool. His face was dark, his eyes brilliant, and his jawline like granite.

"Not here," he said grittily. "Not our first time. That should be…in a more appropriate place. A private place, where I can make love to you properly. When I make you truly my wife it will be our real wedding night, slow and sweet and memorable, not a hurried coupling where we could be discovered at any moment."

Of course he was right. What if Ana Maria had decided to join them? Or even Elena, perhaps, thinking she'd like to cool off after her morning's work?

"Go," Marco said, "before I lose my self-control completely." Then he turned and began ferociously swimming away from her, the water parting before his powerful arms.

Amber's legs wobbled as she clambered up the steps. She was shivering, but not with cold. She snatched up her towel, at first holding it to herself like a security blanket, her eyes tightly closed while water dripped from her hair and she tried to orientate herself, until her body returned to something like normal.

When she forced her eyes open everything seemed more sharply delineated than before. She was hyper-aware of the heat of the sun on her skin, the way its light caught the droplets of water that Marco splashed up, the dazzling white of the walls about the pool, the stillness of the trees that grew beyond them.

She fastened the towel firmly above her breasts, the centres still furled and tingling. Wrenching her thoughts away from how Marco's hard chest had felt against them, she wrung out her hair, took several deep breaths and walked towards the gate. She had no idea how long that torrid episode had taken—perhaps only minutes—but she needed to compose herself and get some clothes on before she could face her husband again.

Her husband. It felt strange, alien. Like the man himself.

Last night they had slept in the same bed, although she had been unaware of his presence beside her. He wouldn't wait forever for her to fulfil her marriage vows.

When Amber crossed the courtyard Ana Maria didn't look up from her book, and she met no one on the way to the bedroom. She lost no time in drying herself properly and slipping into fresh undies and a loose cotton dress. She used the dryer in the bathroom on her hair until it was only slightly damp, and fastened it back with a tie.

When she emerged Marco was in the bedroom, wearing jeans, zipped but not fastened, and he was pulling a T-shirt over his head, his damp towel crumpled on the floor.

Averting her eyes from the tantalising glimpse of a rather magnificent male form, Amber walked to her dressing table and began fiddling with the things on its top. Her minimal make-up gone and her hair pulled back from her face, she looked naked—pale and washed-out compared with the warm skin tones of the Venezuelan women, enhanced by their impeccable make-up, drawing attention to dark-lashed eyes and luscious lips. The Internet had told her Venezuelans had won world beauty contests more often than those from any other country.

How could she compete?

Men had sometimes called her beautiful, but she'd always taken it with a grain of salt. She had no doubt that the woman she thought of as Marco's wife—his *real* wife—would have been a genuine beauty. He wouldn't have settled for anything less. Probably from a wealthy and respected old family like his own, she'd have had all the qualities required of a Salzano bride, cultured and knowledgeable about the customs and mores of her class, she wouldn't have been always on the alert in case she inadvertently broke some unspoken rule of conduct.

She'd have been able to speak freely with Señora Salzano in their own language, perhaps viewed soap operas with Ana Maria. And she had given Marco a son. The son he'd adored.

Marco had loved her.

Suddenly Amber was silently crying, hot tears spilling down her cheeks. She saw them in the mirror and shut her eyes in a futile attempt to stop them.

Two hands descended on her shoulders, turning her. Marco said, "There is no need for tears."

Amber tried to pull away from him, scrubbing at her wet cheeks, her voice rising. "I've been bullied into marriage with a man I scarcely know, dragged I don't know how many thousands of miles from my home, family, friends, a job I loved, and from my own country—where I could walk in the bush without worrying I might be savaged by some wild animal—to a strange place in the back of beyond where I can't even speak the language. And you tell me not to cry! Well, *stuff you,* I'll cry a damned river if I want to!"

She sniffed, swiped a hand across her eyes where the tears had miraculously stopped, and said with irritated passion, "Only, I *hate* tears!" They were Azure's specialty. Amber was the strong one. "And don't you *dare* laugh at me!"

Because although he'd listened gravely enough to her list of grievances, perhaps even with some sympathy in his eyes—guilt was too much to read there, surely—at her final outburst Marco's mouth had twitched at the corners, and the skin at the corners of his eyes was crinkling.

He controlled his expression and said, "I beg your pardon, *querida,*" sounding so sincere she eyed him with deep suspicion.

She scowled, and muttered without conviction, "I told you not to call me that."

His mouth was firmly closed and perfectly straight, but the amusement in his eyes hadn't completely disappeared.

"I regret," he said, "that I could not give you more time to become accustomed to the idea of marrying me. There are matters here that require my attention. Naturally you will miss your home for a time. Tomorrow you must speak with your parents, perhaps your sister."

"Is that an order?"

He seemed puzzled, not answering immediately. "It is a suggestion. One I thought you would welcome."

"It's just," she said crossly, "you have a habit of expressing yourself in commands. Like telling me not to go walking alone."

"You could become lost, or come across something unexpected. An anaconda. Or a caiman. Even a rattlesnake."

Amber scarcely contained a shudder, the standard reaction of a Kiwi to snakes and alligators or crocodiles. Ana Maria had shown her several small crocodile-like caimans, but meeting a bigger one alone would have freaked her.

Marco shifted his hands to cup her face, wiping at the residue of tears with his thumbs. "In a couple of hours I will take you to meet some of these dangerous creatures, and will make sure you come to no harm." He patted her cheek and dropped his hands. "I will see you later."

When the door closed behind him, Amber drooped, suddenly too tired even to rouse annoyance at his patronising manner. The wide bed under the silently whirling ceiling fan looked overwhelmingly inviting.

She kicked off the sandals she'd donned and lifted the cover away, then lay down and reached for her book on the bedside table. But she had read only a few pages before her eyelids fell and she let the book drop to her chest.

* * *

Marco stared at the spreadsheet on the screen in front of him. The figures before him refused to make sense.

He kept thinking of Amber—the way her body had felt against his in the pool, how she'd kissed him, with that brief, shy touch of her lips. Then, when he held her closer, she'd opened her mouth to his persuasion and he'd felt the soft mounds of her breasts pressing against him, the tiny hardened peaks that told him she wanted him. That knowledge had increased his own desire, and he'd had to battle for some semblance of control.

When her lovely legs wound about him he'd almost lost it, wanting to tear away the thin barriers of cloth between them and plunge himself into her there and then.

Fortunately, sanity had stepped in just in time. Had he not already taken too much from this woman, driven by his own needs, his wants? He could at least choose a more suitable venue to first slake his growing lust for her.

As she'd just reminded him, he'd torn her from everything—everyone—she knew and brought her to the other side of the world, to a place where she knew nothing and no one. What had she called it—the back of beyond?

He smiled. Even in tears she had delivered him a diatribe, a catalogue of his sins. Which were many, as no one knew so well as he.

And this latest was the blackest of all, as conscience and reason and his father's training in honour, the mark of a true *hidalgo,* a noble man, constantly reminded him. Yet he would not give up. Could not. Fate had presented him with this one chance to fulfil his heart's desire.

When the idea had first entered his mind he knew it was reprehensible, iniquitous. His mother and his dead father would have condemned it. He might have dismissed it out of hand, except for one thing: no matter how much she protested, how often she spat words at him like a cornered she-cat, Amber responded to him sexually. The inexplicable pull of attraction—that wayward, God-given and seemingly arbitrary compulsion between a man and a woman—had grown stronger each time they met, regardless of her efforts to hide it, fight it, pretend it didn't exist.

His disappointment when he'd thought no baby existed had been much more painful than he would have anticipated, biting sharp and deep. Correspondingly, his anger at Azure's refusal to confirm whether the child was his had seared his soul. Even though he had come reluctantly to admire Amber's steadfast defence of her family, his inability to control his desire for her also angered him.

In the end, every other way to a solution proved unworkable. So he'd stifled the grumblings of conscience and heritage, sure that Amber would in time come willingly to his bed. And then…

Then he would get what he wanted, as he almost invariably did. And no one would be hurt.

His absent stare wandered from the computer screen to a framed photograph on top of a filing cabinet. A dark-haired woman holding a little boy smiled back at him.

He let out a sharp breath, went to the cabinet and picked up the photo. Frowning down at it, he ran a thumb over the picture, then opened the top file drawer and dropped the photo at the very back before pushing the drawer shut with a thud.

Amber woke at the soft opening and closing of the bedroom door. She'd fallen first into a light doze, semi-aware of the twittering of birds outside that contrasted with the stillness of the house, while images floated through her mind—her family, Benny's endearing chuckle, Azure's distraught face when she heard that Marco was in New Zealand, and Marco himself in his many moods from fury to cold implacability to unexpected gentleness.

Before sleep overcame her she'd almost imagined herself back home in her own bed, but on opening her eyes she saw the fan circling above her, the high beamed ceiling, and then Marco coming towards her.

She sat up so quickly that for a second she was dizzy. Her hair was dry now, but she checked the pillow behind her with her palm.

"What is it?" Marco inquired.

"I'm afraid I've left a damp patch on the pillow." She hadn't put a towel down. "My hair…"

Marco shrugged. "Concepcion will bring a new one."

How nice to take things like that for granted, Amber thought acidly. To know that if you spoiled something it would be fixed for you, that if you made a mess someone else would clean it up.

Her female friends joked that they could do with a wife, but here a wife wasn't expected to do daily chores. Not if she was married to a Salzano. All Marco required of her was sex and a baby, the former being nothing but a means to an end. If she lay back and thought of England—or of the Salzano empire—he'd be satisfied.

"Did you sleep?" he asked. "Are you ready to go out?"

Sleeping in the daytime made her muzzy. She swung her feet to the ground. "I can do with some fresh air. Give me five minutes while I change."

Marco nodded and turned to look out of the window, for which she was grateful. In the bathroom she spread sunscreen over her face and hands and put on light cotton trousers and a buttoned shirt. Back in the bedroom, survey-ing the row of shoes stowed on the floor of the wardrobe, she asked Marco, "Will sneakers be all right?"

He turned. "If you have no suitable boots."

His boots had heels, which made him seem even taller when she'd laced her sneakers and he came towards her again. "You may need a jacket," he said. "And bring your video camera."

She picked up the camera, from which she had down-loaded her morning's work onto her computer, ready for more filming. "You don't mind?" she queried him.

He shrugged. "You did not buy it for nothing."

He had watched her choose the camera at the duty-free store, apparently intrigued by the fact she knew exactly what she wanted in her purchase and how to find it.

Outside, a short way from the house, a dozen or so horses were corralled in a large enclosure. Two were tied to the railing, already saddled.

"This is Domitila." Marco patted the neck of a dappled grey mare with powerful shoulders and graceful legs who snorted and turned her head to nuzzle at his shoulder. "Come and meet her." He petted the mare's straight, short head, and the pointed ears flicked in greeting.

Her alert eyes turned to Amber as Marco stepped back.

"She's lovely," Amber said, caressing the velvety nose.

"She is a direct descendant of the conquistador horses who were left to run wild. Our feral horses are small but very strong and hardy. Crossbreeding with Thoroughbreds from Europe and North America produced a unique strain suited to our land. Domitila has no vices. You will be safe."

He untied the reins, and Amber refused his help to mount, but let him tighten the girth and adjust her stirrups.

Marco vaulted easily onto the other horse, a dark bay with a black mane and tail, who tossed his head and danced a bit before Marco urged him forward, along the drive and then onto an unsealed road.

"You have seen capybaras today?" Marco asked as they came upon a family of them making their slow way to a pond.

"Yes. They're amazingly tame."

"They are the fourth or fifth generation that has not been hunted or molested on the *hato*. Also," Marco added dryly, "they are very lazy. A biologist who came here to study their behaviour gave up after a few weeks of sitting around waiting for them to do something other than eat, sleep, and cool off in a pond or lagoon, where they also mate—reputedly up to twenty or thirty times a day when the mood takes them."

Amber laughed, and he grinned at her, making her stomach flip. She had never before seen him look as relaxed, and she felt a loosening of the tension that was always there between them. She raised her brows scepti-cally, wondering if he was pulling her leg, as her own com-patriots sometimes did, teasing gullible tourists. She said, "No wonder they're tired."

Marco laughed. "They do no work," he pointed out.

They walked the horses a bit further while Amber became used to Domitila and let the horse get to know her. It was she who increased the pace when they left the hacienda environs with its corrals and outbuildings behind and headed along one of the road-cum-dykes.

In the distance she saw what looked like huge red poppies among the pale grasses, until one soared into the sky, followed by dozens of others.

"Scarlet ibis," Marco explained.

A scattered herd of cattle grazed knee-deep in the pale, coarse grass. Humpbacked, creamy animals sporting wide, lethal-looking curved horns, Amber thought they appeared underfed, with prominent bones and long, skinny legs, unlike the fat, sleek cattle she knew.

"They are bred to withstand the conditions in this country," Marco told her. "We have only two seasons, the dry and the wet. Before the rains begin these beasts will be sold or moved to better pasture for fattening."

In time they reached open forest, which became thicker as they approached a bend in the river that fed it. Tall palms pushed above other trees, and something dropping rapidly through the branches startled Amber and made Marco's horse shy and skitter backwards until his strong, capable hands brought it under control.

Amber's placid mare simply ignored the large rust-red monkey now hanging with one hand from a branch only a metre or so from them and regarding Amber with a quizzical expression that made her laugh.

The monkey grinned, and then swung away into the tangle of trees and creepers while the riders continued until they reached a wide stretch of water that Marco called a lagoon.

A flock of storks took off into the sky, and at the water's edge two long crocodile-like caimans basked, open mouths displaying rows of pointed teeth. As she pulled on the horse's reins they turned and, moving surprisingly quickly, slid into the murky water.

Marco halted his horse and dismounted to come to Amber's side as she swung to the ground. His hands went to her waist from behind, and into her ear he whispered, "Shh."

Silently he pointed to a huge rock near the edge of the lagoon, in its shadow something like a heap of smooth, muddied stone.

Her breath caught when she realised it was an enormous, coiled snake, and she involuntarily took a step back, coming up against Marco's lean, hard body. His hands tightened and she felt laughter shake his chest but he made no sound. "Anacondas are not poisonous, though they can bite. Do you want to film it?"

"It isn't moving," Amber pointed out. "That thing would hardly show up at all on film."

Marco left her and moved cautiously forward. When she saw the snake's greenish-brown body ripple and it began to uncoil, Amber stifled an urge to scream. Then Marco lunged, and when he straightened he had a firm grip on the snake's head while its sinuous body twisted in protest, its pale pink mouth gaping.

Amber's hands shook as she focused the camera and started it running. Surely what Marco was doing was dangerous? The snake was as thick as his powerful thighs, and must be at least six metres long. Yet he held its writhing body as nonchalantly as if it were an animated toy, even when its tail end began to coil about him.

"That's enough," she told him in strangled tones.

"Do you want to touch it?" he asked.

Touch it? The last thing she wanted, but an unwilling fascination, mingled with misguided pride that made her not want to appear a wussy female in front of him, interfered with her sense of preservation and propelled her forward.

She put a hand gingerly on the snake's skin, surprised to find it warm and dry, the muscles beneath strongly flexing in its effort to escape.

The intricate, symmetrical design of its tiny scales, olive-green with gold spots, was beautiful, and she fancied that its small gleaming eye held a fear equal to her own.

Stepping back, she said, "Let it go."

When Marco did, she raised the camera again and filmed the anaconda slithering away, sliding its entire body with remarkable speed into the water.

"Did you get a good shot?" Marco asked.

"Yes. But you've no need to show off your machismo for me," Amber replied rather tightly. "I wouldn't have had a clue what to do if that thing had attacked you."

He laughed. "I have been doing this for tourists since I was a boy." Then he looked at her closely. "She was not big enough to harm me. The females can grow to three times that size. And I am not defenceless." He indicated a sheathed knife tucked into his belt. "But your concern touches me."

His voice belied the sentiment, and Amber swung away from him, pretending to study the water. The light was fading now and she realised that the several twin glowing objects on the water's surface belonged to caimans, their scaly bodies submerged and only their eyes showing.

Marco said quietly, "This is when the animals come to drink. If we are patient we will see others. But you will need this." He produced a small can of insect repellent, took her hand and sprayed the cool liquid down both sides of her arm, doing the same for the other, then sprayed some into his hand and smoothed it over her face and neck before doing the same for himself.

Amber sat entranced beside Marco on a convenient flat rock while birds of so many species that she finally stopped counting flew overhead, roosted in the trees or cautiously dipped their beaks into the lake's edge.

Marco knew all of their names in English as well as Spanish—yellow-knobbed curassow, sun-bittern, white-throated spadebill, fuscous flycatcher, pale-eyed pygmy-tyrant and dozens more. Some were beautiful, some strange, many sporting unbelievably bright colours. Red, green, blue, yellow and everything between.

Pink flamingos stalked en masse on the other side of the lagoon. A fox and an ant-eater slunk down to slake their thirst. A family of skittish white-tailed deer approached and warily drank, shying away from the lurking caimans with their sharp teeth.

It was dark by the time Amber and Marco returned to the hacienda under a wide sky lit by an aloof white moon and millions of stars.

As José led the horses away Amber turned to Marco. "Thank you," she said. "It was amazing."

In the dim light she couldn't see his expression when he said, "You can thank me properly later. But first we will shower and eat. You must be hungry."

"Starving!" she admitted.

Marco laughed and put a strong, warm arm loosely about her as they walked to the house.

After showering, she put on a flared skirt and sleeveless silk blouse decorated with tiny tucks and narrow lace, then pinned up her hair and used eye shadow and lipstick, knowing the other women in the household would as usual be faultlessly groomed.

In the mirror of her dressing table she saw Marco emerge from the bathroom wearing only a towel.

When he dropped it to dress she hastily averted her eyes, but the imprint of that brief sight lingered.

Remembering the anaconda with its fearsome, sensuous

beauty, both fascinating and dangerous, and the way he'd effortlessly held it helpless until it pleased him to release it, she shivered. Obviously he had learned young to dominate the animals that inhabited his domain, but had he in some mystic way absorbed some of their nature?

She wondered if she would have been able to bring herself to agree to Marco's infamous proposition if he'd been old, fat and ugly, with bad teeth. Or if she hadn't felt the inexorable pull of his undoubted attraction for women, despite trying to fight it. Her acquiescence to his ultimatum hadn't been quite so selfless as she'd liked to think.

CHAPTER NINE

MEALS at the hacienda were apparently leisurely, an opportunity to talk with other members of the family, and in the evening to exchange news of their day. It was late by her standards when Marco took her up to her room, and this time he said good night to the others, came in with her and closed the door.

"Have you recovered from your jet lag?" he asked her in a neutral voice.

She could say no, or that she was tired, but it would only delay the inevitable. "Yes," she said, annoyed that her cheeks were flushing and her voice sounded husky. "I think so."

He nodded, and considered her. "You look very lovely tonight," he said. "I like this." He touched one of the tiny pearl buttons that fastened her blouse. "It's pretty."

"It's cool," she said.

"Cool *and* pretty." His eyes laughed at her. He raised his hand and cupped her cheek, his thumb caressing her lips. "You enjoyed our afternoon?"

Amber swallowed. "You know I did. Your visitors must be blown away by their experience here. I was."

"Then perhaps—" with both hands he tipped her face to him "—you can thank me now more warmly."

Reluctant to give in easily to what appeared to be a demand for her compliance, Amber hesitated. A thought wormed into her mind. Had some of the attractive young women who toured the *hato* under his guidance taken up similar invitations from their handsome host? He'd probably been spoiled for choice.

"Is this how you expect your female visitors to express their appreciation?" she asked.

His mouth tightened, and a dangerous glint appeared in his eyes. "No," he said shortly. "Only my wife."

Then his dark head came down and his mouth exacted a sweet, subtle punishment, taking what he wanted from her, apparently uncaring that she refused to kiss him back.

When he raised his head, she stared defiantly into his glittering eyes, even when his hands slid from her cheeks to her neck and settled on her bare shoulders. "Do not test my patience too far," he warned.

"Are you threatening me?"

His hands left her. "I am trying to make this easy for you. In the pool yesterday you were not averse to my lovemaking. Why do you deliberately jab these little barbs at me?"

"Maybe it's in my nature," she retorted. "You don't really know me at all—any more than I know you." Something hard and cold coming from deep within her spurred her on. "How many women have you been with?"

"That need not concern you," he answered, his head lifting at an arrogant angle as if she'd insulted him. "I was faithful to my wife—my first wife—as I will be to you."

Of course it was none of her business. She didn't know why she'd asked, except that for some reason the possibility of being one of many made her angry.

Being reminded that Marco had been married before, to

a woman he had presumably loved and cherished, didn't help her perverse mood. "Thank you," she said.

Not that there was much she could do about it if he strayed. She was locked into this marriage, had agreed to carry out its terms and wasn't in the habit of breaking her word.

Marco didn't look at all mollified. If anything his expression had grown more austere, and she realised that her reluctant acknowledgement of his promise might have sounded like sarcasm. "I can see," he said, "that you are in no frame of mind to consummate our union tonight. I will sleep elsewhere."

Torn between a miserable awareness that she'd spoiled the delicate rapport they'd built earlier, and a savage satisfaction at routing him, Amber watched him wrench open the door and leave, snapping it shut behind him.

The satisfaction quickly drained. It had been a petty victory at best, and she suspected Marco had come out of it with more battle honours than she.

Not to mention that he would ultimately win despite her desperate efforts to salvage her pride and some measure of autonomy from this debacle. No matter how much she twisted and turned and snapped at him, or how deeply she despised herself for her body's astonishing response to his male charisma, she had no choice in the end but to surrender.

CHAPTER TEN

MARCO was gone before Amber went down for breakfast. If he'd returned to their room earlier to gather some clothes she hadn't heard him.

Señora Salzano returned her *"Buenos días"* with a restrained smile and a gracious nod. Elena returned the greeting politely but without enthusiasm, and Ana Maria jumped up to escort Amber to the table and urged her to fill her plate.

Sitting down again, Ana Maria said, "You look a little tired, Amber." Then, her eyes sparkling with mischief, she asked, "Is my brother's machismo too much for his bride?"

Amber flushed, but was saved from answering by Señora Salzano speaking sharply to her daughter in Spanish. The woman understood English better than she spoke it.

Ana Maria looked abashed and told Amber, "I didn't mean to embarrass you."

Mustering a smile, Amber shook her head. "I'm used to being teased by my sister."

Ana Maria smiled. "And *we* are sisters now, you and I—since you married my brother."

* * *

Amber spent the morning with Marco's sister on the court-yard terrace. While Ana Maria was busy with textbooks and a laptop computer, Amber read a book she'd bought at one of the stopovers on the long flight. She'd phoned her parents and assured them she was well and comfortable, and talked about the amazing wildlife with real enthusiasm.

Near lunchtime she heard the sound of a car drawing up outside, and shortly a young man appeared at the open end of the courtyard. He strode quickly across the flagstones and leapt lightly up the steps to the terrace.

Ana Maria jumped up, laughing, and ran towards him.

A wide grin on his face, he opened his arms to her and she flung herself into them, squealing, "Diego!" hugging him back and speaking in excited Spanish.

Amber uncertainly stood too. Ana Maria took the young man's hand and dragged him over to introduce them. "Diego is back early from visiting his family," she said, and then turned to him. "We were expecting you tomorrow when the next tourists are due."

"I was anxious to meet Marco's new bride," he said. "Elena told me the news." Bowing over Amber's hand, he lightly kissed it. "I see he has chosen well. She is *una belleza.*" His eyes sparkled with appreciation as well as curiosity. "I congratulate him."

Amber gave a small tug at the hand he still held, and he relinquished it with a little moue of regret.

He was probably in his late twenties and hadn't missed out on the family good looks, with thick dark hair and brown eyes, and a lady-killer smile. "So," he said. "What do you think of our little hacienda?"

Amber laughed. *Little?* "I think it's very impressive, and the birdlife and animals are simply fabulous."

He chatted for a while and left to greet his aunt.

At lunch Marco was absent. No one remarked on it, and Amber didn't want to admit her ignorance of her husband's routine or whereabouts. She gathered it was normal for the *llaneros* to start work at dawn in order to avoid the heat later in the day. If they were working far from the hacienda they would take food with them.

Diego flirted outrageously with her, making Ana Maria laugh. His aunt murmured reprovingly once or twice, but his exaggerated contrition made even her lips twitch, and he lightened Amber's mood.

Marco arrived late for dinner, stopped briefly in the dining room to apologise to his mother and greet Diego and, scarcely looking at Amber, left to get out of his dusty work clothes and have a shower.

When he reappeared, newly shaved and with his damp hair slicked back, he kissed Amber's cheek before seating himself at the head of the table. He accepted Diego's congratulations on his marriage with a nod, and after a glance at Amber cut off the younger man's fulsome compliments on his choice with a curt, "Don't embarrass my wife, Diego." Followed by something in Spanish before turning his attention to his plate.

Diego murmured, *"Perdón, por favor,* Amber,*"* seeming only slightly abashed, his eyes dancing, and she had to smile back. His light chatter made up for his cousin's taciturnity, and she was glad of the distraction.

She went upstairs early, but after donning a light lawn shift-style nightgown over matching bikini panties and removing the bedcover, she sat against the pillows leafing though fashion magazines Ana Maria had loaned her,

some of them in English. She was too keyed up to concentrate on a book.

Outside she could hear men's voices, a group of *llaneros*
chatting and laughing, and then music—haunting guitar
music accompanying a Spanish song that seemed redolent
of love and loss. Long after the music had ceased, and she'd
heard Señora Salzano and Ana Maria enter their rooms,
Marco hadn't appeared. She wondered if he was talking to
his newly arrived cousin—or had he returned to wherever
he'd slept last night?

Eventually she switched off the bedside light and tried
to will herself to sleep. The room was suffused with cool
moonlight, and after a while she opened her eyes and stared
at the high, white ceiling with its solid supporting beams.
A wave of homesickness washed over her.

Turning onto her side, she curled her legs up, and for a
short while let tears flow. Then she heard the quiet turning
of the doorknob, and held her breath as Marco slipped into
the room and the door clicked shut behind him.

Amber closed her eyes. She had been ready to talk
things out, try to come to some understanding, and was un-
reasonably aggrieved that he'd taken so long to follow her,
as if he should have known she was waiting for him.

He made hardly a sound, but she sensed that he'd moved
nearer. After minutes seemed to have passed she risked
opening her eyes the tiniest slit, and saw he was standing
at the window, one hand resting on the wall beside it as he
leaned slightly forward, the moonlight silhouetting his
proud, resolute profile and laying a silver patina on his
black hair.

As if he felt her gaze he straightened and dropped his
hand to his side, turning towards the bed.

Amber hastily closed her eyes again, willing her breathing to evenness.

Again there was a pause, but now he was so near she could smell the soap and aftershave he'd used, hear his breathing. Invisibly she stiffened, every nerve on the alert. Then she felt the lightest brush of something warm across her damp cheek—Marco's lips—and heard the harsh drawing in of his breath, followed by a whispered exclamation, and through her eyelids caught the sudden flaring of the bedside light as he switched it on.

She had to open her eyes then, covering them with the back of her hand and rolling over so her back was to him when he loomed over her.

He pulled her hand away and looked down at her, his lips tight. "Am I so fearsome," he said, "you must cry yourself to sleep?"

"I'm not afraid of you!" Amber injected scorn into her voice and sat up so that she was more nearly level with him. Bad enough being caught for a second time crying like a baby, let alone having him think he could intimidate her.

"You relieve my mind," he said gravely. "Then why have you been weeping into your pillow? Perhaps you missed my presence in your bed?" He shifted to sit on the side of it, facing her with his arm across her legs, his hand on the sheet beside her hip.

Amber glared. He was uncomfortably close to the mark. "What I miss is my home, my family."

"Ah." He actually looked sympathetic. "That is understandable. You have spoken to them?"

"Yes."

"Good. If you wish, you may do so every day and talk for as long as you like."

As if she needed his permission. But to be fair, he was paying the phone bill. She made a conscious effort to excuse his habitual air of command as a result of being in charge of this vast enterprise. "I'm sorry if I was a bit sharp last night," she said. "Only I felt you were pushing me into a corner, making me kiss you."

He looked at her steadily for a long moment before he said, "Then I too am sorry, Amber." He picked up her hand that was clutching the edge of the sheet and kissed it, retaining his hold as he lowered it. His voice deepening, he said, "If you had just said no I would have respected that. I want very much to make love to you, when you are ready." He raised his other hand and brushed at her cheek with his thumb, wiping away the last trace of tears. "Have I not told you I am not a brute, to take a woman by force?"

He could have, she knew. The walls in this place were thick, the doors solid wood, and even if someone had heard her scream, no one in this house would willingly cross Marco or interfere in his marriage.

She supposed his ancestors had not been so enlightened, their women given little choice, any resistance easily and ruthlessly overcome.

The blood of the conquistadors still ran in Marco's veins. His methods might be more subtle, but when it came down to it she had no option but to meet his demands, however he couched them.

In that respect she was no different from the helpless Indian maidens who became spoils of war, or the aristo-cratic, sheltered *señoritas* whose marriages were arranged for dynastic reasons.

Procrastination was pointless. She took a deep breath and said, "All right. Tonight, then. Now."

Before she lost her nerve.

Marco had been looking down at the hand he held, his thumb roving back and forth over her skin. He looked up, his eyes searching as she met them with what she hoped was a fearless stare, ignoring the colony of butterflies that had taken residence in her stomach. "Why now?" he demanded, his eyes narrowing.

Amber shrugged. "It's as good a time as any. The sooner we…start, the sooner I can get pregnant and you'll have what you wanted. And then…you said you'd let me go."

Her insides went hollow at the very thought of leaving after having his baby, but she thrust that aside to be dealt with later. Right now all she wanted was to get this over with. She didn't have to *enjoy* it.

"Well?" she challenged him belligerently.

Marco for once was apparently at a loss. At last he said, "If that is what you want."

"I said so, didn't I?" Her voice had ratcheted up a notch. Trying to loosen the knot of nervous tension that threatened to choke her, she said, "Unless you're exhausted after chasing cattle or whatever you were doing all day?"

A gleam entered his eyes. "I am not so exhausted as that."

Abruptly he stood up and began unbuttoning his white shirt, his eyes holding hers.

When he let the shirt drop to the floor her heart seemed to leap into her throat. She would have liked to ask him to turn off the light but didn't want him to know she was having an attack of shyness. As his hands went to the tooled leather belt he wore, her gaze involuntarily followed. He tugged at the silver buckle, and the belt joined his shirt on the floor. His bronzed feet were bare.

He opened the waistband of his trousers but didn't

unzip them, saying, "Move over, *querida*," as he threw back the sheet.

Amber obeyed, inwardly quivering with nerves, automatically pulling down the hem of the short gown when it rode up on her thighs, then thinking how stupidly prudish that was.

The bulk of Marco's magnificent, half-naked body obscured the bedside lamp and threw the farther half of the bed into shadow. He adjusted the pillows before leaning on one elbow and surveying her like a connoisseur appraising a work of art. One he wasn't sure was worth its price.

His free hand fingered a lock of her hair and tucked it behind her ear. "You are naturally blond?" he asked.

"More so when I was a kid," she answered huskily. "I use lemon rinse when I wash it."

A smile touched his mouth. "Ah, sweet yet sharp." He leaned forward and inhaled the scent of her hair, then dropped a kiss on the top of her head, another on her forehead. With kisses he closed her eyes. His mouth wandered across her cheek to her ear, and his tongue found the small indentation below.

Amber lay perfectly still, fighting her body's responses and the sensation that she was melting inside.

Marco's hand trailed from just under her chin down her throat, paused on the pulse beating at its base, pressing gently with a finger, then moved under the satin of the nightshirt to cup her shoulder while his tongue explored the hollow his finger had discovered.

Amber forced her eyes wide open, trying to dispel the feelings he was arousing, determined not to give in to them. Somehow it was important to her self-respect that she retain control over her body even as she allowed Marco to do whatever he willed with it. He'd had his way in everything else. The only thing she could deny him was her active participation.

He lifted his head and looked at her flushed face, her stubbornly closed mouth, and she stared back at him defiantly.

"I see," he said softly. "You wish to make this a war of wills, *mi esposa.*"

My wife, he was reminding her. Amber clenched her fists, held rigidly at her sides. "I'm not fighting you."

A smile holding both arrogance and irony briefly touched his mouth. "We will see how long your *resistencia pasivo* will last."

He began unfastening her nightgown with agonising slowness. At last he parted it, revealing her breasts, that to her utter chagrin she knew were visibly reacting to his intent gaze. Lower down the minuscule panties did very little for modesty.

She heard Marco expel a breath, and turned her head aside. "*¡Exquisita!*" he said. "You are even more beautiful than I had dreamed."

He circled each peaking breast with a finger, then began drawing closer to the centre of the right one, which throbbed, aching for his touch.

When it came, she dug her teeth into her lower lip, clasping at the sheet with her hands as he teased and tormented. Then his hair brushed like silk against her skin and she felt his mouth, his tongue, caressing, tasting, stroking. Involuntarily her eyes closed tight and she forced herself to stay still until she could bear it no longer without betraying herself, and cried out, "Stop!"

He did, to take her chin in his hand and look into her eyes, his own glittering with night fire, his cheeks darkened, a faint sheen on his forehead.

She knew he saw the flush that warmed her face, the glazed look in her eyes. His gaze shifted to her mouth, swollen where she'd bitten into it, and then his head came down, his lips gently taking her bruised one between them, his tongue moistening the small hurt, easing it.

She felt his bare chest against the pebble-hard evidence of her unwilling arousal and was torn between shame and her growing desire to reciprocate the tender, tantalising kisses he was bestowing on her mouth.

He began kissing her throat, her shoulders, the inner crook of her left elbow, the smooth skin over the tiny veins in her wrist. He kissed each finger in turn, then took one in his mouth and sucked on it, his tongue playing around it, and gave it a painless nip with his teeth before returning his attention to her breasts.

She heard her own breath quicken, and could do nothing to hide it or the hammering of her heart when Marco put his palm over it, while his mouth wreaked havoc on her senses, until she gave a small, involuntary moan and moved restlessly on the bed.

Marco gave a brief, breathy laugh, and his mouth moved lower while she clenched her teeth. She hadn't known that her navel was an erogenous zone, but then, every inch of her skin seemed to be equally so. Everywhere he touched with his mouth, his hands, his body, her nerves seethed with answering desire. When his hand glided over the satin panties and cupped her between her legs, she knew he'd recognise the proof that she was indeed ready for him. But he didn't simply tear off the last barrier between them, instead dispensing with his own trousers first, then slipping a finger inside her panties and beginning a slow, relentless stroking.

"Don't," she whispered, despite the reluctant pleasure he was giving her, draining her will. Her head thrashed from side to side in desperate negation, even as her legs parted of their own accord. *"Please!"*

Immediately he stopped what he'd been doing, his hand moving to her breast, caressing, gently tweaking, and that was almost worse—her body was bathed in fire, every skin cell alive, needy, longing, while her mind frantically fought for control. Her lips parted on a long drawn-in breath, and then Marco's mouth was on hers, open and hot in a merciless, passionate, searing kiss, his tongue an instrument of erotic torture, sending her mindless, while she could feel between her thighs the hard, proud crux of his manhood demanding entry.

When his mouth left hers Amber was dizzy, floating on a sea of wanting, needing. The tumbled sheets, the bed, the world itself seemed far away. She hardly felt Marco remove her panties, and when he poised himself over her, his eyes like black jewels, his male scent an aphrodisiac, his mouth rigid with superhuman control, she stared back at him with fierce, silent craving.

He entered her slowly, as if afraid of hurting her, and she couldn't help lifting to him a little, wanting him deeper, wanting him to fill her, wanting him…

She heard the harsh sigh of satisfaction he breathed against her cheek, and then he thrust powerfully, deeply, lifting his head to watch her face, and she closed her eyes, closed herself around him, felt her body convulse, lost herself in unbelievable, shuddering delight, heard her own voice cry out wordlessly and at last raised her arms and wrapped them tight about his shoulders.

CHAPTER ELEVEN

DIMLY she was aware that Marco was speaking in Spanish, his voice low, sexy, urgent. She heard him say her name—Amber—and then *querida, bella, muy buena,* and other words that she didn't recognise.

Then he gave a long, guttural moan and she felt his muscles tense under her hands, his body quiver as it was taken over in his turn by the uncontrollable pleasure that was like no other. Amber clung to him, her fingers unconsciously digging into his flesh, her own pleasure was heightened by the knowledge that Marco shared it, that he was buried deep inside her, their limbs twined about each other, their bodies fused together as if nothing would ever part them.

She was still having tiny aftershocks when Marco finally collapsed against her, then rolled over, holding her to him, the movement intensifying the sensation so that she let slip a small, surprised, "Oh!"

He must have felt the rhythmic spasms she couldn't stop, and his hands shifted from her waist to stroke over the curves below and hold her at the top of her thighs while he rocked her, encouraging her, and she felt him harden again inside her. Half-horrified and yet impelled by primeval instinct that held her in thrall, she moved against him, driving herself to the goal she knew was within reach, felt him match her rhythm, find the apex, until they fell together into the void once more and she couldn't stop her whimpering cries.

Exhausted, she dropped her head against Marco's dampened shoulder, inhaling a salty aroma mixed with the essence of his skin scent.

Marco stroked her tumbled hair, murmuring, *"¡Maravillosa!"* Marvellous.

He kissed her cheek, then pressed a long, slow kiss on her mouth before easing himself away.

Her body felt weightless, as if it were no longer flesh and blood but something ethereal, drifting on air.

He tended her, found her panties and her nightdress and covered the nakedness he'd so thoroughly explored. "Go to sleep," he whispered, and kissed her drooping eyelids closed. Then he kissed her again on her mouth, his lips lingering, tender. Moments later his arm came around her and his hard, lean body warmed hers.

She gave a long, luxurious sigh and slid into sleep.

Sunlight and the twittering of birds woke her. The pillow next to hers was dented, the sheet cold. She realised she'd missed hearing Marco get up and leave, even missed breakfast. Hastily she scrambled from the bed and made for the bathroom and a lukewarm shower.

Coming out, she grabbed a towel and caught her reflection in the mirror—saw that her lips were full and red, her eyes luminous and languorous. Bedroom eyes.

At the washbasin she rinsed her face over and over with cold water, hoping to eliminate the telltale signs.

Downstairs she apologised to Señora Salzano, who insisted on asking Filipa to bring a tray for her, saying, "You must eat, to give Marco a strong healthy *niño*."

"I'm not pregnant, señora!"

"Who knows? A *bebé* does not make its presence known *inmediatamente*."

Amber realised the *señora* might be right. The thought gave her peculiar feelings—a flash of panic, followed by something much more complex, compounded of wonder and denial and a flutter of excitement.

Ana Maria was studying, apparently, and there was no sign of Diego or Elena. After eating her delayed breakfast, Amber took the tray to the kitchen herself, then went upstairs to transfer more film to her computer, and spent the morning editing yesterday's pictures. The editing programme was new to her, and she was still working it out by trial and error when Marco arrived for lunch, startling her and making her realise how quickly the time had passed.

He strode across the room to stand behind her chair. His hand caressed her shoulder and he bent to place a kiss on her cheek. He smelled of leather and dust and the hot sun. "What are you doing?" he asked.

She told him, and he said, "Something to send your family?"

"Not only them. I thought while I was here I'd try my hand at making a documentary for television. I might be able to sell it back in New Zealand if it's good enough."

Marco's hand dropped. "Lunch is on the table," he said, and headed for the bathroom.

Apparently Diego had been with Marco, checking a camp where the next group of tourists had booked two nights. They talked about it at the table.

"They sleep in tents?" Amber queried.

Diego flashed her his supersmile. "There is a lodge to keep our visitors safe. Is bad for business if the customers get eaten." He made his hands into claws and pantomimed a snarling wild beast, then sat back, grinning as Amber and Ana Maria burst out laughing.

Amber caught Marco watching her, unsmiling, a strange expression in his eyes.

Diego said, "We take guns along as a precaution, but if the tourists do as we say there is no problem. Personally," he added darkly, his expression changing, "I would rather shoot one of them than a puma or jaguar, if they get in its way."

"Unfortunately—" Marco's dry voice broke in as Amber raised her brows in disbelief "—shooting our guests is also not good for business, Diego."

Diego shrugged. "I tell them there are plenty of *hombres estúpidos* in the world but not so many pumas left, so I must take care of the pumas first. They laugh, but maybe there is a bit of doubt." He held up a thumb and forefinger no more than a centimetre apart. "*Diminuto.* Is enough." He grinned again at Amber.

She said, "I'm sure the customers love you, Diego." He must be a hit with the women.

"Anytime you want your own guided tour, *bella señora,*" he said, "I am happy to show you."

"I'd love to film a puma in the wild," Amber told him. "Or a jaguar." Impulsively she asked, "Is there any chance I could join your group tomorrow?"

"*Sí!*" Diego's eyes lit up, but Marco cut him off with an unequivocal, "No!"

Disappointed, and irked at the imperious veto, Amber demanded, "Why not?"

Something flashed in Marco's eyes, but he said calmly, "Be patient, *querida.* I will take you myself to the *campamento,* when it is empty of strangers and we will be alone." He smiled slightly, in his eyes a deep, challenging spark, and it was as though only the two of them were in the room. A tiny shiver spiralled through her, and she couldn't speak.

Could the others at the table read the silent reminder of last night? She saw Elena glance from her to Marco, then dip her head and dig her fork into a piece of beef.

Ana Maria said, "You have had no *luna de miel,* have you, Amber? Though the *campamento* is not…um…*muy lujoso…*" She asked Marco, "What is the word?"

Amber too turned to her husband inquiringly. Neither phrase had yet entered her limited Spanish vocabulary.

"It is not luxurious," he supplied, and to Amber, "My sister does not think it suitable for a honeymoon."

A honeymoon? Amber stared at him. He lifted a dark brow, saying, "We can talk about it later." Then he turned to Elena and they began discussing the preparations for the visitors.

Amber drew in a breath. If this had been a normal marriage she'd have jumped at the offer of a honeymoon in the jungle among free-roaming animals. When she and her sister were younger they'd sometimes camped with their parents during school holidays, at a beach or national park.

She was suddenly overwhelmed by a longing for lush green paddocks where sleek, fat cattle and woolly white sheep grazed; for cool, thick, green bush that held no dangers, and deserted beaches where it was safe to walk barefoot on miles of smooth, soft sand.

Ana Maria murmured to her, "Amber, are you all right?"

Despite the girl's lowered voice Marco must have heard.

His head turned sharply from Elena towards Amber in midsentence, and when she instinctively looked at him his gaze was piercing.

She returned her attention to his sister and forced a smile to her lips. "I'm fine," she said.

"You look a little tired," Ana Maria told her.

"There is a reason for that," Marco said.

Ana Maria's face brightened with delighted comprehension, and Diego gave a knowing chuckle.

Marco went on, "My wife is unused to our climate and she has been tiring herself with her explorations. Today, *querida,* you must have a nice long siesta."

Tempted to tell him she would do exactly as she pleased, perhaps go for a nice long walk or take Domitila for a nice long gallop across the *llano,* Amber kept the smile in place, the devoted bride in front of his family.

After Filipa had cleared the plates from the table, Marco was the first to rise, coming round to pull out Amber's chair and take her hand so that she had no choice but to accompany him upstairs. Behind them she heard Diego murmur something, followed by a giggle from Ana Maria and then Elena's voice, short and sharp in rapid Spanish.

When Marco had closed the door of their room behind them, Amber tugged her hand from his and crossed to the window, staring at the expanse of blue-green grassland drying to pale brown in the sun, with the inevitable flock of birds wheeling under a cloudless sky, then dropping as one into a distant clump of twisted trees.

"Come," Marco said from somewhere behind her. "Ana Maria is right. You should rest."

"I'm not tired." Her voice was brittle, and she didn't turn

from her stance at the window. After all, she had slept late that morning.

"No?" Silently Marco had crossed the huge rug that covered the old boards, and his hands descended lightly on her shoulders. "*Bueno*. I too do not wish to sleep."

She felt his fingers push aside her hair, which she'd left loose before hurrying downstairs, and then his lips were on her neck, pressing little kisses in one spot, then another, and another. His hand slipped the wide boat-neck of her cotton top off her shoulder and he kissed the smooth curve, his hair cool and soft against her cheek. His other hand went to her midriff, sliding under the shirt.

Amber closed her eyes. Already he was aroused, and unwilling or not, so was she. Memories of last night danced in tantalising, erotic pictures behind her eyelids, and her body remembered too wanton and wayward, ignoring her mind's effort to assert control.

What was the use? Marco already knew he could break down her inadequate defences, bring her to humiliating, quivering acquiescence—and more than that, much more: to a primeval, raging lust for a man she surely should loathe.

His ancestors had conquered with fire and sword, cruel and rapacious, taking what they fancied—gold, jewels, land…and women. Marco's weapons were his hands, his mouth, his naked body, his intimate knowledge of female anatomy—in short, his skill at pleasing a woman—to achieve his conquest over her. She should be grateful that it was a gentle though ruthless seduction rather than a brutal, uncaring slaking of crude sexual appetite.

Even now, as he turned her in his arms and she opened her eyes, saw the fierce masculine beauty of his face, the glitter of passion in his eyes, she knew her own face reflected the fever of desire, her skin going taut and hot, her eyelids involuntarily falling again as he bent to her, his mouth working dark magic, spinning her into an abyss of mounting, dangerous sexual hunger.

He swept her up in his arms, and she wound her own arms about his neck, her head nestled against his shoulder until he reached the bed and tumbled onto it, still holding her.

With a kind of bitter resignation, she thought hazily that if she couldn't rouse enough self-respect to resist, she might as well enjoy the moment. When he set about swiftly removing her clothes, she tore at the buttons on his shirt, and it was her hands that fumbled with the buckle of his belt, unzipped his trousers, helped haul them off. She wanted him, wanted to be held close, kissed, stroked, wanted to explore his body with her hands and mouth as he had hers last night. Wanted the sweet oblivion that only he could give her, when for a little time nothing mattered but this need to have each other, hold each other, giving and receiving the greatest physical pleasure a man and woman could experience.

When it came, her whole body stiffened in Marco's embrace, and her parted mouth drew in a breath and held it until her body released its tension and wave after wave engulfed her in delight, gifting her the fulfilment she craved. She felt his answering surge inside her, and thought she would die, drowned in exquisite sensation. Surely no one could bear this much pure enjoyment, going on and on for so long?

Then it was over, and she lay panting, dizzy, spent, unable to move, her hair tumbled around and over her face, her limbs boneless, while reality slowly trickled back into her consciousness.

Marco leaned over her, his hair rumpled. She vaguely

remembered burying her fingers in the thickness of it, holding him to her as his tongue did exciting things to her breasts. He looked pleased, triumphant. His hand lifted her hair away from her face and he smiled down at her—a lazy, satisfied smile—then kissed her softly, erotically, savouring her mouth with all the finesse of a connoisseur tasting some exotic new dish.

Then he gathered her into his arms and tucked her head against his shoulder, stroking her hair. It felt good, her resting place against his skin warm and comfortable. She was utterly filled with a sense of wellbeing, of contentment. For now, she refused to think about what had brought her here, or what was to come. On that defiant thought she dozed off.

Marco's movement woke her sometime later as he carefully eased himself away and left the bed, to pull on his trousers with his back to her.

Opening her eyes, she drew in a quick, horrified breath as she saw the red marks on his shoulders. She sat up, dragging the sheet over her bare breasts.

Instantly he turned. "I'm sorry I woke you. I have work to do." Taking in her expression, he said, "What is the matter?"

"I…your shoulders," she said. "Did I…?" She looked down at her fingernails, which perfectly matched the crescent-shaped red indentations she'd seen on his skin.

Her hands went over her mouth in embarrassment, then she quickly lowered them to readjust the sheet.

Marco laughed. "Yes, you have put your mark on me, *mi tigresa pequeña. De nada,*" he said, picking up his shirt to pull it on over the small wounds. "Do not worry. They are proof of your affection for your husband, no?"

His *little tigress* sent him a hostile glance. It had no visible effect. He laughed again, and with the shirt still open he bent over to kiss the top of her head. Drawing away, he pulled her inadequate covering down a little and said huskily, "You have the marks of *amor* on you too." She followed his gaze and saw two patches of pinkened flesh on the upper slopes of her breasts.

Marco perched on the edge of the bed and leaned towards her, planting a kiss on each telltale sign, making her catch her breath against the dissolution of her insides. "Such delicate skin," he murmured. "I will try to take more care next time."

Abruptly he stood up. "You tempt me to neglect my duties. But unfortunately I must leave you, *mi amante.*"

When he'd gone Amber found her Spanish dictionary and looked up *amante.*

It meant *lover.*

Or possibly *mistress.*

It was no use trying to pretend she was indifferent to Marco's lovemaking, though she told herself she was merely fulfilling her part of the bargain they had made.

The day she informed him as neutrally as she could that she wasn't pregnant, he merely nodded and said, "There is plenty of time, *querida.*"

One afternoon she summoned the willpower to turn him down when he made a move during siesta, saying she wasn't in the mood, it was too hot. Marco shrugged, said calmly, "As you wish, of course," and moved to the other side of the bed, to lie on his back with his hands behind his head, staring at the ceiling, the fan in the centre sending cooling air over the bed.

Amber turned her head away and tried to persuade herself the jittery tension and restlessness she felt had nothing to do with sexual frustration.

After a while Marco got up and said, "I'm going to swim." He didn't invite her along, and she wouldn't let herself ask. She swam with Ana Maria quite often, and sometimes Diego joined them, splashing them and horsing about until they ganged up on him and fought back. Even Elena joined them now and then. But Marco often seemed to prefer having the pool to himself.

The next day he didn't appear for lunch or siesta time, but when he followed her to bed that night and reached for her Amber discovered in herself something she had never suspected. In answer to Marco's gentle consideration she responded with a ferocious, frantic ardour. Driven by confused feelings of frustrated need and the hard, cold lump of frozen tears that seemed to be her heart, she kissed with furious passion, teased with her hair, her hands, her body, used his body to heighten her own desire and, like the tigress he'd called her, bit and scratched, turning their bed into a battlefield, though it only made him laugh in pleased surprise. Which finally freed her inner rage.

She was lying on top of him then, her breasts filling his hands, and she began pummelling his chest with her fists, her teeth clenched, until he caught her wrists in his big hands and turned her over, trapping her with her wrists pinned against the pillows as he thrust into her again and again with all the violence and heat and fury that she craved. The world exploded around them and she lost herself, her mind, her body shattering into a million shards of glittering, unbelievable, seemingly unending pleasure until she fell into a dark, velvety void.

A deep animal growl came from Marco's throat as he reached his own climax, culminating in a long, harsh sigh.

It was minutes before he released her, and she returned

to a consciousness of where she was and what had just happened. Finally she rolled onto her stomach, appalled at her own behaviour, too mortified to face Marco, yet still tingling all over with the luxurious, lethargic aftermath of frenzied, out-of-this-world sex.

Marco touched her hair, then swept his hand slowly down her spine, over the curve of her behind, and back up again. He went on lazily stroking her with his warm, soothing hand, murmuring to her in musical Spanish until she drifted into sleep.

Amber phoned her parents each week, confining the conversation mostly to life on the *hato* and the fun she was having filming its animal inhabitants. It wasn't difficult to wax lyrical about the wildlife and the food, the harsh beauty of the *llanos*. She also spoke to her sister, both of them skating over the reason she was so far from home. Amber was unsure if Rickie was around to hear.

Azure put Benny on the line, and Amber realised how much she missed the little boy. Listening to his baby babbling, she thought if she felt this strongly about her nephew, how could she ever leave her own baby?

Would Marco cast her off as soon as she'd fulfilled her promise to give him a child? He'd said she could leave then, but also that in his faith marriage was forever, and surely sexually at least he was satisfied? If they had a baby together that must create a stronger bond.

Tourist parties and backpackers came and went, sometimes with a few days between.

A bird-watching club from Britain stayed for several days, excited by the variety of species they spotted in so short a time. Then a trio of scientists studying the climatology and ecology of the *llanos* dined with the family and talked with Marco and Diego about balancing cattle management and wildlife preservation.

Amber realised that Señora Salzano quietly kept her hands on the reins of the household, ensuring the hacienda was clean and well kept despite its age, the guest accommodation serviced by women who lived in neat, pink-washed houses nearby. She oversaw supplies and meals and worked with Elena to ensure their guests' comfort. And, she ran a project to make white cheese commercially along with some of the *llanero* wives.

Every member of the family had their responsibilities. Amber sometimes felt superfluous to requirements, but offered help where she could.

Something inside her seemed to have broken on that night of ferocious lovemaking with Marco. She hoped it wasn't her spirit. Their sexual encounters were intense; her rage had faded and the ice around her heart was melting.

Marco was unfailingly thoughtful and courteous, although sometimes she sensed a restraint in him, as if he were holding back. Occasionally she caught him looking at her with a brooding expression, his eyes black and unreadable, his mouth taut, perhaps impatient for news of a pregnancy.

If only she could forgive him for the way he'd manipulated her, trapped her, might they build a true relationship based on sexual compatibility and parenting a child—or children?

Any child of this mockery of a marriage deserved a stable, happy home—not two parents at loggerheads. She could keep on sniping at Marco, hold on to her bitter resentment and turn into a shrew, continually carping on how unwillingly he'd got her where he wanted her. She might manage to hurt him a little, but in the end she'd hurt herself more, become the kind of person she would never want to be, unhappy and full of spite.

Or she could accept there was no way out of this situation and try to turn it into something more than a convenient arrangement.

One Sunday the family piled into two cars and drove to a white adobe church where a priest came once a month to say Mass for the *rancheros* on their parcels of land.

Marco introduced Amber to the silver-haired priest before the service. Afterwards a dozen or so men came to shake Marco's hand and be introduced to his bride. Women hung back with shy smiles, children either clinging to their skirts or scampering around after each other.

The priest took Marco aside, and whatever Marco said made the other man frown and shake his head, glancing at Amber, who stood waiting beside Señora Salzano. But then he gave an apparently reluctant nod and raised his hand in a blessing before Marco rejoined the family.

Amber waited until they were alone to ask, "Does the priest disapprove of me?"

"No. The padre is displeased that I have not yet arranged a church wedding."

"A *church* wedding?"

"Here in Venezuela couples must have a civil ceremony for legal reasons, but it is traditional to be married in a church afterwards. That is regarded as the real wedding."

"He doesn't feel we're really married?" After a little thought, Amber said slowly, "What about your mother?"

"She is religious. For her it is important."

Maybe that was the reason the *señora* seemed rather distant with Amber, though always gracious. And why

Concepcion, though respectful, often looked at her with polite disdain, and at Marco with sad disapproval.

Did Marco regard their marriage as real? she wondered. Maybe he'd left himself a loophole. He might still be able to marry again if he sent her home.

She began to adjust to life on the *hato,* enlivened by Ana Maria and Diego, both happy to help her with her Spanish, which she studied every afternoon. Señora Salzano gradually became less aloof, seeming pleased and approving when Amber tried to converse with her in broken Spanish or asked to help with some household task. Even Elena accepted her presence on a day trip with a new bunch of tourists, pointing out good subjects for filming. Although Elena's manner remained cool, she seemed a different being, casually dressed with her hair in a ponytail, her make-up disappearing in the sun.

Again Amber had to tell Marco there was no pregnancy. And again he said there was plenty of time.

She started filming the day-to-day life of the ranch. The brown-skinned, sun-wrinkled *llaneros* saddled up at first light, Stetson-type hats on their heads but, astonishingly, many wearing a type of sandals on their feet. They rode out to move the wandering cattle to fresh pasture or bring them into the yards near the hacienda, where they would separate and brand the yearlings, draft some beasts for sale or butcher a few for the hacienda's meals.

One day she filmed them as they brought in a small herd of the feral horses that roamed the plains, and the *llaneros* set about taming their new mounts, making critical comments on one another's efforts and laughing whenever a rider hit the dusty ground.

Ana Maria took Amber to watch, saying, "In the old

days they used whips and spurs, but Marco won't allow that. Some of the old *llaneros* laughed at him, said no horse would obey until it was properly broken and afraid not to. But he showed them they were wrong."

A snorting, white-eyed mare, according to Marco the matriarch of the herd, had been driven in with the others, but eluded all efforts to catch her. Marco and a couple of men had isolated her and she was alone in a large corral. A day later Marco rode into it and they closed the gate behind him. Ana Maria had persuaded Amber that his technique was worth seeing.

A coiled rope hung on his saddle. He had his horse approaching the mare at a walk. The *llaneros* perching or leaning on the surrounding rails fell silent.

The wild horse shifted as the other drew near, and when they were a few metres apart she lifted her head and galloped off to another corner of the enclosure.

Marco and his mount followed. Everywhere she went, horse and rider remained at her side, sometimes turning tightly to evade lashing hooves and threatening teeth, but always coming back to mimic her movements.

Eventually the mare seemed to tire, realising there was no escape. She stood with her head down and Marco reached over to touch her at the shoulder, talking quietly, soothingly and gently rubbing.

She twitched away, but took only a couple of steps, and when he did it again she only turned her head as if asking what he was up to.

Marco dismounted, still talking, the lasso in his hand, and although she eyed him suspiciously, when he put a hand again on the horse's strong neck she shuddered and tossed her head but didn't run.

Marco appeared to have endless patience, and Amber found she was holding her breath when he tried to slip the noose over the horse's head. The mare evaded it and trotted to another corner of the corral. He followed on foot, his own horse plodding after him. Maintaining eye contact, he went on murmuring, stroking, and after a few more feints he was able to slip the noose over the mare's head.

She tried to shake it off, then ran, but Marco vaulted onto the other horse, following as before, gradually shortening the restraint until, miraculously, he had the wild mare trotting alongside him, apparently happily.

In the following days Amber filmed him working the horse, persuading her to trust him, until he had her trotting in a circle. She ceased backing away at his approach, and soon was following along when he walked the other horse.

Then he tried a saddle, which she did her best to buck off, and only when she had accepted that, he mounted her for the first time.

The mare trembled at the strange sensation, turned its head and made a tight circle, apparently in an effort to see its rider, then kicked out, trying to dislodge him. Marco stayed as if glued to the saddle. Within a week he had the mare obeying his every command.

Marco's way with females, it seemed, extended even to horses.

Ana Maria suggested Amber show her edited videos to the family on the big TV screen in the *sala*. Diego and Ana Maria were predictably lavish with praise, and Marco and his mother seemed impressed.

Finally even Elena said reluctantly, "They look…quite professional!"

Amber forgave her for the obvious surprise, pleased at the young woman's reluctant respect. "It's a top-of-the-range camera," she said. "And I learned a lot about filming from the people I used to work with."

Diego said, "We could use some clips from them on our Web site—if you allow it, Amber."

"You'd be very welcome," Amber told him warmly. "Tell me which ones you want."

A few days later, after she'd been swimming with Ana Maria, Elena and Diego, as they returned to the house the two young women fell behind, gossiping about fashion.

Amber said to Diego, "Elena is getting used to me, I think. She seemed a bit…shy, at first."

"Shy?" Diego laughed and glanced back. Leaning closer, he whispered, "I think my poor cousin hoped Marco would choose her."

"Choose her?" She looked at him inquiringly.

"Marry her."

"They're cousins!" Amber stopped to face him so abruptly she stumbled and bumped against him.

Diego steadied her. "Elena is cousin to Marco's wife— I mean his first wife." Then anxiously he asked, "You know he has been married before?"

"Of course I know."

The other two caught up with them, Ana asking, "Are you all right, Amber?"

"Fine." Amber tried not to look at Elena as Diego dropped his hands. "I tripped, that's all."

The four of them entered the house together and separated to dress. When Amber reached the bedroom, Marco was standing at the window, already showered and dressed in a white shirt open at the neck, with dark trousers.

He turned, taking in the towel tucked over her swimsuit, and her bared legs. "What were you and Diego talking about?" he asked as she crossed to the wardrobe. He must have seen them in the courtyard. "Secrets?"

"No! Nothing really." Relaying Diego's revelation would be unfair to Elena.

"Don't take my cousin's compliments too seriously," Marco said. "He is *un coqueto,* likes to flirt."

"I know that." Amber found a blouse and skirt in the big wardrobe. A little nettled, she said, "He told me Elena is a cousin by marriage."

"*Sí.* That makes her family. Her father died when she was seventeen. There was very little money left for her or her mother. Elena took a degree in business administration, and she is very useful here."

So he'd offered her a home and a job, probably paid her way through university. "What about her mother?" Amber asked. "There was nothing useful for her to do here?"

Rather coolly he said, "She did not want to move from the house she had lived in since she was a bride. She prefers to stay there with her memories."

It must have been a happy marriage. Amber wondered if Marco's parents had been happy together. A large framed photo of them on their wedding day, posed rather stiffly and smiling at the camera, hung in the *sala.*

Struck by a thought, she said, "What happened to your wedding photographs? And your son's photos? I haven't seen any pictures of them around."

"They are safe. Before I brought you here I asked my

mother to remove those on display. It did not seem…tactful to leave them."

"Oh." He'd been thinking about her feelings. "But surely you miss them—I mean, their photographs. I'd understand if you want them put back."

He gave her a penetrating look. *"De nada,"* he said dismissively. "Their images live in my heart." He touched his hand to the place, and Amber could think of nothing more to say, shamed by a pang of envy in her own heart.

She turned and walked to her computer, open as she'd left it before going to the pool, the screen blank. She pressed the start button and the screen sprang to life with her latest effort at editing her videos.

Marco came to her side. "You are very good at this," he said.

"Thank you. There's so much to film here. But..." She hesitated. "I had a feeling you didn't like my plan to make a documentary and send it to New Zealand—if I can find someone to buy it."

"Send it? I thought you meant after—" He paused, then gave a soft little laugh. "Perhaps I misunderstood. You may film as much as you like."

Misunderstood? Light dawned. He'd thought she meant when she returned home after her role here was finished.

That night, as she lay against his chest after making love, Marco said, "We have no visitors this week. I will take you to the *campamento* as I promised."

CHAPTER TWELVE

THE *campamento* was a two-storey building with a wide balcony running along its length that gave a view of a tranquil lake. There were two big rooms with bunks, but the one Marco ushered Amber into was smaller, boasting two queen-size beds shrouded in mosquito nets, and its own bathroom.

At sunset they sat on the balcony drinking wine, and watched dozens of flamingos at the edge of the lake standing statue-like until something in the water disturbed them and they took off in a panic-stricken pink cloud.

Marco handed Amber binoculars and she saw the caiman, frustrated in its quest for prey, turn with a petulant flick of its tail and submerge, its body scarcely rippling the water. A turtle sat unperturbed on a broken, dead branch near the water, and rainbow-feathered parrots flocked, chattering, in the nearby trees.

Stunning scarlet, black or green ibis flew down to dip their long beaks in the water, and a group of monkeys approached, scattering when the three-metre-long caiman leaped at and very nearly caught one, ending up snapping in frustration on the shore.

The next day Marco collected fishing gear and took

Amber on a leisurely river trip in a flat-bottomed boat, motoring gently through blankets of mauve water hyacinths, across which jacana—brilliant yellow beneath their wings, black on top—daintily trod as though walking on the water. Kingfishers dived for their dinner, and pinkish freshwater dolphins performed elegant synchronised leaps. Otters glided by or floated on their backs, and wading birds almost five feet tall stalked along the river bank. "Jabiru," Marco called them, and pointed out a flock of whistling ducks.

Shaded by trees where yellow butterflies were as numerous as leaves, he stopped and they fished from the boat. Amber caught a saucer-size silver-and-apricot fish with a huge mouth and fearsome teeth. Torn between pride in her catch and sadness at the plight of the fish as Marco efficiently dispatched it with a quick blow to its head on the side of the boat and tossed it into a bucket, she asked, "What is it?"

"Piranha," he said nonchalantly, and she recoiled, beset by memories of lurid tales and old TV movies of hapless minor characters or evil arch-criminals being devoured in minutes by hordes of piranha.

"They are good eating," Marco said, "but bony. We need more to make a meal."

Back at the *campamento,* instead of dining in the big room lit by oil lamps, he built a fire on sand near the water and barbecued their catch, serving it up with corn patties and plantain.

In the bedroom afterwards they made love in a leisurely, languorous fashion, miles from any human eyes and ears, to the chittering, cawing and hooting of night birds and the booming calls of howler monkeys.

As she lay against him, replete, in the distance Amber heard a deep roar, and lifted her head to listen as it was answered by another.

"Jaguars," Marco told her, stroking her hip. "The female is calling for a mate."

"This is the mating season?"

Marco gave a low laugh. "For the jaguar there is no particular season. Like us. But the male must wait until the female indicates she is receptive to his attentions. They are solitary creatures, coming together only for a short time to mate."

And stayed together just long enough to make babies, Amber thought.

The following day when they strolled along the lakeside, Marco pointed out the clear prints of a jaguar among the bird prints and snake trails.

Every day brought new discoveries and showed Amber new aspects of her husband. He could move as silently as a ghost through the tall grass of the plains or the green thickets of palms and bushes, and from twenty paces he could spot a green iguana hiding among the leaves of a tree, or an armadillo snuffling around its roots.

Although he carried a gun and a knife during their excursions, he had a passionate and protective love for his homeland, its wild creatures and its displaced indigenous population, as well as for his own heritage, and wrestled with problems of providing justice and fairness for all while preserving the economic base of the country.

She learned more about the complications of South American politics than she'd ever seen in the news. And more about her husband—his childhood on the *llanos,* his introduction in his teens to the wider world and the family's other business interests, his father's death and Marco's expansion of those interests to safeguard the family while redressing past wrongs, even against the advice and grumblings of old-guard friends and family.

One night she dared to ask, "Tell me about your wife."

She was lying in the crook of his arm while he absently stroked her hair. The stroking stopped, and after a short silence he said, "You are my wife, Amber."

"You know who I mean. I don't even know her name."

He was silent so long she thought he was going to refuse. Finally he said, "Her name was Emilia. She was very young when we married—barely nineteen. I too was young—it seems now a long time ago. She was pretty and sweet-natured, a good mother. I had known her since we were children. I think both our families expected we would marry one day, although nothing was ever said aloud."

"But you loved her?" She couldn't imagine Marco being pressured into marriage.

"Everyone loved Emilia. And she gave me Aurelio, our son, the most precious thing in the world to both of us."

He fell quiet and Amber said softly, "Aurelio. It's a nice name." Tentatively she asked, "What happened to them?"

"An accident." His voice thickened. "We were in Barinhas. I had a meeting with some politicians and landowners there, and Emilia wanted to take Aurelio shopping. He was growing at an astonishing rate, always needing new clothes or shoes."

Even now there was a note of pride in his voice. He paused again before going on. "We had arranged to meet for lunch once the meeting was over. I came out of the building where it had been held and saw them on the other side of the road. I waved. So…*stupidly!*" His voice grew harsh. "Aurelio was usually a sensible boy, but not used to the city. I remember how his face lit up, and his smile…he had such a smile, like the sun coming out on a cloudy horizon. Emilia had her arms full with parcels and bags, and anyway he thought he was too big to hold his mother's hand. I saw him step off the kerb without looking, but I had no time to shout at him, send him back, before a truck came around the corner…"

Amber held her breath, her stomach knotting, and wished she hadn't started this.

"I was too far away to do anything," Marco said, his voice now devoid of all emotion, but his accent becoming stronger. "I could see what was going to happen. Emilia— poor, brave Emilia—saw too. She dropped her parcels, her handbag, and dived—she seemed to be flying—to reach Aurelio, save him, get him out of the way. She must have known she would be killed. But it was no use. They both died instantly." His flat tone turning to harsh despair. "It all seemed so slow, and yet I could do *nothing!*"

"Oh, Marco!" Amber put her arms about him, offering what comfort she could, unable to imagine how he'd felt when his wife and child were killed before his eyes.

Tears filled her own eyes. "It wasn't your fault!"

"Everyone told me that," Marco said wearily. "It makes no difference."

Her tears spilled onto his skin, and he touched her face. "Amber…you are crying for me?"

"All of you," she said shakily, trying to wipe the tears away with one hand, trying to stop. "You and Aurelio and Emilia."

And maybe she was crying for herself too because, she realised, somewhere along the rocky road of their unconventional relationship she had fallen in love with this complicated, multifaceted man, who didn't love her and surely never would. She could give him her heart, her life. But his heart lay in a cold grave with his adored son and the gentle, courageous and selfless woman who had been destined for him from childhood—his beloved, *real* wife.

"Don't," Marco said, brushing his fingers across her wet cheeks. "They are beyond hurt, and I have become accustomed to mine. These things do not leave one, but they are past." He kissed her, holding her face in his hands. "You, Amber, have the power to give me happiness again. And I want you also to be happy." He kissed her once more. "I will do my best to make it so."

On their last day they caught a glimpse of a jaguar, its tawny coat marked with irregular circles, but it disappeared with a flick of its tail before Amber could get a shot of it with her camera.

Later they heard roaring quite close, and after hunting around for spoor Marco promised her a better opportunity.

Just before dusk the jaguars began to call again and, following the sound, Marco led Amber on a twisting route from the lake to a place where they peered through screening bushes at a magnificent spotted jaguar about twenty metres off, basking in the remains of the sunlight, flicking its tail and occasionally showing long, curved teeth to let out a full-throated roar, its ears twitching. As Amber focused her video camera an answering roar came from somewhere not far off.

"She awaits her mate," Marco whispered. "He is close now."

Within minutes a long, dark shadow rustled the grass and bushes, and a sleek black form materialised, emitting a low growl.

Marco had told her that black jaguars were sometimes born among a litter of spotted siblings, and she caught her breath at its sinuous, dangerous magnificence.

The female immediately leapt up and faced the intruder, snarling and being snarled at in return, both animals lashing their tails and showing their curved, pointed teeth. To Amber it didn't look like a love match.

The jaguars circled warily, feinting as if about to charge, then both reared and clashed against each other in a growling, hissing frenzy of claws and fangs, rolling over and over, scrambling for dominance.

Amber lowered her camera for a moment, and Marco murmured, "She is testing him to be sure he is a worthy mate for her. But he is strong and virile. She will submit to him in the end."

Now the black beast was on top, snarling, and the female suddenly stilled, lying half on her side as he straddled her. Through her zoom lens Amber could see the faint markings of typical jaguar rosettes with centre spots in his glossy coat.

He licked the female's neck and she turned her head, lifting it to nuzzle at him, making a soft sound almost like a purr. Amber let out a quietly whispered, "Oh!"

The male's black head rested on the female's neck, his paws, claws retracted, kneaded her body. Despite the earlier tussle, her hide was unmarked.

The male adjusted their position, and the muscles in his powerful haunches began moving rhythmically.

Feeling like a voyeur, Amber was nevertheless caught in the magic of the moment, there seemed to be such anomalous tenderness in this savage mating.

The female's amber eyes almost closed. The male's

movements stopped and he gave her what looked like a teasing, amorous bite on her shoulder before lifting himself away and trotting out of sight. For a while his mate remained where she was, then lazily rolled onto her back for a few seconds and repeated the movement several times, as if ecstatic, before stretching out, her side rising and falling with her breathing. She looked thoroughly content.

The black male reappeared, stared about suspiciously, his tail weaving the air. He appeared to home in on the two humans watching, his ears pricking up. Amber was almost certain he had seen them.

"Don't move," Marco breathed in her ear. He had the rifle in his hands.

It seemed an eternity before the jaguar turned his attention to his mate and padded over to her, lying down at her side, still watchful as if guarding her. It was getting dark now and his eyes were luminous, eerily glowing. Eventually he yawned, settled his big head between his paws and apparently slept.

"Come." Marco silently rose, and when he helped her up Amber realised her legs were stiff. She followed him as quietly as she could back to the cabin, still spellbound by what they'd been privileged to see.

Making love to her that night, Marco turned her over onto her stomach and she felt his strong body cover her, the gentle nip of his teeth on her shoulder even as he found the slick, yearning centre of her awaiting him, and he filled her over and over while she buried her screams of ecstasy in the pillow.

CHAPTER THIRTEEN

THE day following their return to the hacienda, Marco told Amber, "Next week I must go to Barinhas on business. We will take Madre and Ana Maria, and you can choose a wedding dress. Ana Maria knows all the best clothing stores."

"A wedding dress?"

"As the padre pointed out to me," he said rather dryly, "you were cheated of a proper wedding day. My mother too wants our marriage celebrated in the traditional manner. Perhaps your family would like to be here."

"I don't know if they can afford—"

"I will be happy to pay their fares, and they will of course stay here as guests of the family."

The dress was fabulous. Deceptively simple in style, but made sumptuous with shimmering satin and delicate lace.

She'd argued about using Marco's credit card, but had given in when he said, "It is part of our agreement. There is no need for you to make such an expense."

The reminder had stopped her cold. Sometimes she could almost—almost—forget that theirs was not a normal marriage, that love had played no part in its genesis.

Three weeks later she stood before the long, gilt-edged

mirror in Señora Salzano's room while the *señora,* Ana Maria and her own mother and sister fussed over her.

Ana Maria had taken charge of her make-up and styled her hair, crowned with a circlet of flowers.

"Are you sure about this, Amber?" Azure asked anxiously, when the others had left to check their own appearance. "Tell me truthfully, do you love him?"

Amber replied after the smallest hesitation. "Yes. Marco shouldn't have done what he did, but I don't think either of us understands completely how hard it was for him to let Benny go. He isn't mean or nasty, just…very focused on the things that are important to him."

"And not used to being thwarted," Azure added.

Sometimes she showed surprising insight. "True," Amber conceded. "But he has compromised hugely on this."

Amber had held her breath when her sister arrived with Rickie and their son. She'd seen how Marco had to tear his gaze away from the child sleeping against Rickie's shoulder, turning to greet her parents. And how later Azure had watched nervously when the little boy, losing his initial shyness, approached Marco and was lifted into his arms. Amber saw the fleeting tension in her husband's face.

When Benny reached up and patted his cheek, he'd smiled and then looked across at Azure, also watching him with anxious eyes. "I have two beautiful nieces," he said. "Thank you for giving me a nephew to love also."

And now he had met Benny, Amber thought, he wouldn't want to give up that link, would he? He'd said he would be an honorary godfather. He wanted to be involved, if peripherally, in Benny's life.

Even if he didn't love her, he'd want their marriage to last, legally at least.

Azure had looked as though she wanted to snatch her child back, and Amber quickly crossed to her side, a smile on her mouth to hide from the others the warning in her eyes.

Gradually Azure had relaxed over the next few days. Now she gave Amber a hug and said, hopefully, "Well, if you're happy, I'm glad it turned out okay. I can't thank you enough for what you did. And you look beautiful!"

Turning to the mirror again, Amber saw that it was true. She hoped Marco would think so, that he would fall in love when he saw her, and never want to let her go.

The traditional solemn marriage rite in the little village church was far more emotive than the brief, cold ceremony back home that she'd never mentioned to her parents or sister. Making her vows in careful Spanish, and then in English for the benefit of her family, her voice trembled, and Marco's hand tightened on hers, his dark eyes burning, compelling.

The church was crowded; members of Marco's extended family, his *llaneros* and the families that farmed around the village all attended, spilling into the square outside.

Giving Amber a warm embrace on the church steps, Marco's mother said, "Now you are really married to my son, you must call me *Mamá* Salzano."

She had arranged a huge wedding feast at the hacienda.

There was dancing and singing to the sounds of Venezuelan harps, four-string guitars and maracas far into the night, and when Marco and Amber danced the *joropo* together, all of the guests erupted in thunderous applause, clapping in time to the music.

It began almost like a romantic waltz, the music slow as Marco held her close and then expertly swung her to his side, his head turned to hers and his lips only inches from her mouth. His strong hands guided her through a series of simple steps that she followed faultlessly, and the music quickened to a fast, foot-stamping crescendo. He never took his gaze from her face except to twirl her, always bringing her back into his arms. Marco gave her a dazzling smile as they whirled ever faster, his eyes alight with pleased surprise.

"How did you learn our national dance?" he asked as he held her in his arms after the final flourish. He kissed her quickly on the lips and waved to their audience.

"Ana Maria," she said breathlessly, "taught me. And I've watched the *llaneros* dancing it with their women."

He laughed. "What other secrets are you keeping from me, *mi esposa?*"

Amber shook her head. *I love you* was a secret too new and fragile to express. He had never asked for her love, never offered love to her. If he couldn't reciprocate her feelings he might find the confession an unwelcome burden.

But today they had been married in his church, and he too had made vows. If she gave him what he wanted so badly he might come to love her, even if only out of gratitude.

When they finally went to bed, as dawn broke over the vast flatlands, perhaps she imagined that Marco's lovemaking was extra tender, adoring her body almost as if this were their true consummation. As if he'd really meant it when he promised to love and cherish her until death.

The celebrations went on for three days before the guests began to leave. Elena had worn a wistful look as she gathered with the family at the church, and Amber had felt sympathy, but even Elena was swept into the dancing and partying, one young man particularly attentive.

Saying goodbye to her family at the end of their week-long stay, Amber was relieved that their lack of Spanish and

Señora Salzano's limited English precluded any in-depth conversation about how she and Marco had met.

As the *hato* returned to normal, Amber realised that with the whirlwind preparations for the wedding and the excitement of seeing her family, she had lost track of her monthly cycle, which had never been reliably regular.

And maybe that was exactly why she'd missed a period. Stress—even the pleasant kind—could be a cause.

A test with the kit she kept in the bathroom was less than conclusive. The instructions said false negatives were more likely than false positives. She forced herself to wait another week.

This time there was no doubt.

It was Sunday morning and later they would be going to church, but she'd visited the bathroom early, when the sky was a pale, luminous pink. Marco was still in bed but awake, propped against the pillows with his hands behind his head, looking…enigmatic.

She said, "It looks as though I'm pregnant."

The words seemed to fall into a void between them. She wondered if he'd heard.

He lowered his arms with no discernible change of expression. "I have wondered when you were going to tell me."

Of course he'd have been keeping an eye on the calendar. This, after all, was why he'd married her. Try as she would to forget that, the reality every now and then hit her like a splash of icy water, bringing to the fore the persistent hidden ache she couldn't quite ignore.

Lately—ever since what she thought of as their "real" wedding day—when they made love, he had been extra gentle, sensitive to her every move, every murmur or sigh of pleasure, satisfying her fully while holding back himself. Not that passion was lacking, but she felt a subtle difference in his touch, his kisses. In and out of bed, he treated her like something precious and breakable. Last night she'd dared hope it meant his feelings were changing, becoming deeper. She'd gone to sleep in his arms bathed in a warm glow of cautious joy.

Had all that careful handling been not for her, but to protect the baby he had guessed she carried? She said, "I wanted to be sure of a positive test before saying anything."

"We will see a doctor to be certain, make sure everything is as it should be."

His voice was neutral, and she stood uncertainly in the middle of the room, feeling suddenly alone and frightened, all last night's warmth and wonder seeping away. The responsibility of having created—co-created—a new life, another human being, struck her as something so huge and powerful she wasn't ready for it.

"Are you all right?" Marco flung back the covers and strode to her.

She wanted him to take her in his strong arms, hold her close. Instead he stopped and lightly laid his hands on her shoulders, soothed the goose-flesh on her arms but otherwise didn't touch her.

"I'm fine," she said mechanically. Physically she didn't feel any different. Without knowing what she had expected of Marco, this calm acceptance somehow bothered her.

"I will make sure you are taken care of," he said. "You and our son."

Amber didn't doubt it. He would do anything necessary to ensure this baby was born safely, and that meant taking care of the woman who housed it. Her body, that he enjoyed so much, admired and caressed and played like a violin, bringing it into singing, extraordinary harmony with his, would become distorted and clumsy with the burden of his child. Unattractive.

She should remember that for him sexual pleasure was a bonus, a nice perk. Basically she was no more than an incubator for Marco's longed-for child.

He said, "Is there anything you need? Anything I can get for you?"

Amber shrugged out of his hold. "All I need right now," she said, retreating to the bathroom, "is a shower."

So cool, Marco thought as Amber closed the door between them. Foolishly he had hoped, after the harmony of their brief "honeymoon," the solemn religious marriage ceremony and all they had shared since, that she would be happy to share this with him, to stay with him as his wife and the mother of their child.

A strange, black heaviness descended on him. There was no going back now. And more than ever the burden of guilt weighed on him, coupled with dread.

She is not Emilia, he told himself. Aurelio's birth was a freak event, Emilia was so small, almost delicate. This will be different. Yet fear laid an iron hand on his heart.

What madness had possessed him to think Amber would ever look forward to having his child? He had done this to her and now there was no going back.

May God forgive me. But it was not God's forgiveness he craved. And how could he dare even ask for Amber's?

The specialist Marco insisted on consulting said Amber needed a good, balanced diet and moderate exercise to keep healthy and prepare her body for labour. Marco vetoed horse-riding, and she was limited to walking and swimming, with gentle workouts on the home gym that Ana Maria religiously used. It was much less fun now Ana Maria had returned to university. "Mamá Salzano" was quietly pleased and joined her son in ensuring Amber had adequate food and rest, and did nothing that could harm the baby.

Amber began to feel like a prisoner.

Occasionally she persuaded Marco or Diego or even Elena to take her out in one of the all-terrain vehicles with her camera. With Diego she had updated and extended the Internet site, which now featured several clips of her work. She was also editing a feature and researching TV outlets for it.

But she'd explored only a small part of the vast estate, seen relatively few of its wild inhabitants.

The rains came, and came, and came—day after day, flattening the coarse grasses of the *llanos,* soaking the ground, flooding huge areas of the plains.

Marco regularly flew her to Barinhas for checkups, but after two ultrasounds, because of the baby's position in the womb, medics were unable to determine its sex.

"If they'd said it's a girl," she asked, flying home after the last test, "would you have wanted a termination?"

"An abortion?" His brows knotted fiercely. "Certainly not! You are not to think of such a thing."

Well, at least they were of the same mind on that. She would never have agreed.

The day Amber first felt the baby move, she was in the courtyard alone, tending the flowers in their pots, a duty she had taken over as something she could do without incurring Marco's displeasure.

She dropped the secateurs in her hand and put her palm to her abdomen, thinking maybe she was mistaken, but again she felt the movement, a fluttering of her tiny passenger, unmistakably something she'd never felt before.

Thinking Marco was working in his study with Elena, she went inside and along the passageway, eager to share the news with him, and threw open the door without knocking, to find Elena standing alongside the filing cabinet, gazing at a framed picture in her hand.

When Amber entered, Elena quickly turned away, and the picture hit the corner of the open drawer, smashing the glass with a sharp sound. It dropped to the floor.

Elena seemed frozen in horror, and Amber quickly crossed to pick up the picture. "I'm sorry, Elena," she said. "I didn't mean to startle you."

She turned the frame, broken at one corner, to examine the damage and pick out the rest of the ruined glass, only then seeing the smiling woman and child in the photograph.

Elena snatched it from her, holding it to her chest. Her eyes were wide and her lips trembled.

"I'm so sorry," Amber reiterated. "The photo isn't damaged," she said gently. "We can get another frame. It's Emilia, isn't it? Marco's wife, and their son."

Elena nodded, still clutching the picture close. "It should be on the top of the cabinet, where he could see it from his desk. I found it at the back of the drawer." Her dark eyes flashed and her pretty mouth twisted bitterly. "All Emilia's pictures are gone, except in my own room. He tries to forget her now because he is *loco* for you."

I wish! Amber thought wryly. Had he placed the picture there so that he could secretly take it out and remind himself of his double loss? Remember when he and Emilia had been together with their little boy, a happy family?

Aloud she said, "He won't forget her, Elena." Her voice was husky with effort. "I know he loved her very much. He had her pictures put away to save my feelings. I don't suppose he realised how much it hurt you."

Disturbed by Elena's tragic, hostile stare, she crouched to pick up some glass.

"Amber?" Marco's voice made her jump, and a sliver of glass dug into her palm. "What are you doing?"

Amber hastily stood, and Elena, looking totally miserable, dumbly held out the picture for him to see.

He frowned. "You dropped it?"

Amber said quickly, drawing his attention, "Elena's not to blame. I am. I came in after she found it and I—"

He wasn't listening, taking one stride to catch her wrist and look at the blood welling on her hand. *"¡Ay, Dios mío!"* he exclaimed. "What have you done to yourself?"

"It's nothing—I was cleaning up the broken glass."

He said something explosive in Spanish and then, "We have staff to do that! Elena—call Filipa, tell her to bring the first aid kit." Grabbing the waste paper bin near the desk, he ordered Amber, "Put the glass in here."

"Shouldn't it be wrapped?" she objected, not wanting someone to cut themselves when disposing of the bin's contents. But at his hiss of impatience she complied. Blood was welling from the small wound at a surprising rate, and she didn't want it to fall on the beautiful woven rug.

She looked about for a box of tissues, but Marco had pulled a folded, unused white handkerchief from his pocket, and he pressed it against her palm.

When the maid brought in the first aid kit he took it from

her and dressed Amber's hand himself, then told Filipa to sweep up the rest of the glass and dispose of it, and she hurried out of the room.

Elena stood by silently watching his ministrations, still holding the photograph, then suddenly burst into a torrent of Spanish too fast for Amber to follow, except for her own name and Emilia's, until Marco said something curt and harsh, and she ran from the room with the photo.

Amber said, "She's upset. I'm really sorry about the damage to the photo."

He looked at her closely. "Why did you do it?"

For a moment she gaped at him. "It was an accident!"

What had Elena said in that passionate outburst? Amber had been taught at an early age that telling tales was mean and ignoble, unless to prevent actual physical harm. The habit of a lifetime prevailed. "There's some misunderstanding," she said weakly.

Filipa arrived holding a short broom and a shovel and began sweeping up the rest of the glass, and Amber closed her lips, unwilling to continue the conversation in front of the maid, even though the woman evidently didn't understand a word of English.

"You admitted you were to blame," Marco said.

Amber shook her head. "I'd rather not discuss it now." Nor did she feel this was the time to tell him that she'd felt his baby move. That moment of euphoria and excitement had passed. "I have things to do before dinner," she said, and slipped past Filipa to return to the patio and the dead blooms she'd been snipping off.

At dinner a subdued Elena avoided Amber's anxious eyes, later slipping off early to her room. When Amber and Marco were alone later preparing for bed, she asked him, "What did Elena say this afternoon before she rushed off?"

"Quite a lot," he said. "But it need not concern you."

"Neither of us meant to damage the photograph." Amber briefly told him what had happened.

He merely nodded, his expression not giving anything away. When she added, "I think Elena was distressed that you'd taken her cousin's picture from its place. Would it disturb you if it were repaired and put back there?"

Marco's short laugh was oddly harsh. "Is that what you would like me to do?"

"For Elena's sake, yes." Perhaps for his too she thought, suppressing the pang that gave her. "I appreciate you were trying to save my feelings, but I can't ignore or forget that you were married to someone else and had a child with her. It's been the elephant in the room ever since I came here."

"Elephant?" Marco shook his head, his brows rising.

"The thing that everyone pretends isn't there," she explained. "Even though it's so big you can't miss it."

"Ah," he said, enlightenment in his face. After a brief pause he said, with a strangely resigned expression, "Very well. I will tell Elena to get a new frame and return the picture to its accustomed place." Under his breath he muttered something else, but she caught only the word *penitencia*. Penance? She didn't dare ask.

Within a few days the photo reappeared on top of the filing cabinet, in a new frame. Amber didn't ask where that had come from—perhaps Elena had removed another picture from it. She seemed to mellow towards Amber from then on, and one day when they were alone she said abruptly, "I'm sorry for those things I said to Marco about you. You are not what I thought. He told me you asked him to put Emilia's picture back."

"I have no idea what you thought. Or said to Marco."

Elena flushed. "That you were a…a gold digger, I think is the English term. That you had hypnotised him with sex, made him forget the sweetest, prettiest, most loving wife any man could have, who adored him."

Almost exactly the same words that Marco had used to describe Emilia.

"He won't forget your cousin," Amber said, thinking how ironically far off the mark Elena's view was. "Nor Aurelio. He can't, and I wouldn't want him to. Only…I would like him to be happy."

Elena gave her a strange look. "I, too, would like that for Marco," she said. "Are *you* happy, Amber?"

"Of course." *Was* she? Certainly closer to it than she had expected before leaving her homeland. She and Marco had sex less often lately, but he was solicitous when she had bouts of nausea or was simply tired. When they did make love he was cautious, afraid of hurting her or the baby despite the doctor's assurance there should be no problem. Every night he slept at her side, and as the months went on he spent more time at the hacienda. Yet somehow he seemed emotionally to be growing more distant.

Amber remembered wistfully their closeness at the *campamento,* when he'd even allowed her to comfort him over the loss of his son and his wife. All that seemed to have disappeared under a mask of courtesy and care that held little real warmth.

He was pleased that she had developed a growing appreciation of his country, its language, customs and turbulent history. Once he took her to Caracas for several days, where they attended concerts and exhibitions, and she absorbed the rich cultural life of the city with its diverse population and the constant throb and strum of music combining Spanish and African, indigenous Indian and modern American themes and rhythms.

At last she went into labour and was taken to the hospital to give birth. The following hours were a blur of pain and effort, with doctors and nurses giving encouragement and efficiently guiding the process. Marco held her hand in a hard, warm grip while he stroked her hair or wiped her forehead with a cool cloth and talked in a calm, reassuring voice, telling her she was brave, beautiful, magnificent, in English and in Spanish.

Then it was all over and she felt a surge of relief and euphoria like nothing she'd every experienced before.

A tiny bundle of warmth was placed on her breast and she looked into fathomless dark eyes that blinked sleepily from a round little face with a rosebud mouth, and scarcely heard the voice of one of the medical staff say, "Congratulations, *señora*. You have a beautiful baby girl!"

She must have slept for hours. When she woke a nurse was lifting the wailing baby from a bassinet beside the bed, depositing it into Amber's arms as soon as she'd managed to sit up. The nurse helped her bare her swollen breasts and beamed with satisfaction as the baby nuzzled about and found its target, settling comfortably to suckling.

Amber would never forget that moment, when absolute love and awe filled her, gazing down at the oblivious little face with its curved cheek and minuscule nose and cap of wavy dark hair, while unbelievably small, fragile fingers clutched at her skin.

After the nurse left, Marco entered, carrying a huge bouquet and looking big and handsome and turning Amber's heart over just at the sight of him.

She admired the flowers and he put them on the cabinet at her side before pulling over the visitor's chair and seating himself. "How do you feel?" he asked Amber.

"Wonderful," she answered, glancing up at him. Oddly shy, she went back to gazing at the baby.

"Your parents are on their way," he said, making her raise her eyes to him in surprise. "I thought you would like to have them with you."

"That's thoughtful of you," she said. "They'll be thrilled with their new grandchild." She guessed that he had insisted on paying the fares. "You're very generous, Marco. I'm grateful."

He too seemed somehow uncomfortable, even stressed, his eyes deeper in their sockets, the skin stretched over the bones of his face. "You have no cause to be grateful to me, Amber," he said. "I am sorry for what I have put you through."

The guilt of a new father after watching a woman deliver his child in blood, sweat and tears. Some women in labour, she'd been told, cursed the man who had made them pregnant. She'd simply been grateful that he was there with his calm, steady support; although, she had seen the sheen of sweat on his brow that matched hers, seen the tautness of his jaw suggesting an inner tension.

All she felt now was a serenity like no other. Only one faint shadow remained. Unable to imagine that Marco didn't share her feelings for this tiny scrap of humanity that they had created, that he had helped her coax and push into the world, she said, "I know you wanted a boy, but maybe next time…"

"Next time…?" He got up suddenly, pushing back his chair so hard that it started to topple and he grabbed it and put it upright. "*You* can say that?"

The baby abruptly stopped suckling and wriggled inside her covering, making little snuffling noises. Amber lifted the infant against her shoulder, closing the gown over her breasts. A cold sense of foreboding crept up on her. Recalling what Marco had said about his first wife—that after her difficult childbirth he wouldn't subject her to another—she said, "I'm strong and healthy. There's no reason I can't have another baby, in time."

"I hope you do," Marco said in a strangely muffled tone, "but not mine."

The chill increased, and her voice sounded thready when she said, "What do you mean?"

He wasn't looking at her, instead staring at the floor, hands thrust into his pockets. She saw his knuckles through the fabric as if he'd clenched his fists. "I have booked a flight for you and your baby to fly to New Zealand with your parents, in ten days' time. A one-way ticket."

Shock made her dizzy and speechless. Her limbs seemingly made of lead, she turned and placed the baby back into the bassinet, tucking in the covers as if the trivial action were the most important task in the world.

Her heart was leaden too, beating slowly, suffocatingly. "*My* baby?" she repeated.

"Of course I will pay for her upbringing, her education—anything she needs," Marco said, his tone colourless. "Or that you need." He might have been discussing the care of his cattle. "Apart from that…I'm sure you will give her a good upbringing."

Amber's heart was splintering into a thousand pieces.

At the same time anger began to simmer, breaking through the paralysing cold and fear that gripped her.

Marco had counted on a boy, and because she'd given him a girl he was cutting his losses, denying the baby the right to know her father, hurling Amber's unspoken love back in her face. Sending them away because she'd failed in the one thing he'd wanted from her, the one thing he'd married her for, that she'd almost lost sight of because she'd foolishly, *idiotically* fallen in love with him.

Fallen in love, forgetting how cold-bloodedly he'd engineered their marriage, how ruthlessly he'd exploited her love for her family, her fear for the future of her sister's baby, forgetting the very basis of her relationship with him—that if she didn't meet the conditions he'd laid down he'd dispense with her. As he was dispensing with the child he didn't want.

"You *bastard!*" she spat. "You heartless, selfish, sexist barbarian!"

She should have seen the signs—they'd been there. The practised seduction, the efforts to resign her to her fate with cunning and patience, his encouragement of her filming, the magical "honeymoon" at the *campamento,* enchanting her with its wildlife and putting his own spell on her with his lovemaking.

And then, after she was pregnant, a gradual withdrawal, an aloofness she was unable to penetrate. Because he thought he'd achieved his goal, and all he had to do now was wait until his child—his *son*—was safely born.

Even today he hadn't even glanced again at the baby. Not once. How could she have thought she loved this calculating, manipulative, unfeeling man?

Marco's jaw set tight. "I said I would let you go."

"When I gave you a son!"

He shrugged, with a seeming effort. "It makes no difference. I have arranged for your parents to stay at a hotel near here. It is best if I don't see you again." Something happened to his voice then, a sort of cracking. "Thank you, Amber, for our time together. I apologise from the bottom of my heart for what I did to you. It is impossible to make it right. I have been all you say—selfish, arrogant, a barbarian. I can only try my best to make it up to you."

He turned and opened the door, even as she tried to absorb that, make sense of it. "Marco?" she said to his implacable back.

He ignored her, stepping into the corridor.

She shoved back the bedcovers and somehow got hurriedly to her feet. *"Marco?"*

He might have been deaf.

"Marco!" Reaching the doorway, she held onto it because she was dizzy. Dimly she could see him rapidly walking away from her, skirting a couple in front of him, nodding to a passing nurse.

With an effort she stepped out into the corridor, screaming at him with all the energy and fury she could muster, "*Marco Salzano,* don't you *dare* walk out on me—on your daughter!" She tried to say more, but her lips wouldn't work and the corridor was turning darker. Then, even though her eyes were open, she saw only blackness and finally nothing at all.

Leaving the room, Marco resolutely kept his eyes focused straight ahead. He was doing the right thing—far too late, but he had to go through with this. Had to, however inadequately, give back to Amber whatever he could of her own life. And sacrifice his baby, his and Amber's beautiful baby girl. No matter that it hurt so much he was afraid to look at her.

Taking long, rapid strides, he passed a couple in the corridor, stifling an urge to shove them out of his way, so black was his mood.

He had always known that a child would bind Amber to him. But he also knew that he wanted more from her than a reluctant commitment, more than her lifelong bondage for the sake of her child. More, much more, than her sexual surrender and the delights of her body.

He wanted her love. Even though he'd tried to blind himself to his own need at first, *that* was the real, underlying reason he had been unable to fly home and leave her in New Zealand.

And how could a woman like her love a man who had descended to such depths to win her? She could feel nothing but hatred for such a man.

The nurse he automatically nodded to as he strode away from any chance of happiness gave him a startled look. He realised he appeared the antithesis of a delighted new father, with a scowl on his brow and his eyes bleak with steely determination—and grief.

His guilt had increased daily with the progress of Amber's pregnancy, peaked as she struggled in agony to deliver his child.

Now her voice, sounding both desperate and angry as she called his name, challenged his cowardly retreat, made him wince. He gritted his teeth and kept walking.

He heard a muffled thud, an exclamation, and turned to see the nurse hurrying towards a crumpled form outside the door of one of the rooms.

Amber.

Without thought he was running back, passing the nurse halfway and dropping to his knees beside the still, ashen-faced body, choking out her name.

The nurse arrived beside him, checked Amber's pulse, asked, "She's your wife, *señor?*"

"Yes." Marco said. "My wife." *My wife, to have and to hold...* But he must not think that.

Deathly afraid, he obeyed the nurse's brisk request to carry the patient back to her room.

Gently he lowered Amber to the bed, relieved to see her eyelids flutter and consciousness return as she focused dazed green eyes on him.

"Marco," she said. Her hand moved, apparently aimlessly, and he caught it in his, smoothing back her tumbled hair from her cold forehead with the other. She seemed to be comforted by that, her eyes closing, a hint of colour returning to her cheeks.

He held his breath, thinking his heart was going to burst with fear and love. It had been the same while she was having the baby, her lovely face contorted with effort, sweating, gasping, grunting—praying. He had never felt so helpless in his life, nor so guilt-stricken, not even after Emilia and Aurelio died, when in the depths of despair he'd blamed himself for not being able to save them.

Nor when he'd brought Amber to the home that held their ghosts, unable to shake the feeling that he was betraying their memory by wanting another woman with a desire so fierce and relentless that he'd forced her into an insane bargain. Not able to even face their photographs, pretending to himself as well as his mother that it was Amber's feelings he was sparing.

Amber, who hadn't cared anyway. Who, far from being

upset by reminders of a previous love, had urged him to restore Emilia and Aurelio's portrait to its place.

While he had squirmed with an irrational jealousy of her easy friendship with Diego, she had not felt even a twinge of that emotion.

Because she did not—could not—love him. This too was his fault—the pallor of her skin, her bloodless lips, the coldness of her hands, the glazed look in her eyes.

It had taken all his willpower to walk away from her, set her free to live her life without him. But with the daughter he had loved from the first moment he'd seen the wet, bloody, slippery little tadpole that she was at birth. He'd been afraid to look at her as she lay on her mother's breast taking her first breaths. He'd known right then, with the piercing pain of imminent loss, that he had no right to hold either of them, neither her nor her mother.

A doctor hurried into the room after the nurse and Marco allowed them space to take her blood pressure, check Amber's pulse again, ask questions that Amber weakly answered. Finally they left, saying, "You fainted, is all. Don't get out of bed too quickly. We'll leave you with your husband." And to him in Spanish, "Ring the bell if you are worried."

Marco stared down at his sleeping daughter. He lifted his gaze to Amber and saw her eyes widen, knew she had seen his suffering. "Thank you," she said, "for coming back."

He shut his eyes tightly, turned away to swipe with an impatient hand across the hot stinging of his eyes and, making himself face her, said in a guttural voice, "Do not thank me, Amber. It is what you call coals to Newcastle."

For a moment she looked blank, then to his surprise she

emitted a shaky, girlish giggle. "You mean coals of fire, I think. It wasn't your fault I fainted."

"You are wrong. Everything that has happened since we met is my fault. I have sinned against God and against you. Against my own...morals, principles. I told myself I was entitled, that because you had conspired with your sister to hide her son from me it was not criminal to force you to be my wife. But the truth was, I wanted *you*. You. And a baby—your baby—to hold you to me."

"But—"

"I will keep my promise to let you go," he ground out, against every instinct, "but—" momentarily he closed his eyes again, composing himself "—*why* did you call me back? You have made it doubly hard."

Amber had seen the anguish in his eyes. *"Why?"* she asked, afraid to believe in the hope that stirred inside her. "Why is it so hard?"

He opened his eyes, and they blazed. "Because I cannot live without you—no, I must. I will not ask you to forgive me for the unforgivable. This is the penance I deserve. It is for your sake, and for hers." His gaze flickered to the crib, and then he seemed unable to drag his eyes away. "A part of you—and a part of me also. At least that knowledge you cannot take from me."

Amber blinked. "I don't want to take anything away from you, Marco!" What was he saying? "You kept insisting on a son, but...you *want* her? You think you could love her?"

He groaned, actually groaned aloud. "Of course I want her!" he growled, and drew a harsh breath. "I have loved her from the moment I first saw her. Almost as much as I love you."

Amber stared, momentarily unable to speak. "Me?"

"*Madre de Dios!* How can you not know? I have loved you since—I think since I first knew you were not your sister. You were so fierce to protect your family, so determined to defy me, even though I knew that in another time, another place, we might have been lovers. I *had* to have you, keep you at my side. I was *loco*—arrogant and *estúpido* enough to think I could make you love me."

Amber felt hope slowly becoming certainty, then a starburst of revelation.

Marco loved her. Hadn't she seen it in everything he'd done since taking her to his home—in every gesture, every touch, every look? In his patience and determined gentleness, his care of her even when she repudiated it, impatient with his over-protectiveness.

She swallowed, found her voice. "What you did was monstrous—" she saw him wince at that "—and if you ever pull a stunt like that again, I'll…I'll…haul you over those red-hot coals from Newcastle," she finished lamely. "It's what you deserve. But—" she looked at the baby, obliviously sleeping at her side "—you gave me the best gift of my whole life. For her sake alone I'd forgive you, if I wasn't already in love with you."

Marco shook his head. "In love with me?" He seemed dazed.

"*Yes!* And if you send me away I'll come back to Hato El Paraíso and camp on your doorstep, in a tent if I have to. With our baby. You wouldn't do *that* to your daughter, would you?"

Marco sank heavily on the bed, taking both her hands in his. "No, *querida*. Never." Regaining some of his usual manner, he said, "I will not have it! But you must be sure this is what you want, because I may never let you go. Oh, holidays, *sí*. For a little while, to see your family. Not to leave me, to tear my heart apart."

"I couldn't," Amber said simply. "And besides, I won't deprive our baby of a father. She needs you, almost as much as I do."

"As I need you, *mi corazón*," he said fervently. *My heart.*

She'd never thought Marco could sound so humble. It was almost scary that she could do this to him, a man who had never shown vulnerability before.

Then he leaned over and kissed her, and she held him close with her arms about him, goading him from gentleness to passion until he wrenched himself away, saying, "Enough! You are not fit yet for this." He stood, drawing in deep breaths, his hands clutching the rim of the bassinet. "Have you given her a name?" he asked.

"No. Do you have any preference?"

Marco shook his head. Then he said, "*Sí*. Generosa. In honour of her mother. Its meaning is *generous*."

Amber tried the name. "Generosa." She looked at the baby. "Genny for short? Or Rosa. She looks like a rose."

As if she had heard, the baby stirred, opened her eyes, screwed up her face and sneezed. Both her parents laughed, enchanted at what they had made between them. Marco leaned down and whispered, "Generosa?"

She stared up at him, gave a contented little grunt and closed her eyes again.

Marco leaned down and kissed her forehead. "Generosa," he said. "I think she approves."

"Yes." Amber held out her hand to him, and he took it again in his, raising it to his lips.

"You must rest," he ordered sternly, tucking her hand under the covers.

For once Amber would be happy to obey. When she was not so tired she would teach him to be less autocratic, for their daughter's sake. Already she imagined a teenager with Marco's black hair and strong will, dark eyes flashing at his protective restrictions. She smiled. "You can go now," she said. "I suppose you have things to take care of."

"No. Only you," he assured her. "I am yours," he promised, "for as long as you want me."

"I want you. Always." She closed her eyes, serene in the knowledge that he was watching over her and their child, that whatever predators or demons he had to fight, from outside or within himself, her very own conquistador would keep them safe for the rest of their lives.

HAWAIIAN SUNSET, DREAM PROPOSAL

BY
JOANNA NEIL

When **Joanna Neil** discovered Mills & Boon®, her lifelong addiction to reading crystallised into an exciting new career writing Medical Romance™. Her characters are probably the outcome of her varied lifestyle, which includes working as a clerk, typist, nurse and infant teacher. She enjoys dressmaking and cooking at her Leicestershire home. Her family includes a husband, son and daughter, an exuberant yellow Labrador and two slightly crazed cockatiels. She currently works with a team of tutors at her local education centre to provide creative writing workshops for people interested in exploring their own writing ambitions.

CHAPTER ONE

'He's not doing very well at all, is he?' The young woman's voice was choked with emotion, and her eyes filled with tears as she looked at Amber. 'Isn't there something more that you can do for him? Nothing seems to be happening.'

Amber removed the printed trace from her patient's heart monitor and taped the paper strip into his file. The readings were erratic, showing a dangerous, uncoordinated rhythm. 'I know this must be a very difficult time for you,' she said in a quiet voice, turning towards the girl, 'but I want you to know that we're doing everything we can for your father. I've given him an injection to take away the pain, and he's receiving medication through a drip in his arm to try to prevent things from getting any worse.' There was a defibrillator on standby in case his condition deteriorated, but she wasn't going to point that out to her patient's anxious daughter.

The girl pulled in a shaky breath. 'He looks so dreadfully ill. I know he hasn't been well these last few months, but this has come as such a shock. As soon as I saw him, I knew it was bad. His secretary called me at the university to say that he was unwell and that they'd called for an ambulance… I was in the middle of a lecture, and I rushed over there as quickly as I could.'

She gulped, sending a worried glance towards her father. 'She said he had been in his office, trying to get through a backlog of work, when he suddenly felt nauseous and short of breath. At first he thought he was suffering from a bad attack of indigestion, but then things got worse and he felt this awful pain in his chest…a crushing, vice-like pain.'

She broke off and dabbed at her eyes with a tissue. 'By the time I arrived at the office, he had collapsed and the paramedics were there. It all seemed to have happened so quickly.'

'The paramedics gave him emergency treatment before they brought him here,' Amber told her. 'They did everything that was possible to make sure he arrived here safely.'

Martyn Wyndham Brookes had been conscious when he'd arrived at A and E but, despite his pain and discomfort, his one thought had been for his daughter. 'She's very young,' he had managed to say, 'and she's a long way from home…studying at university. She always wanted to come to London.' His face had been haggard with pain, but his concern for his daughter had been obvious as he'd looked anxiously at Amber, and she had hurried to reassure him.

'We'll look after her, I promise,' she'd told him gently. 'I'll have a nurse take care of her…but right now we need to concentrate on making you feel better.' She had taken to him straight away…such a strong, warm-hearted man.

Now, after he had lapsed into a drowsy, semi-conscious state, she felt it was time to explain to his daughter what had happened. 'I suspect he's had a heart attack,' she said, 'and that there's a blood clot blocking an artery somewhere and causing problems with his circulation.'

Tears trickled down Caitlin Wyndham Brookes's cheeks. 'That's what the paramedic said…but that's bad, isn't it?'

'It's something we're used to dealing with,' Amber said. She studied the girl's pale features. 'Is there anyone we can call for you…someone who might come and be with you?'

Caitlin shook her head. 'My mother died some years ago, and there's no one over here…just my friends at university.' She gazed at Amber in an agitated fashion. 'Isn't there something more you can do for him? What if you have to go off and deal with other patients? I know you have others to see, and it's so busy here. There are so many patients being brought in… I want somebody to be with him all the time, someone in a senior position.'

The flow of words stopped suddenly, as though she was taking stock of what she had said. 'It's not that I'm doubting your ability,' Caitlin tried to explain, 'but he's just lying there, looking so frail… It isn't like him at all…he's always been so tough, so busy, on the move all the time.' Distress caused her voice to waver, and Amber hurried to soothe her once more.

'We'll know much more about what's happened to him when we've done all the necessary tests. It will take a little while for all the results to come back, though. In the meantime, we're taking good care of him. He's receiving oxygen through a face-mask, and his condition is being observed the whole time with the aid of the heart monitor and various other machines. If I'm called away to attend to another patient, I'll still know what's going on, because the nurses will alert me to any change as soon as it happens.'

She frowned as she ran the stethoscope over her patient's chest. Initially, his heart rate had been alarmingly fast, while his pulse had been barely discernible, but now the heart rhythm was becoming chaotic and everything about the man told her that he was gravely ill.

'Unfortunately, we don't have any records for him, over here in the U.K.,' Amber said, turning to look at the girl once more. Caitlin Wyndham Brookes was twenty or so years old, a slender young woman with black hair expertly cut into a smooth, jaw-length bob. Her eyes were grey, sombre at the moment, much like an overcast, rain-drenched sky. 'You mentioned that he lives overseas for most of the year,' Amber added. 'Do you know who looks after his medical care back home?'

'He has his own doctor in Oahu…in Hawaii.' Caitlin glanced at Amber. 'I suppose I could try to get in touch with my step-cousin over there. He'll be very concerned about my father—they're so much like father and son. My father took Ethan under his wing after his parents died, and there's a real bond between them.'

She hesitated for a moment, thinking things through. 'Ethan would probably be able to have a word with the doctor back home, if that would help, and I know he'll want to be kept informed about what's happening over here.'

Amber nodded. 'That would be great. As he's so far

away, it might be quicker and easier if he could fax the information we need, or perhaps send the bare essentials by e-mail. If you were to go and have a word with our nurse, I'm sure she could help sort things out.'

Sarah, the nurse on duty, was happy to oblige, and Amber sent her a grateful glance as she led the young woman away. Sarah gave her a discreet smile in return, her fair hair making a silky swathe across her shoulders as she nodded with gentle perception. 'I'll take a few details and see if we can find out any more information.'

She could see that Amber had enough on her hands, dealing with a difficult situation that could take a turn for the worse at any moment. Much as she wanted to help in any way she could, Amber was finding it distracting, trying to keep the young woman calm throughout everything.

Amber turned her attention back to her patient. Martyn Wyndham Brookes was in his mid-fifties, a tall, personable man, she guessed from talking to the paramedics, with black hair streaked with threads of silver. She gathered that he was a wealthy man, a man of some standing in the international business community. According to the paramedics who had brought him into hospital, his U.K. office was situated in Docklands, occupying a prestigious block that overlooked the grand vista of the river Thames.

It seemed, though, that illness was no respecter of wealth or position. Martyn's condition had gone downhill rapidly, and Amber knew that it was going to take all her skill to help him to recover. His features were ashen, his skin had taken on a clammy appearance, and he was no longer attempting to talk.

'How's it going?'

She glanced up to see that James, her boyfriend, a senior house officer like herself, had come to join her. She looked at him with affection, feeling as though a faint glow of sunshine had come into her life. 'Things could be better,' she said in a low tone. 'It's always good to see you, though. How are things with you?'

He shrugged, draping an arm around her shoulders, so that she immediately felt warm and cherished. 'So-so. It's been pretty stressful around here, lately, with one thing and another. We're still waiting on the results of job applications, aren't we, and our contracts here come to an end within a couple of weeks? Have you heard anything yet?'

She shook her head. 'Nothing, so far, though I haven't had time to check my hospital mail box yet to-day. We've been so rushed in here.'

He gave a brief, half-hearted smile. 'I expect you'll come through it all right. You're very good at everything you do. Look at the way you sailed through your exams. No one is going to turn you down. You applied for a top-notch job in emergency medicine and you're bound to get it.' Even as he was singing her praises, there was a flat note in James's voice that made Amber glance up at him, a frown indenting her brow.

He let his arm fall to his side, leaving her feeling suddenly bereft. Something was clearly wrong with him, but she had no idea what it might be. James had not been his usual self for some weeks now. At first she had thought it was the pressure of exams weighing him down, along with the aftermath of results, but now she was beginning to wonder if it was something more than that.

'I don't think it's as cut and dried as it seems. I'm waiting to hear the news just the same as everyone else. From what I've heard, it's all down to the computer system matching up job applications with employers. There were some terrible glitches, apparently.' She frowned. 'It's all a bit worrying, isn't it? Sarah said that there have been quite a few mix-ups, and a lot of people have missed out on getting any kind of job. Some junior doctors have been talking about leaving medicine altogether.' She shook her head in sad reflection, causing her burnished chestnut curls to quiver in response. 'It's such a waste, after all those years of training.'

She looked back at her patient. He seemed to be oblivious to everything that was going on around him, but perhaps that was just as well, given how desperately ill he was.

'I doubt you'll have any problems,' James said. 'All the senior staff speak very highly of you, and you could pretty much do anything you want. I guess it puts me in the shade.' His mouth made a rueful shape, and Amber sent him another quick look, wondering what had got into him to make him appear so downbeat.

'You sound as though things are becoming too much for you,' she murmured, sending him a sympathetic smile before checking the pulse oximeter reading to see how her patient was doing. The machine kept bleeping, warning her that the level of oxygen in his blood was falling as his circulation became more impaired. She decided to check with the consultant about starting him on thrombolytic drugs to try to dissolve, or reduce, the size of any clot that might have formed.

'I'm really hoping that we'll be able to work together

at the London University Hospital. We've worked well with one another here in A and E, haven't we?' Amber studied James closely, seeing the troubled look in his eyes. 'Perhaps we could have lunch together later today and talk things through? I'm fairly sure that you won't have any trouble getting the research job you were after.'

'Maybe. There aren't that many people lining up to study my particular area of enquiry into asthma. It all depends whether the powers that be can come up with the funding.'

He straightened up, looking more at ease with himself, and moved away from her, towards the door. 'I'll go and check in the office again to see if any more news has come in.' He looked at the man lying motionless in the bed. 'Poor chap. It looks as though he's having a rough time.'

Amber nodded, brushing a hand over her temples to tease back tendrils of hair that threatened to obscure her vision. Her chestnut-coloured hair was a shoulder-length mass of wild curls, a genetic gift from her mother that needed to be ruthlessly tamed with clips or scrunches. They shared the same eye colour, too, a soft, jewelled green.

'I want to start him on thrombolytics,' she said, 'but until I have the results from the lab, I'm working in the dark a bit. My boss is operating on a badly injured patient right now, and I don't want to disturb him unnecessarily, but I don't think I can afford to wait.'

'I know what you mean. It's a balancing act, knowing when to prescribe and when to bide your time. I'd be inclined to interrupt your boss if I were you.' James walked towards the door. 'I'll be back down here in a few minutes to see how you're doing—I only came to see if you had heard anything about the job you applied for. Someone said letters were being given out this morning but for now I need to go and check up on a patient. Do you want me to check your box for any letters while I'm there?'

'Yes, thanks.' Amber nodded and turned her attention back to the businessman, writing up his medication notes on the chart as Sarah came into the room. Sarah shot a glance towards James as they passed each other in the corridor, and a small frown started up on her brow. Martyn's daughter was by her side, but Caitlin was pre-occupied just then, speaking to someone on her mobile phone. She stayed in the doorway, and Amber guessed Sarah had asked her not to bring the phone into the room.

Amber put the chart to one side and looked once more at the chest X-ray in the light box. Martyn's heart was enlarged, and that was not a good sign.

Sarah inspected the settings on the infusion meter and made sure that their patient was receiving the right amount of medication through a drip in his arm.

'Is everything okay with you and James?' she asked in a quiet voice, throwing a brief glance in Amber's direction. 'He doesn't seem to be his usual self these days, does he? It's hard to pinpoint, but there's definitely something…'

'I was just thinking the same thing,' Amber answered cautiously. 'I think the world of him, as you know. We've been together for over a year now, and I thought everything was fine, but just lately I'm not so sure. He doesn't smile as often as he did, and he has a sort of hangdog air about him, doesn't he?'

Sarah nodded. 'It's probably the aftermath of exams, and waiting around for results and job offers,' she remarked. 'It seems to have affected everyone. My boyfriend's gone into a bit of a decline, too. We've just not been having any fun lately.'

'I dare say things will get better.' Amber looked across the room at Caitlin, and saw that there was an awkward air about her, a reticence, as though she was in some way holding back. 'Was there something you wanted to ask?' Amber murmured.

Caitlin indicated the phone. 'It's my step-cousin, Ethan,' she said, in a hesitant fashion. 'He asked me to put him on speaker-phone. He wants to be involved in everything that's going on.'

'That's fine with me.' Amber nodded. 'Just don't bring the phone any closer to the medical equipment, or it might cause interference.'

She checked Martyn's pulse. It was thready, his features were drained of colour, and she was worried in general about his condition. 'It must be frustrating for your cousin to be so far away and not know what's happening.'

'But not for much longer, I hope.' A male voice cracked in a whip-like fashion across the room. His tone was concise and authoritative, and Amber braced herself in startled recognition of the fact that he must be able to hear every word that was being spoken. 'I'd like to talk to the doctor in charge of my uncle's case,' he said.

'That would be me,' she answered. 'I'm Dr Amber Shaw. I'm the senior house officer in A and E. I was on duty when your uncle was brought in. I take it you are Ethan Wyndham Brookes?'

'I'm Ethan Brookes without the Wyndham. Yes, my

cousin explained the situation to me. I understand you've been taking care of my uncle, and I'm grateful to you for that. I heard that you have him on anti-coagulant therapy to prevent any more blood clots from forming, but his condition seems to be deteriorating.'

'Things are going very much as we might have expected,' Amber told him. 'As I explained to your cousin, we're still waiting on the results of tests, but they should be here very soon.'

'Hmm. But in these situations time is of the essence, isn't it? So, I'd like to speak to the consultant in charge, if I may?'

He posed it as a polite question, but Amber was in no doubt that it was a request. She guessed from his deep, well-modulated and assured tones that he was used to having things his own way. He would be somewhere in his mid-thirties, she imagined.

'Of course, I'll put you in touch with him as soon as possible, but he's in Theatre at the moment. Perhaps I could assist you in the meantime? I'd like to reassure you that we're doing all that we can to make your uncle comfortable.'

'I'm glad to hear it. My cousin and I are very worried about her father.'

Amber had the feeling he didn't want to be dealing with an underling at all, but she made an effort to remain calm and not take it personally.

'I'm very well aware that this is a difficult time for both of you,' Amber murmured, 'but I can assure you that everything that can be done is being done. Your uncle has received the recommended treatment so far…oxygen, aspirin, glyceryl trinitrate and painkilling medication, as well as blood-thinning drugs. I've already cleared the way for him to be taken up to the angiography suite. As soon as my boss has finished in surgery, he'll come down and assess your uncle's state of health.'

'So you're thinking about operating on him?'

'It's a possibility, if his condition will allow us to do so. We may be able to find the clot that's causing the damage and remove it by means of a catheter. That might do away with the need for more intrusive, major surgery, but I have to say that Mr Wyndham Brookes's condition is very precarious. From the looks of his X-ray there could be an underlying disease that might cause more problems. That's why it would be extremely helpful for us to have access to his medical records.'

'I'm already onto it, and I'll send them to you as soon as possible. In the meantime, I'd like to set up a video link with his hospital room. I know you have conferencing capabilities, so it shouldn't be too difficult to arrange.'

His suggestion took Amber's breath away. This man clearly knew what he wanted, and didn't see why he shouldn't sweep every obstacle to one side in order to get things done.

'Is that going to be a problem for you? Perhaps I should speak with your chief administrator?' Perhaps he had heard her swift intake of breath. Ethan Brookes sounded as though he had no time for shilly-shallying. If she couldn't deal with it, he would go to someone who could.

'That won't be necessary,' she murmured. 'Your uncle is in a private room, so I'm sure we can accommodate your request, as long as his daughter has no objection.' She glanced at Caitlin, raising her brow in a faint query.

'I'd like that,' Caitlin said. 'It will make me feel better to know that Ethan's looking on.'

Amber wasn't at all sure how she felt about it. Having her every move watched by a stranger wasn't something she welcomed, but technological advances meant that it could be done, and if it was something that helped unite families in their hour of need, who was she to object?

'My boss should be here within a few minutes,' Amber said. 'I'll speak to him about it, and if he agrees, we'll call on one of our technicians to set it up. Now, if you don't mind, I need to give my full attention to your uncle…unless there was something else that you urgently wanted to discuss?'

'No…it will keep. Thanks for your co-operation,' Ethan said. The speaker-phone link was cut, and Caitlin went out into the corridor to finish her conversation with him in private.

Amber drew in a deep breath. It was one thing to deal with worried relatives close at hand, but having difficult, long-distance discussions with someone she had never met was a first for her.

A few minutes later, she left Martyn in Sarah's care, while another nurse took Caitlin away to show her to a waiting room. There she would be able to sit in comfort and talk about her concerns to the nurse with the aid of a reviving cup of tea. Having Caitlin looked after took a great deal of the strain off Amber's shoulders and left her free to go and check on her other patients.

When her boss came down from Theatre, Amber grabbed the opportunity to update him on Martyn's condition.

'We'll take him up to the catheter suite as soon as the team is assembled,' the consultant agreed. 'As to the video link, I see no reason to object.' He gave a brief, wry smile. 'Besides, I've heard of the Brookes's international fruit-shipping company. I read about their goings-on in the newspaper from time to time. These people are high-powered, influential individuals. Let's not get on the wrong side of any of them, if we can help it. Call the technician and ask him to sort out the video link. Anything to keep them happy.'

Amber lifted a faintly arched brow. Her boss wasn't someone who usually worried too much about following protocol and treading carefully around people, so if he thought it expedient to appease Ethan Brookes, who was she to argue?

'Professor Halloran,' Sarah interrupted, 'you're needed in the resuscitation room. One of your pacemaker patients is in difficulty.'

The consultant nodded. 'Okay, I'll be along right away.' He sent a brief glance towards Amber. 'Prepare Mr Wyndham Brookes for surgery, and I'll be along as soon as possible.'

Amber did as he asked, leaving a nurse to call in the technician to set up the video link. Martyn was barely conscious, but she spoke to him gently, explaining what they were going to do.

'Professor Halloran is the best cardiac surgeon we have,' she told him. 'He'll use X-ray images to look at your blood vessels through our cardiac monitor, and that should help him to find exactly where the blockage is. He'll most likely insert a very thin catheter into a blood vessel of the top of your leg, and then he'll use specialised instruments to remove the clot that's causing the problem.' She looked into his grey eyes. 'Do you understand what I'm saying?'

He nodded almost imperceptibly. 'I do.'

'Is there anything that you'd like to ask me about it?'

'Nothing. Thank you. I'm very tired.' He tried to lift his hand and made a frail attempt to pat hers as it rested gently on the bedclothes beside him. His breath came in quick gasps. 'I know you'll do your best for me. You mustn't worry if it all goes wrong.'

Amber felt the quick sting of tears behind her eyelids. Somehow, this man had managed to reach her inner core, the place where she tried to keep her feelings hidden. In the short time she had known him, she had found an affinity with him, and she realised that she cared deeply about what happened to him.

'Nothing will go wrong,' she said softly. 'I'm going to take good care of you, I promise, and you have to know that Professor Halloran is the very best.'

He didn't speak any more after that, but lapsed into what seemed like an exhausted sleep. The heart monitor began to bleep, the trace showing a chaotic descent into a dangerous rhythm, and Amber called for help. 'I need a crash team here—now. Call for Professor Halloran.' Her patient was going into shock, and cardiac arrest was imminent. 'He's in V-fib.' Ventricular fibrillation meant the heart was unable to pump blood around Martyn's body and without swift intervention he would die.

James and Sarah rushed to the bedside. Sarah started chest compressions, while James set the defibrillator to analyse the patient's rhythm and prepared to deliver a shock to Martyn's heart. Amber was aware of Caitlin standing in the room, watching everything that was going on, tears rolling down her cheeks, but she couldn't let that distract her. She worked quickly to secure Martyn's airway with an endotracheal tube and ensure that he was receiving adequate oxygen through a mechanical ventilator.

'Stand clear, everyone,' James said. As soon as the shock had been delivered, Sarah continued compressions. Amber checked for a pulse and looked to see if the rhythm of the heart had changed.

'He's still in V-fib,' she said. 'Let's go again with a second shock.' By now, Caitlin was making small sobbing sounds, and Amber was aware of another strange background noise, an odd swishing sound that she couldn't quite make out.

James set the machine to deliver the second jolt of electricity, but Amber could see it hadn't had the desired effect. 'Keep up the compressions,' she said. 'I'm going to give him a shot of adrenaline.'

They continued to work on their patient, but after a while, when Martyn's response was still insufficient, Amber added amiodarone to his intravenous line. She wasn't going to give up on this man, no matter how resistant his condition seemed to her efforts.

'You can do this, Martyn,' she said, under her breath. 'Come on, now, work with me. You're going to the catheter suite and you're going to come through this. Don't let me down.'

James glanced towards Caitlin, clearly disturbed by the girl's distress, but he could see that Sarah was tiring and moved to take over the chest compressions. Sarah watched the monitors and recorded the readings on a chart, while Amber worriedly assessed the nature of the heart rhythm and debated whether to add atropine to the medications she had already given him.

Professor Halloran came into the room, taking everything in with one sweeping glance. 'How's he doing?' he asked. 'Do you have a normal rhythm now?'

Amber checked the monitor and turned towards him. 'We do,' she said, relief sounding in her voice, and Professor Halloran nodded in satisfaction.

'Well done, everyone.' He turned his attention to the flat screen of the computer monitor that had been set up on a table across the room. He held up his hands in a thumbs-up sign. 'He's back with us,' he addressed the screen, and now, at last, Amber realised where the swishing sound had been coming from.

The screen was filled with the image of a man standing on what appeared to be a wooden veranda, surrounded on all sides by a balustrade. He was looking towards them, long limbed, lean and fit, with broad shoulders that tapered to a slim, flat-stomached midriff. He was wearing casual clothes made of fine-textured cotton that would be cool and comfortable in the heat of the Hawaiian summer. In the background she made out a palm tree and the clear blue of ocean waves lapping on a golden, sandy beach.

'I see that,' the man said. 'I saw it all, as clearly as if I had been there.' He moved closer to the webcam, and Amber realised that the computer must be situated on a ledge in front of him. The screen showed him now in clear view, blotting out most of the background, and she was aware of the strong, angular lines of his face, of thick, black hair cut in a way that perfectly framed his features. Most of all, she was stunned by his clear, blue eyes, the exact colour of the sea, that appeared to be looking right at her.

'We'll take your uncle up to the catheter suite right away,' Professor Halloran said. 'It's important that we get to work as soon as possible.' He glanced at Amber. 'I'll leave you to bring him up in the lift, Amber, while I go and prepare.'

Amber nodded, dragging her gaze away from the image on the screen. She was glad to have something to distract her. There was something about the way Ethan Brookes looked at her that was infinitely disturbing. It was as though he could see into her very soul, and that was an unnerving thought.

Even more unsettling, though, as her gaze swivelled to the doorway, was the sight of James, deep in conversation with Caitlin.

'I don't know what to do,' Caitlin was saying. 'He's all I have in the world.'

'You're not alone,' James murmured. 'I'll look after you. I'm off duty for a while now, and we can talk. Maybe we could even get together later this evening when my shift finishes. I know you'll probably want to talk some more. These things can hit you very hard. It's a worrying time.'

The girl lifted tear-drenched eyes towards the young doctor, and James reacted in the way that men have reacted throughout time. He melted in the face of her vulnerability, draped an arm around her and gently led her away. It was an innocent, caring gesture, but somehow, seeing his tenderness and concern for this young woman, it rocked Amber to the core. James hadn't taken his eyes off Caitlin's face. He looked at her with compassion and something else, something akin to adoration. He appeared to be totally, utterly smitten.

'Dr Shaw? Are you with us?' Ethan Brookes's voice cracked across the void, and Amber blinked, coming back to reality and trying unsuccessfully to blank out the image that was imprinted on her mind.

'I should thank you for your prompt action,' he said, and she lifted her gaze towards the screen once more.

Those steely blue eyes raked over her, as though he was making a thorough assessment of her. 'You've bought my uncle a little more time, and I'm grateful to you for that.'

She gave a brief, noncommittal nod in his direction. 'That's what I'm here for,' she murmured.

'Yes, but it's obvious that you're also young and relatively inexperienced. You did well to cope as you did…but I'm wondering if I should arrange for a private specialist to come and take charge of my uncle's case. I don't want anything left to chance.'

She braced her shoulders. She was a senior house officer, more than capable of doing what was required. 'Of course, that's your prerogative,' she murmured. 'It wouldn't be wise to delay proceedings, though. He needs to go to surgery now, and we have his full permission to go ahead…so if you'll excuse me, I need to go and take him there.'

'I understand that. I won't get in your way…now… and thanks again for what you did.'

Ethan Brookes was thanking her, but his words had an empty ring about them. The image of his cousin and her boyfriend came into her mind once more, and right now she couldn't help momentarily wishing that the Brookes family had never come into her life.

CHAPTER TWO

'WE'VE done all that we can for him for the moment,' Professor Halloran told Amber as they left the catheterisation suite some time later. 'We may have cleared up the immediate problem, but Mr Wyndham Brookes is still a very sick man.'

Amber nodded. 'At least you managed to remove the blood clot that was causing the trouble. It's unfortunate that he has a lot of other things to contend with alongside that.' Martyn was lucky to be alive, but from the results of tests and the indications they had discovered during the operation, his quality of life was going to be severely restricted.

'I expect his nephew will want to know exactly what we've found,' Professor Halloran added, 'although the medical notes he sent us were a good pointer to the cause of the problem.' He frowned. 'Ethan Brookes is certainly keen on being kept fully involved, even though he's living thousands of miles away. Maybe you could explain to him that his uncle will need to take great care with his health over the next few months.'

'Are you not going to talk to him yourself?' Amber looked at her boss in surprise.

'Yes, I will…later. Right now, I have to go back to my pacemaker patient. His needs are greater right now.' He gave her a beaming smile. 'Besides, I've every confidence in you. Talk to Miss Wyndham Brookes, as well. I'll speak to both of them this afternoon, when I'm free.'

Amber was glad he had such faith in her to do the right thing, though she suspected it was a ploy…he was a much better surgeon than he was at talking to patients. As to speaking to Martyn's nephew herself, she was conscious that Ethan wasn't entirely pleased that she was the one taking day-to-day responsibility for his uncle. He wanted the best…but Professor Halloran was not readily available to be there for him one hundred per cent of the time.

She went back down to A and E and went in search of Martyn's daughter. She could understand how distressing this situation was for the girl, but the image of James consoling her and leading her away with his arm draped protectively around her had been running through her mind over and over again as if in a film loop these last few hours.

Perhaps she was taking things too personally, though. Wasn't it entirely natural for any normal, thinking person to want to comfort someone in their hour of need? James was a good, kind man. She ought to be pleased that he was so considerate towards others.

While she had been in the catheter suite, James had apparently been working his way steadily through the mounting list of patients who had arrived at A and E. He met her as she walked over to the central desk in the unit a few minutes later.

'I picked up this letter for you from your mail box,'

he said, handing her an envelope. 'It looks official, so it could be news of the job you applied for.'

'Oh, thanks.' Amber frowned, looking at the logo on the envelope. He was right…the letter probably contained the information she was waiting for. She glanced up at him. 'Did you hear anything about the job you were after?'

His mouth made a downward turn. 'Yes. It turns out I didn't get the job. The letter was waiting for me when I went back to the mailroom. They appointed another candidate, but wished me luck for next time.'

Amber felt an immediate rush of sympathy for him. 'Oh, James,' she said, reaching out to give him a hug, 'I'm so sorry. I know how much you wanted that post. You must be feeling really down about it.'

He nodded briefly, trailing an arm around her in return. 'I was almost expecting to be turned down, but it came as a shock, all the same.'

'It must have done. What will you do now?'

He gave a negligent shrug. 'I'll have to think about some of the other research projects available. They weren't nearly as appealing as this one, but at least I stand some chance of getting one of them.'

'Sorry to interrupt, Amber,' Sarah said as she approached the desk, 'but Mr Wyndham Brookes has just been brought back down to his room. His daughter is feeling anxious because he doesn't look too good…and I think she's been looking at the medical notes that were sent over from Hawaii—that was never going to make her feel better. Her cousin advised her against it, and so did Professor Halloran, but she was determined to go ahead anyway. Do you want to come and have a word with her?'

'Yes, of course. I'll come along right away.'

Amber sent a worried look in James's direction, but he was already lifting up a patient's chart from the tray on the desk, and she started to turn, getting ready to walk away with Sarah.

James frowned. 'I feel sorry for the girl. It's bad enough that her father has been taken seriously ill, but she's a long way from home and virtually on her own.'

'I expect she appreciated you trying to help her,' Amber murmured. She slipped the envelope into her pocket. If it was bad news about the job she'd applied for, she'd rather deal with it when she was on her own back in her rented apartment. 'You were very kind to her. I imagine she'll look to you for help from now on. I heard you telling her that you would be free to talk to her after your shift finishes.'

'That's right. Do you mind very much?' James asked softly. 'I know we said that you and I would have dinner together later on today, but she's not coping very well, and I don't like to leave her without support. Maybe we could all get together to eat. She might appreciate having a woman around.'

'I'm not so sure about that.' Amber's expression was subdued. 'I don't think I'm her favourite person at the moment. She was quite distraught, and I had the distinct impression she thought I wasn't doing enough to help her father. It happens, doesn't it, when people are ill and the situation isn't improving?' She had the feeling that Caitlin had passed that view on to her cousin, but to his credit he hadn't made any comment on that—to Amber, at least.

She sent James a thoughtful glance. 'But you go ahead and meet up with her if that's what you want to do. I have a thousand things to catch up with back at the apartment.'

It might have been her imagination, but she thought she detected a look of relief passing over James's face. Was he finding it too much of a strain lately, being the second half of a couple? Over the last few weeks she had noticed subtle changes in his manner towards her, though she had tried to tell herself it wasn't happening. Now it cut her to the quick to have to take on board the changes in him. She didn't want to believe that their relationship was falling apart, but all the signs were beginning to point in that direction.

'I might do that, if you really don't mind? I said I would help her as much as I could.' He made a fleeting smile. 'It's strange, but it appears we have a lot in common. It turns out Caitlin's studying pharmaceutical sciences and wants to go into clinical research, much the same as me. It's an odd world, isn't it?'

Amber nodded. So they were on first-name terms already, were they? Her gaze was bemused as she watched him walk away. She set off with Sarah towards the patient's private room.

'I don't think I would have had the confidence to give him the go-ahead to meet up with another woman,' Sarah commented in a low voice as they walked along the corridor. 'Seems like a risky proposition to me.'

Amber gave a shuddery sigh. 'I've a feeling you could be right, but without trust, what is there? If I tried to stop him, it would make me appear selfish and uncaring, and for his part he'd probably end up feeling thwarted and resentful.'

'You're too good for this world,' Sarah commented

dryly. 'In fact, you have a lot in common with Martyn Wyndham Brookes, now I come to think of it. I feel really sorry for him. He seems like such a lovely man. Even though he was very ill when he first came to us, he managed to thank us for what we were doing for him. He was appreciative to all the nurses. He's one in a million… I suppose it must have been great for his daughter to have him come over to the U.K. to work for a few months while she's studying here.'

'I should imagine so. I take it for granted that my parents are fairly close at hand, though we don't see each other as often as I would like. It must be a bit lonely for Martyn's daughter, being so far from home.' Amber was making an effort to put all thoughts of James and her patient's daughter out of her mind. It was all supposition up to now, and she could be wrenching her heart unnecessarily.

'A great experience, though, coming to study at one of the best universities around. And she has a dishy cousin keeping in touch with her.' Sarah grinned. 'Now, that does make me envious…except I wouldn't want to be related to him. He's much more like eligible-bachelor material.'

Amber gave a rueful grin. 'Are you sure he's eligible?'

'Oh, yes. Professor Halloran told me so. The family's rich, and he's always in the papers because some flighty madam wants to get her hooks into him.'

Amber gave a dismissive laugh. 'I don't believe that for a minute. I have a feeling that he's way too grounded to allow anyone to take advantage unless he wants it. Just talking to him puts my defences on alert.'

'That's because you're ultra-cautious—and you're much more of a touchy-feely kind of person. Talking to him via a screen and a microphone isn't the same as meeting up with someone face to face. Technology just doesn't do it for you, does it?'

'You should have been a psychologist,' Amber remarked with a faint smile. 'Is he online right now, do you know?'

'Yes, he is,' Sarah murmured. Her mouth relaxed into a soft smile. 'He spoke to me to ask how things were going in the catheterisation suite. I'd have given anything to stay and chat with him,' she added in an undertone, 'but his cousin beat me to it, coming into the room and wanting to tell him what she'd heard.' She rolled her eyes heavenward. 'He has everything, doesn't he? Good looks, energy and a fabulous office practically on the beach.'

'Perhaps he works from home,' Amber suggested. 'If his family owns an international fruit-shipping company, it could be that they live on site. Imagine being at work and watching the waves roll onto the beach while you cool down with a glass of something iced and delicious, made by your own company.'

Sarah chuckled. 'I doubt I'd get very much work done in those circumstances,' she murmured.

When Amber walked into Martyn's room a moment later, she saw straight away that he was in a state of exhaustion. Of course, he was still drowsy from the anaesthetic, but the readings from the various monitors showed her that he was very weak and that his heart was struggling. She checked his medication, adjusting the infusion meter, before turning to his daughter, who was sitting, waiting anxiously by his bedside.

The computer monitor with the video link was set up

so that Ethan Brookes would be able to see both his uncle and his cousin. Amber did her best to ignore the webcam while she spoke to Caitlin. She was aware of Ethan's image in the background, though, his features alert, his gaze watchful, and though she nodded towards him briefly out of politeness, she preferred to set about dealing with the flesh-and-blood person who was in the room with her.

'Professor Halloran asked me to let you know that he removed the blockage in your father's artery,' she told Caitlin. 'His circulation improved right away, and he should soon start to feel much better. Even so, it looks as though there has been extensive damage to his heart, and I'm sorry to say that I don't believe he will ever regain perfect health. It's important that you know that.'

Caitlin's gaze was cool and remote. 'Wouldn't he have stood a better chance if he had been operated on earlier?'

It was a faint barb, but Amber deflected it easily enough, knowing that the young woman was deeply upset and trying to come to terms with her father's illness.

'No, I'm afraid he wouldn't,' she said gently. 'Your father was already struggling with a heart that had been weakened by an infection of some kind. It must have occurred a while ago, and unfortunately it means his heart muscle is unable to pump at normal strength. The body tries to compensate for this, and as a result fluid builds up in the lungs, liver and legs.'

'What treatment are you planning on giving him?' Ethan Brookes's deep voice cut into their conversation. 'There are things that you can do to help him have a better quality of life, aren't there?'

'Yes, we can certainly do that.' Amber turned to look

at the computer screen. Ethan Brookes's blue eyes seemed to pierce her like lasers, as though he would accept no prevarication. 'We'll give him medication that will enhance the capacity of the heart muscle. Professor Halloran has prescribed a cardiac stimulant. What we want to do is make the heart's pumping more effective, and at the same time reduce congestion.'

She turned back to Caitlin. 'I know this is going to be hard for you to accept,' she said softly, 'but your father is never going to be the man he once was. He's very frail and once he's up and about again he'll find that he's short of breath if he tries to do too much. He'll have to take things slowly and that means he will need a long convalescence.'

Caitlin looked bewildered. 'He's never going to tolerate that. He's always been so vigorous. The business has been everything to him, and I can't see him sitting back and taking a passive role.'

'I don't believe he'll have any choice,' Amber said in a quiet voice. 'He can look forward to a reasonable quality of life if he takes things easy. Perhaps you can help by encouraging him to do that?'

Caitlin looked at the computer screen, sending her cousin a look of complete bewilderment. 'The business is everything to him,' she said. 'How is he going to be able to hand over the reins?'

Ethan's reply was brisk. 'I'm his partner,' he remarked in a matter-of-fact tone. 'I'll have to step in and make decisions for him.'

'But you've never been involved one hundred per cent in the business,' Caitlin protested. 'How is that going to work? You know what he's like. He'll never sit back and allow others to take over.'

'You'll have to leave it to me to sort things out,' Ethan said. 'I'm more worried about how you're going to manage. You still have a few weeks to go at university before you have to come home, don't you? Do you want me to come over and help you out?'

Caitlin shook her head. 'No, I couldn't ask that of you. I know how busy you are, and you'll have even more on your plate now that this has happened. You can't afford to take time off from your work. I'll manage. Don't worry about me. I have friends who will help me to get through this, and it's comforting to have this link set up so that I'm able to talk to you this way. It helps to put my mind at rest knowing that you're at the other end of a phone.'

Amber looked at her with renewed respect. Maybe she was growing up fast because of what had happened to her father. She wondered what it was that kept Ethan Brookes so busy, if he wasn't taking an active role in his uncle's business. What kind of work was he involved in?

'Will you keep me informed of what's going on over there, Dr Shaw?' His voice cut into her thoughts, and she blinked, looking up at the screen.

'Of course. I shall take a personal interest in your uncle's welfare. It may be that once he's up and about, we can refer him to our rehabilitation unit. They're very good at helping people to get back on their feet and helping them to learn how to cope with their limitations.' She studied him briefly. 'I understand how difficult this must be for everyone to take on board, but if you have any worries or questions, you only have to ask and I'll do my best to explain things.'

Ethan nodded. 'I know it can't be easy for you, relaying everything to me from such a long distance, but I do appreciate what you have been doing up to now. I should warn you, though, that illness and frailty won't keep my uncle down for long. Even though it seems that he might be easy to manage at the moment, once he's sitting up and taking notice you're likely to find him quite a different kettle of fish.'

'I'll try to bear that in mind,' Amber said. She wondered why he was warning her. Did he not think her capable of dealing with a difficult patient? She doubted Martyn would ever cause her a problem...he seemed to be a likeable man, through and through.

She glanced towards Caitlin. The girl was talking softly to her father, lightly stroking his hand in a gesture of affection, and Amber decided that for the moment she was calm enough and probably had as much information as she could handle. It would probably be best to leave her to come to terms with her father's condition at her own pace.

She looked back at the flat-panel computer screen, taking in the breathtaking sight of the Hawaiian seashore in the background. 'Every time I see you, you're close by the beach,' she murmured, focussing once more on Ethan. 'I had assumed that you were talking to us from your workplace—perhaps I was wrong about that? I must admit I've been envying your lifestyle.'

He gave her a fleeting smile that lit up his features. 'I should have explained,' he said. He waved a hand at the villa behind him. 'This is where I live. I've been trying to call the hospital from here whenever possible. You perhaps don't realise that it's actually very early in the morning over here, not long past sunrise, and I haven't even had breakfast yet, let alone set off for work. Besides, if I were to ring from the office, my uncle would soon become agitated. He likes to keep his finger on the pulse of what's going on, and any sign of his workplace would be enough to bring his blood pressure up.'

'You're right... I hadn't even thought about the time difference. It's late afternoon here.' So late, in fact, that she was due to finish her shift shortly. 'Anyway, from what I can see of it,' Amber murmured, 'you have a beautiful home.'

'Thank you. I certainly appreciate it,' Ethan said. 'Maybe at a time when neither of us is quite so busy, I'll show you around the inside, via the webcam.'

'I think I'd like that,' Amber agreed. 'It won't be quite the same as being there, but I'm sure to get something of the feel of the place.' Maybe technology wasn't so bad after all. She smiled. 'All that sand and sea and palm trees waving in the light breeze make me long for my summer vacation. Not that I'd ever be likely to go as far as Hawaii.'

Perhaps it was the smile that caused it, but Ethan's eyes widened a fraction as he looked at her intently. After a moment or two his gaze moved slowly over her, as though he was seeing her properly for the first time, and she was suddenly conscious of the clothes she was wearing—a skirt that fell smoothly over the curve of her hips to drape softly around her legs, and a snugly fitting cotton top. What did he make of her? she wondered. Did he only see her as young and inexperienced, incapable of taking proper care of his uncle?

'I'm sure you would love it here,' he said. 'I'll be sure to show you the landscape all around when you check in again.'

At that moment, Martyn made a faint groaning sound, and Amber turned immediately to look at him. She moved closer to the bedside. 'How are you feeling?' she asked.

'A bit sore,' Martyn answered. 'And very tired… It's as if all my energy has drained away.'

'That's to be expected,' Amber told him. 'It's nature's way of telling you to take things easy.'

'That's not what I'm used to,' he said with a wry smile. His gaze wandered to the computer screen. 'I thought I heard voices,' he murmured. 'Ethan, my boy, I'm glad you're there. What's happening at the plantation?' He paused to drag in a shaky breath. 'Are you managing to keep on top of things?'

Amber raised her eyes heavenward. Caitlin and Ethan had been right when they'd said he wouldn't let go. Here he was, slowly coming round from the effects of an injection that had made him woozy and tranquil, and he was already asking questions. 'I'll leave you in the care of the nurse while I go and look in on my other patients,' she told him. 'Have a chat with your family, but don't go tiring yourself. You need to rest.'

She gazed at the screen and sent Ethan a look that spoke volumes. He nodded, and gave her a smile in return. 'I'll make sure of it,' he said.

Amber took her leave of Caitlin, and went to check on the rest of her patients in A and E. Before too long it was time for her to go off duty and make her way home.

Once she was back in her apartment, the reality of everyday life began to creep in, and weariness swept over her as she recognised that she was totally, utterly alone. She had no doubt that James would have finished his shift and be comforting Caitlin right now, and that left a bitter taste in her mouth.

She reached into her pocket and drew out the letter James had given her. She had been busy these last few hours, but it had taken all her reserves of will-power to keep herself from opening it until now. All her hopes for the future lay within the contents of this envelope, but James hadn't even asked her what it contained. Perhaps he assumed all would be well…or maybe his priorities had changed, now that Caitlin needed his support.

She tore open the envelope. 'Dear Dr Shaw,' the letter began, 'I am sorry to inform you that, due to a filing error, your application was mislaid, and unfortunately the position you applied for has been filled in the mean-time. Please accept our deepest apologies for the mix-up.'

Amber scrunched the letter into a ball and pulled in a shuddery breath. All her dreams were gone in the blink of an eye. She was devastated.

She had worked hard throughout her training to become a doctor, and her one ambition was to specialise in accident and emergency medicine. Now that opportunity had been denied her, and she was to all intents and purposes going to be out of work within a few weeks. It was too late to pursue any other job offer because all the specialist applications were closed.

She wandered around the apartment, seeing nothing, struggling to take in the news. There was no point in ringing James to confide in him, and seek to find consolation together. If he had cared enough, he would have phoned her by now to ask how she was getting on, and she could only guess that he probably had other things on his mind.

Instead, she rang her mother. She, at least, would want to know the result of all her efforts, and Amber had already found a voice message on her answering machine asking her to get in touch.

'Oh, Amber,' her mother said, 'I never dreamed that they would turn you down… Well, they haven't, have they? It's all down to administration errors. Is there anything you can do now? Will there be other jobs you can apply for?'

'I doubt it,' Amber said in a resigned tone. 'It's too late now to sort anything out. All the specialist positions that would have interested me will have been filled by now. The most I can hope for is that I can apply for a locum post. I might be able to fill in when people are sick. It means going from one hospital to another, where I'm needed, perhaps, or working for short stints on contract—a few months at a time, maybe.'

'It might not be so bad as you imagine,' her mother commented. 'Perhaps something will turn up.'

'Let's hope so,' Amber murmured.

They chatted for a little while, about her mother's work as a graphic artist, and Amber enquired after her father, who worked as a general practitioner at the local health centre.

'He's out on call, at the moment,' her mother said. 'There seems to be a spate of people going down with flu. I think he's overworked and stressed just now—one of the doctors is off sick, and another is away on leave, so the practice is under a bit of a strain. He's had to take on a good share of his workload, as well as his own.

We're both under a good deal of pressure at the moment and things are a bit tense between us at times. I have deadlines to meet, and nothing quite goes the way I want it. I told him what we both need is a good holiday.'

Amber could see how that prospect would be tempting. She could do with a break herself. She had a picture in her mind of boats tethered on a gently sloping beach, while waves lapped desultorily at the shore, leaving white ribbons of foam to fringe the golden sand. Exotic birds would fly from one palm tree to another…and there, in the forefront, gazing at the vista before him, stood a tall, bronzed figure, his blue eyes half-closed against the glare of the sun.

She pulled herself together with a jolt, frowning as she said goodbye to her mother. Why on earth would an image of Ethan Brookes come into her mind that way? Didn't she have enough problems to deal with, without him popping into her mind every other minute?

CHAPTER THREE

'YOUR temperature's way too high, Jack,' Amber told her patient, 'so I'm going to give you something to try to bring it down, along with medication to stop you from being sick.'

'Thanks. I feel really rough.'

'I can imagine how bad it must be.' She glanced at his arm. 'That's a really nasty sore you have there,' she said with a frown as she examined him. 'Do you recall how it happened?'

Jack grimaced. 'I was bitten by an insect of some kind—a sandfly, I think.' He was a man in his early twenties, a man who should have been full of vigour and zest for life, but at this moment his skin was sallow, and there were beads of sweat breaking out on his brow.

Amber nodded. 'I don't suppose that it happened in this country, did it? Have you been overseas at all, lately?'

'I was in South America,' Jack said. 'I worked there for a couple of months until recently.' He glanced at her. 'Do you think that's what's causing my illness—the fact that I had an insect bite? That's what my mates think.' His face contorted as another spasm of nausea washed over him and he struggled to overcome the urge to vomit. 'I didn't feel too bad until I arrived home in the U.K.,' he managed. 'I seem to have gone downhill ever since then. I've never felt as ill as this before.'

'It does seem quite likely that's what happened,' Amber told him. 'I'll do a biopsy, and take some blood for testing. Once we have a clear idea what we are dealing with, I'll be able to treat you more specifically.'

Jack looked worried. 'Some of my co-workers have been telling me that this sort of illness can be hard to treat. Some even said that people don't always recover. Is that true?'

'What kind of friends are these who say something like that?' Amber asked, raising a brow in astonishment. She gave him a reassuring smile. 'Let's wait until we have the results, shall we? What I will say is that I haven't lost a patient yet to an insect bite.'

Sarah mopped his brow with a cool flannel. 'She's right,' she said with a faint chuckle. 'We only bring in lay-consultants after we've been scratching our heads for a couple of weeks, because we reckon after that length of time anybody's guess is as good as ours.'

'You're making fun of me,' Jack said. He gave them a weak smile. 'You wouldn't be doing that if you felt the way I did.'

Sarah patted his hand. 'Only kidding,' she murmured. 'Dr Shaw knows what she's doing. She won't let you down.'

Amber made quick work of collecting the samples she needed. 'If it's true that you were bitten by a sand-fly,' she said, 'especially a female sandfly, then it's quite possible that you have a parasitic infection. They can be really nasty and make you feel truly awful, because they attack your immune system and lower your resistance. If that's what has actually happened, we'll put a drip in your arm and treat you with a medication that will kill off the parasite. It won't happen overnight, though. Sometimes it can take several weeks for the treatment to take effect.'

Jack made a face. 'I'm not going anywhere in a hurry,' he said. 'I wouldn't have the energy.'

Amber left him with Sarah a few minutes later. She had been working for a good part of the day in A and E, but now it was time to go and check up on her patients on the surgical ward.

She called in on Martyn first of all. James was there, talking quietly to Caitlin, while Martyn was sitting in a chair at the side of his bed, balancing a laptop computer on his knees and frowning in concentration. He looked weary, a few lines of strain showing around his mouth and forehead, and Amber was immediately on the alert. James and Caitlin were oblivious to anything around them, smiling and sharing anecdotes with one another about life at university.

'I thought I'd drop by to see how you're getting on,' Amber said, greeting Martyn and nodding towards James and Caitlin. 'I see you have company, though, so I'll make this a quick visit.'

James got to his feet. 'I've been looking for you all morning,' he murmured. He came over to her and gave her a hug. 'I heard about the job,' he said quietly. 'That was really bad news. I was so sure you would get it. The whole system is chaotic.'

'I suppose I can't complain,' she said. 'A lot of us are finding ourselves in the same boat, unfortunately.' It felt good to have his arms close gently around her. It was a light, comforting embrace that showed her he cared, but she couldn't help thinking it had come too late. A couple of days had passed since she had received the letter, and this was the first time he had mentioned the subject. She returned the embrace and then, much as she would have liked to prolong the contact, she gently broke away from him, turning her attention towards Martyn. It didn't seem right to be hugging, however brief and innocent the gesture, in front of a patient and his relative.

'I hear you've been trying to walk about a bit,' she said, giving Martyn a brief look to try to assess how he was doing. 'That's good. Try to do things gradually, though. We don't want you to tax yourself too soon and end up having a relapse.' She frowned. 'Sarah tells me you've been making a lot of phone calls these last few days…and that's fine, if it's to keep you in touch with family and friends to generally cheer yourself up—only Sarah has the idea that you've been talking to people at the office and getting yourself into a state.'

He looked at her, very much like a little boy on the receiving end of a telling-off. 'It's just that I'm feeling so much better,' he said, using a placatory tone. 'And it's all down to your care and attention. You don't need to worry about me. I'm doing really well. You saved my life and I'm always going to be in your debt. I wouldn't dream of doing anything to undo all your good work.'

Amber sent him a knowing look. 'Don't even begin to think you can wind me around your little finger,' she admonished him. 'I'm onto your tricks. Your nephew warned me about you.'

'That was very well said.' Ethan's deep, male voice came from across the room, causing Amber to give a startled jump. She frowned at the screen that showed his image. Was that man forever going to be sneaking around and putting in an appearance when she least expected him?

She glanced at the watch on her wrist. 'Aren't you up and about again at an altogether unsociable hour?' she asked. Why couldn't he turn up when the night shift was on duty and she was safely out of the way? But perhaps he had always been an early riser…and that thought only added to her discomfort. What business did he have looking so fit and energetic when the sun was barely up in his part of the world?

'Do I detect sour grapes?' Ethan said, lifting a dark brow. 'I guess you've been hard at work for several hours by now. How is it that you're still looking after my uncle when your job is supposed to be in Accident and Emergency?'

'Professor Halloran asked me especially to look after Martyn,' she explained. 'But, in fact, my work is divided between A and E, the surgical ward and various other wards. I like it this way, because it gives me the chance to follow up on people who have been admitted to hospital from A and E. That doesn't usually happen with these senior house officer jobs, but I've found I really like being able to do that. It gives the training more depth, and that's why I applied for this particular rotation.'

'Didn't I hear you saying that you'd missed out on getting a job to go to after this one?' Martyn looked up from his laptop, a faint line indenting his brow. 'Most of the junior doctors' contracts come to an end soon, don't they?'

Amber sent him a fleeting glance. Although he had appeared to be engrossed in what he was doing, he had obviously been listening in to her earlier conversation with James.

'That's true,' she told him. 'Somebody mislaid my application and by the time it turned up, the job I applied for had been filled. Now it looks as though I'm going to be joining the ranks of the unemployed.'

Martyn shook his head. 'I don't know what the world is coming to,' he said. 'Now, if I was in charge—'

'You'd be running us all around like a bee after honey,' Ethan interjected. He strode across the veranda of his property, his body long and lean, exuding health and vitality. 'You need to learn to take a back seat. Don't think I haven't heard about all the requests for changes at the plantation. You seem to forget that I'm in charge right now. I'll make the decisions so you don't need to worry about anything.'

'But you need me to guide you,' Martyn insisted. 'You haven't been involved with the day-to-day running of things up to now, and you have enough to do with the practice back home. You can't possibly do two full-time jobs, and if we don't get the new machinery up and running we'll be falling behind schedule.'

Practice? What practice would that be? Amber wondered, but Caitlin began to speak just then, diverting her thoughts. 'You know you shouldn't be getting involved with any of this,' Caitlin told him. 'Ethan is perfectly capable of dealing with everything. You just don't like to let go, do you?'

'It isn't that at all,' Martyn said, using an appeasing tone. 'It's just that I can see from all these work logs that the technicians haven't been on the site yet. We need them to service the equipment.' He nodded towards his laptop screen. 'Someone needs to gives them a nudge to get things moving.'

'So you've logged into the company's intranet, have you?' Ethan murmured. 'Is there no stopping you?' He was frowning, his blue eyes darkening like clouds rolling in off the sea. Behind him the sky was lit up with the glow of sunrise, colouring the landscape with a burst of flame-coloured light.

'I don't know what you mean,' Martyn said, assuming an innocent air. 'After all, I'm not back home at the plantation, or in the U.K. office, so I have to keep in touch with what's going on, one way or another.'

Amber walked over to him and peered down at the computer. 'This is a top-of–the-range laptop, isn't it?' she murmured, sounding impressed. 'A super-duper internet machine with all kinds of bells and whistles. May I take a closer look?' When he acknowledged her with a nod, she carefully placed her hands on the computer, turning it lightly so that she could see what was on the screen. 'Oh, so you're not using this for playing solitaire or amusing yourself with films…that's what you told Sarah you wanted the laptop for, wasn't it? But, then, you weren't exactly being upfront with her, were you?'

She looked sternly down at him and Martyn's face took on a faintly sheepish look. 'I do want to do those things. It's just that I haven't quite found the time just yet.'

'Well, I'm afraid it's too late now, because your office is closing, as of this minute,' she informed him. With one swift movement Amber lifted the computer from him and closed the lid. 'I'm confiscating this,' she said, moving away from him. 'You'll get it back when I've decided you've had sufficient rest.'

'You can't do that,' Martyn protested, his jaw dropping open. Clearly, no one had ever thwarted him in such a way before.

'Can't I?' She studied him thoughtfully. 'I believe I just did.'

She heard a stifled chuckle and glanced in the direction of the video link. 'I do believe he's finally met his match,' Ethan said, giving her an appreciative look. He made a thumbs-up sign. 'Perhaps Professor Halloran wasn't so far off beam in keeping you in charge here after all,' he added in a musing tone. 'I had wanted to bring in our own consultant, and I'd have gone ahead and done it if Martyn hadn't vetoed me.'

Martyn glowered at both of them. 'I may yet change my mind,' he threatened. 'I'm sure I have the number of one or two specialists who can be relied on to do things my way.'

Amber wasn't fazed by his reaction. 'By all means go ahead,' she said. 'You still won't get your computer back until you've had a good, long rest.'

Caitlin put a hand to her mouth, but whether that was to cover her amusement, or to hide the extent of her shock, Amber wasn't sure. Either way, James lightly touched the girl's arm and murmured, 'I have to go back to work now. It's good to see that you're bearing up well.' He nodded towards Ethan. 'You can rely on Amber to take care of things. She's always been a force to be reckoned with.'

He smiled at Amber, and went with her to the door as she sought to find a safe place for the laptop. 'Are we on for lunch later today?' he asked.

She nodded. 'That would be good.' She looked at him closely, but she couldn't read his expression and she wasn't at all sure what was going on with him lately. Perhaps he wasn't able to decide what he really wanted. He seemed to be blowing hot and cold, but then again who was she to judge? These days her emotions were a mishmash of confusion and disappointment, only enlivened every now and again by one of his smiles.

Once she had disposed safely of the laptop into a secure locker, she went back to Martyn's private room. Caitlin had gone to get herself a cup of coffee, and Martyn was alone, still sitting in the chair by the bed.

'I need to check your blood pressure,' Amber said, and Martyn obligingly held out his arm, though he still had a disgruntled look on his face. Amber stared about her to see if Ethan was still online, but the screen was blank, and she wasn't sure whether she felt relief or disappointment about that.

'He's gone to work,' Martyn said, following her gaze. 'Like you, he's a doctor, only he has a private practice within the main hospital back home. He trained in emergency medicine. It's all he ever really wanted to do, but he has other interests besides that, including half-ownership of the plantation. Until now he's been a silent partner.' He gave a faint scowl. 'Only, just lately, he's starting to have a lot more to say for himself on that score.'

A doctor… That probably explained a lot, Amber mused. Ethan would understand only too well what was happening with his uncle. It was no wonder that he wanted the very best care for him, knowing how very ill he was.

'That's because he cares about you, and doesn't want you to over-extend yourself,' she told him as she wrapped the blood-pressure cuff around his arm. 'He said he'll sort things out, and perhaps you should let him get on with it without trying to interfere.'

'And what would you know about running a pineapple plantation?' Martyn said grumpily. 'My grandfather started the project, and I have to keep up the family tradition. There's more to it than simply planting seeds and harvesting the crop. If we don't keep up to date with our research projects, we won't be able to develop new varieties of fruit, and our produce will become vulnerable to the ravages of pests and diseases.' He gave her a mournful look. 'That's why I need my computer back, or, at the very least, my mobile phone.'

'All in good time,' Amber said in a peaceful tone. 'Nothing major is going to happen in the next few hours, except that you're going to lie back and relax. I'll switch the TV on for you, if you like, and you can amuse yourself with the afternoon film or a house make-over programme. It's what you need, something pleasant and unchallenging to send you to sleep.'

'I don't want to watch a film,' he said in a terse voice.

'You can't go on the way you did before.' She indicated the blood-pressure monitor. 'Look at that,' she commanded him. 'The reading is way too high. You've just miraculously come through a very difficult and worrying time, and you're not doing anything to help yourself.'

'Is everyone in your family the same as you?' he

asked, narrowing his eyes. 'Is there a stroppy gene mixed in somewhere with all the usual ones?'

'I'm not altogether sure about that,' Amber murmured, releasing the cuff. 'My father is efficient, hardworking, always striving to do better, but he's generally easy to get along with. My mother is usually very calm and sensible, though she does have her moments when she decides enough is enough and makes her feelings clear to everyone around her.'

She frowned at him. 'I know exactly what she would say to you right now… "Nature, time and patience…three great physicians. Let them do their work."'

'Hmm.' Martyn studied her curiously as she put away the monitor. 'That's quite an unusual saying, isn't it?'

'Is it?' Amber raised a brow. 'My mother says it all the time.' Perhaps they didn't use that phrase where he came from.

His gaze trailed over her features. 'Does she look at all like you? Your hair colour and all those natural curls are something quite out of the ordinary, aren't they? Perhaps you've inherited them from her?'

'Well, from the pictures I've seen of her as a young woman, we're very much alike. Some people have commented that we could have been mistaken for twins if all you had to go on were the photographs.' She frowned as she reached for his chart. 'I'm going to add another lot of tablets to your regimen,' she said. 'We need to get that blood pressure down.'

'Is your mother a medical professional, the same as you?' He was looking at her thoughtfully, and she guessed his interest was caught because he liked to know about people in general. Perhaps that was what gave him an edge in the business world—that, and a tendency to overwork.

'No. My father is a GP, as it happens, and I suppose it was being around him and seeing how much he helped people that made me want to go into medicine. My mother is a graphic artist. She's very talented— she studied in London initially, and then she found work with an advertising company. They used to have their premises quite close to where your offices are situated now, come to think of it...only, that was years ago, before I was born. Your place wasn't built back then, was it?'

He shook his head. 'We moved into the Docklands building a few years ago. We were always based locally, though.'

'Well, I don't think my mother really liked working in the city, and eventually she decided to move to Henley-on-Thames. In fact, it was when she moved there that she met my father. They had a whirlwind courtship by all accounts, and were married within a very short time, a matter of a few weeks, I heard.'

'Do you have any brothers or sisters?'

'No.' She was pensive for a moment or two. 'I've always thought it would be nice to be part of a big family, but it didn't happen. I think my mother had problems when she gave birth to me, and perhaps that's why she didn't have any more children. I was born prematurely, and I think both my parents were a little shocked that they had a child within that first year of marriage. My father said it seemed like no sooner were they married than they had to set about preparing a nursery. At least they don't seem to hold it against me.' She gave him a quick grin, and in return his features relaxed and his eyes took on a glimmer of amusement.

'And look at you now…totally in command and still ruling the roost. You're not going to give in and let me have my technology back any time soon, are you? I could really do with having my mobile phone.'

She shook her head. 'Definitely not for a while. I want you to get well again, and there's no point in you blustering,' she said. 'Ethan and Caitlin warned me that you'd be too much to handle, but I don't believe it for a minute. You might growl and snarl a little, but you're a pussycat really, aren't you?'

He smiled. 'You've seen through me,' he said. Then he reached out and grasped her hand when she would have moved away from the chair. 'Sit down on the bed near to me and talk to me for a while, will you, if you have time? It's very boring in here, you know, and you're such a sweet girl, an angel to look at, and you brighten my day like nothing else. Tell me about your family life…where you lived, where you grew up.'

She smiled back at him and obligingly sat down. Sarah would page her if any problems cropped up and nothing urgent was happening right this minute, as far as she could tell. 'I grew up in Henley-on-Thames,' she said. 'It was all very peaceful, and my mother managed to do some of her work from home, which was great. Then my father started his own medical practice and we lived on the premises. Over the years the practice grew and he took on partners.'

'It sounds idyllic. Your father must be very proud of you, having achieved so much. I know you're a very good doctor. I've seen it for myself, and everyone says so.' He didn't let go of her hand, but stroked it gently as though reassuring himself that she was real, flesh and blood.

'Am I interrupting something?' Ethan's voice cracked like a pistol shot across the room.

Amber gave a faint gasp and swivelled around to glower at the screen. 'So you're back again,' she murmured. 'I thought you had gone off to work. How is your uncle supposed to get any rest when you keep popping up every few minutes?'

Ethan's eyes narrowed on her. 'So I *am* interrupting.' He nodded, as though confirming an inner thought. 'That's interesting. You seem inordinately put out by me being around, in virtual form if not in the flesh.'

'Perhaps I am,' she answered tautly. 'It's very offputting to have you appear out of nowhere like that every so often and, besides, all that, as I've explained to you in detail, Martyn needs to rest.'

Okay, so Ethan *was* a relative, and visiting hours in the hospital were fairly lax, but there had to be a limit as to how much her nerves were to be put through their paces, surely? Who else would stand for it? Not Professor Halloran, that was for sure, though he would never be around long enough to put it to the test.

'He isn't likely to get much rest with you holding his hand that way, is he?' Ethan's gaze was full of censure, and Amber felt a surge of guilt sweep over her. What was he implying? She wasn't doing anything wrong and in, fact, it was Martyn who was holding her hand, but perhaps from where Ethan was standing it looked suspicious. 'His blood pressure's already high, according to the nurse,' Ethan added, 'and any time now it's likely to be off the charts.'

Amber glanced at Martyn, expecting him to rush to her defence, but he was chuckling softly. 'Children,' he said in a droll tone, looking from one to the other, 'let's not have any bickering, please. It isn't good for the patient to be caught in the middle, now, is it?'

'Oh, you're impossible. You're both as bad as one another.' Amber withdrew her hand from Martyn's grasp and got to her feet. 'He'd probably recover much faster if he was left in peace for a while,' she informed Ethan curtly, 'without you coming on line to constantly remind him of all the work issues that are floating around. I suggest you limit your video meetings to prearranged times.'

'And if I don't?' Ethan's brows rose.

'Then I might just arrange for the video link to be cut from this end,' she said. 'I doubt either of you would want that.'

Martyn glanced at Ethan, a glimmer lighting his eyes. 'Feisty, isn't she? Beware the woman who doesn't embrace technology,' he warned.

Ethan gave a short laugh. 'I've battled with worse opponents,' he countered. 'Besides, I'm the one who has Professor Halloran's loyalty and support, so I'm not likely to worry about empty threats, am I?' He placed his hands palms flat against the back of his hips and proceeded to lightly stretch his spine, looking every inch the cock of the walk, much to Amber's annoyance.

'Anyway,' he added, 'I just came back to say I've spoken with the manager at the plantation, and he says they're on the ball with the seed development programme, so you needn't have any worries on that score. And the technicians will be along to service the new equipment this morning.'

'So now—' he broke off to direct his remarks towards Amber '—I shall go off and begin my stint at the hospital. I shall come back on line first thing in the morning…your morning, my evening. I doubt I'll be in any mood to do battle by then, but don't count on it.'

Amber's green eyes flashed, shooting sparks at the screen, but Ethan cut the link, leaving her to vent her frustration inwardly. She turned back to Martyn. 'Obviously the "I'm in charge" gene is fully functional in your family, or is it just the males that possess it?' Caitlin obviously didn't, from what Amber could glean, because she was soft and vulnerable, the kind of woman who wanted to know that there was a man around to take care of her.

Martyn laughed softly. 'Ethan's all right, once you get to know him. He tends to be a bit guarded about women having designs on the family fortune, but that's only because both he and I have experienced the unfortunate side of opposite-sex relationships. For my part, women seemed to want to comfort me after my wife died, but I could see perfectly well through those that had an ulterior motive, and to be honest, no one could ever replace my beloved Grace.'

He was thoughtful for a moment. 'As to Ethan, women tend to be a little more subtle in their approach. If his mother was alive, I dare say she would set him straight on their various whiles, but unfortunately both his parents were killed in a boating accident when he was in his teens. I think it's made him tougher, in a way. He's found his own path in life, and he hasn't done too badly for it.'

'Caitlin said that you took care of him. I expect that means he's more like a brother to her than a cousin.'

'Yes, that's true. That's why he looks out for her all the time. Of course, it wasn't just me who took care of him. Grace was like a second mother to him. Unfortunately, we lost her a few years back, when she had a bad asthma attack. I'm pretty sure that's why Ethan took up medicine…he watched Grace battle with asthma and he wanted to learn how to make a difference in people's lives.'

'I'm sorry. You must miss her dearly.' Amber's words were heartfelt. He looked and spoke like a man who had cared deeply for his wife.

'Yes, I do.'

The nurse came to bring him his medication just then, and Amber decided it was time to take her leave. 'I need to go and look in on my other patients,' she said. 'Behave yourself, and don't think you can wheedle the nurses into giving you your computer back. It isn't going to happen.' She gave the nurse a meaningful look, and the girl nodded.

'You can rely on me,' she said. 'Sarah's been telling me all about his workaholic ways. She said we should put a note in his file to warn everyone.'

'What a great idea,' Amber agreed. 'I'll go and do it right now.' She grinned in Martyn's direction, and as she left the room she heard him complaining to the nurse about people who took it on themselves to dictate his life.

Martyn was a good man, but he needed someone to be firm with him and ensure that he lived to fight another day. Ethan was doing his best for him, trying to put his mind at ease, but there was only so much he could do from a distance. She had been wrong to condemn him for coming back and forth on line, but the man made her jumpy, putting her on edge every time he came into view, and she had no idea why she should feel that way.

CHAPTER FOUR

OVER the next few days, Martyn's condition improved steadily. He would never be the active man he once was, but there was more colour in his cheeks now, and his breathing was much easier as the medication helped ease the congestion in his lungs.

'When is he going to be able to leave hospital?' Ethan asked one day, when Martyn had been taken to the X-ray unit for follow-up checks, and Amber was sitting by his bed, writing up his medical notes.

'I would say that he should stay here for at least another week,' Amber told him, 'and then he would be better off having a couple of weeks in rehab. He's quite shaky on his feet and he needs physiotherapy to help him regain his strength.'

'But you won't have anything to do with what goes on in the rehabilitation unit, will you?' Ethan said, giving her a quick look.

It seemed an odd question for him to ask. 'I'll be able to check up on his progress from time to time,' Amber replied, 'but you're right, there will be other doctors in charge over there.' She studied him. 'Why do you ask? Are you still concerned about my involvement in his care?' She had thought he had grown used to her being around, and that he had finally accepted that she was the one making the day-to-day decisions in consultation with Professor Halloran.

'You've looked after him very well. I've no complaints on that score. What concerns me is that you and he seem to be growing closer by the day,' Ethan murmured. 'I'm not sure what to make of that. Video links have their limitations after all, but I do know that my uncle is taking a very special interest in you.'

'I don't know why you should think that way, and I'm sorry you feel it's a problem,' she said. 'I like your uncle. He's a thoughtful and considerate man, and he always thinks of others, even when he's struggling to manage things for himself.'

'He certainly thinks about you a lot.' He studied her fleetingly, as though trying to work something out in his head. 'He seems concerned that you have no job to go to when you finish your contract here. I don't see why that should be his problem, do you?' His gaze seemed to home in on her very much as though he had a target in his sights.

Amber was taken aback by his comments. 'It isn't anything that he should be worried about, obviously,' she answered on a cautious note. 'Anyway, I don't believe he thinks about me all the time, any more than he does about other people.'

'He's very curious about you. In between bombarding me with questions about the business, and making suggestions for ways we can advertise our products, all he wants is to sing your praises to me. I've not seen him this animated in quite a while.'

Amber gave that some thought. 'He's certainly been using his phone a good deal lately, so much so that I've had to threaten to confiscate it again. He may have been trying to contact advertising agencies, now I come to think of it, but I don't believe his fever of activity is all to do with business. I know he's been talking to friends.'

In fact, she thought he had on occasion been talking to an investigative agency of some sort… She had overheard the odd snatch of conversation from time to time when she had walked into his room, though he usually finished the call when she approached. Perhaps he was checking into the background of a prospective employee. 'I just have the feeling that he is a very compassionate man who cares about everyone and everything.'

'That's true.' Ethan nodded. 'He's always been that way. Grace used to say he had a heart big enough to embrace the world, and sometimes she worried that people would take advantage of him.'

Amber could see how that might happen. 'Perhaps he can't help himself,' she murmured. 'He asks me about my other patients, and he's even been wandering down the corridor to visit one of them whenever he feels up to it—a man who went down with a parasitic infection. I've been able to follow up on the man more closely because I was the one who initially liaised with the tropical diseases unit.'

She frowned. 'Martyn seemed quite worried about how Jack was doing, and I wondered if it was something that he had ever suffered from, though I can't find anything in his notes to that effect.'

'I have the feeling it was more that he was impressed by your ability to diagnose the condition in the first place, given that you're a fairly junior doctor. He told me all about it. He seems to think that other people might have missed the diagnosis, but, then again, he isn't a medical man. I guess he's interested in Jack because he's done lots of interesting things on his travels. Oh, and he said he was curious to know if you had studied tropical medicine.'

'He has been asking a lot of questions, hasn't he?' Amber smiled up at the screen. 'I did think about it at one time, as another string to my bow, you might say. I thought it might come in useful if I ever travelled the world, but other things got in the way. I decided that I was really interested in accident and emergency work, and I pinned my hopes on specialising in that. Then the job fell through, as you know.'

'So you still don't know what you'll be doing when you finish there?'

She shook her head, causing a ripple of curls to quiver and dance in chaotic disorder. 'I don't have a clue. I asked my father if he had any vacancies at the surgery, but things seem to be running very smoothly there and they can't afford to take on anyone else.'

Sarah came into the room just then, and Amber finished making the notes in the file before standing up.

'Is there a problem, Sarah?'

'Not really. It's just that Jack's ultrasound results have come back and I think you need to take a look at them. His liver and spleen are enlarged, so it looks as though the treatment's not working as effectively as you hoped.'

'All right. I'll come and see what's to be done. There is another treatment, but I would have preferred not to use it unless it was really necessary. There are some toxic side-effects that can affect the kidneys, so I need to be very careful how I administer the drug, and he'll need to be monitored very closely.'

She glanced towards the computer screen, taking in Ethan's brooding stare. 'I expect I'll talk to you again later,' she said. She was getting a little more used to him constantly being around, and there were even times she found herself looking forward to seeing him. It was only when he questioned her motives, albeit in a round-about way, that she began to feel aggrieved.

He nodded. 'Later.'

Jack was still very unwell, and it was a worry knowing that his liver and spleen were affected. Amber explained to him about the new medication, and with his permission she began to set it up. It would take time before it worked its magic, and Amber waited anxiously for results.

Another week passed by, and very gradually she began to see a change in the young man. 'It looks as though we've cracked it at last,' she told him as she checked through the latest batch of blood test results.

Jack smiled. He looked much better than he had previously, and Amber was pleased to see a sparkle back in his eyes.

'Your girlfriend is going to be so thrilled when she comes to see you at visiting time,' she said. 'It'll take a few more weeks of treatment until you're properly clear, but you're definitely on the way.'

'It's brilliant news. My parents are going to be over the moon, as well.' He was still smiling. 'They've been worried sick about me.'

Amber left him to absorb his good fortune and went off in search of James. She just had to share this with him. Every day they came together to talk about the highs and lows of their work, and this was definitely a high.

'I saw him go into the patients' day room a few minutes ago,' Sarah said. 'He told me he was looking for one of his asthma patients but, to be honest, I think the room has been empty for the last hour. Martyn sometimes ambles down there in the late afternoon, but he was waiting for Ethan to get in touch last I heard.'

'Thanks, Sarah,' Amber murmured. 'I'll go and check in there first of all.'

There was a spring in her step as she walked down the corridor and hurried towards the room. Martyn would be glad to hear the news, too, because he had kept up his interest in Jack's case, wanting to know if the side effects had caused any problems. Luckily, they hadn't.

She pushed open the door to the day room. James was in there, though his back was towards her, and as soon as she saw his lean, familiar figure, she brightened. But then he half turned and with a shock she realised that he was not alone.

Caitlin was there with him, and they had their arms around one another, locked in an intimate embrace. He was kissing her, but as they heard the sound of the door opening, they broke apart.

Amber stared from one to the other, her heart taking a downward leap in her chest, her throat closing in a surge of emotion. Then she swivelled around and hurried out of the room. Her worst fears had come crashing down on her, and she had no idea what to do or how to cope.

'Is something wrong?' Martyn asked. He was walking slowly along the corridor towards her and now there was a look of concern on his face. 'What is it? Has something happened to a patient? Is it Jack? Has he taken a turn for the worse?'

She looked up at him, unable to speak for a moment or two. Then, 'Jack's fine,' she told him briefly. 'He's absolutely fine. His treatment's working.'

Martyn turned to follow the direction she was taking. 'Will you slow down?' he asked. 'Where are you going?'

She didn't answer him, but at that moment Caitlin and James came out of the day room, and on hearing their voices Martyn half turned with her to look towards them.

James looked pale, his features sombre, but Caitlin's face still wore the bemused look of a girl who didn't know what was happening in the world around her.

'Will you walk me back to my room?' Martyn said, looking at Amber. 'I'm feeling a bit shaky. I was going to watch TV in the day room, but I think I've changed my mind. I've just remembered that there's racing on the radio, and I'd rather listen to that in my room.'

'Yes, of course,' Amber said. The last thing she wanted right now was to have company of any kind, but Martyn was a patient, and his needs had to come first. They started to walk along the corridor, leaving James and Caitlin behind. Perhaps James thought better of following her, seeing that she wasn't alone. The relief Amber felt was small consolation.

'Are you still worrying about finding a job?' Martyn asked once they were back in his room. 'You haven't seemed to be your usual self these last few days. I know you've been concerned about Jack not improving as fast as you would have liked, but you're doing all you can for him, aren't you?'

Amber helped him into his chair. He sounded as though he was having difficulty breathing, and she guessed that the effort of walking to the day room had placed a strain on his heart. 'Just you try to relax for a while, and get your breath back,' she said. She poured him a drink of juice from the jug on his bedside table, and offered him a tablet to dissolve on his tongue and ease the spasm of pain in his chest.

He accepted both, and then leaned back in his chair, gathering his strength.

'Jack is feeling much better,' she told him. 'The treatment seems to be working at last, and we've managed to keep the side effects down to a minimum. With any luck, he'll be going home at the end of the month.'

'That's brilliant news.' Colour was gradually coming back into Martyn's cheeks, and Amber watched him, concerned for his well-being and trying to push the image of James and Caitlin out of her mind.

Seeing them together that way had come as a tremendous shock, but now, as she slowly absorbed the reality of the situation, she was trying to analyse how she truly felt.

Was it something she had known all along—that she and James had drifted apart? Would it have happened even if Caitlin had not come along? What was it that James had said? *'You can rely on Amber to take care of things. She's always been a force to be reckoned with.'*

Perhaps that's where the trouble lay. She was self reliant up to a point, whereas Caitlin was young and vulnerable, and she brought out the protective instinct in James. It didn't matter that Amber might be filled with self-doubt from time to time. She tried her best to deal with each problem as it came along, and it was a matter of pride to her that she should try sort things out for herself instead of wearing her heart on her sleeve. But maybe James didn't want a woman who was on equal terms with him, and that was a sad truth that Amber was trying to take on board.

Her shoulders slumped. She was empty inside. There was nothing left. No dreams to cherish, no soul mate to walk hand in hand with her through life, no job to help her seek solace in helping others…no future. All that lay before her was an endless, bleak desert.

Martyn stirred, and she realised that he was studying her thoughtfully as he shifted in his chair. His condition was beginning to improve, and she could see that he was frowning, preoccupied now that he was feeling a little more rested.

'Would you like me to switch the radio on for you?' she asked. The headphones were on a hook on the wall behind him and she made to reach for them, but he shook his head.

'I've changed my mind,' he said. 'I don't feel like listening to the radio after all.' He pulled in a deep, steadying breath. 'I'm glad Jack is feeling better. It will be good for him to go home.' He hesitated. 'I keep wondering what's going to happen when I go back home— back to Hawaii, I mean. Life is never going to be the same for me again, is it? I'm beginning to realise that I might struggle in some ways without help. Here in hospital it's reassuring to know that someone is always on hand to help out, but I won't be able to rely on that back home, will I?'

'You'll have Ethan, won't you?' Amber frowned. 'He's a doctor, and he's your nephew…he isn't going to leave you to cope on your own, is he?'

'He has enough to do, with the plantation and his work at the hospital. I can't ask him to do any more.'

'What about Caitlin? Her university course finishes soon, doesn't it? Won't she be on hand to take care of you?'

Martyn pulled a face. 'She's very young, and she has her life ahead of her. I can't ask her to stay home and look after me. Besides, she plans to take up a post in pharmaceutical sciences at the university hospital in Oahu. Her exam results here in London have been excellent, and she's assured of a place there.'

Amber shook her head. 'I don't understand how you can be feeling concerned about what will happen back home. In your circumstances, you could have someone take care of you twenty-four hours a day…though I can't see you putting up with that state of affairs for very long. I don't think you're temperamentally suited to have someone by your side for that length of time.'

Martyn began to smile. 'You understand me so well, don't you? And how long have we known each other? A very short time.' He was thoughtful for a while, and then said, 'Of course, there is a solution to my problem. You would be my perfect choice…who could be better to look out for me?'

Amber stared at him. 'I'm not sure that I follow your drift,' she said.

Martyn leaned forward in his chair, his face brightening as though everything was becoming clear to him. 'It's like this… It occurs to me that with you being out of work, you might just want to think about coming over to Hawaii to take care of me—on a part-time basis,' he hurried to add. 'I wouldn't want you to feel that you needed to be there all the time. You could always take up a part-time post at the hospital. I have contacts that could fix you up with work. I know they're short of people in the emergency unit.'

Amber was stunned by his proposition. 'But there must be all sorts of people you could ask to do that,' she said, 'people who live near to you back home.'

'Possibly,' he agreed. 'But I know you, and I like you. I've become very fond of you over these last few weeks. More to the point, I trust you, Amber. Think of it as a great opportunity. Not only could you work in Emergency, you could learn more about medicine in a different country, a different climate.' He watched her as though he was trying to gauge her reaction. Then he leaned forward and reached for her hand, clasping it between his palms. 'Couldn't you do with a break right now…sun…sand…sea…? What could be better?'

'I… You've taken me completely by surprise,' Amber managed. 'I don't know what to say.'

'Say yes,' Martyn urged her. 'You don't have any reason to stay here, do you? Except your family, of course. But we could arrange for you to link up online, or even for them to come out to see you.'

'I don't know.' Amber was frowning, trying to take it all in. What was there for her here, except heartbreak and unemployment? Her whole life had changed over these last few weeks. Her career would soon be on hold, and this very afternoon her love life had come crashing down around her. Why shouldn't she take the easy way out and try to escape the tragedy? Wouldn't it be the chance of a lifetime to go and work on a tropical island in the Pacific Ocean?

'Well then, let's say that you come out for six months, to give it a try? That way you wouldn't be committing yourself for ever. What do you think?'

'What does she think about what?' Ethan's voice broke the silence, crackling through the air and slicing through Amber's reverie like a knife. 'Am I missing something? Why are you two holding hands again?' His voice was etched with suspicion and his blue eyes raked over her, so that Amber felt her defences spring up in an act of self-preservation.

Why was he so concerned about her relationship with his uncle? Did he really think she was trying to inveigle her way into his uncle's heart? It hurt that he should think so little of her.

'Your uncle has just offered me a job in Hawaii,' she said. Her jaw lifted. 'And I'm thinking of accepting it.'

Ethan gasped, but Martyn's hands tightened on hers, and a smile lit up his face. 'You won't regret it if you do, I promise you.'

She smiled at him. 'We'll see. Just give me a little while to think things through,' she said. 'I'm not sure that making snap decisions is a good idea.'

'I know you'll make the right choice.' Martyn was irrepressible now, and she could see he believed it was a done deal. That gave her pause for thought. It was one thing to rile Ethan by making rash statements on the spur of the moment, but Martyn deserved better. His offer was genuine, she was sure of that, because he wanted the best for both of them, and it would only be fair to give the idea due consideration.

Ethan, on the other hand, was ready to take issue with her on the mere suggestion that she and Martyn were cooking up plans between them.

She gazed across the room at the screen. Ethan's gaze drilled into her, and she could feel the frustration that fed the flame that burned in his eyes. Did he think she had manoeuvred Martyn into offering her this opportunity?

That was his problem, she decided. She'd had enough of being let down by men and the system in general. It was time to take charge of her life, instead of allowing events to buffet her here and there in whimsical fashion. If Ethan didn't like the option she chose, that was unfortunate. Martyn was offering her a way out, and she would give his suggestion some serious, deep thought.

CHAPTER FIVE

'I can't wait to be back on the island,' Martyn said, 'but it shouldn't be much longer now, all being well.' In the background, the quiet drone of the plane's engines seemed to confirm what he was saying. 'Of course, the delay at the start of the flight didn't help, did it? Though I expect we'd have had to wait much longer if you hadn't stepped in and helped the flight attendant.'

'I felt sorry for her,' Amber murmured. 'There isn't really any treatment for a perforated eardrum, except for painkillers and maybe antibiotics. But she certainly wasn't able to come with us on the flight in that condition, so it left the airport authorities with a problem to solve, didn't it? They had to quickly find someone to replace her.'

Martyn pulled in a long, deep breath. 'It all turned out fine in the end, though, thank goodness. And now we're on the last leg of the journey.' He smiled softly. 'It seems such an age since I last set foot on Hawaiian soil, and yet really it's only been a few months.'

'Perhaps it feels that way because so much has happened to you in that time,' Amber suggested. 'You've been very ill.' She frowned. 'In fact, I was worried in case you wouldn't be well enough to fly, but you seem to have surprised us all.'

'I was determined to make it,' he said with quiet satisfaction. 'I have to go home. I don't know how much longer I have on this earth, but I want to die on Hawaiian soil.'

Amber reached for his hand and gave it a gentle squeeze. 'Please don't say that. You've been doing so well.'

'Only with your help,' he said. 'You mustn't worry about me. I'm content. I'm glad that I've been given a little more time.' He gave her an appreciative, gentle smile, before leaning back in his seat and slowly closing his eyes. Within minutes, he appeared to have drifted into a light doze.

Amber gazed out of the window of the plane. She still found it hard to believe that she was actually sitting here by his side, getting ready for the approach to the island. Her mother's warnings and the echo of her parental anxiety were still ringing loud and clear in her head.

'But it's so far away, and you don't know this man or these people,' her mother had said.

'Why don't you speak to Martyn yourself?' Amber had suggested. 'I'm sure he'll be able to put your mind at ease.' Her mother had agreed to do that, but in fact her father had made his own checks to see that all was well. He had spoken to the hospital authorities on the island and verified that the job she was going to did indeed exist, and though Amber protested that she was perfectly able to take care of herself, she was pleased that they cared enough to make sure that she would be safe.

Her mother was still agitated, even after she had spoken to Martyn. 'This is all so sudden,' she said, 'and I can't think why he wants to take you halfway across the world.' For a moment Amber thought she sounded very much like Ethan. Ethan was definitely guarded about Martyn's sudden decision to ask her to come to Hawaii with him, and she still had the feeling he thought she might somehow have manipulated his uncle into taking this action.

'Are you sure you know what you're doing?' he quizzed her, his blue eyes narrowing on her. 'My uncle might be physically frail, but he won't be alone out here. Hawaii is my land, my territory, and my family is everything to me. I won't stand by and see any of them hurt.' It was a warning she took to heart. She didn't blame Ethan for his attitude…it was good that he cared so much for his uncle, but it was unnerving to know that he was suspicious of her motives. Clearly she couldn't look forward to everything being plain sailing when she arrived in Hawaii.

As to her mother, Amber couldn't quite see what she was worried about. 'Everything's been properly sorted out,' she told her. 'The arrangement is that I'll have my own house—well, it's a bungalow, really—but it will be fairly close to the big house where Martyn lives. I'm not sure whether his nephew lives with him, but I think it was Ethan's idea that I have my own place.' He didn't want her getting too close to Martyn, that was for sure, but she wasn't about to say that to her mother and cause her to worry even more.

'Aren't you surprised that Martyn has taken to you this way?' her mother asked. 'He's given you no real reason for wanting you to go out there, has he?'

'He's set up a job for me,' Amber said. 'Perhaps he

was concerned that I was going to be unemployed. Anyway, I start work at the hospital two weeks after I arrive in Oahu.'

At least, after talking to Martyn, her mother was no longer putting obstacles in her way. She seemed reconciled to the fact that Amber had made up her mind, and she seemed slightly appeased when Amber promised to stay in touch.

'I want you to talk to me every week, and tell me what's going on,' her mother said. 'We'll set up one of those video cam links that you told me about.'

'I'll do it as soon as I get there,' Amber said. 'Honestly, you're worrying over nothing. Didn't you feel reassured after you spoke to Martyn? He's really a very good man, you know. Dad spoke to him on the phone, didn't he? And he didn't have any problem with him.'

Her mother was still fretting. 'He spoke to his nephew, too, but he didn't seem too keen on the idea. I'm just taken aback by the whole thing. This has all happened so quickly,' she said. 'I can't get used to the idea.'

That was the only explanation her mother gave for her anxiety, and Amber did her best to set her mind at rest. Her mother didn't usually react this way to new situations and Amber thought it a little odd that she should be so unsettled about it even now.

'You'll be able to come and visit me, won't you?' Amber murmured. 'You and Dad are due a holiday, and I'll be back after six months anyway.'

'So you say. He said you could stay on, didn't he?'

'Either way,' Amber said softly, 'we'll find a way to keep in touch on a regular basis and we'll meet up after a few months.'

Ethan's attitude didn't surprise her. He was the one person who was still not reconciled to the situation in any way, and Amber was uncertain how she was going to deal with him. He had said he would meet them at the airport, and already she was bracing herself to cope with that.

Martyn stirred in the seat beside her. 'Caitlin asked me to ring her as soon as we arrived. We're running late, though, aren't we, with the delay at the airport? I expect she'll be working herself up into a state, wondering what's happened.'

'I'm sure she'll be fine. She strikes me as a fairly level-headed young woman.' She glanced at him. 'Are you all right? You look a little pale. Are you worried because you've left Caitlin behind?'

'Not really,' Martyn said. 'I just don't want her to be anxious, that's all. She was apprehensive about my leaving, and a little concerned about not coming with me, but I knew she wanted to stay on in the U.K. for a few weeks more, and I gave her my blessing.' He smiled and patted her hand. 'I'm just a little tired, that's all… nothing to worry about. I shall be fine once I'm home. I'm really looking forward to it.'

Amber sat back in her seat and tried to relax. Caitlin had stayed behind to finish off her last few weeks at university, although in truth her exams were behind her, and there was no real need for her to remain. James was the reason she had decided not to come home. She didn't want to tear herself away from him, and he was only too happy to have her around for as long as possible.

'I'm so sorry, Amber,' he had said. 'I don't know how it happened. I think the world of you, you know I do. I was in love with you, and then Caitlin came into my life and all at once everything was topsy-turvy.'

Amber wasn't sure any longer how she felt about the situation. She had thought she loved him, but now that it was over, her heart was still in one piece and there was just a numb feeling where once she used to care.

She looked out of the window at the landscape below. Right now, they were flying over beautiful coral reefs on the approach to the island of Oahu. The sea was a startling, vivid blue, the surf lapped at the edges of Oahu's golden Waikiki beach, and looming up ahead of them was Diamond Head, the crater of an extinct volcano, magnificent with its ridges and steep rock faces. Calcite crystals glimmered in the sunshine, sparkling like the jewels that gave the crater its name, and the sun overhead gave the rim of the crater a golden glow.

'That mountain range is the Koolau Range,' Martyn said, pointing out the peaks in the far distance. 'Soon we'll be coming into Honolulu airport.'

Amber felt her heartbeat quicken. Would Ethan be there to meet them, as he had promised?

Martyn was using a wheelchair, so they were last to get off the plane, but everything about the disembarkation procedure was made smooth for them, and it was only a short time later that they found themselves in the passenger greeting area.

Amber thought she might have trouble picking out Ethan among the crowd, but he was the one who found them, and he came towards them, his stride long and brisk. He was much taller than she had expected, and altogether he made an impressive figure. His skin was lightly bronzed, his hair midnight black, and he was wearing cool, casual clothes, light-coloured trousers and a blue shirt, worn loosely so that it skimmed his hips. He had with him a straw-coloured canvas holdall.

'It's good to see you again, Martyn,' he said, placing the bag over the backrest of the wheelchair and reaching out to clasp his uncle's arms in greeting. 'You look much better than I had expected. Did you manage to get plenty of rest on the journey?'

'I did.' Martyn smiled. 'It all went very well…but, then, I had Amber to look after me.' He glanced in Amber's direction, and Ethan turned and took a step towards her.

'Amber… *Aloha*,' he said. He reached for her, his large hands closing around her arms in a firm but gentle grip. 'Welcome to my homeland. I must thank you for taking such good care of my uncle.' He released her, adding, 'I have something for you.' Then he turned for a moment and took a small package from the canvas bag. Opening it, he drew out a perfect white orchid, before dropping the packaging back into the bag. 'A beautiful flower for a lovely young woman,' he said, slipping it into her hair just behind her right ear.

His gaze travelled over her, taking in the soft lines of the dress she was wearing, a sleeveless, gently flowing affair that was designed to keep her cool. 'You're even more exotic than I could ever have imagined. It was one thing seeing you on a computer screen, day by day, but here, in the flesh, is something else entirely. You're a knockout, an astonishingly beautiful young woman.'

Then, before she could even draw breath, he reached for her once more, tugging her towards him, his arms gliding around her to hold her close, so that she was

totally wrapped in his embrace. In that instant everything went out of her head. She forgot all about time and
place, and all she was aware of was the feel of him, the
strength of his arms around her and the warmth that
emanated from his body.

He kissed her lightly on each cheek, and Amber felt
her pulse quicken and realised that her heart had begun
to pump for all it was worth. A surge of heat ran through
her from head to toe, and when he finally released her,
she felt sure that her face must be filled with hot colour.

'No wonder my uncle was reluctant to part company
with you.' He said the words in a soft undertone, and
Amber felt the skin at the nape of her neck begin to prickle.

He didn't let her go entirely, though, even then. His
hand remained, palm flat against the small of her back,
and while she was glad at that moment of its steadying
support, she was also conscious of the heat from those
long fingers spreading like wildfire through her veins.

Ethan was more than just a mere man, she discovered. He was a tower of strength and authority, his every
look and gesture shot through with a thread of steel that
left no one in any doubt as to who was in command. And
through it all he exuded the smouldering charisma of a
red-blooded male intent on stalking his prey.

Amber had the distinct feeling that she was the one in
his sights. She hadn't expected him to welcome her in such
a way, or even at all, and she couldn't help wondering if
this was a tactical manoeuvre. Perhaps he had decided that
if there was no way of stopping her from coming here, he
would watch her every move and bide his time.

'Shall we go?' he said, finally releasing her and taking hold of the wheelchair handles. Amber took the op-

portunity to gulp air into her lungs. 'We have a thirty-mile drive ahead of us, but I thought we might stop on the way for something to eat and drink.' He glanced at his uncle for confirmation. 'It's up to you, Martyn. It depends whether or not you want to go straight home. I know you've had a very long flight, and you've probably eaten on the plane.'

'We did,' Martyn said, 'though airline food is never completely satisfactory, is it?'

'That's true.' Ethan handed him the canvas bag. 'There are cool drinks in there. I thought you might need something to perk you up.'

'Thanks. Actually, I think a short stop along the way might be a very good idea. I expect Amber might appreciate the chance to see something of our island, and maybe stretch her legs for a while.' Martyn looked at her to see what she thought of that idea, and Amber nodded.

'The island is beautiful,' she said. 'Just seeing it from the plane was enough to make me want to explore further.'

'We'll make a stop about halfway, then,' Ethan said. 'The road follows the coast for some distance, so you'll be able to look out and see the beaches and harbours along the way. If you look to your right, as we set off along the road, you'll see the mountains. The range stretches along almost the whole of the windward side of the island.'

He led them to his car. It was a gleaming silver saloon, beautifully upholstered inside and air-conditioned, so that the ride was wonderfully smooth and comfortable. Amber sat beside Ethan in the front of the car, giving Martyn more space in the back so that he could relax.

Ethan glanced at her from time to time, making light conversation and telling her about various landmarks along the way, while Martyn was content to doze some more. The road hugged the coastline for a while and beyond the built-up areas Amber caught glimpses of curving bays and rocky shores. As they left the coast behind and travelled northwards through the interior of the island, Ethan pointed out the volcanic mountain ranges on either side.

'That's the Waianae Range to the west,' he said. 'Just now we're passing through the central valley that divides those mountains from the Koolau Range.'

The scenery was breathtaking. She saw lush, tree-covered slopes, carpeted with ferns and decorated with the occasional outcrop of white blackberry flowers. Here and there she caught glimpses of water tumbling down a rock face or rivers winding their way through the valleys.

Up ahead, as they passed through a small township, she saw lakes on either side. 'In a few minutes we'll be driving by the plantation,' he said. 'We won't stop there today, because I think it might be too much for my uncle to cope with. I'll take you to look around it another day, if you like, when you're both rested and we have more time.'

Ethan glanced in the mirror at his sleeping uncle. 'He looks better than he did,' he murmured with a slight nod towards the back seat, 'but I suspect he's going to struggle much more than he had bargained for. This illness has taken its toll on him, hasn't it?'

'I'm afraid so.' She kept her voice low. 'Whatever the infection was that cut him down, it left a legacy that has permanently damaged his heart. He'll need to be very careful, whatever he does…and that means he should be shielded from any kind of stress. I think you should ask him to steer clear of getting involved with the plantation and any problems that crop up.'

'That's like asking a bubbling volcano to keep the pressure down,' Ethan said with a smile. 'You know what he's like. *Caution* isn't in his vocabulary.'

'Yes, I know. But I'm serious about this. No matter what we do with medication, it will only ever be palliative. As a doctor yourself, you must know that. We can improve his quality of life, but there's nothing more we can do to repair the damage, either surgically or with different drugs.'

He shot her a quick look. 'Knowing that, why did you choose to come with him? There isn't much that you'll be able to do to help him, is there?'

Her gaze meshed with his. 'I came because he asked me to, and because I've grown to care for him a lot over these last few weeks. He said he would feel better if he knew that I was with him. He trusts me, and he has confidence in me.'

'Isn't that misplaced confidence if you've admitted you can't do any more for him?'

'I don't think so. I've been upfront with him, and he's under no illusion about his limitations. It's more to do with peace of mind than anything else. He said he wanted to have me close by. He felt that you had enough on your plate with your work and the plantation, and he didn't want to be fussed over by strangers, by doctors he didn't know.'

'Hmm.' His gaze flicked over her. 'I can't help feeling there's more to it than that, but we'll see. He always was one to play his cards close to his chest.'

Amber frowned. She'd been as honest as she could, and yet she had the strong impression that he still suspected her motives…or maybe he thought his uncle was the one with a hidden agenda. Surely he knew his uncle better than that?

'We'll make a stop at a restaurant just up ahead,' Ethan murmured, changing the subject. 'Do you like chicken?'

'I do.'

'That's good. Among other things, they serve mouthwatering chicken dishes with rice, and delicious pancakes topped with ice cream and fruit for dessert. And they make a great mai tai, as well.'

'I've never had one of those.' She sent him a quick glance. 'What's a mai tai?'

His brows rose. 'You don't know? Oh, then you're in for a treat.' His smile lit up his features and watching the way his mouth curved in a crooked fashion caused Amber to catch her breath. There was no doubting that he was an extremely good-looking man. No wonder the girls didn't want to leave him alone. He made Amber's knees go weak, and she had thought she was immune.

'They're a mix of dark rum, light rum and orange curacao,' he explained, 'with a generous slosh of orange and lime juice, syrup and grenadine, all poured over shaved ice. There's a dash of orgeat in there, as well, a type of syrup made from almonds, sugar and rosewater. If you're lucky, it'll be garnished with a slice of pineapple and a cherry.'

'That sounds like a drink and a half.' She managed to stop herself from running her tongue over her lips in anticipation, but he must have guessed her impulse because he gave a soft laugh. 'It looks as though I've tempted you,' he murmured, a glimmer in his blue eyes.

He had the ways of the devil, she decided. He had a hot-blooded, take-charge manner and she had the feeling he would do his utmost to work his fiendish magic on her so that before too long she wouldn't know whether she was coming or going.

'You're right,' she said. 'I'm so thirsty I can almost taste it. It must be the mere thought of relaxing in the heat of the day that's made me feel that way.' She would never admit that thoughts of having him sweep her into his arms had stirred her blood and caused all manner of wild imaginings to jump inside her head. Simply being in the car with him was enough for her to handle right now.

Martyn woke up as Ethan drew the car into the parking lot at the restaurant. 'Excellent,' he said. 'This is the perfect place for Amber to get a taste of Hawaiian life. I couldn't have chosen better myself.'

He turned down the use of the wheelchair. 'I can walk the short distance to the restaurant,' he said. Ethan helped him from the car, steadying him as he set foot on firm ground.

'Just smell that lovely fresh air.' Martyn looked about him and gave a beaming smile. 'Life is so good, isn't it?'

'It can be,' Ethan answered, glancing towards Amber.

She didn't know what was going through his mind, but she decided to push any doubts into the background and concentrate instead on enjoying the spectacular surroundings. It seemed to Amber that there was colour in everything, beautiful bright splashes of green in the palms that decorated the forecourt and gardens of the restaurant, with brilliant sunspots of scarlet hibiscus and bright yellow bromeliads in the shrubbery.

They ate at a table outside, and as Amber sipped her mai tai and gazed around at the vista of hills and valleys all around, she reflected that just a few weeks ago she would never have envisaged that she would be sitting here in paradise. It would have been truly perfect except for the one flaw that she found hard to push to the back of her mind…the fact that Ethan was there. She was conscious of his brooding gaze resting on her in quiet, unguarded moments, and she had no way of knowing what he was thinking.

'If you're both finished, perhaps we should move on,' he said some time later. 'I expect you would both like to get home and settle in. We're coming to the end of a long day.' He looked at Amber. 'You probably want to unpack and get used to your new surroundings.'

'Yes,' Amber said, 'That would be good.'

'Originally I was going to suggest that you stay up at the house with me,' Martyn said, 'but it's probably better this way. You'll have some privacy.'

'As I understand it, the bungalow is close by the house, so I'll be able to drop in on you easily enough if you need me.'

'That's right,' Martyn agreed. 'Ethan pointed out to me that the bungalow was empty, and it's still within the grounds of the main property, so it will be ideal.'

'But you must let me know any time if there's a problem, or you want help of any kind,' Amber said. 'That's what I'm here for, to take care of you.'

'I'm sure it will all work out very well.' He smiled. 'Anyway, Caitlin will be in the house with me when she comes home, and in the meantime Molly will be on hand to help out if I'm stuck.' He glanced at Amber. 'Molly is my housekeeper,' he added. 'I didn't want you to feel that you have to be at my beck and call all the time. It's just reassuring for me to know that you will be around, and perhaps you'll be able to keep me company some evenings.'

'Of course.' Amber sent Ethan a quick look. 'I suggested that we set up a pager system so that I can go to him right away if he needs me,' she said. 'You should be on the link, too.'

He nodded. 'I'm with you on that one. I've already set the wheels in motion.'

He helped his uncle back to the car and saw him settled comfortably. Watching them, Amber couldn't help thinking that their relationship was more like that of father and son. She could see the affection in Martyn's eyes when he looked at Ethan, and she knew from the gentle and considerate way that Ethan attended to his uncle that the feeling was mutual.

The journey to Martyn's house didn't take more than half an hour. Dusk was closing in when Ethan finally pulled into the driveway, and Amber was immediately impressed by the beautiful villa that Martyn called home.

It was a two-storey house, colour washed to a pale sand finish, with sloping roofs at different levels, while the veranda was made up of white-painted hardwood decking.

'Now, this I recognise,' Amber said with a smile, looking at Ethan. 'It's where you stood when you made the video link.'

He nodded. 'And if you go just around the corner you'll see the bay in all its glory.'

'I can already hear the sound of the sea,' she murmured, tilting her head so that the faint breeze caught her hair and lifted the soft tendrils. 'I can smell it on the air, too. It's lovely.'

'You have a beautiful home,' she said, turning to Martyn. 'Let me help you inside. You look weary.'

'I am, but I'm happier than I've been in a long time.' He glanced at Ethan. 'It was good of you to take time out to come and fetch us. I know how busy you are. If you want to drop my cases off, I think I'll go straight up to my room.'

'Of course. I'll help you.'

Martyn shook his head. 'It's all right. Molly and Ben are here. They'll see to everything. You take Amber along to her place and make sure that she settles in all right.'

Molly opened the door and greeted him with an expansive smile. 'Oh, it's good to have you back,' she said. She was a woman of around fifty years of age, Amber guessed. She had the honey-bronzed skin of a native Hawaiian, and she introduced the man alongside her as Ben, her husband.

'You leave everything to us,' Molly reassured Martyn. 'Ben will take your cases upstairs and unpack for you, and I'll lay out your things ready for bed.'

Martyn greeted both of them in turn, and then he turned to Amber and gave her a hug. 'You should have everything you need at the bungalow. If there's anything missing, just let Ethan know, and he'll put it right. If you don't mind, I'll show you around in the morning. I think I've had enough excitement for one day.'

She returned the embrace. 'Of course I don't mind.

That will be great. You go and get some rest and I'll see you tomorrow.'

He nodded. 'Come and have breakfast with me.'

'I'll do that.'

The bungalow was just a short walk along a winding path through overhanging trees and shrubs. Martyn showed her the way, helping her with her cases, and waiting while she put the key into the lock. It was a neat house, white painted, with soft green wooden shutters at the windows and the all-important veranda going all the way round the building.

'You'll be able to sit out on the sundeck,' Ethan said. 'From the back of the house you can look out over the seashore. It's really beautiful first thing in the morning.'

He carried her bags inside. 'You want these put anywhere in particular?' he asked. 'The bedroom is through there.'

'That will do fine,' she murmured. She peered in through the doorway and saw a pastel-coloured room with pale carpets and filmy drapes at the windows. The bed was large, covered with a beautiful, floral-print duvet that picked out the colours in the drapes and in various ornaments around the room. There was a built-in dressing table and several glass-fronted wardrobes with drapes that matched the window curtains. In all, it was a beautiful room.

'You have your own sitting-room through there,' Ethan pointed out, dropping off the cases and showing her into a light, airy living space with glass doors opening out onto a terrace. 'There is your sea view,' he said indicating the area beyond the doors.

Amber gave a soft gasp. 'It's incredible,' she said

softly. 'I think I must have died and gone to heaven.' Through the doors, she could see the vast sweep of a bay, with rocky promontories pushing out into the ocean, and as the sun was setting the sky was lit with orange flame, throwing up silhouettes of the coconut palms and broad-leaved ironwood trees that grew along the shore. Close by the doors was a mango tree, heavy with fruit that were beginning to turn from yellow to red. All she had to do was reach out and pick one.

'I knew I would find everything so different out here, but I don't think I ever imagined it would be as lovely as this…right on my doorstep.'

He gave a faint smile. 'I suppose we get used to it, living here. Perhaps we take it for granted.' He turned around to look at the room. 'Do you think you'll be okay here? You have a writing desk, TV and music centre, and of course there's a computer.'

She was nodding, still too bemused to answer properly. The furnishings were beautifully upholstered in soft, warm colours that were easy on the eye. 'I can't think of anything else I could possibly need.'

He started to walk towards the door. 'That's good. Through here is your kitchen. It's not tremendously big, but there's enough room for a small table and chairs, and of course you have a cooker and a microwave. The fridge has been stocked for you, along with the freezer, but if there's anything you're short of, I can fix that for you. I'm only next door, so you only have to give me a shout.'

'Next door? You mean, up at the house?'

He shook his head. 'I was staying there temporarily while Martyn was in the U.K. I have my own place further along the coast, but since I'm spending more time at the plantation these days, it's easier for me to live here. My bungalow is right next to this one. If you look out of the kitchen window, you'll see my back door.'

Amber glanced about the kitchen while she tried to take that in. It gave her time to think, and to adjust to what he was saying.

The units were made of wood, finished in a soft apple-green colour, so pale as to be restful on the eyes, with some of them glass fronted, and there were lots of shelving units and bottle racks, along with all the modern fittings anyone could want.

She glanced through the window. The back of his bungalow was just a few paces away, as he had said. From here, she would be able to see him sitting out on his veranda whenever he decided to take the air, and the same would go for him.

'I hadn't realised you would be my neighbour,' she said. 'Well, I thought you might be up at the house from time to time, but Martyn told me you had your own place a few miles away.'

He smiled, coming over to her and sliding an arm about her shoulders. 'Did you really think I would stay away and leave you to your own devices?' His fingers trailed through the silky hair at her nape. 'That was never going to happen.'

His long body was close to hers, so close that she could feel the beat of his heart against her breast. It thumped out a steady rhythm, a relentless drumbeat that let her know he was in control, he was watching her, and he had everything worked out.

'You don't trust me at all, do you?' she murmured.

'Not a centimetre,' he answered softly. 'Not even a hair's breadth.' His head lowered, so that his cheek was close to hers, his lips just a breath away. 'I can see very well why my uncle is so taken with you. You're everything a man could want, and I'd be a liar if I said I was immune to your charms. But just so that you know, I'll be close by. I'll be watching everything you do, every move you make.'

He dropped a kiss lightly on her mouth, a touch that was feather-like and as insubstantial as thistledown, and yet the imprint of that kiss stayed with her long after he was gone. She felt the burning embers of it as though he had branded her with flame. It was a kiss that said, Beware, be careful what you do, because I may show you the consequences of any action you take.

CHAPTER SIX

AMBER stared, bleary-eyed, at herself in the mirror in the bathroom. How could she have slept for so long? No sooner had her head touched the pillow than she had fallen into a deep, deep sleep, and yet she didn't feel refreshed. She felt a little odd.

Perhaps was still suffering from jet-lag. It had certainly been the longest journey she had ever undertaken, enough to put the strongest person out of synch. Somehow, though, she had the notion there was more to it than that.

This was to all intents and purposes the beginning of a new phase in her life. She had come all this way to start afresh. Wasn't that the reason she was here? Yes, Martyn had said he wanted her help and she had agreed to stay with him through these difficult months of recovery, but if she was honest with herself, hadn't she also been running away from the situation back home?

In truth, the thought of James getting closer to Caitlin day by day had been more than she could bear, and maybe Ethan was right to suspect her motives in coming here. Wasn't she doing this job under false pretences? What made her think she could make any difference in

Martyn's life? Shouldn't she have stayed at home and tried to make the best of things? Some kind of work would have come along eventually, wouldn't it? But instead of waiting to see what might happen, she had taken the coward's way out.

She stepped under the shower and hoped that the warm spray of water would gradually wash away her doubts. Perhaps it was strange that she was feeling this way, when she ought to be overwhelmed with happiness at finding herself in an idyllic tropical paradise, but Ethan's warning was running persistently through her head, and it had played like a haunting refrain throughout her dreams last night.

She stepped out of the shower a few minutes later, wrapping a towelling robe around herself before going into the bedroom to dry her hair.

She switched off the hairdrier after a few minutes and heard a faint knocking sound coming from the front of the house. 'Amber, are you there? Are you awake?' She set the drier down on the dressing table and became aware of Ethan's voice, threaded through with a faint note of frustration. How long had he been knocking?

Pulling the robe more closely around her and securing the belt, she hurried to answer the door. 'I'm sorry,' she said, stepping back a little and inviting him in with a small wave of her hand. 'I didn't hear you above the noise of the hairdrier. Have you been waiting long?'

'A few minutes. It doesn't matter.' He looked her over from head to toe, an appreciative glint coming into his blue eyes as he surveyed the creamy expanse of her shoulder where the robe had slipped a little, and then his gaze moved to trail along the length of her smooth, lightly tanned legs. Instinctively, she drew the lapels of the robe together.

'I realise time's getting on,' she said. 'I must have slept through the alarm, but I was hoping I'd still make it in time to have breakfast with Martyn. He said the meal would be later than usual.' Then she frowned as another thought struck her. 'Is he all right? I rang the house last night and gave Molly the instructions for his medication.'

'He's fine, don't worry about it. He's suffering a bit from the effects of all the travelling, and asked me to tell you that breakfast will be delayed even further. I'd have left you alone, but it occurred to me that you might not find your way about too easily. There are footpaths going off in all directions around here, some leading to the beach, others to the coastal path. It's easy to be confused with all the trees and greenery obscuring the view.'

He walked through to the kitchen. 'Since I'm here, shall I make some coffee? You look as though you could do with a cup of something. Adorable as you look with that confused, sleepy expression, I think you'd appreciate being wide-awake for a tour around the place. We could take a walk down to the beach while we're waiting for Molly to cook breakfast, if you like?'

'That sounds like a good idea.' It was almost like being on holiday. Having someone take over the running of the household and see to all the catering was way beyond her experience. Ethan lived in a completely different world from her. 'Does she always make breakfast for you?'

'Whenever I'm around, or when Martyn is home… along with lunch, dinner, supper or whatever takes her fancy. Molly's a great person to have around. Her husband, Ben, does all the odd jobs around the place, and keeps the grounds in order.'

'Wow. How the other half live.' She smiled. 'I'm impressed…and coffee would be lovely, thanks. I haven't figured out yet how to use the grinder, so I made do with juice last night. It was delicious, though, like nothing I've ever tasted before.'

'That would be the produce from our plantation,' he murmured. 'It's fresh as can be, so I'm glad you like it.' He walked over to a cupboard and took out a bag of coffee beans. 'We grow this on our land, too, but we don't export it in large quantities. The locals really like it, and it's an indulgence I look forward to every day. It keeps me awake when I have a long day at the hospital. Come over here and let me show you how to work the machine.'

Amber did as he asked, and he began to assemble the various parts of the apparatus. 'You fit the blades in here, see, and then set it on the stand, like so… It can be a bit tricky… Here, you come and try for yourself.'

She gave it her best effort, but the whole thing was seated wrongly and he reached around her to give the base a twist. 'It's a bit awkward if you don't know how. It's a new gadget, one of those "do everything except wash the dishes" types… It doubles up as a food mixer, blender, grinder. That's why there are so many parts to it.'

She felt his arms go around her and he took her hand and showed her how the mechanism worked. She felt the heat rise in her as his body moved closer to hers. His thigh was touching hers, his chest was nudging the length of her back, and his arms were closing in on her like an embrace.

'The whole thing was disassembled while no one was living here,' he said. 'This bit plugs into the mains electricity. And now you just tip in a few beans, see, like this?'

'Yes, I see,' she managed. It was hard to think straight with him holding her that way. 'It was just that I didn't know how to put it all together, but it's clear now that you've shown me.' Now that the gadget was assembled, the rest was plain sailing, but he hadn't stepped back from her, and she was altogether too conscious of his nearness. She could feel the warmth of his body through the towelling robe, and he was close enough that she registered the restrained power locked in his broad shoulders.

She added the coffee beans.

'That's good. Now fix the top cover in place, switch on, and away you go.'

She followed his instructions and the aroma of freshly ground coffee filled the air. He breathed it in, and bent his head towards her so that she felt the faintly roughened texture of his face against hers. 'Isn't that something special? The test will be in the final brew, of course.'

'I… Yes…' she said huskily. 'Um…perhaps I should go and get dressed. I wouldn't want to keep Martyn waiting for too long.'

A glimmer of amusement crossed his face, and she realised that he had known full well what he was doing, all along, and he was well aware of how flustered she had become. Right now he had the upper hand, and it was disconcerting to know that he would exert his control over her at any opportunity.

He eased back from her, and she fled to the bedroom, her heart beating out a frantic rhythm and her cheeks flushed with soft colour.

The coffee was steaming gently in the percolator when she returned to the kitchen. By now she was much more composed, and it helped that she was wearing clothes that were much less controversial, a T-shirt and white trousers, and her hair was tied back in a more orderly fashion, so that only a few tendrils escaped to trail along her cheeks.

He handed her a mug of the hot liquid, and she added cream and sugar before sipping the contents. 'Mmm…it tastes like a small piece of heaven,' she murmured. She had herself under control now, and Ethan could do his worst. She wouldn't rise to his bait.

Perhaps he sensed the change in her, because he let go of the playful mood and concentrated on finding out if everything in the house was to her satisfaction.

'It's more than perfect,' she said. 'I hadn't expected any of this. It's like a home from home—more so, in fact. I could never have aspired to anything like this. When Martyn first put forward the possibility of me coming out here, I thought I would have a room in the main house, perhaps, or at the most, a small flat. After all, my job was to come out here and keep an eye on your uncle, and make sure that his medication was appropriate…but, of course, that doesn't involve very much. We might need to vary the dosage from week to week to ensure that his heart pumps adequately, but otherwise things should run pretty smoothly.'

'But you do know that he's very fond of you? That can't have escaped you. He was determined to keep you close at hand.'

'It's a mutual feeling.' She sent him a quick look. 'I know you think there's more to it, but I like your uncle very much. I took to him right away. I believe he asked me to come here because he wants the reassurance of a friendly face close by. As a doctor, you must know yourself that when someone has been near to death they become apprehensive about the future. Caitlin is busy with her own life, which is only natural because she's young and on the threshold of everything, and Martyn is too generous a man to expect her to come home with him and take care of him.'

'My uncle has never been short of company or lacked friends about him. Come to that, he has Molly and Ben with him the whole time. They live in at the house.' Ethan returned her gaze with a penetrating stare. 'There's more going on here than my uncle is letting on. He is a very wealthy man, and he is used to having things his own way. Maybe you don't know any more about it than I do, but all I can say is that I will protect him in any way I can. He's more than an uncle to me. He's been like a father, and I won't stand by and see him hurt in any way.'

'And it's right that you should do that.' She tilted her head to one side, giving him a questioning look. 'Perhaps we could call a truce…at least we could put up a united front to help him get through these next few months with as little stress as possible.'

'A truce?' He came over to her and lifted her hand, placing it between his palms. His grasp was light but firm, and having him hold her that way sent a strange thrill of excitement coursing through her body. He raised her hand and held it to his lips, brushing softly over the smoothness of her skin. 'A truce, sealed with a kiss. Now, that's something that should stand the test of time.'

He looked at her, his gaze brooding, the pressure on her hand increasing momentarily, and then he relinquished his grasp on her and she felt a sense of confusion, as though something momentous had happened, but she couldn't quite fathom what it was.

'Let's go for a short walk along the bay,' he said after a minute or two. 'You can tell me a little about the job my uncle found for you at the hospital. I expect you'd like to go and look around there some time before you start, and maybe see something of the town. We can arrange all that over the next day or so. You start work there in a couple of weeks, don't you?'

'That's right.'

They set off to walk along the sand just a short time later, and Amber stopped every now and again to gather up shells that had been washed ashore by the incoming tide.

'It's a surfers' paradise along this part of the coast,' Ethan told her. 'The ocean is calm now, but in winter the waves are higher than any you'll ever see.'

Amber looked out over the ocean, shielding her eyes from the glare of the sun. 'What's that I can see in the water?' she asked. 'I can't quite make them out.'

'They're green turtles,' he told her. 'They nest further along the coast, and sometimes they come up on the beach. Occasionally, you'll see whales or dolphins out at sea.'

They watched the turtles for a while, and then Amber went on with her search for shells. She had taken off her sandals and was walking barefoot across the warm, wet sand at the water's edge. Ethan pointed out white-breasted sanderlings hopping to and fro, searching for small crustaceans or insect larvae that might dwell among the damp grains of sand, all the while deftly avoiding the incoming waves.

There were turnstones, too, searching for any tasty morsels that might be lurking under rocks and seaweed. Every now and then they would take flight, moving their prized finds out of reach of other birds.

After a while, Ethan suggested that it was time they set off for the house. 'Molly will be waiting for us,' he said. 'She was planning on giving us quite a feast, though I doubt Martyn will manage very much of it. He wasn't eating too well in hospital, was he?'

'He'll have to take things gradually, and with any luck his appetite will improve.'

She had certainly worked up an appetite herself by now, and her earlier sleepiness had dissolved, blown away by the faint breeze and the exhilaration of walking along this beautiful bay. The fact that Ethan had made it his business to charm her along the way had probably helped.

Molly had been true to her word, Amber discovered as Martyn showed her into the dining-room just off the main kitchen. The table had been laid with a variety of colourful dishes to tempt the palate, along with a coffee pot, cream and sugar and jugs filled with freshly squeezed juice.

'I hope you settled in all right last night,' Martyn said. 'I'm sorry I couldn't show you around the house, but tiredness suddenly swept over me.'

'I'm amazed you coped as well as you did,' Amber told him. 'I thought the idea was that you should take things easy, so you did exactly the right thing in going to bed.'

'Well, I had a wonderful night's sleep. Come and sample some of Molly's glorious food. Ethan, you sit yourself down opposite Amber, and both of you eat up. I really want you to enjoy this breakfast. It's a special occasion with all of us together this way.'

Ethan sat down by Martyn's right-hand side. 'You should try these delicious Hawaiian wraps,' he told Amber. 'You can make them yourself in a matter of minutes, and they're a wonderful start to the day.'

Each wrap consisted of a tortilla filled with egg that had been scrambled and mixed with lightly browned chopped ham and red and green peppers. There was a hint of pineapple in there, too, and the wraps were served with wedges of watermelon.

'You're right,' Amber agreed, adding one to her plate and taking a bite. She savoured the mouth-watering flavours. 'What a lovely way to begin the day.'

'Molly's made my favourite, the Hawaiian royal,' Martyn said. 'It's made with Portuguese spicy sausage, green onions and eggs over a bed of rice. If you add a touch of mustard to the dish, it's absolutely out of this world.'

He helped himself to the food, but Amber noticed he only ate a very small amount. He looked better than he had done in a long while, but she knew that he had to be careful.

'I hope you're going to sit back and relax now that you're home,' Amber said, giving him a quick glance.

'Certainly, I am,' he murmured. 'I had it in mind that, since Ethan isn't working today, he could show you around, maybe even take you into town to look over the hospital where you'll be working. It's entirely up to you, of course. You might prefer simply to spend some time on the beach.'

'We've already been down there this morning,' she told him. 'It was a wonderful experience.'

Martyn looked pleased. 'That's good.' He dabbed his mouth on a serviette and then put the linen to one side. 'I thought I would go and spend some time in my study,' he said. 'I want to reacquaint myself with a few things.'

'You mean, you're going to be looking over the plantation records, don't you?' Ethan said, giving him a stern look. 'Do you really think that's a good idea?'

'Absolutely, I do,' Martyn said with a smile. 'I can't think of any better way to spend my time. I love that plantation. It's been my life's work.' He pushed back his chair and carefully stood up. 'Forgive me if I leave you two together for a while,' he said.

He put out a hand to stop her when Amber would have stood up and gone with him to see him out of the room. 'I can manage,' he said, 'and if I have any problems later, I know how to get in touch with you.' He indicated the pager that was clipped to his belt. 'I don't anticipate any trouble, and I have Molly and Ben to look out for me. You should concentrate on settling in and getting used to your surroundings. Perhaps I'll see you later this afternoon?'

'Of course, if you're sure you'll be all right?' Amber sent him a doubtful look.

'I'll be fine.'

Martyn left the room, and Ethan commented softly, 'He's a strong-willed man, and it doesn't do any good to try to oppose him, once he's made up his mind. He knows what he wants, and sometimes it's less wearing on him and everyone else to let him have his way…or

at least to let him think he has what he wants.' He gave
Amber a thoughtful look. 'So, what would you like to
do today? I could take you to see the sights, or perhaps
you'd like to do some shopping in town?'

'Actually, I think I'd quite like to see the plantation,
if that wouldn't be too much trouble.'

His eyes narrowed on her, and she wondered if he
was debating with himself why she would want to see
the source of the family's wealth, so she hurried to explain, 'I've heard so much about it, and it seems to be
very dear to Martyn's heart. Perhaps once I've seen it,
I'll understand more.'

'That would be no trouble at all. It's just a short drive
away from here. In fact, now I come to think of it, I believe there will be a *luau* later on today, to be held on
one of the beaches nearby. It's one of the events staged
by the company, and the proceeds will go to local char-
ities. It will go on late into the evening, and I think it's
something you might enjoy.'

'That sounds good to me,' she said brightly, but then
she frowned. 'Your uncle asked if I would spend some
time with him this evening. Is it something that he
would enjoy?'

'I'm sure he will, though I doubt he'll want to stay
to the end. I'll let him know what we're planning.'

With that decided, they spent the rest of the morning
and part of the afternoon wandering around the plantation. Amber was amazed by the sheer size of it, and she
was impressed by the colour and beauty of everything
around her. There were hundreds of plants and trees of
many varieties, and it was clear that these were of interest to visitors of all ages. She saw lots of children ex-

citedly rushing about while their parents tried valiantly to keep up with them.

'We don't just specialise in pineapples,' Ethan told her. 'As I said, we grow coffee, along with cacao, bananas, papayas and mangos.'

'It looks as though you grow flowers, as well,' Amber said, her eyes widening as she tried to take in everything about her. 'I've never seen so many varieties, and such beauty.'

'The hibiscus is native to Hawaii,' he explained, 'but we grow flowers for the traditional leis, the garlands that people wear around their necks, as well.'

Amber was overwhelmed by the scale of everything. 'I had never imagined it would be as vast as this,' she murmured. Just to get around the place, they'd had to use a motorised cart. 'No wonder Martyn worries about it. It's such a responsibility.'

'We employ a lot of people,' Ethan said. 'I suppose the key to good management is to delegate. It's something Martyn's going to have to learn to do.'

It was mid-afternoon when they returned to the house. Amber discovered Martyn sitting out on the veranda, taking the air, so she went and sat beside him and told him all about the tour. He seemed pleased that she appreciated the extent of his life's work.

Amber chatted with him for a while and made sure that he was feeling as well as he said he did. She took his blood pressure and checked his pulse, and then looked at his tablet dispenser to see if he had taken his medication on time.

'*Aloha auina la*…good afternoon,' Molly said, coming out onto the veranda with a tray of cold drinks. She placed it down on a table. 'I hope you had a good day with Mr Ethan,' she added, looking at Amber. 'You don't need to worry about Mr Martyn. I took good care of him. I made certain that he took his tablets at the right time.'

'Thank you for that, Molly,' Amber said with a smile. 'I felt sure that I could rely on you to remind him.' She looked at the tray that Molly had set down. 'These drinks look delicious.' There were jugs of various kinds of fruit juices, decorated with slices of pineapple, cherries and limes.

Molly returned the smile. 'Enjoy,' she said, leaving them and going back into the house.

Amber turned back to Martyn. 'So, do you feel rested?' she asked him. 'Will you come with us to the *luau* later on?'

He nodded. 'Yes. I'd like that. I'm glad that Ethan mentioned it to you. It will be a good way for you to celebrate the beginning of your time here.'

Amber sat with him for a while longer, until he looked at the watch on his wrist and suggested that it was time to start getting ready for the *luau*. 'Ethan said he would come and pick us up at six, so perhaps we should prepare for the evening.'

Molly appeared out of nowhere and began to help him to his feet. 'Do you want Ben to give you a hand?' she asked. 'He's finished clearing the weeds out of the vegetable garden, so he's got nothing at all to do right now.'

Amber didn't hear his muffled reply. As the hours wore on, she was becoming more and more doubtful about why she was actually there. Martyn didn't need her, that was for sure. He had ample help already.

It didn't take her long to get ready for the party. She

changed into a simple shift dress that clung softly to her curves. It would be cool enough to counteract the heat of the evening, and yet it was dressy enough for the occasion. She let her hair hang loose about her shoulders and added a dab of lipstick to the generous curve of her lips.

By the time Ethan called for them, she was up at the house, ready to help Martyn into the car.

The beach where the party was taking place was just a few minutes' drive away. Ethan parked in the shade of trees, and then took Martyn's arm and helped him to a seating area set back a little from the water's edge. Amber went to join him at the table, her senses taken up with the sights and sounds all around her.

Hawaiian music was playing in the background, and girls dressed in traditional costume, wearing leis around their shoulders and flowers in their hair, were dancing barefoot just a short distance away. The scent of roast pork came from a barbecue stand just to the back of her, and all the tables were set with platters of fruit, a variety of salads, along with bowls of chicken, rice and sweet potatoes.

Amber leaned towards Martyn. 'If you keep spoiling me with treats like this, I'll never want to go home.'

Martyn gave a soft laugh and squeezed her hand. 'I'm really glad that you like it here. Relax and enjoy yourself.'

'I thought you might like to try some of our island cocktails,' Ethan said, coming towards them with a tray of drinks. He glanced from one to the other, and Amber knew that he had witnessed the gentle show of affection between herself and his uncle. She tried not to let it bother her. Ethan could think what he liked. She wasn't going to let him put her on the defensive all the time.

'Perhaps we should drink to King Kamehameha,' Ethan said, pushing a long glass of something golden towards Martyn and handing her a cocktail glass filled with a bright red concoction and decorated with fruit and a sparkler that fizzed coloured light in all directions. He raised his own glass and then sipped slowly from it.

'King Kamehameha? I don't think I know anything about him.'

'He was a king who founded a dynasty out here. It's said that when he was born his grandfather was warned that he would slay the chiefs and usurp his position when he grew up, so his grandfather ordered that he should be killed.'

Amber stared at him in horror. 'Tell me that didn't happen.'

'It didn't happen.' Ethan smiled. 'Instead, the child was hidden away and brought up by a childless couple, who kept him safe. Then, five years later, his grandfather discovered that he was alive. He was full of remorse for what he had tried to do, and so the boy was allowed to return to court, where he was taught the ways of court diplomacy and served as a loyal aide to his uncle. After that, he became a successful warrior and fought wars to unify Hawaii. I suppose the slaying of chiefs was to do with enemies rather than any family hostilities.'

'And so now we celebrate with feasting and music,' Martyn said.

Just then there was a blaze of light all around as torches were lit and someone began to blow into a conch shell. An expectant hush descended on the gathered crowd.

'What's happening? What does it mean?' Amber asked in a whisper.

'The royal court is arriving by boat,' Ethan told her. 'It's all symbolic. The fire dancers will signify the battles that were fought, and after that it will be time for celebrating. There will be dancing and feasting and generally making merry.'

It was all good fun, and as darkness fell the entertainment began in earnest. Amber's eyes widened as the fire dancers swooped and swirled and flirted with danger.

'You look as though you're enjoying yourself,' Martyn said softly. 'I'm glad about that. It's good to see a sparkle in your eyes.' He looked around and saw that Ben was coming towards him. 'I'm going to let Ben take me home now,' he added, and when Amber would have stood up to leave with him he shook his head and laid a hand on her shoulder. 'You stay and have a good time,' he murmured. 'I expect Ethan will dance with you and show you how we celebrate our good fortune out here. I'll see you in the morning.'

She watched him go, a slight frown gathering on her forehead, and then Ethan was urging her to go and dance with him, just as Martyn had said. He reached for her, clasping her hand and drawing her out on to the flat sand where people were swaying to the rhythm of the music.

His arms curved about her, and perhaps it was the intoxicating effect of the cocktails she had been drinking, but it seemed after that as though the world was made of pure sensation. She was aware of his hard body pressed against hers, the nudge of his leg against her thigh, the gentle glide of his hand over the small of her back, drawing her ever closer to him. And over all was a canopy of stars, sprinkled against the backcloth of a midnight sky.

The haunting music lulled her senses, filling her being, and she and Ethan moved together in harmony with the gentle rhythm. It was perfect, sensual, a throbbing heartbeat of heavenly experience, and even though she realised she had sipped just a little too much of the alcoholic drinks that Ethan had been bringing her throughout the evening, it was the fact that he was holding her that was making her feel this way.

Why did Ethan have this effect on her? She barely knew him. She had only met him a few weeks ago, and yet all her thoughts were taken up with him. As he lowered his head towards her, it seemed like the most natural thing in the world that he should kiss her. His lips descended, touched, tasted, settled, lingering to explore the sweet, curving line of her mouth.

Her whole body tingled with the exhilaration of that kiss. It spread through her like flame, burning like a fever. She kissed him in return, her lips clinging, tasting, savouring the feel of him, so that her whole world took on a golden, warm glow.

'You see,' Ethan murmured, reluctantly dragging his lips from hers, so that they could both come up for air, 'you and I could have it all. You fit so perfectly into my arms as though you were made for me alone. I could give you whatever it is that you want.'

He gazed down at her, his blue eyes glittering in the darkness. 'I'm here, now… I want you, and I know you feel the same way about me. I can feel it in the way your body quivers next to mine, in the way your lips soften when I kiss you. Isn't that the truth? Don't you feel it the same way I do, running through your veins like quicksilver?'

That was exactly how she felt. Her soft, feminine curves were crushed against him, and she wanted to be even closer, if that was possible, but the music was sounding a drumbeat in her head, and the thunder of her heart was overwhelming, setting off an alarm throughout her body.

She pressed a shaky hand against his chest. 'I don't know what I want,' she said raggedly. 'This is all happening so quickly. I only know it's too soon… It's this Hawaiian paradise weaving its spell on me. I've had too much to drink, and I'm not thinking straight.'

She tried to ease back from him, to allow a faint, cool breeze to clear her head, but he wasn't about to let her go.

His gaze meshed with hers. 'I have wealth and power, too…you can have whatever you want. You only have to say the word and it's yours.'

Amber was bewildered. 'I don't understand… Why would you say something like that?'

'You already know the answer to that one, don't you?' His hands caressed her, smoothing over the curve of her hips and lightly pressuring her towards him once again. 'I wanted you the first moment I saw you. You're so beautiful…you stir a man's blood until he doesn't know what he's doing any more.'

She started to shake her head. This sort of thing didn't happen to her. She was caught up in the island's spell, and her inhibitions had dissolved in the heat, and everything from then on had gone haywire.

'I can give you your heart's desire,' he said softly. 'You only have to say the word and it's yours. I owe you a debt for ever because you saved my uncle's life.'

She frowned, mist swirling inside her head. 'Is this all because of your uncle?'

'We can work this out between us.' Ethan's voice was soft, hypnotic. 'Are you so set on letting him lose his heart to you? He's not himself these days. All he can talk about is that he's found you and that he feels blessed because you agreed to come out here with him. What kind of hold do you have on him?'

'I don't have a hold on him.' She gazed at him in consternation. Surely he couldn't really believe what he was saying? 'This doesn't make any sense at all.'

'It all seems perfectly clear to me. He's ill and he's not thinking straight. You saved his life and he wants to repay you for that in some way, but he's taking things to the extreme, and you're going along with it, sucking him in deeper. Why don't you let me save you from yourself? He doesn't need to be hurt in any way. We can sort this out, you and me. You decide what it will take for you to leave him be.'

Amber stared up at him, letting his words flow over her until they began to rain down on her like a cold shower. Everything he had done, everything he had said had been a pretence, a mockery. He didn't care for her at all. He simply wanted to get her away from his uncle.

'How could you?' she asked. 'How could you say such things to me?'

She turned away from him and started to run along the path that led away from the beach. She would not listen to what he had to say. She ignored him when he called her name. All she knew was that she had to get away from him. She had to go back to her temporary home, and she would do it under her own steam. She wanted nothing more to do with him.

CHAPTER SEVEN

'WHAT's going on with you and Mr Ethan? Have you and he had words?' Molly was preparing food in the kitchen, getting ready for an early breakfast. She was cooking omelettes, wonderful, fluffy creations that Amber knew from experience melted in the mouth, but now she paused, looking directly at Amber.

'What makes you say that?'

Molly gave her an old-fashioned look. 'You think I don't know about these things? Hah!' Molly shook her head and began to deftly slice peppers, wielding the knife like an expert before tossing the brightly coloured chunks into the pan with the eggs. 'It's going on too long. I see you, this last couple of weeks, avoiding looking at each other, not talking unless you have to.'

'Um…I suppose you could say we had a difference of opinion, if you like. But we're fine, really.' Amber sent Molly an anxious look. 'I was hoping it didn't show. Neither of us wants to upset Martyn in any way.'

'*Uwe!* I think he probably guessed already.' Molly gave the eggs a quick stir, then angled the spatula towards Amber, shaking it briefly, 'You think he doesn't know what's going on? You're wrong. That man knows everything.'

'Oh, dear.' Amber thought about that for a moment or two. 'But if he does know, it doesn't seem to bother him at all.'

Molly smiled. 'He's very wise. He knows these things have a way of working themselves out. Me? I think you need to sort it out.' She sniffed the air. 'The bagels are done…you want to fetch them out of the oven?'

'Yes, of course.' Amber picked up the oven gloves and slid the tray out, tipping the freshly baked bagels onto a warm platter. 'Will it be all right if I take one of these to go? I'm supposed to start work at the hospital this morning, and I want to be there early so that I have time to familiarise myself with everything. I've already spoken to Martyn about missing breakfast.'

'That's fine.' Molly indicated the array of fillings set out on the worktop. 'Help yourself to bacon and tomatoes. I made you some salad. You want to take that with you? It's in the fridge.'

Amber smiled and dropped a quick kiss on her cheek. 'You're an angel,' she said. 'I love you to bits.'

'Heh-heh. Me, too. You good for Mr Martyn. He's perked up no end since you've been around.' Molly tipped the omelettes on to a plate. 'You take care in this new job. Don't let them boss you around. You're just a slip of a girl, but you know what you doing.'

Amber grinned. She hoped Molly was right about that. A new job, a new hospital, different people to get to know…it all promised to be quite an experience.

She had bought herself a small car, refusing Martyn's offer of help, and so the journey to the hospital was an easy one. She knew the route fairly well, since Ethan had shown her the way a few days ago. He had stayed with her while she'd looked around the place where she would be working and then he'd disappeared on an errand while she'd met the people who would be her colleagues.

Molly had clearly picked up on the atmosphere between the two of them. This last couple of weeks had been fraught with problems, since both she and Ethan had their own particular grievances and were thrown together daily in their contact with Martyn. It had been difficult being in the same room with Ethan, let alone having him as a neighbour, but they had come to an agreement of sorts. They had to be together for as long as she was in Hawaii, and so they would make the best of things, for Martyn's sake.

They both knew where they stood. Ethan didn't trust her and she was always guarded in her dealings with him.

She tried to put all that behind her as she drove along the valley road. The lush, forested slopes had a soothing effect on her, so that by the time she arrived at the hospital she was on good form.

The hospital was a modern building in the middle of a thriving town. Surrounded by lakes and green hills, it was pleasing on the eye, a pleasant place to work. Her job here was to help out in Accident and Emergency, with an element of going out to treat patients outside of hospital, if necessary. As she understood things, she would be working alongside a consultant and senior house officers. Her immediate boss was a young Hawaiian doctor, a registrar named Kyle. She had met him on that first visit and he seemed friendly and confident about what he was doing. There was a monthly rota system in operation for callouts.

'How are you doing?' Kyle greeted her cheerily as she was trying to find her bearings.

'I'm all right, I think,' she said. 'I've said hello to all the doctors and nurses on duty, I know where the charts and the lab forms are stored, and I've discovered where all the equipment is kept. So I think I'm about ready to make a start.'

'That's great.' He handed her a chart. 'Your first patient shouldn't be too difficult to handle. She's a young girl who was walking on the beach when she felt something wrap itself around her foot. Then she was stung, but someone has already removed the spine that was stuck in her foot.'

'So what kind of creature stung her, do we know?' She glanced through the notes, but there was no answer in there.

'I'd guess a stingray,' Kyle said. 'They have an appendage that has sharp, sword-like stingers that can do some real damage. The stingers are filled with venom, so you have both a puncture wound and a poison to deal with.'

'Thanks for that,' Amber acknowledged him. 'I'll go and take a look at her.'

'Okay. Let me know if you have any problems.'

'I will.'

The girl was about fourteen years old, and she was clearly in a distressed state. She'd been vomiting, and appeared to be feeling faint.

'Hello, Lara,' Amber greeted her. 'I'm Dr Shaw. Let's see what needs to be done about your injury, shall we?' She smiled at the girl's mother, letting her explain what had happened.

A nurse had already cleaned the wound, and Lara was soaking her foot in water that was as hot as she could bear. The nurse frequently checked the temperature and added more hot water.

'You need to keep your foot in water for just a few more minutes,' Amber said after she had examined the girl. 'You have already been soaking it for about forty minutes, haven't you?'

Lara nodded. 'I've got a terrible headache. I feel awful.'

'I know you do. These things are not very pleasant, are they? The hot water should deactivate the venom and it also helps to ease the pain, but I'll give you something to take for that anyway. I think the best course of action would be for me to infiltrate an anaesthetic into the wound, and that should help tremendously. I'm going to give you an antibiotic, as well to counteract any bacteria that might be lurking there.'

She left Lara soaking her foot while she prepared the anaesthetic, and once that was done, the nurse gently dried the area.

'All we need to do now is to put a dressing on it,' Amber said when she had finished. 'You should be feeling much better very soon.'

'It feels good already,' Lara said. 'It's such a relief. It was a horrible pain.'

'Well, next time you go wading in waters where there are stingrays, perhaps it would be a good idea to wear some kind of waterproof sandal, or at least shuffle your feet so that you can see if there are any rays lurking close by.'

She left the girl with her mother a few minutes later, and went to report back to Kyle. 'I think we have a satisfied customer back there,' she said. 'I hope all my problems are going to be as easy to solve as that one.'

Kyle laughed. 'You should be so lucky. In fact, we've just had a call to say that there's been a boating accident off the coast. We wouldn't normally expect you to go out with the crew on your first day, but the doctor who's actually on call isn't feeling so good, and the boss thought we should give you the option. How are you with lifeboats? Do you feel up to going on board to help out?'

She nodded. 'That's fine by me, if you're sure you have enough people on hand here.'

'We'll manage. Go and get kitted up in the locker room. The nurse will show you your uniform. You need to be ready to go in five minutes. The boss will meet you at the ambulance bay.'

Amber hurried to get ready, and she was waiting at the ambulance bay with a minute to spare. She looked around for the emergency vehicle, but as it came into view, her heart sank. Ethan was holding open the passenger door for her, leaning across from the driver's seat.

'Over here,' he said.

Her jaw dropped. 'Are you the boss? Don't tell me you're in charge of callouts?'

'Okay, then, I won't.' He shrugged. 'Are you going to get into the car? We don't have time to debate the issue.'

'You didn't tell me that I would be working alongside you,' she said with a frown as she slid into the seat beside him. 'You might have warned me. I thought you worked in a different hospital. According to Martyn, you were based nearer to Honolulu.'

He started the engine and headed for the main road. 'That's true, or at least it was true, but when Martyn was taken ill I had to work closer to home so that I could take over the running of the plantation. I transferred to the local hospital.'

'You must have known we'd end up working together.'

'Not necessarily. I didn't know you were going to volunteer for the on-call work, did I? That wasn't part of the plan originally. It was just something you and Kyle worked out between you.' He checked the road conditions in the mirror and then indicated that he was turning onto the coast road. 'Anyway, what's happened has happened, and we have no real choice but to make the best of it.'

She pressed her lips together. He was right, and, no matter what her feelings were on the matter, it was time to start thinking about the work ahead. 'So tell me about this accident at sea. What can we expect?'

'Apparently, a mast snapped on a sailboat and people were injured when it fell. A woman phoned the accident in.' He sucked in a sharp breath. 'She said her husband and brother were injured, along with her young son. It looks as though her husband has come off worst because he has collapsed. The brother has some sort of head or facial injury, and the boy has a possible fractured wrist.'

'So our role is to treat them as best we can and then send them on to hospital,' she said. 'Presumably they'll be transported by lifeboat?'

He nodded. 'Yes, unless we need to transfer anyone urgently, in which case we'll call for air support. I doubt that will be necessary. They're not far off the coast, so it shouldn't take us long to get there.'

He kept his attention on the road the whole time they

were speaking, and Amber could see from the rigid line of his jaw that he was unusually tense. Perhaps he was worried about what lay ahead of them and was desperate to reach the injured people as soon as was possible.

In fact, they were on board the sailboat within fifteen minutes. The lifeboat stayed alongside while Amber and Ethan tended to the injured people.

Ethan turned his attention to the man who was most seriously hurt. 'It looks as though he has abdominal injuries,' he said. His expression was grim. 'I'll put in an airway to support his breathing, but we need to stabilise his spine in case there are other injuries.'

'I'll help you with that as soon as I've seen to the other two,' Amber said. She had already decided that the man with the facial injury needed urgent attention, but the boy, Shaun, who was about twelve years old, was in a distressed state.

'Try to keep him calm,' she told his mother. 'Support his arm and wrist with a pad of rolled up clothing. I'll come and see to him as soon as possible.'

Her priority with the injured man was to put a tube down his throat to secure his airway before swelling would prevent her from doing it. He was slipping in and out of consciousness, and on examination it appeared that his jaw was broken and that meant it was going to be a tricky process.

'What will you do?' the man's sister asked. 'I tried to stop the bleeding but I couldn't. And I was so worried—I didn't know what to do for my husband. I know the mast hit him across his abdomen but I didn't know what to do to help him.'

'Dr Brookes will look after your husband,' Amber answered. 'He's doing everything that needs to be done. As to your brother, I'm going to clear his mouth and throat of any obstruction,' she told her. 'I'll use suction to do that. I'll have to keep doing it every now and again to make sure that his throat is clear, and once I'm satisfied that his breathing is stable, I'll put a bandage around the crown of his head and his jaw to keep things in the right position.'

She was already working on him as she was speaking. She added a second bandage around his forehead to keep everything in place. 'We'll arrange for a specialist to operate on him as soon as we get back to the hospital,' she said.

As soon as she had done what was necessary, she turned her attention to the boy. 'Can you tell me what happened?' she asked him.

'I fell,' he said. He was much calmer now, and she guessed that the shock of the accident had caused his initial distress as had the pain and discomfort he'd suffered. 'Well, my dad pushed me out of the way so that I wouldn't get hurt when the mast fell. I put out my hand to stop myself falling and I felt the bones go.' He looked at his wrist and hand. 'It's an odd shape, isn't it?'

'Yes, it is. That's because the bones have cracked and moved out of place,' she explained. 'I'm going to give you something to take away the pain, and we'll put a splint on your arm so that it doesn't move and cause any more damage. When we get to the hospital, a doctor will give you an anaesthetic—something to make sure that it doesn't hurt—and then he'll put the bones back into the right position. You'll have to wear a cast for a few weeks while the bones mend.'

He nodded as though he understood, and Amber worked quickly to relieve his pain and support the wrist.

'Is my dad going to be all right?' he asked. He sent his father a surreptitious, worried look. 'And what about my uncle Sam? His face is a mess.'

'Your uncle will be much better once he's had an operation to fix the bones of his jaw in place,' she said, 'and Dr Brookes is doing everything that he can for your father.' She glanced at Ethan to see how he was coping and then looked back at the boy. 'If you're all right for the moment, Shaun, I'll go and help him.'

'Yes. Help him, please.'

Ethan was listening to his patient's heartbeat through his stethoscope at that moment. 'How is he doing?' Amber asked in an undertone.

'Not too well, by the look of things.' Ethan's mouth made a flat line. 'His heartbeat is very slow, and I suspect that there's internal bleeding. We need to get him to hospital and into surgery as soon as possible. I'm giving him intravenous fluids to ensure that he doesn't go into shock, but we have to be very careful not to overdo it and cause even more problems.'

'Shall I ring ahead and tell the trauma teams what's happening?'

'Yes. And arrange for an ambulance to meet us by the shore.' He twisted around to look at the man's son. 'I know this is hard for you,' he said. 'Your father's a good man, and his first thought was to protect you. You can be proud of him.' He studied the boy, and Amber guessed he was wondering how much information he could take on board.

'He needs an operation to repair any damage that

might have been caused inside him when the mast hit him,' he said. 'We're doing everything we can to make sure that he'll come out of this all right.'

Shaun seemed to cope with that well enough. His mother put an arm around him, and they clung to each other for comfort.

Ethan turned back to his patient, and Amber could see that he was deeply concerned for him. He pressed his lips together and simply watched him for a moment, and she realised that he felt a deep empathy for the little family.

It was only then that she remembered what Martyn had told her about Ethan's parents. They had been killed in a boating accident, he'd said, when Ethan had been in his teens. Was Ethan thinking about that right now? Perhaps that accounted for the sadness in his eyes.

She knelt down beside him and laid a hand lightly on his shoulder. 'Are you all right?'

He sent her a brief sideways look. Her gaze meshed with his, and in that moment a fleeting, unspoken understanding passed between them.

'I'm fine.' With a faint inclination of his head, he indicated the man with the broken jaw. 'I see you managed to stop the bleeding. That was good work. He looked a mess, but you managed to sort things out and soothe the boy at the same time.'

'It wasn't too difficult.' She was already dialling the number for the hospital. 'We should tell the lifeboat people that we're ready to move Shaun and his mother. That will give us more room to manoeuvre. Perhaps a couple of the crew could help us move the father onto a spinal board.'

He nodded, and she set things in motion while he

tended to his patient. Soon the men from the lifeboat were escorting the woman and her son from the sailboat.

'You're good at this, aren't you?' Ethan said glancing up at her. 'Calm, efficient, focussed. Perhaps my uncle was right when he thought you would slot into this job as though you were made for it. He's a people-watcher, you know. He doesn't say a lot, but it's all going on inside his head.'

All the while he was talking, he was checking his patient's vital signs, and Amber's respect for him was growing by the minute. This was a side of the man she hadn't seen before. This was the professional, the man who was dedicated to his career. She could see it in his every action. He was thorough, taking time to do a good job, making sure that his patient was stabilised before he was moved.

'Perhaps I should return the compliment,' she said. 'You've been totally focussed on what we're doing right from the start. You didn't waste a second in getting here, and you had all the equipment that you needed right on hand.'

'It's essential that you do that,' he murmured. 'The emergency car is always stocked for every journey, and we each have a pack of essential equipment. That's why yours was waiting for you when you decided to come with me. And you made up your mind fast—that was very surprising.' His gaze narrowed on her. 'But you didn't know I would be the one going along with you, did you, back then?'

She didn't answer him. Why would she rise to his bait?

The lifeboat crew came to help lift the injured man on to the stretcher, and they quickly transported both men to their vessel. From then on it was a matter of minutes before the accident victims were on their way to hospital.

Ethan followed the ambulance. He drove carefully, but fast, and she guessed he was anxious to make sure his patient was safe. They didn't speak about things that had gone wrong between them or how they were going to proceed from now on. Amber had made her decision to work with the emergency service, and if that meant working alongside Ethan, so be it. She was through with trying to defend herself. Let him do his worst. She had the measure of her opponent, and from now on they would meet on equal terms.

Amber's working day finished just after lunchtime. It was a good arrangement, as far as she was concerned, because it gave her most of the afternoon to keep tabs on Martyn's progress, and there was still the glorious opportunity to explore the rest of this beautiful island. The one flaw was that her patients were still in surgery when she had to leave.

'I'll give you a call and let you know how they're doing,' Kyle told her. 'Ethan asked to be informed, as well. He had to go off on another emergency.'

'Thanks, Kyle. I appreciate that.' The man with abdominal injuries was her main concern, but they had been able to get to him within minutes of the accident happening, and those minutes were precious when lives were at stake.

Martyn met her at the door of the main house when she arrived there about an hour later, after taking time to freshen up back at her bungalow. He seemed to be in a thoughtful mood, as though he was preoccupied with something.

'How was your day?' he asked. 'I heard you met up with Ethan.'

'How did you know that?' She was astonished. 'I didn't know myself that we would be working together until shortly after I started my shift.'

They walked into the sitting-room. 'It was on the local news. The press were in touch with the lifeboat crew, and they broadcast it on the local radio station and on the TV.'

'Good heavens. It's a small world, isn't it?'

'It certainly is.' He sat down on an elegant cream-coloured sofa and waved a hand towards the chair opposite. 'Sit down, and tell me about your day. How did you and he get on?'

'We were fine,' she murmured. 'It came as quite a shock to me, I can tell you, to find that we were working together, but when you have to look after people who are ill or hurting, the job is really all that you have in mind. It's a bit like being on autopilot, I think.'

He looked faintly relieved. 'He's a good doctor, Ethan. His colleagues were upset when he had to leave his job at the other hospital, but they're hoping it won't be too long before he decides to go back.'

Amber sent him a guarded look. So he had known all along that Ethan had changed hospitals. Still, why would he think it mattered one way or the other to her? She had been out of work, and a job in Hawaii was a prize by any standards.

'You look as though you're mulling something over,' she said, studying him. 'I could see from your expres-

sion when you opened the door that you were preoccupied. What's troubling you? Anything in particular?'

His expression sobered. 'I'm not quite sure how to
tell you this,' he said. 'It's good news for me, but I'm
not sure that you will feel the same way.'

She frowned. 'Have you found someone to replace
me? Is that what you're trying to say?' Perhaps he had
taken on board Ethan's doubts about her and decided
that since they weren't getting along, things would have
to change. They hadn't drawn up a contract of any sort
after all, and the only concrete things she had were the
job at the hospital and her airfare home.

His brows shot up. 'Good heavens, girl. Why on
earth would you think that way? Is it something Ethan
said? You shouldn't take any notice of him. He has his
own ideas about how things should be, but they don't
always match up with mine.'

Amber stared at him. So Molly was right. He did
know what was going on between her and Ethan, but he
wasn't putting any store by it.

'No, it's nothing to do with Ethan.' It was only half
a lie, but she censored it with herself because she didn't
want anything to disrupt the harmony that existed
between the two men. 'I was never quite sure why you
asked me to come out here. You don't really need me.
You have all these people to help you out, and you have
your own doctor on the island, as well as Ethan to watch
over you. I accepted because I'd really taken to you as
a person, and because Hawaii seemed like the answer
to my prayers.'

He gave her a thoughtful look. 'And you had split up
with your boyfriend, James. I admit to feeling a bit

guilty about that, because it was my own daughter who came between you…but, to be honest, I never thought you and he were right for each other.'

Her eyes widened. 'You don't miss anything, do you?'

'Well, it was fairly obvious. And that friend of yours, Sarah, told me a bit about what was going on…only because I prised it out of her, you understand. I'm a nosy soul. Always have been. Grace used to say to me, "Stop interfering. Let people get on with their own lives. They won't thank you for intruding." But I've always been the same. I need to know what's going on around me, and if I can help people out, or change things for the better, that's what I'll do. Ethan's the same in some ways. He knows what he wants and he sets out to get it.'

'Hmm.' He was certainly right about that. Ethan had tried several devious ways to detach her from his uncle, and when they hadn't worked, he had taken a step back. She didn't imagine for a minute, though, that he had given up. 'But you still haven't told me your news. What is it?'

He frowned. 'I don't want you to be upset by this. I never thought that James was the right man for you. It seemed to me that he couldn't quite cope with your ways of handling things. You were always in control of a situation, and you were good at exams, good at your job, whereas he always seemed to be a little bit in your shadow. I'm sorry to say that, Amber, because he's a good man, just not the man for you.'

She looked at him, a slow chill creeping down her spine. 'Are you saying your news is about James? Is that what this is about?'

'I am. I'm sorry.' He leaned forward in his seat as

though he wanted to be closer to her, to comfort her. 'You see, Caitlin called this morning. She said that James has asked her to marry him, and she said yes to him. They want to hold the ceremony out here on Oahu.' He frowned. 'I know how difficult that will be for you.'

Amber pulled in a sharp breath. This couldn't be happening. Not here, not now. She had come all this way to where she'd thought she was safe. And now her world was crashing down around her. How could James do this to her? It was like rubbing salt in the wound.

'When is this supposed to happen?' she asked.

'Next month. They don't want to wait. They made up their minds that this is what they want to do, and they say can fit in the wedding and honeymoon before they both start work at the university over here. Apparently James has secured a research post alongside Caitlin.'

'Oh…oh.' It was more of a shudder than a word. She felt her heart plummet to the pit of her stomach. Not only were they getting married out here, they would be living and working here, too.

Her head was in a whirl. 'I need to think about this,' she said. 'I don't know what to do. Perhaps I should go away.' She twisted around as though she would make her escape right there and then. 'I can't stay here and watch this happen.'

He began to shake his head. 'That's not the real you talking, the girl who takes control of her life and gets things sorted.'

'Oh, but it is,' she said. 'Don't you see? I'm a coward. I don't have any backbone. I ran away once, and I can do it again.'

'But you won't.' He spoke softly, his voice gentle

with understanding. 'And it wasn't as though you were actually running away from James, was it? It might have seemed that way, but there were other things going on at the time.'

She stared at him dazedly. 'I don't know what you mean.'

'I don't think James was the crux of things. After all, you stood by and watched what was happening and said nothing. You could have kicked up a fuss and tried to work things out between you, but you didn't. You accepted what was going on.'

He paused. 'Why should you blame yourself for finding an easy way out? Your career had been messed up through no fault of your own. Who wouldn't have taken the opportunity to come and live in a land of sunshine and be pampered for a while? You're simply human, and you accepted the perfect solution when it was offered to you.'

She hadn't spoken and he looked at her to see if she was listening to what he said. 'Amber, please don't act hastily. It may seem like the end of the world to you right now, but it may not be as bad as you think.' He hesitated, letting his words sink in. 'Besides, I really do need you here with me, you know. A wedding is a big thing to organise, and just the thought of it makes me feel drained of energy. You have a way of revitalising me, and I don't like to ask this of you, but this is my daughter, and I have to give her my support. I can't do it on my own, Amber. Please don't run away again.'

'Run away?' Ethan's voice ricocheted around the room as he pushed open the door. 'Why would she be running anywhere?' He walked towards them, looking from one to the other, a deep frown drawing his brows together. 'What's going on?'

Amber stood up, a wave of nausea threatening to overwhelm her. She wasn't at all sure what to make of Martyn's announcement, but to have Ethan witness her discomfiture was more than she could bear right now.

'This has nothing whatever to do with you,' she said. 'This is a private conversation between me and your uncle.' She knew it was the wrong thing to say as soon as she'd said it, it was ill mannered and intolerable, but her mind was reeling in shock, and Ethan's arrival had sent her spinning into a vortex of confusion.

Why did he have to turn up like a bad penny when she was at her lowest ebb? How could she fight her demons with him around? Wasn't he the worst demon of all?

She needed to get away from here and go somewhere to lick her wounds in private. Why should Ethan witness her downward spiral? It wasn't fair. Life wasn't fair. It was full of trip wires and traps that had been laid for the unwary and she was finding herself tangled up in every one of them.

'Amber? What's happened? What's wrong?' Ethan was frowning, his gaze homing in on her as though he would pin her down right there and make her give him an answer.

Amber stared at him, caught in the glitter of those blue eyes like a trapped animal. He, of all people, would rejoice in her downfall.

Then she looked at Martyn, and saw how pale he had become, and her heart crumpled. He was ill, and it was up to her to ensure his well-being, but she had let him down at the first hurdle. His glow of happiness had been blotted out by a grey cloud, and it was all her fault.

'Martyn, I'm sorry,' she said. 'I didn't mean to cast a shadow on your good news. I just need to think this through.'

'It's all right,' he murmured. 'I understand.'

'I'm glad someone does,' Ethan said in a brisk tone, 'because I certainly don't. Is anyone going to enlighten me?' He glared at both of them, his brows drawing together in a dark line, his stare threatening retribution.

'Not now, Ethan,' Martyn said wearily. 'Just give it a while, will you?'

Amber had been glued to the spot, but she suddenly found that strength had surged back into her legs. She turned away and hurried out of the room.

CHAPTER EIGHT

'YOU still haven't told me what caused the upset the other day.' Ethan threw Amber a sideways glance. He was at the wheel of the emergency vehicle, heading at top speed towards the coast, and all Amber could see of the landscape was a blur of trees and blue sky. 'Why would you be thinking of running away?'

'Would you just concentrate on your driving instead of asking questions?' She gritted her teeth. 'I'd as soon get there in one piece.'

'There's nothing wrong with my driving.' He raised a dark brow. 'I took an advanced driving test and passed with flying colours.'

'Yes, and I suspect *flying* might be the operative word.'

His mouth quirked in response, but Amber was relieved when he slowed down to a pace that she could cope with. 'Is that better?' he asked.

'Much better. Thank you.' She began to breathe more easily. 'I know we have to get there quickly, but there's a limit to how much risk I want to take.' She frowned. 'The lifeguards are already on the scene, aren't they, and they're trained in resuscitation methods?'

'That's true, but we're closer at hand than anyone else, and if we can get there before the ambulance, the boy has a greater chance of survival.' He glanced at her. 'I didn't mean to scare you. Are you okay?'

'I'm fine.'

By now he was slowing down even more, turning the car on to the slipway used for towing boats on and off the beach. He applied the brakes.

Amber had the passenger door open as soon as the vehicle stopped, and then she sprinted across the flat, smooth sand to where she could see the lifeguards at work. Ethan kept pace with her.

'How's he doing?' Amber asked the lifeguard who was working on the boy. She put her medical bag down on the sand.

'Not too well. We brought him out of the water as quickly as we could, but he was already unconscious. We've been working on him for a couple of minutes and there's been no change.'

The lifeguard continued with chest compressions while Ethan went down on his knees and started to assess the boy's condition.

Amber guessed the child was about ten years old, and there was a graze across his temple where the surf-board had hit him as he overturned in the water. His worried parents were standing nearby, looking ashen faced and weepy.

She checked for a pulse. 'It's barely discernible.'

Ethan quickly introduced an endotracheal tube into the boy's throat. 'I need suction,' he said, but Amber was already by his side, ready to clear the boy's airway and enable Ethan to attach the oxygen supply.

Once the child's airway was assured, Ethan inserted a gastric tube so that they could draw water or debris from his stomach. Amber started to set up two intravenous lines, so that he could be given fluids and medication, while Ethan taped electrodes in place on the boy's chest so that his heart rhythm could be monitored.

'Let's get him warmed up,' Ethan said, as soon as they were finished. They could already hear the sound of the ambulance siren in the distance, and by the time the paramedics arrived their patient was wrapped in a blanket. They worked together to carefully transfer him to a body board to protect his spine. Then they strapped him securely in place.

Ethan handed over their patient into the care of the paramedics, while Amber tried to comfort the boy's tearful parents. 'We'll get him to hospital straight away, and the medical team will take over as soon as he arrives. They'll take good care of him.' She knew that the boy's problems were far from over. He would need careful nursing to ensure that his heart rate and blood pressure returned to normal, and any lung complications could be averted or dealt with.

'I'd like to follow up on him at the hospital,' she told Ethan, when the ambulance started to pull away. 'We don't have any immediate calls to make, do we?'

'No. I'm with you on that one,' he murmured. 'I always follow up on the patients I've brought in. I like to know what happens to them.'

They went back to the car and Ethan set the engine in motion. 'It's uplifting whenever there's a good outcome.'

'Like the man who collapsed on his boat after he was hit by the mast.' Amber smiled. 'I heard he'll be coming out of hospital soon. And his brother-in-law is on the mend, too.'

'It turned out well in the end, didn't it? I felt sorry for the young lad. It was a scary situation for him, and he was clearly worried about his father, but he managed to hold it together very well.'

Amber glanced at him, wondering whether she should ask him about what had happened to his own parents or whether it would be best to leave it alone.

In the end she said softly, 'I guessed you were worried for the family and that you understood exactly what they were going through. Martyn told me what happened to your parents. It must have brought it all home to you.'

He nodded and didn't seem to mind that she had brought up the subject. 'I was a little older than the boy when the accident happened, so perhaps I was better able to cope with it. Like him, I was on board the boat at the time, and it was a frightening experience. We were caught up in a sudden storm at sea, and the waves were higher than any I'd ever seen. I think the boat must have been blown off course, and there was a problem with the onboard electronics. My father managed to radio for help, but he was tossed against the framework of the cabin and suffered a head injury. My mother and I went to help him, but she collapsed. They said later that she must have suffered a heart attack.'

Amber closed her eyes briefly. 'I'm so sorry,' she said. 'That must have been dreadful for you.'

He grimaced. 'I suppose I was luckier than most. My uncle took me in and looked after me as if I was his own. He said I was like the son he never had… And Grace, my aunt, was like a mother to me. I could never get over the loss of my parents, but Martyn and Grace made my life whole again.'

'It must make you very sad to see him so ill.' She frowned. 'I felt bad that I upset him the other day. It grieves me to think that I might have been the cause of him having a relapse.'

'You didn't do anything to make his condition worse,' Ethan murmured. He turned the car on to the road leading to the hospital. 'His heart is weak, and it's only the tablets he's taking that are helping him to keep it all together. I knew some time ago that things were bad, and I didn't want him to go over to the U.K. because I thought it was too risky. I warned him, but he wanted to see how Caitlin was doing, and he was determined to look in on the U.K. offices to make sure things were shipshape.'

'Even so, it can't have helped when I reacted the way I did.'

He drove into the hospital car park and threw her a sideways glance. 'What was it all about? I know he told you that Caitlin was getting married, but why would that cause you any problems?'

He parked the car and cut the engine. Then he remained still, waiting for her answer.

She sighed. 'She's marrying my ex-boyfriend…only he wasn't an ex until he met her.'

He frowned. 'So you and James were an item? How long had you been together?'

'About a year.'

His eyes widened. 'So it wasn't a passing fancy. No wonder you were upset at the news. That must have caused you a few qualms. And did Martyn know this the whole time?'

'Yes, apparently he did.'

'No wonder you took Martyn up on his offer to come over here. It must have seemed like a heaven-sent opportunity.' He gave a soft whistle, thinking things through, and she sent him a sharp look.

'Don't gloat,' she said. 'I didn't come here with any designs on your uncle, neither did I develop any ulterior motive. I was out of work through no fault of my own, and I was ensured a job out here. You've had me wrong the whole time.'

'Have I?' He gave her a thoughtful, brooding look. 'It still doesn't account for my uncle inviting you over here and setting you up in a place of your own. He'd have treated you like a regular princess if he'd had his own way.'

'Which he didn't—and, like I said, don't gloat.'

He held up his hands as though to admit defeat. 'I'm not rejoicing in your misfortune. I wouldn't do something like that.' He studied her for a moment or two. 'So how do you feel about James coming over here now that you've had time to get used to the idea?'

'Humiliated, embarrassed, hurt—how would you expect me to feel? He threw me over for another woman, and I don't know how I'm supposed to deal with that. Maybe you have some ideas about what I should do. You seem to have plenty of ideas about everything else.'

He blinked, jerking back a little in his seat. 'Whoa. Don't pin this one on me. I'm just trying to work out exactly what's going on here.'

'Well, I'm not going to run away, that's for sure. I

know you'd probably be glad if I chose to do that, but I realised that it was out of the question as soon as I saw Martyn relapse. He's getting weaker by the day, and I don't want to be the cause of any further downward spiral. I'm sorry if my staying here doesn't suit you.'

'I didn't say I thought you should leave.' He gave her a direct look, a glimmer of light starting up in the depths of his eyes. 'If I remember correctly, what I actually said was I thought you should turn your attention towards me. That way we both stand a chance of getting what we want.'

She glowered at him. 'You're impossible,' she said, reaching for the handle and pushing the door open. 'I can't talk to you when you're like this.'

She slid out of her seat and started to walk towards the doors of the accident and emergency department. She would concentrate her attention on the boy who had nearly drowned. He, at least, was worthy of her anxiety.

The boy gradually recovered over the next few hours, and the following day the doctors were able to remove the tube from his throat. He sat up and began to pay attention to his surroundings, and his parents were exhilarated to have their son back.

Over the next few weeks, Amber concentrated on trying to boost Martyn's strength. She made slight changes to his medication, giving him diuretics to lower the pressure in his arteries and heart, along with tablets to improve the heart's pumping ability. Gradually, he seemed to be better able to cope.

The wedding plans went ahead, and Amber did her best to ignore the preparations going on around her. The wedding was to be held on Martyn's land, with a terraced and grassed area close to the beach set aside for the actual ceremony. A wedding planner came to organise the seating arrangements, and soon there were visits from flower arrangers, caterers and all the other people who would be involved in making this a wedding to remember.

James and Caitlin arrived home the day before the ceremony was due to take place. Martyn embraced both of them and invited them into the house where Molly was busy laying out a welcome home feast in the dining-room.

Ethan greeted Caitlin like a long-lost sister, giving her a hug and at the same time lifting her off the ground and twirling her around in and exuberant show of affection. 'It's good to see you again,' he said. 'Congratulations on the new job. When do you start?'

She answered him, talking excitedly about all the changes that were taking place in her life. 'It was such good fortune that James managed to get a job in clinical research alongside me. It was what we both wanted.'

Ethan acknowledged that, and turned to James. 'So, James,' he said, giving him the once-over, 'you're going to tie the knot and whisk my cousin away to the Caribbean for your honeymoon, are you? You must be a pretty fast worker. You only met a short time ago, didn't you?'

James nodded. Perhaps he became aware of Amber standing a short distance away because he sent her a cautious glance, before answering Ethan in a low tone. 'It was more of a love-at-first-sight kind of thing,' he said, shifting his gaze to Caitlin by his side.

Caitlin slid her hand into his. 'We both knew right away that we were made for each other.' She, too, glanced towards Amber, a worried look on her face.

'I guessed it must be something like that,' Ethan said. 'And, of course, being able to connect with both of you through the video link at the hospital it meant that I already had the chance to get to know James.' He moved towards Amber, who had been helping Molly set platters of food on the table. 'It's how I first came across Amber, too.'

Amber gave a faint smile, acknowledging that. He was making an effort to include her in the conversation, and that was probably more for Martyn's sake than anything else, since his uncle was looking a bit fraught about the situation when he thought no one was looking at him.

But Ethan took her completely by surprise with his next move. He slid an arm around her shoulders and drew her close to him. 'She's the light of my life.'

The pressure of his arm about her slowly increased, as though he was giving her a hidden warning not to try to pull away. And then he looked down into her eyes with the expression of a man who was totally in love. Only Amber wasn't fooled for a moment. She could read the hidden message in those glittering eyes, and it was telling her that she should go along with this pretence, not only for her sake but for Martyn's, as well.

She gazed up at him. He was way out of order, wrapping her close this way and crushing the softness of her curves against his long body. If she could have aimed a surreptitious kick at his ankle without giving rise to suspicion, she would have, but everyone was watching them intently, and she had no choice but to smile through this mockery of a love match.

It was bad enough that he was teasing her this way, but even worse was her unwilling response. Ethan's hand seared her skin where it rested on the curve of her shoulder. He let it glide downwards until it rested lightly on the curve of her hip, and she felt the instant clamour of her nerve endings as sensation rocketed through her. He knew exactly what he was doing. With one gentle caress he fired up her senses as though she was the candle to his flame, and her whole body went into meltdown. How could he torment her this way? Why wouldn't he leave her be?

But she knew the answer to that, didn't she? He was putting his uncle's mind at rest and wiping away any guilt that might linger in his cousin's mind at the same time.

She could see that Martyn was pleased that they were supposedly over their differences and heading for something more meaningful. There was a glimmer of amusement in his eyes. If only he knew the truth of the matter…

Still, perhaps it was better this way. He could see his daughter married with a clear conscience, and his blessing would go with them when they set off for the Caribbean.

She carefully detached herself from Ethan's embrace. 'I promised Molly I'd help with the food,' she said. 'Excuse me, will you?'

Caitlin followed her a short time later, coming into the kitchen and looking anxiously across the table towards her. 'I'm so glad you've managed to find happiness for yourself,' she said. 'You must think I'm a terrible person.' There was a catch in her voice as she added, 'I didn't know, to begin with that you and James were a couple. If I had done, I probably wouldn't have let things go as far as they did. By the time I found out, it was too late. I'd fallen for him completely.' She looked at Amber, her gaze sincere, apologetic. 'Can you forgive me?'

'I never blamed you,' Amber said. 'You were going through a very difficult time, with your father being seriously ill, and I could see that you turned to James for comfort. It doesn't matter. Don't worry about it.' She was thoughtful for a moment or two. 'Perhaps he and I were never really suited anyway. We got on very well together, like true friends, but there has to be more if you want to sustain a relationship.'

Caitlin seemed to take comfort in that. 'I'm glad you don't feel too badly towards us,' she said. They spoke for a while longer about various things and then she glanced around the kitchen. 'Molly has done us proud again, hasn't she? Shall I take that bowl of rice through to the dining room?'

'Yes, she has. Thanks, that would be helpful.'

Caitlin went back into the dining room and Amber gathered up a tray of nibbles and headed after her. She saw James and Ethan talking to one another as though they were old friends, and she decided that she would like nothing more than to slip away at the first opportunity.

She couldn't, though. They were ready to sit down and eat together, and the talk was all about the wedding the next day.

'You brought your dress in London, I heard,' Molly said, looking at Caitlin and placing a basket of crusty rolls on the table. 'I can't wait to see it.'

Ethan came and sat next to Amber. He offered her a dish of chilled tropical fruits. 'This is your favourite starter, isn't it? Well, next to Molly's scrumptious prawn cocktail, at least. What's your fancy today?'

She looked at him from under her lashes. How did he know about her favourite food? Was he a people watcher, like his uncle? Or was it simply a case of getting to know the enemy? 'You don't need to keep up a pretence with me,' she said, keeping her voice low. 'I believe James already has the message. That stunt you pulled earlier was enough to grab his attention—and everyone else's too. Even Martyn fell for it.'

'You can't have too much of a good thing,' Ethan murmured. 'Let's make sure they swallow it hook, line and sinker, shall we? Then the wedding will go off smoothly and the young couple will go off happily on their honeymoon.'

'I'm not playing your games,' she muttered under her breath. 'Enough is enough.'

'Enough?' He lifted a dark brow. 'Believe me, angel, I haven't even started yet.'

She looked up at him then, and he smiled at her, his mouth curving in a way that found its mark, a bone-melting, heat-seeking-missile kind of smile that laid waste to her defences and left her floundering.

He was incorrigible. Worst of all, she had the feeling he would be true to his word, and her knees grew weak at the thought. How could she withstand the on-slaught of his carefully prepared manoeuvres? Heat pooled in her abdomen at his mere smile, so how on earth could she cope with a full-blooded ambush?

On the morning of the wedding, the bustle of prep-arations moved up several notches. The caterers set out a banquet fit for a king. There were Caesar and Waldorf salads and fruit starters, a selection of appetisers, which included spinach and cheese brochettes, and there was filet mignon, along with spiced chicken and seafood dishes. For dessert there were all kinds of delicious sweets to choose from…tropical fruits, whipped cream and chocolate mousse were just a few.

Outside, in the grounds of the house, rows of elegant white-painted chairs were set out on the lawns by the terrace, and standing columns adorned with splendid flower arrangements had been placed alongside the seating area. There was a bridal archway festooned with fragrant roses, and to one side was an area laid out with tables and chairs where people would sit and eat after the ceremony.

Beyond the immediate area, the curve of the bay provided a jewelled backcloth, where the glitter of sunlight on the blue ocean vied with white ribbons of surf that were left by the gentle waves rolling up on the beach. A cluster of palm trees would provide the setting for photographs of the bride and groom, and altogether Amber couldn't think of a lovelier way for a couple to be married.

'How are you doing?' Ethan asked softly, coming alongside her as she stood on a low promontory, breathing in the salt tang of the air and gazing out at the ocean. 'Just a short time now, and everyone will be taking their seats for the ceremony. How are you coping with all that?'

Her mouth made a crooked shape. 'Are you afraid that when the minister says, "Does anyone here know any good reason why this couple should not be married?" I'll interrupt and say, "Yes, it should have been me"?'

He laughed. 'I'm pretty sure you wouldn't go that far.' He slid his arms around her. 'But how do you really feel?'

'I don't know,' she answered truthfully. 'It's very strange, but I don't feel anything. Perhaps I just want it to be over, so that life can get back to normal, or at least as normal as it can be out here when my home is in the U.K. My whole world is upside down right now.'

'Well, we have a whole day of celebrations ahead of us, good food, music, dancing. Let me help you through that, at least. We can think about getting back to normal later.'

'I don't need help,' she said. 'I'm okay, and I just want to be left to deal with things my own way.'

He sucked in his breath. 'Oh, I don't think that's a good idea at all. You have way too many devils to fight…least of all the fact that your ex-boyfriend might wonder how you feel about all this.' He gazed beyond her to the house where all the preparations were going on at a fast pace. 'You haven't spoken to him about that yet, have you?'

'I haven't had the chance. Obviously, we talked before I left England for Hawaii, but the wedding plans came as a complete shock.' She listened to the waves lapping at the shore, lulling her with their own soft, calming refrain.

'I expect he wants to know that all is forgiven…but maybe you've moved on since then?' He drew her closer to him, winding his arms around her so that there was no escape. Then he lowered his head to hers and in the next moment he had claimed her lips, crushing their softness in a kiss that was more thorough and passionate than anything she'd ever experienced.

His hands slowly stroked the length of her spine, trailing over the curve of her hips, and a wave of delicious sensation coursed through her. It felt as though her entire body was fused with his in an explosion of pleasure that left her weak with desire.

How was it that he could make her feel this way? She had never been so emotionally out of control before. It was as if he had lit a spark within her that flared briefly and within seconds had ignited a conflagration. Her whole body yearned for him. She needed him. She loved the way he was holding her, kissing her, thrilling her with his gently stroking hands. He made her feel cherished, as though they were the only two people in the world and there was no need for anything else.

And then he was slowly releasing her and she stared up at him in a haze of bewilderment. She wanted that sweet bond to go on for ever, and yet he was carefully easing himself away from her

He looked beyond her and said quietly, 'Hello, there, James. Forgive us for cluttering up your parade. You must be anxious for the ceremony to go ahead. Not long now, huh?'

'That's right.' James looked uncertain, and more than a little bemused, and Amber gazed at him in shock. She had not heard him approach.

He was halfway along the path towards them, but he had half turned as though he had started to go back the way he had come. She wondered if he would have walked away without disturbing them if Ethan had not spoken. Perhaps he thought neither of them had seen him, being engrossed in that kiss.

'I just came to see if Amber was all right,' James added, turning to face them full on. 'So much was going on yesterday and this morning, and we haven't been able to talk up to now. I didn't want to go through the ceremony without at least saying a few words, but it looks as though I needn't have worried.'

She found her voice. 'I'm fine, James,' she said huskily. 'I wish you and Caitlin all the luck in the world. I'm sure you'll have a wonderful marriage.'

'Thank you.'

By her side, Ethan maintained a watchful, cautious look over James. His hand still lay possessively on the curve of her hip, and all at once it dawned on Amber that Ethan's actions were not as innocent as he would have her believe.

He must have known all along that James was heading towards them. Perhaps he had seen him come out of the house.

His actions had to have been deliberate from the first. He had meant James to see them kiss. This whole episode had been for James's benefit.

The knowledge washed over her like a cold shower of rain. She felt cheated, filled with dismay because her foolish mind had let her believe for just a small space of time that Ethan might actually care for her.

Instead, though, it was all a game to him. A ruse to ensure that his cousin would go off contentedly into her marriage and James would harbour no doubts that Amber's feelings for him had been well and truly extinguished.

That last was the only part that gave her solace. She watched James walk away from them towards the house, and it came on her with stunning clarity that her relationship with him had never been the real thing. It had been a friendship built on tender affection and mutual respect, but it would never have lasted a lifetime.

It seemed that Ethan was the only man who could make her feel truly alive and at the same time full of emotional contradictions. He confused her, provoked her, startled in her feelings she'd never known she possessed, and through it all he sparked a fire that raged throughout her body, an all-consuming inferno that threatened to destroy her.

For the unpalatable truth was that Ethan didn't love her. He was simply playing a part, and when the game was over, she would be the loser.

'I'm going back to the house,' she told him now. 'Molly asked me to help her give out the corsages, and I still have to change and get ready for the ceremony.'

Over the next hour, guests began to arrive, along with the minister who was to conduct the marriage ceremony, and before too long the formal proceedings began.

Caitlin wore an exquisite dress of white silk, and James was splendid in a crisp, perfectly tailored suit. They made their marriage vows while Amber looked on and realised that she was actually pleased for them.

She had expected that she might feel empty inside or lost in some way as she saw James married, but instead she was completely at ease. Her thoughts had an unsettling way of dwelling on a different man entirely, a man with jet-black hair and startlingly blue eyes, but perhaps that was because Ethan was by her side, and she was conscious the whole time of him surreptitiously watching her.

With the ceremony over, the celebrations began. They ate at the tables on the terrace and listened to the traditional speeches, and after a while musicians moved into place on the specially erected dais and began to play lilting Hawaiian music.

Amber danced alongside the women in the wedding

party, and there was a good deal of fun and laughter as they practised the traditional hula. Molly put a circlet of flowers in Amber's hair and placed a lei around her neck.

'Now you dance, see, flowing movements of your arms and hips, and you become one with the waving palm trees and the flowing sea.'

Amber was wearing a cotton top and a softly draped skirt that flowed around her legs as she danced barefoot with the rhythm of the music.

'They say the hula was first danced by Hi'iaka, goddess of Hawaii, of the hills, the lands, the cliffs and caves,' Molly said. 'She was given the task of bringing home the love of her sister's life, Lohi'au, but of course things went wrong, and her sister, Pele, wreaked havoc. Pele was the goddess of the volcano, the spirit of molten lava, and Hi'iaka tried to appease her with the dance... So, you see, the hula is more than just a dance. It tells a story, and you become part of the story when you dance.'

Several of the male guests came to join them in the dancing, and Amber had no shortage of partners. Then Ethan came to claim her for himself, and the next few hours became a blur of sensation, of being held in his arms and swaying gently to the sensual rhythm of the music, of feeling the warmth of his body next to hers. She loved the way he nuzzled the soft skin of her throat, the way his hands lightly caressed her.

She wished the closeness were for real, that it was something more than just a pretence, because she was fast discovering that whenever she was with him she felt as though she could take on the world. All was well, and nothing could ripple the reservoir of contentment she felt in his arms.

The cherished moments came to an end, though, when James and Caitlin prepared to leave.

Perhaps that was just as well, because with each hour she spent with Ethan she found herself being sucked deeper and deeper into a whirlpool of emotion that she couldn't comprehend. How could she feel this way about a man who teased and mocked her and had voiced his suspicions about her from the first?

The bride and groom left in the middle of the evening while the celebrations were still in full swing, and the guests went to see them depart. The couple left in the bridal car for the hotel where they would spend the night before setting off for their honeymoon the following day.

Amber waved them off alongside Martyn, wishing them good fortune and showering the wedding car with flower petals.

When they had disappeared out of sight, Martyn turned back to his guests. '*Mahalo nui loa na ho'olaule'a me la kaua,*' he said. 'Thank you for celebrating with us. My daughter is starting a new life with her new husband, and I'm sure we all wish them well. Please stay and enjoy the party. The dancing and the music will go on until the early hours.'

Amber glanced at him as he stepped back from the driveway and turned to walk along the footpath. 'How are you coping? You look very happy. This must have been a wonderful day for you.'

He nodded. 'It's been a good day, but I'm tired now. I shan't stay for the rest of the party. I'm glad I was able to see her settled. I think she's made a good match.' He sent her a thoughtful look. 'And how is it with you? You seem to be bearing up—perhaps you realised that he wasn't the right man for you after all. You've much too feisty a spirit to be content with James for long.'

'I expect you're right.' She walked with him back to the house. 'I'm inclined to say what I think, and I haven't the patience to bide my time or debate the whys and wherefores of a situation if I see something that needs doing.'

Martyn smiled. 'That sounds a lot like Ethan's character…though I've noticed of late he's played his cards close to his chest. I know he made out that you and he had something going between you at lunch yesterday, but I'm guessing that was for Caitlin's benefit. His intentions were good, I'm sure. And it had the desired effect. Both Caitlin and James seemed reassured.'

She studied him for a moment or two. 'Nothing much gets by you, does it?' She smiled. She might have known he wouldn't be fooled.

'That's true. I know Ethan too well, and I've pretty much picked up on your vibes over these last few weeks. Don't think too harshly of him, will you? I have a feeling you and he are actually more in tune with one another than you think. It would make me very happy if you and he were to get together.'

Her eyes widened. 'You wouldn't be trying to play matchmaker, would you?' She wouldn't put it past him. There was a lot going on in Martyn's head, much more than he let on.

'I wouldn't dream of it,' he said, but there was a wicked glint in his eyes that told her he was fibbing. 'Anyway, I'd be wasting my time, wouldn't I? Ethan does exactly as he pleases…and you're more than a match for him when it comes to down to it.' His mouth curved. 'Caitlin, now…she takes after her mother, gentle, uncontroversial, a peacemaker. It seems to me that she and James are very well suited.'

Amber helped him to his room. 'Would you like me to get you a hot drink to help you sleep?'

He shook his head. 'I shan't have any difficulty in sleeping, even with the party going on,' he said. He eased himself into his bedside chair. 'Ethan will wind things up when the time comes. He knows what to do and he always does the right thing. I feel secure leaving everything in his hands…the plantation, the house… He knows what needs to be done.'

Amber sent him an anxious look. His thoughts seemed to be drifting, and he wasn't making much sense. Perhaps he was more tired than he realised. 'I'll ask Ben to come and help you to bed,' she murmured. 'Is there anything I can get for you?'

'Nothing, my dear. I have everything I could want. It's been a good life.'

Amber frowned. She stayed for a while, waiting as he drifted into sleep. Then she carefully checked his pulse and tried to reassure herself that all was well with him.

A few minutes later, she hurried downstairs and asked Ben if he would go and help him prepare for bed.

'You look worried,' Ethan said, catching up with her as she left the kitchen. 'Is everything all right with my uncle?'

She shook her head. 'I think so, but I'm not sure. He's not quite himself but, then, it has been a long day, and a momentous one, for him. I think he must be very tired.'

'I'll look in on him in a while,' Ethan murmured. 'Are you going to stay and enjoy the rest of the evening?'

'I'll stay for a while,' she said. 'I want to make sure that Martyn is all right.'

'Good. Maybe we could keep each other company. A few more dances in the moonlight would be good, don't you think? It would be a crime to let such a beautiful night go to waste.'

'That's true enough…but you really don't have to play games with me any more, Ethan. James and Caitlin aren't here any more, and your uncle has gone to bed. You can relax and be yourself.'

'I was never playing games,' he murmured. 'Don't you know that?' His blue gaze travelled over her, sweeping down from the burnished chestnut of her hair, over her slender, feminine curves and along the length of her shapely legs. 'I was deadly serious. Always.'

Amber's eyes widened. 'Always?'

His mouth made a crooked shape. 'When it comes to knowing what I want, I wouldn't let anything get in my way…and I've wanted you from the first, Amber.'

A ripple of heat washed over her, bringing soft colour to her cheeks. She shook her head. 'But you're talking about purely physical feelings,' she said, 'and I think there has to be a lot more on offer than that.'

She wasn't going to let him bamboozle her with his smooth way of talking. He'd been messing with her emotions ever since she'd arrived in Hawaii. She had the notion he'd be more than content with a wild, passionate affair, and when those initial feelings fizzled out, it would be a simple case of 'goodbye and thanks'. The fact that her heart would be broken into little pieces wouldn't matter a jot to him, would it?

His eyes took on a glimmer of amusement. 'Does there? I'd say physical had a lot going for it.'

'Yes, and so does self-respect…my self-respect.'

He laughed softly as she brushed past him on her way to the terrace. His hand whipped out and circled her wrist like a lasso. 'You can run, but you can't hide,' he warned. 'You stir my blood with every move you make, and the temperature's rising.'

'Then I suggest you go and take a cold shower, Ethan,' she murmured. She wrenched her arm free from his grasp. 'It'll do you the world of good.'

She hurried outside, glad of the faint breeze that fanned her cheeks, but all the while she was conscious of Ethan's blue gaze searing her flesh and his gentle laughter echoed inside her head.

CHAPTER NINE

'I CAN'T imagine what Mr Martyn's up to,' Molly said. 'He's had these lawyers come up from town to see him. They've been shut in the study with him this past hour.' She placed a steaming pot of coffee on the dining table, and added a jug of cream alongside a dish of brown sugar.

'It does seem a little odd,' Ethan murmured, helping himself to savoury rice from a dish on the hotplate at the side of the dining room. 'He usually tells me what's going on, but all he's said is that he needs to make some firm arrangements concerning the plantation.'

'Surely he would tell you what those arrangements were?' Amber queried lightly. She chose a light salad for herself, and some pasta blended with tomatoes and aromatic herbs.

They went to sit at the table, while Molly disappeared into the kitchen. 'I know he's anxious that if anything should happen to him, all the legalities are firmly in place,' Ethan commented. 'He knows that I will take care of things since I own half anyway, but he wants to make sure that Caitlin's interests are assured. He'd already set up a trust fund for her, but I imagine, now that she's married, he feels he needs to tie up any loose ends.'

'That sounds logical enough to me.' Amber frowned. 'It's worrying me that he's doing all this, though. Even though his illness has slowed him down these last few months, he was always lively in his mind, but now he seems to be a little withdrawn, preoccupied almost, and very weary. I can't change his medication any more... There's nothing else I can give him that will help. Instead, I have to look on and see him growing weaker by the day.'

'You shouldn't blame yourself in any way.' Ethan sent her a quick look. 'You've done as much if not more than anyone could. I don't think he's concerned by what's happening to him. In fact, he seems more content than he's ever been.'

'Perhaps you're right.' She poured coffee for both of them and paused for a moment to savour the hot liquid. 'He was certainly happy to see Caitlin settled. He was so pleased when she sent him the photos of her Caribbean honeymoon, and he told me he really likes the way she's decorated their new house in town. It's quite close to the university where they'll both be working, he said.'

Ethan nodded. 'They're holding a house-warming party some time this week, aren't they?'

'Tomorrow evening.' She sent him a wry glance. 'Seems to me you need a secretary to remind you of all these things.'

He chuckled. 'Why would I bother when I have you and Molly to remind me what's going on? And if I wasn't there on time, Caitlin would soon be on the phone, asking me what had happened.' He shot her a look from half-closed eyes. 'Seems to me I'm surrounded by women who think it's my life's work to keep appointments.'

'You should count yourself lucky to be on the receiving end of all that attention,' she retorted. 'Though from what Martyn told me, you've never been short of women wanting to stick around.' She frowned. 'He said it was something of a problem, so it's probably no wonder you were suspicious of me when we first met.' She looked at him from under her lashes. 'Perhaps you still feel that way?'

He paused in the act of spearing prawns with his fork and studied her for a moment or two. 'Actually, it was more a case of overwhelming jealousy than suspicion. I had a pretty bad case of wanting what Martyn prized for himself.' His blue gaze meshed with hers.

She sat back in her chair, her eyes growing large. 'You had it all wrong.' She was quiet for a moment, a line knotting her brow. 'Martyn's a good-hearted man who saw a way to help me out. He acted out of benevolence, that's all.'

Ethan shrugged. 'Whatever his motives, I could see right away all the qualities that Martyn saw in you. You're kind, thoughtful, a brilliant doctor, beautiful, and decisive, too. You don't hang around waiting for things to happen, you think things through, decide on a course of action, and away you go.' His mouth curved. 'You and he are very much alike.'

'Perhaps that's why he took to me.' She stirred the pasta with her fork. 'You're a lot like him, too, only with a tougher exterior.'

He put a hand over his chest as if he was in pain. 'I'm a mere mortal. If you cut me, don't I bleed?'

'Pish.' She made a short, derisory sound. 'I doubt it. You'd never allow anyone to get that close. Your armour's intact, not a chink to be seen anywhere. How else have you managed to keep all those women at bay?'

His eyes half closed, his gaze narrowing on her. 'Maybe I never met one that I'd trust enough with the key to my heart. I can definitely be hurt too, you know.'

'Is that so?' She looked at him guardedly, not sure how she felt about another woman trampling over the man she was growing closer to day by day. 'Has someone wounded you?'

He picked up his coffee cup and held it in both hands for a while, staring at the dark liquid, but she sensed he wasn't really seeing it. 'My family was taken from me,' he said. 'First my mother, who I loved dearly, and then Grace, who cared for me as her own and teased me and made me smile again.' He pulled in a shuddery breath and then swallowed some of the coffee. 'I let two lovely, good-natured women into my heart, and they were ripped from me. I told myself I would be very careful who I ever let in from then on.'

She gave a soft sigh. 'I can't imagine what it must be like to go through that. I've always had my parents close at hand.' She ran a fingertip lightly around the rim of her cup, giving herself time to think. 'Of course, Martyn must have suffered along with you when he lost Grace. I'm assuming his parents lived long and healthy lives?' She looked at him for confirmation, and he nodded cautiously.

'They did, though his parents divorced when he was a youngster, and his mother married again, so you might say he's had a chequered life.'

'You wouldn't think so, from all that he's achieved. He said his grandfather started the plantation... How did you come to own half of it?'

He put his cup down. 'It was partly an inheritance from my parents. My father took an interest in it along with Martyn, and the rest became mine because I bought into it. I learned a lot about how to cultivate land over the years, and it was always taken for granted that I would follow the family tradition, but I wanted to go into medicine. After what happened to my mother and Grace, I wanted to learn how to take care of people. I needed to know that I could do something to make their lives better.'

She put down her fork and laid her hand gently on top of his. 'You do that every day,' she said softly. 'I've seen the way you handle the most difficult cases, and you're very skilled at what you do.'

He made a rueful face. 'But not skilled enough to help my uncle. I wish I could find a miracle of modern medicine that would make him whole again.'

They both knew that wasn't going to happen, and by mutual consent they turned to other topics of conversation over the next few minutes.

They were finishing off dessert as Martyn came out of his study and saw the lawyers on their way out to their cars. When he came back, he looked like a cat that had licked the cream. 'That's all sorted, then,' he said, coming into the dining-room.

'What's sorted?' Ethan dipped his fork into a melt-in-the-mouth banana coconut cake, before glancing up at his uncle.

'Oh, tidying up a few odds and ends. There were

some minor alterations to be made to Caitlin's trust fund, and a couple of papers I needed to sign to secure a piece of land for the plantation. I wanted to expand the coffee growing side of things, and I've been after that land for some time. Anyway, it's all done now, and I'm well pleased.' He looked from one to the other, smiling, and then glanced at the sideboard where the dishes on the hotplate were steaming gently.

'Have you two saved me some lunch? I hope you haven't polished off all the chicken… And there had better be some of that banana cake left.' He looked pointedly at Ethan's rapidly vanishing dessert.

Ethan immediately looked guilty. 'Ah…banana cake… Now, that could be a problem. You do know it's my favourite, don't you? I actually crave it sometimes.'

Martyn frowned and ran his glance over the table. Coming towards them, he lifted up a ceramic cover and peered at the cake stand underneath. 'Hah,' he said, giving Ethan a narrowed look before his mouth curved into a crooked smile. 'Just as well for you that there are a couple of slices left.'

Amber watched the repartee between the two of them and relaxed. It seemed that Martyn was back to his old self, and Ethan was on top form. Maybe, if she gave it time, he would even let her within warming distance of his heart.

They went to Caitlin's house-warming party the next evening. Martyn was in jovial mood, enjoying the opportunity to mix with all the family and friends his daughter had invited. There were distant uncles, aunts and cousins, and they all seemed intent on having a joyful get-together.

Amber kept a careful eye on Martyn to make sure he

wasn't overdoing things, but he appeared to be coping well enough. Whenever she looked his way, he was chuckling at something someone was saying or admiring the gardens that Caitlin was trying to cultivate.

'He seems to be doing fine, doesn't he?' Ethan said, coming over to her and handing her a glass of rum punch.

'Yes. It's lovely to see him looking so cheerful.' She sipped her drink, enjoying the exotic flavour, and after a while she laid her glass down on a nearby table.

He slid an arm around her waist. 'Come and see the palm grove,' he murmured. 'Ben and Molly offered to keep an eye on Martyn for a while.'

He led her to the foot of a grassy hill some short distance from the house, where ferns grew in abundance and trees made majestic silhouettes against the skyline. Darkness was falling, and the air was heavy with the scent of tropical flowers. The faint clicking sound of a gecko could be heard in the distance. It was peaceful out here, away from the bustle of people and the background hum of gentle music.

'This must feel a little strange to you,' Ethan said, 'meeting our family, while yours is so far away. You said, a while back, how difficult it was getting used to being away from home.'

She nodded. 'I thought I would be all right, but I've never been away for such a long time before. Of course, I talk to my parents on the phone, and I see them over the video link, but it isn't quite the same. I think they've been arguing lately, but I can't get to the bottom of what's happening. They seem a bit tense with one another. I know my father's busy with the medical practice. My mother is still a bit out of synch with everything.

She isn't usually rattled easily, but my coming here didn't sit well with her for some reason.'

'Will they come over here to visit, do you think?'

'I hope so.' She leaned back against the trunk of a palm tree and gazed around. 'They talked about coming here in a couple of months. I'm sure they'll love it as much as I do.'

'The romance of the island is finding its way into your heart. It happens to everyone after a while. It casts a spell on you, and you never want to leave.'

He came to stand in front of her, laying a hand on the bole of the tree just above her head, and then he leaned towards her, dropping a kiss lightly on her mouth. 'I hadn't expected it to happen,' he said softly, 'but you've made a huge impact on my life. You caught me unawares, and now I can't stop thinking about you, day or night.'

He gave a half-smile, his gaze running over her. 'Especially in the night.' He kissed her again, teasing the softness of her lips with the brush of his mouth, enticing a flurry of expectation within her nervous system, stoking the flame that burned inside her.

He ran his finger along the line of her throat and let it trail downwards, shifting over the full curve of her breast, until his hand came to rest beneath its ripe mound, cupping her gently.

Heat pooled in her abdomen, and Amber felt her legs go weak. He moved closer, his long body lightly pressuring hers, his kisses filling her with sweet anticipation. She wanted this to go on and on. For this moment he was hers, and hers alone.

She wound her arms around his neck, loving the feel of him, her mouth softening beneath his. He kissed her face, her throat, and dipped lower to brush his lips over the creamy swell of her breasts.

Then the reality of the world intruded on them. The sound of voices erupted from the house some distance away, and the spell was broken in an instant. Ethan eased himself away from her as the noise increased, and chattering people spilled out onto the garden terrace. Amber straightened, moving away from the palm tree, looking towards Caitlin's new home.

'People are getting ready to leave,' Ethan murmured. 'I suppose we'd better go and find my uncle and round up Molly and Ben.'

She nodded. The tantalising, wonderful moment had gone almost has soon as it had occurred, and she felt an overpowering sense of loss. She loved Ethan. It came to her in a startling flare of revelation that threatened to overwhelm her with its forcefulness. Her life would never be the same again. She loved this man, and she realised now that she had never felt this way before. It was all-consuming, a love that she knew with certainty would stay with her for all the years to come.

And yet she couldn't help feeling that it was a revelation she could have done without. For Ethan had made no sign that he loved her in return. He wanted her, desired her, but that was not at all the same thing.

They walked back to the house and took their leave of Caitlin and James just a short time later. 'That was a good party,' Martyn told his daughter and her new husband. 'It's lovely to see you settled here. I just know you're going to be very happy.'

The journey home was a short one, and Amber left Martyn to chat with Ethan for a while. 'It was a great night,' she said, 'but I have to make an early start in the morning. I'll see you both tomorrow.'

Over the next few days, she tried to concentrate on her work at the hospital. The rota meant that she was based in the Accident and Emergency unit this month, while another doctor went out on calls.

Ethan had been asked to go and help the bosses at his former hospital with planning arrangements to co-ordinate emergency services throughout the region. It meant that Amber saw very little of him during that time. He dropped in on Martyn every day, to see how he was doing, but mostly he worked late into the evenings and continued with his emergency call outs as usual.

'Mr Martyn has appointed extra people to take charge at the plantation,' Molly told Amber one day at breakfast. 'I think he was worried that Mr Ethan would find it too much to cope with, running the business, as well as working at the hospital.'

'Is Ethan all right with that?'

'Am I all right with what?' Ethan came into the dining room and helped himself to a buttered croissant along with apricot preserve. He sat down at the table, biting into the croissant and wiping crumbs from his mouth.

Amber watched him in fascination. How was it that everything about him drew her attention and held her absorbed whenever he was around? 'Are you all right with having managers appointed to take over from you at the plantation?'

'I'm fine with it,' he said, taking another bite and pouring a cup of coffee. He lifted the pot and raised a questioning brow, indicating Amber's cup. She pushed it towards him and he gave her a refill. 'I asked him to make the changes,' he said, putting the coffeepot back on its stand, 'and I suggested the people I wanted to fill the slots.'

'Does that mean you're going back to your job at the main hospital?' Amber asked. She finished off her omelette and laid down her knife and fork, taking a sip of hot coffee.

He shook his head. 'We're setting up a new joint system, making it a smoother process to deal with emergencies. I'll probably be based at both hospitals. It should prove interesting.' He finished off his coffee and looked around. 'What's happened to Martyn this morning? Is he running late? He's usually joined us by now.'

'I looked in on him, but he said he was still tired and said he would have a bit of a lie-in this morning,' Molly said. 'I told him I would take a breakfast tray up to him.' She indicated the tray she was preparing. The plate was covered to keep the food warm, and she was adding freshly squeezed orange juice along with croissants and preserve. 'I'll take this upstairs now and see if he's feeling more rested.'

Molly left the room and Amber glanced at Ethan across the table. He had just finished off his third croissant and was starting on a plate of scrambled eggs and ham.

'What?' he said. 'Something wrong?'

She hid a grin. 'Nothing at all. I've no idea where you put it.' There wasn't an ounce of fat to spare on him. He was long and lean, with muscles honed to perfection, and she guessed that was a result of him being constantly on the move, full of energy. He was bursting with vitality, always up for the next challenge.

'Hmm.' He looked her over, starting with the silky

length of her hair, and moving down to linger on the smooth, bare flesh of her arms before gliding over the fullness of her curves. 'I'd say you had things just about right. No need for you to diet, obviously. That heavenly feminine shape is perfection itself.'

Warm colour flowed into her cheeks. He had caught her out in staring at him and paid her back in kind. Did he really like the way she looked? A little glow started up in her.

Molly came back into the room just then. 'Mr Ethan…' she said, and then she stopped.

'Yes, Molly, what is it?' He glanced towards the doorway where she stood, and for a second or two Molly simply stayed there, just looking at him and saying nothing.

It was clear that the housekeeper was upset, and both Ethan and Amber stood up to go over to her.

'Molly, what's wrong?' Ethan placed an arm around Molly's shoulders, looking down at her as though he would comfort her in any way he could.

'It's Mr Martyn. I don't know what to do. You should go up to him.'

Ethan nodded and sent a quick glance towards Amber to let her know that she should take care of Molly. Then he strode out of the room and went quickly upstairs.

'Come and sit down, Molly,' Amber urged, helping her into a seat. 'What's wrong with Martyn, do you know? Is he struggling for breath?'

Molly shook her head. 'I don't think he's breathing at all. I think he's gone, passed away. He was just lying there, so peaceful, and I thought he was sleeping, but he didn't wake when I spoke to him, and then I realised that he'd gone.'

Molly reached for a hanky from her pocket and began to wipe her eyes. 'He was such a lovely man.'

Amber stared at her in shock. She tried to comfort her, and all the while she was thinking that she should go to Martyn, but Ethan was with him and if what Molly had said was true, Ethan might want to be alone with his uncle for a while. If he'd needed help, he would have called her, wouldn't he?

She waited, desperately wanting to hear him shout her name so that she could go to help. That would mean that something could be done, wouldn't it?

But Ethan didn't call, and Amber stayed with Molly until Ben came to see what was happening and find out why Martyn hadn't arrived to go through the list of jobs for the day with him.

'Will you stay with Molly, Ben? I need to go and find out how Ethan is coping.'

Ben nodded, and turned to comfort his wife. Amber hurried out of the room and went in search of Ethan, stopping to knock quietly on the door of Martyn's room.

'Ethan, are you all right in there? Is there anything I can do to help?'

He didn't answer, and it was a while before she heard him walk across the room towards the door. 'There's nothing anyone can do,' he said. 'It's too late. It's over.'

She looked beyond him to where Martyn was lying on the bed. Like Molly had said, he seemed to be at peace, the remnants of a faint smile on his face, and she said huskily, 'I'm so sorry, Ethan.' Tears were trickling down her cheeks, but she let them fall. Martyn had been good to her and to everyone around him, and it was only fitting that his loss should be mourned.

Ethan didn't say very much at all over the next hour or so. It was as though he was in shock, and Amber reflected that they were all in much the same state.

Over the next few days she helped the family with the arrangements that had to be made, and she stood with them alongside Molly and Ben as Martyn was finally laid to rest in a secluded corner of the cemetery where his ancestors were buried.

She helped prepare a reception for family and friends who came to pay their respects, and she was amazed by the number of people who came to grieve for him. 'He was such a well-respected man,' his plantation manager said. 'His name will go on for years to come. Everyone who knew him will have something good to say about him.'

Ethan thanked everyone for coming to the house. 'Caitlin and I have been overwhelmed by your thoughtfulness and consideration,' he told the gathering. 'We've lost a truly great man, a man who did so much to provide work for people on the island, and who has been responsible for serving a community way beyond these shores. I know he would want to thank you for the help you gave him over the years, and he would value the work you do in keeping on with the traditions he set in place.'

Amber walked around as though she was in a daze. She mingled with people in the house, and spoke to visitors who assembled outside on the terrace. She comforted Caitlin as best she could, and through it all she wanted to wrap her arms around Ethan and hold him close.

He was distant from her, though, wrapped up in his own grief. He was finding it difficult to relate to anyone at all just then, and Amber realised that all she could do was let him know that she was here for him if he needed her.

After a few days Amber went back to work and made an effort to adjust to life without Martyn's presence. He had promised her the use of the bungalow for as long as she needed it, and Ethan had continued to expect her to join them up at the house as before. She didn't know how much longer things would go on this way, though. Now that Martyn had gone, her position in the household was precarious and she was uncertain as to how she should go on.

'The family solicitor is coming over to the house late this afternoon,' Ethan told her one morning as she was preparing to leave for work. 'He wants everyone to meet up for the reading of my uncle's will. Given the intricacies of the estate, it might go on for a couple of hours, so Molly's going to prepare coffee and snacks. We should have enough room for everyone to be seated in the main reception room.'

'Okay,' she said. 'Thanks for telling me. I'll keep out of the way. I have plenty of chores to keep me busy back at the bungalow.'

'No,' he said. 'Leave them for another time, please. The solicitor says you're mentioned in the will, so you should be there.'

Amber stared at him. 'Why would Martyn have left me anything? And how is that possible? He didn't say anything about changing his will, did he?'

'No, he didn't. But, then, he invited the lawyers over to the house a few weeks ago, and he was fairly offhand about his reasons, wasn't he?' He sent her a brief, assessing look. 'I knew something had to be going on with him. It was odd, him bringing you over here in the first place…generous and altruistic maybe, but I always felt there was something more to it than that.'

Amber breathed in deeply. She had no idea what had been going on in Martyn's mind, but it was obvious that Ethan still had doubts as to his motives. She could only hope that the reading of the will would make everything clear, and that the uncertainty could be cleared up once and for all.

CHAPTER TEN

'Now we come to the main bequests,' the solicitor said, addressing the people who were gathered together in the reception room. He had been talking for over an hour already, dealing mainly with issues concerning the continued running of the plantation, the various overseas assets and the gifts and legacies that Martyn had bequeathed to distant family members. Molly and Ben had each inherited a good-sized sum of money and one of the bungalows on the estate. Amber's name had not been mentioned so far, and she was beginning to wonder if Ethan had made a mistake when he had asked her to be there.

Perhaps he simply wanted her to support him through this final ordeal. Hearing Martyn's wishes laid out this way had been difficult, because it was as though he was still speaking to them, letting them know how much he cherished each and every one of them.

Ethan learned that he was to inherit a large chunk of the business, along with a sizeable fortune and the house that they were sitting in at this moment. It meant that he was the main shareholder, owning around sixty-five per cent of the whole.

Amber was startled by that information. Why would

Martyn have left Ethan the house? Shouldn't it have gone to Caitlin? Perhaps it was because of the land that went with it…as a member of the Brookes family, and half-owner of the plantation, maybe it was his true inheritance.

Caitlin was to have another portion of the business, amounting to some seventeen and a half per cent. She, too, was given a sizeable fortune, and her trust fund was to be opened up so that she would have an amount to live on each year. There were also various properties left to her.

'Last, but not least, Mr Wyndham Brookes has made provision for Amber Shaw,' the solicitor said. 'Miss Shaw, for you there is the remaining seventeen and a half per cent of the business, and the bungalow in which you are living at present. There is also a sum of money.'

Amber was already struggling to take in what the solicitor was saying. When he mentioned the amount of money that was to be hers, the colour drained from her face and she thought that she was going to faint. She sucked in a shaky breath. Surely the solicitor had it all wrong? It was someone else who had inherited this fortune, not her.

Caitlin had gasped as the last part of the will was being read out. Amber saw the shock on her face, and when she looked towards Ethan, she saw that he, too, was stunned. His jaw was set in a rigid line, as though he couldn't quite take it in.

The solicitor was still speaking. 'There is a letter for you, Dr Shaw. Mr Wyndham Brookes suggested that you might want to read it in private.'

'There has to be some mistake,' Amber said. 'Why would Martyn leave me anything at all? Perhaps there's been a mix-up over the name?'

He shook his head and gave a brief smile. 'There is no mistake. I believe you will find that everything is explained in the letter.'

The solicitor looked towards Caitlin and Ethan. 'There are letters for both of you, as well. Mr Wyndham Brookes felt that you should know something of the reasoning behind these legacies.'

Amber was shaking as she accepted the envelope from the solicitor. All about her the meeting was breaking up as people went to help themselves to more coffee or stood about in small groups, talking to one another.

'If there is anything you want to ask, or you need any help at all, please get in touch with me,' the solicitor said. He handed her an embossed card. 'My number… You can reach me during office hours with that, but my mobile number is on the card, as well, in case you have a problem at any other time.'

'Thank you.'

She got to her feet and straightened up. Caitlin was wearing a bemused expression, and Amber felt she needed to go over to her. She had to let her know that she had no idea what Martyn had intended.

'Caitlin, this has all come as a huge shock to me. I didn't know this was in his mind. I can't explain it.'

Caitlin nodded. 'I'm not really concerned about the inheritance, or the money side of things but, as you say, it has come as a shock to all of us.'

Amber looked at Ethan. 'Perhaps you should read this letter with me. I've nothing to hide. I can't begin to imagine what it says.'

He shook his head. 'He said it would be best if you went somewhere to read it in private. You should do that, and maybe we can talk later. We've all had a lot to take in this afternoon.' He glanced at Caitlin. 'Are you all right? I know this has been difficult for you.'

Caitlin gave him a watery smile. 'I think I need to go and walk outside for a while with James. I feel as though my father's presence is all around, and I still can't get used to the fact that he isn't coming back.'

Ethan nodded, and watched her leave the room with James at her side. He turned back to Amber. 'I have to go and talk to the rest of the family. Perhaps you and I could meet up in an hour or so and talk things through?'

'Yes, that sounds like a good idea. I'll go back to the bungalow. Like Caitlin said, it's all a bit overwhelming here right now.'

She left the house and walked along the path to the bungalow. It was inconceivable that Martyn would have left it to her. What had he been thinking?

She went into her sitting-room and sat down on the sofa, staring down at the envelope that was still clutched in her fingers. Would the letter tell her everything she wanted to know? What had been going through Martyn's mind when he'd made that extraordinary bequest?

She carefully tore open the envelope and drew out the sheet of paper inside. Martyn's bold, black handwriting filled the page.

My dear Amber, you're probably very puzzled right now, and wondering what this inheritance is all about.

I'll try to explain. The truth of the matter goes back many years, to when I lived in London and our offices were near what is now the Docklands area. We needed the services of an advertising company, and your mother came along to do a presentation for us. I was completely knocked out by her. She was stunning, and I fell for her, hook, line and sinker. We had only known each other for a short time when I was called back to Hawaii to take over the running of the plantation. I wanted your mother to come with me, but she wasn't ready to take that step.

Anyway, we parted company, and I missed her. I wrote to her for a while, but then it became obvious that the distance between us was a huge barrier, and the letters petered out.

I didn't have any more communication with her until after you and I met just a few months ago. I was very curious as to what had happened to her in the intervening years. In retrospect, I'm pleased that she married soon after I left for Hawaii all those years ago. I trust she's had a happy marriage, and she must surely be proud that she has produced such a beautiful, intelligent and caring daughter.

I think it best if I leave it to your mother to explain the rest to you. Take this legacy I have given you and enjoy it. I'm so pleased to have met you, and come to know you, even though it has been for such a short time.

If you need help with anything in the future, you should look to Ethan. He has been like a son to me, and I know he is the one you should turn to for whatever you might need.

Take care of yourself, and have a happy future.
Martyn

Amber read the letter over and over again. He had said so much, and yet so little. Why was he leaving it to her mother to tell her the rest? What more was there to tell?

She began to pace the room. It was astonishing to learn that he and her mother had fallen for one another all those years ago. But perhaps her mother had not had quite the same depth of feeling for Martyn, or maybe the thought of leaving home and travelling halfway across the world with him had been too much for her.

There was a soft tapping at her door, and Amber pulled herself together and went to answer it.

Ethan stood there, looking at her guardedly, and she knew he must wonder what her letter contained.

'Come into the sitting-room,' she said. 'I've opened the glass doors to let the ocean breeze into the house. It's beautiful at this time of the day as the sun's going down. I love looking out over the water.'

His gaze travelled over her. 'Are you going to tell me what my uncle had to say? You don't have to, of course, if you'd rather keep it private.'

'Didn't he explain things in his letter to you?'

He shook his head. 'He simply said that he wanted us to treat you as part of the family. He asked Caitlin to think of you as a sister. For my part, he offered advice as to the best course of action for the future.'

She frowned. 'What would that be?'

He gave a rueful smile. 'Perhaps we should find out what's actually going on here before we start looking into that. Are you going to tell me what he said, or is it something you need to keep secret?'

'It isn't a secret…but it isn't anything I really understand, either.' She handed him the letter.

He read it carefully, and then looked up, frowning as he studied her features. 'He told me that you look very much like your mother did when she was your age,' he said in a quiet voice.

'Yes. That's true, and maybe I reminded him of her. But why has he left so much to be guessed at? Why does he want me to talk to my mother about it?'

'You don't know?'

She gave a shuddery sigh. 'I can guess…but the answer turns my world upside down, and I can't believe that it could be true. Why hasn't he said what he means in the letter?'

Ethan's mouth made a wry shape. 'I'd say that was typical of my uncle. He doesn't want anyone to be hurt and so he's leaving it to the one person who has most to lose to tell you the truth. That way it's up to her as to how much anyone needs to know.'

Amber pressed her lips together. 'So you think I'm actually his daughter? Where does that leave my father…the man I've always called my father? I don't believe he has any idea about this, or surely he would have said something?'

She stared at Ethan, her eyes filling with tears. 'What am I supposed to do? How can this possibly be true?'

Ethan handed her the phone. 'There's only one way to find out,' he said. 'Talk to your mother.'

She stared at the phone. Everything she had ever believed had been turned on its head. In just a few short hours the world, as she knew it, had changed. If her mother confirmed what Martyn had been hinting at, then she was truly his daughter. It meant that Caitlin was her half-sister. And Ethan, what did it mean for her and Ethan? Was Ethan her cousin?

A wave of nausea swamped her. She handed the phone back to him. 'No, I can't. I don't want to know,' she said. 'I can't handle this. Everything was going along reasonably well, and now it's all gone wrong. It's chaos. I don't know who I am any more.' She paced the room once more. 'Besides, it must be early morning back home. I can't ring, out of the blue, and disturb everyone.'

'I expect it will be breakfast-time,' he said, thrusting the phone back into her hand once more. 'Didn't you tell me your father leaves early for the surgery? It's possible that your mother will be alone right now. This is probably the best time of all for you to call her.' He looked at her. 'You can do this, Amber. Deal with it now and find out the truth, otherwise you'll be forever afraid of what you might find out.'

She could see the sense in what he was saying. Could she live her life not knowing if she and Ethan were related? This was something she had to clarify, no matter how painful the answers might be.

She dialled the number, and when her mother answered, she walked into the kitchen and sat down at the table. She didn't know whether Ethan followed her. All she knew was that making this phone call was one of the hardest things she'd ever had to do in her life.

'Oh, Amber, I knew this would happen as soon as you told me he had passed away. I've been dreading this moment.'

'So, is it true…what he's hinting at? Am I really his daughter?'

Her mother's voice broke. 'Yes, it's true.' She gave a heavy, shaky sigh. 'I should have said something before this. He called me and said he had spoken to the lawyers. I knew then I had to say something.'

'But you didn't. Why didn't you tell me from the first?' Amber was struggling to come to terms with what was happening. How could her mother have deceived her for so long?

'I was afraid this would happen…that it would all come out,' her mother said. There was a catch in her voice, and a soft note of resignation threaded through her words. 'It was all such a long time ago now. He swept me off my feet, and I couldn't think straight back then. He was like a whirlwind that blew through my life.'

'But you must have let him go without telling him that you were pregnant.' Amber frowned. 'How could you do that?'

'I didn't know I was pregnant until after Martyn left the country. And then, when I found out, I was so scared. You need to understand that my parents were very strict, and they would never have understood or condoned a pregnancy outside marriage. By then, though, I'd already met your father. I had a job to do in Henley-on-Thames, and your father was working there. We fell in love, and he asked me to marry him.'

She hesitated. 'He didn't know about the baby…or about Martyn. I told him I'd been involved with someone before he came along, but that was all. I said it was over between me and this other man, and I wanted to tell him about the baby, but I was afraid that he wouldn't understand. His parents were much the same as mine. They'd have thought very badly of me if they had realised the truth.'

'Don't you think my father would have guessed?'

Her mother sighed. 'We were very young, and innocent, despite what you might think. I kept quiet and let everyone think that you were born prematurely…even your father. You were tiny, and he didn't seem to suspect the truth. I felt really bad about deceiving him, but he loved you so much, and I couldn't bear to hurt him by telling him how things really were. As time went on, it was harder than ever to let him know what had really happened. We couldn't have any other children and I didn't want to hurt him by telling him that you weren't his. And I couldn't risk your grandparents knowing that I'd made a mistake. They would have thought so badly of me, and I didn't want them to treat you differently because of what I'd done.'

'Surely they wouldn't have?' Amber was finding her mother's confession difficult to absorb. Then her mother made a small hiccuping sound, and Amber wondered if she was crying. 'Mum…you have to know, I don't blame you for any of this,' she said. 'I just needed to know the truth, that's all. This has all come as such a shock.'

'I know. I'm sorry, Amber. I'm sorry I deceived everyone. I knew it couldn't go on, but I didn't know how to put it right without destroying everything.'

'What will you do?' Amber sucked in a long breath. 'I don't want you or Dad to feel badly about this…but he'll want to know why I have this inheritance, won't he? What will you tell him?'

Her mother gave a shuddery sigh. 'I've already spoken to him about it. After Martyn rang to tell me about the changes to his will, I realised I had to tell your father the truth. I should have done it a long time ago.'

'How did he take it?'

'Not very well. I'm still not sure that he's come to terms with it. And then I knew I had to tell you, but I didn't want to do it from such a distance. I thought maybe I could wait until you came home, or until we went out there to see you.'

Amber could see now why her mother had been so unsettled by her meeting with Martyn and her decision to come out to Hawaii. It had set off a chain of events that would have repercussions for a long while to come.

They spoke for a while longer and then Amber ended the call and sat for a while, thinking things over. She turned to see that Ethan was standing in the kitchen, watching her closely.

'You heard?' she asked, and he nodded.

'Shall we go for a walk along the beach?' he suggested. 'I think you need time to absorb all this. It's been a momentous day for you, hasn't it?'

She looked at him, then stood up and placed her hands palms flat against his chest. 'Ethan, I think I should leave this place and go away somewhere. Somewhere far away. I don't think I can stay here and live life the same way as we have been doing these last few months. I have a half-sister I didn't know about, and getting used to that will take me some time, but I don't think I'll ever come to terms with the fact that you and I are cousins.'

She felt very close to tears. 'That's something I can't cope with right now. I need to put some distance between us. I'm sorry. I'm too close to you and it's all wrong. I've fallen in love with you over these last few months and it isn't right. I wish none of this had ever happened.' She tried to move away from him, but Ethan put his arm around her and pulled her close to him.

'You're wrong,' he said. 'We're not cousins at all. In theory, maybe we are, but Martyn was never a blood relative. His father was John Wyndham, and when his parents' marriage broke up, his mother married into the Brookes family. There were no children from that second marriage, and so there are no blood ties. He's my uncle because he was brought up alongside my father. You don't need to worry on that account.'

'I don't?' She stared up at him, scarcely able to believe what he was saying.

'You don't.' He kept his arm around her. 'Let's go and walk along the beach and see if we can find an answer to all this, shall we? I don't want you to go away from here. I want you to stay by my side and let me show you how good life can be. I don't even want to contemplate life without you.'

'Are you sure about that?' They walked out of the house, arm in arm, and wandered down the footpath towards the beach. The sun was sinking beneath the horizon, leaving its fading red light to glow softly in the sky, and all was calm, the serene tropical night like balm to Amber's soul.

'I'm sure,' he said, as they started to walk along the beach. 'I never knew what it was that Martyn was hiding from me, but now I know that he had the best of reasons for keeping quiet. He didn't want to upset your mother's apple cart. He was leaving it to you to find the truth, and to her to decide whether or not she should tell your father.'

He let his hand rest against the small of her back. 'I'm glad this has all come out into the open. All I want now is to let you know how I feel about you. Martyn knew all along, and he gave me his blessing in his letter to me. I love you, Amber. *Aloha au ia'oe.*'

She stood very still and looked up at him. The sand was soft beneath her feet, and overhead the palm leaves danced in the faint breeze. 'I love you, Ethan. *Mau loa*. For ever.'

He lowered his head and kissed her tenderly, holding her close as though he would never let her go. She stayed locked in his embrace for a long, long time. So much had happened, she had learned so many things, but most of all she had learned that she loved Ethan with all her heart.

'He really gave us his blessing?' she asked softly, after a while.

Ethan smiled. 'He said I should put a ring on your finger before some other likely candidate came along and whipped you away from me.'

'That sounds like Martyn.'

'Yes.' Then he frowned. 'What's that noise?' Ethan moved back from her a little, trying to discern what was happening.

Amber could hear a light chirruping sound, and it took a moment before she realised that it was her mobile phone.

She glanced at the display. 'It's my mother,' she said, looking anxiously at Ethan. 'I hope she's all right. I feel as though I messed things up for her.'

He lightly squeezed her shoulder. 'You did what you thought was best. Answer it.'

'Hello, Mum.'

'No, Amber. It's your father.'

'Oh, Dad, I'm so glad to hear your voice. Are you all right? I thought you were usually at the surgery at this time?'

'Well, I was out on call, and I just dropped in home for a while. I could see that your mother was upset.'

'Was she?' Amber was cautious, not knowing what to say. She didn't want to cause her mother any more problems. She frowned and Ethan drew her nearer to him in a gesture of support.

'You know, she told me everything. About Martyn and all that happened. I just wanted you to know, Amber, that it's all right. I was hurt and angry to begin with, but it was more to do with the fact that your mother hadn't told me from the beginning. All along I had a feeling that things weren't quite right, but I loved you and accepted you as my own. The fact is, I love your mother, and I'm glad that she's told me everything now. I just hope that you're okay with it. It must have come as a bolt from the blue.'

'Something like that,' she said. 'But, yes, I think I'm all right with it. It's a lot to take in. I just want you to know that to me you'll always be my dad. You've always been there for me, and that's what really matters. I love you both. Tell Mum for me, will you?'

'I will, Amber. She's here with me, and I'm sure she knows already.'

They cut the call after a while, and Amber turned to look up at Ethan once more. 'I think it's going to be all right,' she said. 'I don't know how they could have kept up the pretence for so long, each one worried about what the other would think.'

'Love does strange things to people,' Ethan murmured. 'It makes you blind, it drives you crazy, it causes you to do all sorts of things to protect yourself from being hurt.'

'Is that what happened to you?' She ran her fingers gently down his cheek.

'In a way. I knew that you were everything I ever wanted, but I was afraid you would leave me high and dry. I tried to tell myself that you weren't for real and you would be heading back home just as soon as you tired of being out here. But you unlocked my heart and crept inside, and now I can't ever let you go.'

She smiled up at him. 'I'm not going anywhere,' she said huskily. She wrapped her arms around him and drew his head down towards hers, kissing him softly, her lips clinging, her body arching against him.

He sucked in a taut breath. 'If you're going to do that, we had better start making plans,' he said in a ragged voice.

'Plans?'

'For our wedding day,' he said. 'I wouldn't want history to repeat itself after all. You're taking me way too close to heaven, and I'm just a mere man. I don't have the willpower to resist you.'

She laughed softly. 'My parents are supposed to be coming over here soon, aren't they? Why don't we arrange it so they're coming for a very special celebration?'

'My thoughts exactly,' he said in a roughened tone. *'Nau ko'u aloha,'* he whispered. 'My love is yours. *Mau loa.* For ever.'

'For ever,' she echoed, and gave herself up to his kisses. The sun had gone down over the horizon, the night was young, and moonlight bathed them in its silvery glow. All was well with the world.

A sneaky peek at next month...

By Request

RELIVE THE ROMANCE WITH THE BEST OF THE BEST

My wish list for next month's titles...

In stores from 18th January 2013:

3 stories in each book – only £5.99!

❏ Undressed by the Billionaire – Susan Stephens, Amanda Browning & Susanne James

❏ A Very Personal Assistant – Jessica Hart, Margaret Mayo & Nina Harrington

In stores from 1st February 2013:

❏ Platinum Grooms – Sara Orwig

Available at WHSmith, Tesco, Asda, Eason, Amazon and Apple

Just can't wait?

Visit us Online

You can buy our books online a month before they hit the shops! **www.millsandboon.co.uk**

0113/05

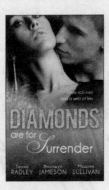
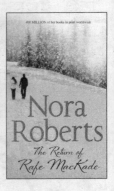

Mills & Boon® Online

Discover more romance at
www.millsandboon.co.uk

- **FREE** online reads
- **Books** up to one month before shops
- **Browse our books** before you buy

...and much more!

For exclusive competitions and instant updates:

Like us on **facebook.com/romancehq**

Follow us on **twitter.com/millsandboonuk**

Join us on **community.millsandboon.co.uk**

Visit us Online

Sign up for our FREE eNewsletter at
www.millsandboon.co.uk

WEB/M&B/RTL4

The World of Mills & Boon®

There's a Mills & Boon® series that's perfect for you. We publish ten series and, with new titles every month, you never have to wait long for your favourite to come along.

Blaze *Scorching hot, sexy reads*
4 new stories every month

By Request *Relive the romance with the best of the best*
9 new stories every month

Cherish *Romance to melt the heart every time*
12 new stories every month

Desire *Passionate and dramatic love stories*
8 new stories every month